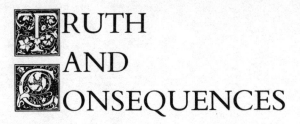

TRUTH AND CONSEQUENCES

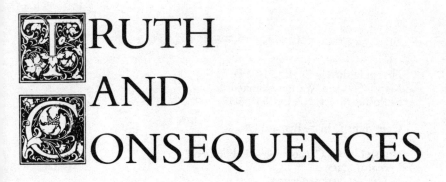

TRUTH AND CONSEQUENCES

Mary Bernard

SECKER & WARBURG
LONDON

First published in England 1983 by
Martin Secker & Warburg Limited
54 Poland Street, London W1V 3DF

Copyright © Mary Bernard 1983

British Library Cataloguing in Publication Data
Bernard, Mary
    Truth and consequences.
    I. Title
    823′.914[F]   PR6052.E/

    ISBN 0-436-04230-4

Printed and bound in Great Britain by
Biddles Ltd, Guildford and King's Lynn

To my grandfather

George Frederick Clarke

avo patrique

PART I

Chapter 1

E MET IMOGEN on his first day in England.

He walked slowly when he got to Canonbury Park South on that bright September afternoon in 1964, digging the Standishes' letter out of his pocket to check the number. Yes, this was it – a dignified four-storey early Victorian house of buff brick, with a small front garden behind iron railings. He climbed the steps to the shiny black door and pressed the brass doorbell.

Silence: no buzz, no footsteps. There was no knocker, but rapping with his knuckles seemed a touch informal. He hesitated, then guessed that what he had taken for a bell-push was just the opposite. Something he had heard of but never before seen – a bell-pull. Gingerly, he pulled it.

A loud clangour, and the door was opened by a dark, friendly-looking woman with a warm smile. 'Hullo, I'm Frances, and you must be Jacob,' she said in a welcoming rush, putting her hand on his arm to draw him into the big square hall. 'I recognise you from Jamie's description.'

He smiled back, rubbing his crinkly red hair. 'Yes, I guess I'm pretty unmistakable.' He hoped she meant his hair, not his height; he was only five foot four, and she had at least three inches on him.

'Is your trunk in the taxi? I'll get Oliver to help you. – Oh, in the left-luggage at Waterloo? Very sensible. And how adventurous to come by tube. Here, let me take your case.' She put it on a mahogany table beneath a large looking glass. 'Oliver!' she called. 'Here's Jacob Harris.'

Oliver came into the hall smiling. 'My dear chap, such a

3

pleasure.' His hand was delicate, but his handshake was firm. 'After all this time. Come into the drawing room, do sit down, what can I get you to drink?' He looked like Jamie: thin-faced, light-eyed, fairish-haired, elegant, slender – and at least six feet tall, damn it. His suit was so well cut that Jacob guessed it must come from Savile Row and blushed for his own jeans, button-down shirt and leather windcheater.

Sitting back with their drinks they searched for topics, keeping off the one subject they knew they shared – Jamie – until they had a better sense of each other. The Standishes started with the weather – so nice that his first day in England was sunny – and his Atlantic crossing. – As boring as that? How disillusioning, one had pictured it as romantic. 'And what made you decide to come over here as an affiliated student?' Frances asked with polite interest.

He shrugged. 'A break before the grad school grind, I guess.'

'So after these two years you'll be going on to a Ph.D?'

'Yes – it'll keep the draft board off my back; and I can't think of anything better to do. I'll probably end up as an academic. Fate worse than death.' He grimaced.

'And why England?'

'Well, Cambridge is good for classics, but that's really just an excuse to spend some time in England. I'm an Anglophile from away back.'

'Really?' Oliver just lifted his eyebrows.

'Not a naive one, I hope' – defensively. 'I don't think I've got many illusions about England. I've been reading the *Observer* and the *New Statesman* for years. So I don't expect a green and pleasant land – I've read things about Rachmanism and council estates and CND and the TUC and, uh, public schools and grammar schools and secondary moderns and comprehensives and class and accents and U-and-non-U and, uh . . .'

'Gracious,' said Frances. 'It's surprising you came at all.'

They all smiled, and Oliver asked, 'But how did you become an, er, Anglophile in the first place?'

'Hmm, I don't know. I've just always been curious about England – maybe because one of my ancestors came from here – my great-great-great grandfather.'

'A . . . a Pilgrim Father?' asked Frances.

He laughed. 'Hardly. An English Jew named Moses Harris. He was press-ganged in the Napoleonic wars and jumped ship in Halifax; but there weren't enough Jews there for him to find a wife, so he drifted south till he reached Boston. It had a good-sized Jewish community, and he got married and settled down respectably as a tailor. He wanted to visit England and see his family again before he died, but he didn't make it.'

'How romantic,' she said. 'And do you still have family here?'

'You know, I've no idea. The letters back and forth stopped in the generation after Tailor Harris's.'

A leisurely dusk was drawing on; the light from the tall front windows was fading to a greenish tone, an indefinite medium in which it was easy to be quiet for a short time. Then Frances said something about music, they found they had tastes in common, and Oliver got up to put on a Chandos Anthem. Pausing with the record balanced between his fingertips he asked, 'Shouldn't Imogen be home?'

'I told her seven-thirty, there's nearly half an hour – she's playing with Fiona.'

The music was astutely chosen – interesting enough to merit attention, though not so absorbing as to command silence; they were free to talk but relieved of having to. Jacob leaned back on the sofa and stretched out his legs comfortably. What about the Standishes, then? Hard to tell. They both had subtle, sensitive, expressive faces. Oliver was unnervingly like his younger brother, even to the sharp nose, narrow, flexible mouth and delicate hands, but he was suave where Jamie was wryly ingenuous; and his defences were in better order. Jacob remembered Jamie's quivering face after he had got him out of the bloody bath. No one would ever have to save Oliver from suicide. Frances was easier in manner, her friendliness less studied; beyond that, they were equally opaque. In turns of phrase, in glances that flickered between them, in fleeting hesitations that sometimes preceded their replies he thought he caught glimpses of – of what? Secret amusement? Secret boredom? Did they, like him, feel a little tense from puzzling out the nuances of unaccustomed tones and gestures?

Probably he was imagining things. He was tired; they might

5

be, too – indeed, Oliver had said that he was a trifle weary from interviewing a politician. Besides, he was in a foreign country; the signals were bound to be different.

'What do you think of England so far?' Frances asked during a quiet passage in the music.

'I haven't seen enough to say. A lot of back yards from the boat train, a sub- a trip on the underground, then five minutes' walk here from the subway st- the tube stop – that is right, isn't it? It's pretty around here, though.'

She smiled. 'It's all right, but it's nothing much really. Tomorrow you must see something of London. – You were going to? Good. We won't be able to take you round: the paper comes out on Sunday, so Saturday is Oliver's busiest day; and I'll have to stay at home with Imogen. But I'll suggest a few things to see.'

He nodded gratefully and settled deeper into the sofa, looking round at the large, L-shaped drawing room. It was furnished with a careful unity of colour: silvery greys and greens for carpets and upholstery, dark green for the walls, upon which there hung nineteenth-century watercolours and the portrait of an eighteenth-century gentleman. There were no curtains; the windows were set in shutter recesses. Scattered about on the tables was a diversity of books and pleasing objects. Though not conspicuously luxurious, the room was exceedingly comfortable; there was no sparseness, no skimpiness, no evidence of war between expensive tastes and inadequate means. The Standishes had enough money to realise their ideas, a sensible modesty of conception, and an eclectic taste. Most of their furniture was solid, unpretentious eighteenth-century mahogany; but an elaborately scrolled, deep-buttoned crimson lady's chair and a florid Victorian footstool fitted in without drawing attention to themselves, as did the dark-green velvet sofa, a glass coffee table and a soft grey leather armchair – all best-of-breed modern, probably from the family's furniture firm. More than their conversation or the music, the Standishes' drawing room hinted at a strong individual sensibility beneath the smooth surface of their hospitality. They might be opaque at the moment, but Jacob thought he would like them: he must have a good deal in common with them when he felt so much at home in their drawing room.

'I do like this room,' he said impulsively through the music. 'It reminds me of my parents' living room.'

After a microsecond of silence Frances said, 'Oh, in what way?'

'Hmm, the feel, I guess – the way you mix things. Aline – my mother – does the same thing. She likes modern Italian things and Sheraton and big chintzy chairs, and she and Isaac make them all go together like . . . like all this.' He gestured largely at everything in sight.

The record ended; as Oliver got up to turn it, the front door opened and shut, and footsteps scattered across the hall. 'There's Imogen.' Frances stood up. 'I must feed her and start our dinner. Oliver, will you read her her story tonight?'

Imogen came to the drawing-room doorway and stood there wordlessly, hanging on the doorknob.

'Imogen, this is Jacob Harris,' Frances said, 'your uncle Jamie's friend.'

'Hullo,' she said, swinging a little on the doorknob.

'Hello, Imogen.' He could hardly see her in the fading light; she was just a small girl, perhaps six years old, with dark hair and a high clear voice.

The kitchen was in the basement: a big room with a russet quarry-tile floor, a scarlet Aga, two big dressers, an enormous butcher's block and an old scrubbed pine table close to the french windows at the back of the room. There was a delicious stew in an orange casserole, and a red wine, for which Oliver apologised after one wincing sip.

Jacob enjoyed it anyhow, but without saying so; he did not want them to think he had a boorish palate. He was rather unsure of himself. There were odd, jarring moments when he felt like a barbarian, though the Standishes were doing, saying, implying nothing but what was friendly and flattering. It was not Oliver's fault that he did not know good wine from bad – and the wine was neither here nor there: mere ignorance; he would learn. He must simply be tired and edgy.

'You'll find Cambridge provincial after living in a big city all your life,' Oliver said in a tone of commiseration.

'Oh, I'll probably be right at home. Malden – where I live – isn't the big city, it's a suburb. Besides, Bostonians always feel provincial, because New York is really the big city.'

'Like Birmingham and London.'

'Not quite,' he said affably, showing off his knowledge of England. 'We Bostonians believe we're superior beings, provincial or no, whereas I gather that Birmingham doesn't have a special relationship with God.'

In the second before they laughed, could he almost hear their minds whirring and clicking and adding a new factor to their sums about him?

'But you'll be coming up to London quite often, won't you, for concerts and the theatre,' said Frances. 'Then we'll be able to see more of you.'

Such nice people; he must be crazy. 'And movies,' he added. 'I'm a movie nut, and Jamie said that the National Film Theatre is the best place for old movies.'

'Oh yes, the NFT.' They nodded politely, and he imagined them telling each other at bedtime: 'My dear, a "movie-nut". So American!'

Chapter 2

E SLEPT LATE; the sun was striking the basement floor at a steep angle through the open french windows by the time he came downstairs. The room was bright, warm and empty, and he was wondering whether to rummage for breakfast or wait until someone appeared, when Imogen bounced down the brick steps from the garden.

'You're up late,' she observed.

'Well, it's only five in the morning where I come from, so for me it's really very early.'

'Oh. Where you come from – that's America. Why is that?'

'Why is what?'

'Why is it early where you come from?'

Jesus. 'It's a bit complicated. The sun rises earlier over here.'

'Why?'

'Uh, let's see, because the earth moves around the sun – no, because the earth spins round like a top once every twenty-four hours, while the sun stands still.' Geography before breakfast was not his idea of how to start the day, but she was waiting expectantly, so he took two oranges from the fruit bowl. 'Here, this is the earth, and this is the sun. Now the sun doesn't really move, even though it seems to – you do know about that?' he asked anxiously; he did not want to find himself disabusing her of what might be, for all he knew, an emotionally important eternal verity, like fairies or Santa Claus. But she nodded as if she had taken in Copernicus with her mother's milk. 'Okay. So we'll put the sun in the middle of the table, here, and move the earth around it. We'll call this speck on the earth-orange "England" and . . . Hmm. I need a second spot for America, and there isn't one.'

'There's a globe in Daddy's study – shall I fetch it?'

Jacob expected an ordinary metal desk globe, but she returned barely visible behind a big ancient globe of sallow leather, and put it down, puffing. 'Will this do?'

'Just dandy.' He mounted the sun-orange on an empty milk bottle in the middle of the table and started rolling the globe round it. 'Of course these are the wrong way round for size,' he remarked offhandedly, one old Copernican to another, as he tried to master the surprisingly difficult knack of spinning the earth on its axis while revolving it round the sun.

'What do you mean?'

'You know – the sun is really much much bigger than the earth, but we've got a great big earth and a tiny sun instead.'

Imogen looked from globe to orange in bewilderment. 'I didn't know that,' she said in a dismayed voice. 'Is it really true?' She looked up at him.

Jacob felt a sudden pang as he met her eyes properly for the first time. They were the most astonishing eyes he had ever seen in anyone, child or adult: heartrendingly beautiful – light hazel, flecked with green and yellow; the iris circumscribed by a dark rim as definite as a pen line; the lashes dark and thick; the eyebrows neat, dark and straight below her dark brown fringe.

9

Not that she was a beauty; the rest of her was ordinary enough, and even her eyes were not unusually large or brilliant in colour. It was their amazing seriousness that made them so beautiful. How could a child of six have such a grave gaze?

'Is it true?' she repeated, her distress concentrated in the curious way the inner ends of her eyebrows were puckered upwards.

'Yes, I'm afraid so,' he said, and they regarded each other with a queerly mutual sympathy.

She turned the globe so that she could see England. Tentatively, reluctant to expose the depths of her ignorance, she asked, 'If the earth is so small . . . how does everybody fit on?'

'I think it's not that the earth is so small,' he offered rather desperately. 'It's really very big; but the sun is so much *bigger*. There's room for us all on the earth – but the sun is so big that everybody on earth would fit onto a tiny corner of it.'

Thin, but it did the trick. She poked London with her finger. 'Then nobody will fall off . . .'

'No, nobody will fall off.'

'Imogen, what on earth – ?' Frances was behind them in the sunny doorway.

'I was just showing Imogen why it's earlier in America than over here.'

'That's very good of you. Have you managed to find any breakfast? I sent her in to help you.'

'We got distracted by time zones,' he said in excuse for Imogen.

Frances smiled generously at both of them and bustled out some breakfast. 'Don't let her pester you,' she advised when Imogen had returned the globe and gone back outside.

'Don't worry, I got into that myself. I'm a pushover for children – I have about a dozen young cousins that I spend time with. Sheila and I – she's my girl – took four of them camping for a week this summer, for instance.'

'Your girl? I'd like to hear about her. But I won't ask now – you should get out and see London. May I ask lots of questions this evening? – Good.' She got him an *A to Z* and pointed out Mayfair and Kensington and Soho and St Paul's and the City and Regent's Park. 'But that's already more than you can possibly see in one day. Don't worry about getting back

10

early; I'll just make you an omelette – we don't have proper dinner on Saturdays, because Oliver doesn't get back till ten or so.'

'Start with a view of the Thames,' Frances had said. 'It's all too easy to forget that London grew up round the river.' So he took the tube to Waterloo, marched out onto Waterloo Bridge shortly before noon – and stopped, staring dumbfounded at something he had never thought to see: a celestial city.

What do you mean? he scolded himself. It's only London. He could not answer his own question; yet for all that he knew well enough what he meant.

First the wide white vista, in the hazy September sunlight: the tawny Houses of Parliament, both bigger and more delicate than they looked in movies; the massive chiaroscuro of Somerset House; and, all along the Embankment, soot-streaked buildings of Portland stone gleaming milkily behind trees, above the muddy river and old boats. Then, rising noble among barbarous tower blocks – cynosure of the whole sweep, though set to one side as if by a superb nonchalance of intention – the monumental, maculate bulk of St Paul's: no mere temple of Christianity, but a holy edifice of civilisation, both sacred and secular, cathedral and capitol of a real and an ideal city.

Only London – yes, but to an American . . . There must be more than one celestial city, he guessed, gazing at his first. Not in America. But he had once seen a photograph of Paris, taken from the Eiffel Tower as a thunderstorm rolled towards Sacré Coeur; and he remembered that his mother had said: 'Jerusalem? A holy city, sure; but for me *the* holy city is Florence.' He had not understood her then; he was beginning to now. For other people there might be, in Asia or northern Africa, other holy places; but for him, as for Aline, the celestial cities would all be European. Face to face with their densities – of history, beauty, meaning, implication – an American – a certain kind of American – an American like Jacob – recognised at once the sustenance he had been starving for and leapt into faith with a convert's fervour.

And where had he got the idea that London was dun and grey? It was luminous; it gleamed. The slight haze diffracted the light without dulling it, so that sharp edges were blurred, harsh shadows dissolved. London was grey as the inside of an oyster shell is grey: iridescent: and St Paul's its black pearl.

What on earth had got into him? Sentimental idiot, victim of wishful thinking. The great vista must be sucker bait, a con trick: vast stage flats in faultless *trompe-l'oeil*, erected by the famously hypocritical English to hide the shabby city he had been prepared for. He would penetrate the façade and break the spell.

Fat chance. All afternoon he walked and rode by tube round central London. Everywhere the light was soft and blooming: along the loud and leafy Embankment, in peaches-and-cream Kensington, on the plum-hued opulence of Mayfair. He was a goner. London was noisy, seedy, tawdry, dirty; but it was also the enchanting city he had seen from the bridge: baggy, elephantine, capacious, huddling up its centuries cheek by jowl, alive with a deep slow pulse. For everything that was ugly there was more that was beautiful – it hardly mattered that Piccadilly Circus was a sleazy second-rate Times Square, when the urbane elegance of St James's Square was just round the corner. He wandered about until dark, meeting London with a delight that was not altogether surprised. He could hardly believe it existed, but he recognised it. He felt at home.

By nightfall he was worn out and wished he did not have to face an evening of strenuous friendliness with strangers whose social dialect was slightly different from his. But it was not like that at all. Frances was warm and welcoming and wanted to hear all about his day; and the combination of her interest and her delicious mushroom-smothered omelette soon revived him.

'And now,' she said, ' now I want to hear all about Sheila.'

'Lord – where to begin? . . . Well, we were at Harvard together, and now she's training to be a teacher of deaf children –'

'Did she read education?'

'No, applied mathematics – computers. That's how we met – in a data-processing course a couple of years ago.'

'But aren't you a classic?'

'Yes, but at Harvard you take a lot of courses outside your special field. In my freshman year I took a computing course and liked it, and after that almost all my non-classics courses were about computers. They're great fun.'

'But how did Sheila get from computers to deaf children?'

'Because she's got, uh, a strong social conscience, and she decided she can't do something just because it's fun; she wants to be of use. And her uncle runs a school for deaf children, so there's a family connection.'

'And what does she look like?'

He showed her the snapshot in his wallet: a girl with fuzzy dark hair, rather protuberant eyes, a beaked nose, full delicate lips and a general look of not having enough flesh on her bones. 'She's not pretty' – in case Frances were trying to think up a compliment. 'But she's . . . remarkable-looking. Like . . . like running water. You want to watch her.'

She studied the photograph and said on an interrogative note, 'I can't really tell what she's like from this.'

'Hmm, well . . . extreme and intense and principled; and she has a crazy sense of humour . . .' He considered. 'I don't know how to describe her. Deep down we're as like as two peas, but you'd never know it, because we're so different on the surface. People usually think I'm nicer than Sheila, because she's always getting prickly and taking stands; but they're wrong. I think the same as her, but I'm too lazy or cowardly to go out on a limb. She's much *better* than me – I'm too easygoing.'

'But you say you're so much alike?' she asked with a puzzled frown.

'Yeah, it's . . . it's as if our pulses go at exactly the same speed; we're like, uh, identical twins separated at birth and brought up differently – you know, the way they score so close on psychological tests.'

'And the two of you are together for good?'

'Heavens, yes. I can't imagine not spending my life with Sheila – though twenty-two may seem young to be saying that – '

'Not at all. Oliver and I got married at twenty-two.'

'And there may be other people as well, you know.' He thought he should establish this right away. He would probably be seeing more of Frances; and, if he got attached to somebody in England, as he hoped he would, he did not want her to think he was betraying Sheila. 'We haven't . . . tied each other down.'

'You mean . . . affairs? – Aren't you taking quite a – ' There was a sound from upstairs: the front door. 'Here's Oliver – just

13

as things were getting really interesting.' She smiled at him companionably.

They went up to the drawing room with coffee and bittermints. Oliver offered brandy and leaned back in the grey chair, nursing his glass, then cleared his throat, looked briefly at Jacob and away, and said, 'Er, Frances and I both want – we never can thank you enough for what you did for Jamie: saving his life –'

' – and seeing him through it all afterwards,' said Frances, 'instead of leaving him to the psychiatrists.'

'But I couldn't do that. I was afraid they'd put him in the booby hatch, and that would have been . . .'

'But most people wouldn't have wanted the responsibility or trouble – you were marvellous.'

'Just so,' said Oliver.

There was a silence. He couldn't think what to answer; the only things that occurred to him – 'No trouble' and 'A pleasure' – were manifestly inappropriate. 'Uh, thanks,' he said, then blurted: 'You know, I was afraid you'd blame me when he decided to go to med school out in Vancouver.'

Oliver made a movement of surprise. 'Good gracious no, my dear fellow. Jamie can only keep out of Standish and Sons by staying away from England for a good long time. Mother's a human bulldozer; if he came back, she'd chivvy him till he either went into the firm or had another breakdown. No, he told us you encouraged him about Vancouver, and we were cheering you on.' He put the tips of his long fingers together underneath his chin. 'I was the lucky one, really. When I wouldn't follow Andrew into the firm, she assumed I was a fluke; she didn't dream that two sons out of three would opt out. So I didn't get nearly as much flak as Jamie.'

'Come off it, Oliver. You *still* get flakked.'

'Now, Frances' – mildly. 'Mother means well. She just got obsessed with the firm after Father's death – having to hold everything together till Andrew reached twenty-one. She's not rational about it.'

'Hmph. I know you think that. *I* think she's just bossy.' She took a deep breath. 'But I am sorry,' she told Jacob. 'We shouldn't be rehashing family quarrels with you here.'

'No, I don't mind,' he said sincerely, pleased that they were enough at ease with him to growl at each other. They would not have done so the night before.

Nice people. He was glad they had invited him to stay with them before he went on to Cambridge. It was a good introduction to England, better than plunging straight into a hothouse student life. Yesterday's momentary tensions must have been imaginary, for today had been completely comfortable, in spite of a few crossed wires when they took his offhand hyperbole literally.

Perhaps he should tone himself down a bit, then, in the interests of perspicuity. It would be well worth the effort, if there were many people like the Standishes about.

Chapter 3

FTER BREAKFAST ON Sunday morning Oliver attacked a hefty pile of all the Sunday papers with professional interest. 'He'll be at that for ages,' said Frances. 'Let's take our coffee outside.'

The big walled garden was mostly lawn, with borders, a huge wisteria, several large rosebushes and, in the grassless shade of a mature beech, a weathered statue of Pan, lifting a shaggy hoof in odd glee and looking sidelong at nothing in particular as he breathed into his pipes with lips pursed from blowing and curved in a slight smile.

'What a wonderful creature,' said Jacob.

'Yes, isn't he. I got him when I took articles –'

'Took articles?'

'Qualified as a solicitor. He was a sort of mascot; and now he's Imogen's god.'

'Her *what*?'

She chuckled. 'She's always known that Pan was a god,

and apparently she thought Jesus looked like Pan; so she was disillusioned last winter when she saw a book with pictures of Jesus, and announced she didn't believe in Jesus any more – not that we'd taught her to, but kids pick these things up – she believed in Pan. And she's believed in him ever since – she brings him flowers and talks to him. It stops short of burnt offerings, but nothing would surprise me. She's a funny child.'

'A Pantheist?' he suggested.

She looked at him startled. 'Why did I never think of that?' she said, laughing, as they went and sat down.

'What kind of law do you practise?' he asked.

'Nothing just now, actually.' She straightened herself on the chaise longue. 'Now I'm working at being a full-time mother to Imogen. I don't believe in leaving a child with nannies, especially an only child. I mean, she needs me here after school and at lunchtime. It's very important not to let an only child feel unwanted.' Her tone was defensive.

Jacob nodded neutrally. It sounded pretty crazy to him, but for all he knew she was right.

She drew in her breath, staring moodily at Imogen, who was wandering towards them across the lawn. 'I'd like to work part time, in fact, but most firms don't want part-time solicitors. And Oliver isn't the slightest help.' She seemed to hear the edge to her voice and, shaking herself, smiled first at him and then, holding out her arm for an embrace, at Imogen. 'After all, the important thing is for me to be here when Imogen comes home from school – isn't it, dear?'

'I think it would be fun to come home by myself and open the door, and nobody would be there.'

'You'd like it for a while, but then it'd get lonely, don't you think?' She hugged Imogen and stroked her hair; Imogen smiled, pliant in her embrace.

'My mother worked full time all my life,' he said, 'so I always had to let myself in after school.' He was not sure whether he was talking to Frances or to Imogen.

Imogen answered. 'Was it fun?'

'I don't know. I never had anything different, so it was just ordinary to me.'

'What does your mother do?' asked Frances.

'She's an architect. Town planning mostly, a bit offbeat.

Harris Associates gets called in when people *don't* want to flatten the whole city centre.'

'Harris Associates – your father's firm?'

'No, Isaac is a Latin teacher. Harris Associates is Aline's baby.'

'A schoolmaster?' She frowned slightly. 'He must be unusual, I mean, lots of men wouldn't . . .' She trailed off with a lazy gesture and half-closed her eyes, as if sleepy.

He couldn't think of anything to say; the subject was boobytrapped. Best to drop it, like tactful Frances. He too leaned back and relaxed, looking at her. Her eyes were like Imogen's, though smaller and not at all arresting; her broad, handsome face showed no signs of age, though none of youth, either; she was simply an adult. Jamie had said that she and Oliver were both twenty-nine. Seven years older than him. A lot older . . . His eyelids drooped in the sleepy sunshine, then closed, and he slid towards sleep.

'He's asleep.' Imogen's whisper carried clearly.

'No, just resting,' came Frances' softer whisper.

He blinked and slid deeper.

Civilisation – this garden – Oliver and Frances – through Jacob's half-sleep threaded a sense of the beautiful ordinariness of the Standishes and their house, their garden, Pan under the beech tree. They were not special, wasn't that the point? Lots of people like them, not isolated, not self-created: a community – communities – rather than the self-conscious enclaves of his experience. It was Pan; Pan showed . . .

'It's lunchtime.' Imogen had leaned close to whisper; when he met her light brown eyes upon waking, he had no sense of place or proportion and momentarily mistook her for Sheila; and then missed Sheila for the first time since leaving home.

It was a comfortable meal; he was at ease with the Standishes. On the doorstep Frances said, 'You'll come and see us soon, won't you? We mean it; it's been a simply lovely weekend;' and Imogen and Oliver made noises of agreement.

He promised to come soon. 'And thanks again for having me – if everybody in England treats me as splendidly as you people, I'll have a hard time tearing myself away in two years.'

17

'Only two?' said Frances. 'Aren't you doing a Ph.D. after that?'

'But not here. Sheila wouldn't like that one bit. No, I'll be going back in two years.'

Chapter 4

ACOB, THANK GOODNESS it's you. I'm still doing canapés; I was afraid everybody had started to *descend*. Brr, it's freezing. Do come down, we can talk while I work. Oliver's unpacking hired glasses in the drawing room.' She was wearing a long mulberry crêpe frock of indefinite shape, long-sleeved and high in front, bare to the waist behind: a very grown-up garment, one that only a tall, well-built woman could carry off. Sheila would have been lost in it; on Frances it was magnificent.

In the kitchen he organised a production line. 'You spread goo on the bits of toast – mmm, delicious,' licking his finger, 'and I'll gussy them up with the pimento.'

'Gussy up? Wonderful – so vivid,' she said in an equivocal tone. 'Now. What have you been doing since last time? Making another hundred friends?'

'Well, I've been meeting a lot of graduate students recently, and –'

'Mummy . . .' It was Imogen, wearing pyjamas.

'What are *you* doing down here?'

'I can't get to sleep.'

'Imogen!' – exasperated. 'Of course you can. Now go back to bed.'

'Can't I watch the party?'

'I told you before, no. It's past your bedtime, you'll get

18

overtired and worked up, like last time. Remember? That wasn't nice, was it? You said you wished I hadn't let you stay up.'

The firm refusal; the cajoling appeal to reason and experience: who could resist? Not Imogen. She stood one foot on the other and looked sullen, but did not ask again. Instead she said, 'But I still can't get to sleep, because – '

'Nonsense, dear. You're just excited.'

' – because you haven't read me my story.'

'Oh, Imogen!' But this time it was Frances who was defeated. 'All right, I'll come – but it'll be a short one.'

The doorbell rang; rang again. Oliver called: 'Frances?'

'I'll read her a story,' Jacob volunteered.

Frances smiled gratefully. 'Jacob, you're a lifesaver.'

Imogen's white room under the eaves had a low sloping ceiling, a frieze of nursery characters, a faded Teddy bear and a row of nesting Russian peasant dolls along the window sill, a jumble of books in the bookcase and a battered blue lamb on the bed. The gas fire was off; she got into bed smartly and pulled the flowered counterpane up under her arms, then remembered the lamb and tucked it in beside her. Jacob sat on the end of the bed. 'So. What would you like me to read?'

'"Wassilissa the Beautiful", please,' she said, enunciating carefully, and handed him *Russian Wonder Tales* open to the page.

'Okay,' he began. '"Wa–"'

'Oh – I'd like to see the pictures too, please,' she said apologetically.

He went and sat beside her. She put one arm round the blue lamb and glanced up at him: a hint. He put his arm round her, and she wriggled close, hugged the blue lamb tighter and said with satisfaction, 'There'. He started reading. Wassilissa was captured by a witch called the Baba-Yaga and given impossible tasks, and each night she took her little doll out of her pocket and set bread and *kvas* before it and said – Imogen said the words with him – '"There, my little doll, take it. Eat a little and drink a little and listen to my grief".' And the doll's eyes would shine like glow-worms, and it would come alive and do the tasks while Wassilissa slept.

Imogen leaned forward to look at the dusky colour plate.

19

'Wassilissa escaping,' she breathed, glancing round to share her delight, then settled back again. When the story ended, she stayed leaning against him contentedly. 'That's a good story, isn't it?'

'A real dilly.'

'What part do you like best? I like the Baba-Yaga's skulls.'

'Me too.'

'Please can I have another story?'

He looked down at her. 'You're trying to get away with murder, aren't you, young 'un?'

She gave him a sly glance and giggled. But he did not mind being taken for a ride. He was comfortable; he liked holding this warm, delicate small creature; he enjoyed her eagerness to share her pleasure; he had even enjoyed the story. 'Okay,' he said, 'one more, then;' and she quickly turned to 'The Little Humpbacked Horse' and nestled in his arm to listen.

She was nearly asleep when he finished. He turned off the light and made for the door.

'Aren't you going to kiss me goodnight?' Her voice was clear in the dark, her tone not demanding, only curious.

He went back and kissed her, and was kissed. She smelt sweet and clean.

Halfway down the dark stairs his step was checked. What was he feeling, that suddenly made his eyes water? Loneliness, desire, tenderness, excitement: all that, penetrating him so strongly that he gripped the handrail, unable to move; and, peering into the haze of his emotions, discerned only – Sheila; Imogen. Sheila and Imogen together. One person or two? Imogen's sweet smell was still in his nostrils; his arm and side were still warm and slightly numb from cradling her. She had made him miss Sheila, was that it? Yes, there was something of a resemblance. Quite a strong one. Imogen could be Sheila's baby sister, or her daughter. That was it: he was missing the daughter they didn't yet have.

What?

He went down two steps in sheer surprise. Much as he liked children, he had never thought of wanting one right away. He and Sheila would have children eventually; but surely they wanted a few years of freedom first. He would be foolish to start hankering after children now.

Yet what else was he longing for this very minute, if not a child, one who looked like Sheila, like Imogen – like both of them, with Sheila's features, eyes bulgy, nose a delicate beak, and the grave gaze they both had? A daughter like Imogen, like Sheila. Yes. Loneliness, desire, tenderness, excitement – for Sheila and her child: their child: for the idea of trading immediate freedoms for such a prize.

Yes. All that. As soon as possible.

Not, however, in the next year and a half. He was standing on a darkened staircase in London; Sheila was an ocean away. And there was a party going on below. Good Lord yes. In full swing, from the sound of it – he must have been upstairs a long time. He shrugged, shaking himself out of the spell, and, suddenly eager for his first London party, bounced down to the ground floor.

Chapter 5

RANCES MET HIM at the drawing-room door. 'You poor man, I was just coming to rescue you. Did she take dreadful advantage of you?' Without waiting for an answer she smiled, touching his arm in an oddly intimate gesture. 'Now. Who shall I introduce you to? Ah – over there, in the velvet jacket. Very interesting man – cartoonist – his wife's nice too, a solicitor. They were both up at Cambridge.' She led him through noisy colourful clusters. 'Steve, I've just been telling Jacob about you. Steve Walker, Jacob Harris. Jacob's up at Cambridge doing a second B.A., just over from America. Oh, and this' – turning to a sparrow-thin girl – 'this is Ann Walker.' She touched Steve's arm, then Jacob's, as if to bind them together, then left them.

'What are you reading at Cambridge?' Steve asked.

Conversations tended to drop dead if he met this stock question with the truth and no more, so he had developed a stock reply. 'Classics,' he said. 'But mostly I go to movies.'

'Me too,' said a dark girl with a melancholy cast of face. 'What are they like in Cambridge these days?'

Almost everybody in the group had been up at Cambridge, and they plunged into reminiscences of past seasons at the Film Society: 'Remember the time a print of *Notorious* caught fire?' They were in their middle twenties, like his graduate-student friends, but, unlike graduate students, already had a place in the real world and the assurance that goes with it; they were more finished and polished, spoke more definitely, had clearer outlines and livelier manners. Their promise was burgeoning into achievement to which they could not as yet see any limits, and they were glossy with confidence without being at all arrogant. A likeable bunch.

The sad-faced girl who liked movies noticed that Jacob was taking little part in the conversation and smiled at him. 'I'm Liz Perrin, by the way. I work on the same paper as Oliver – I'm a researcher.'

'Is everybody here tonight in journalism?'

Liz looked around. 'A lot of us, yes – and TV and theatre and that sort of thing. Like these two.' She nodded at two men who were joining the group. 'Harry Britten designs sets, and Colin Palmer is a director.'

When she introduced them, Harry stared at Jacob with recognition. 'Haven't I seen you before?'

'Uh, not that I know of.'

'At . . . at the NFT?'

'Maybe, I'm there about once a week.'

'Of course – you sit two rows ahead of me.'

'You come all the way from Cambridge just to see films?' Steve Walker asked disbelievingly.

Harry leapt to his defence. 'Why not? I did when I was up. One can't afford to miss what's at the NFT if one's interested in films. The last time I saw . . . Jacob, is that right? . . . was at *Casablanca*. One of the best-scored films of all time.' In a proud aside he confided: 'I'm secretary of the Max Steiner society.'

He went to *Casablanca* for the *music*? Such championship

Jacob could do without. Fortunately the group dropped movies and started reminiscing about a Cambridge pub called 'The Prince', which most of them seemed to have lived in or visited when they were up.

'What were people doing living in a pub?' he asked Liz.

'Liz!' cried a woman who was pretty in spite of a long face and buck teeth.

'Jean!' She introduced him to Jean Fuller, then explained that 'The Prince' wasn't a pub any more. 'It's bed-sitting rooms. Lots of people lived there – Jean and I did – and all sorts of things happened – '

'Happened! Remember the man who kept stealing our underwear off the line?'

A girl with a lively brown china-doll face overheard her. 'Remember that monster!' she cried, joining them. ('Penny,' murmured Liz.) 'He took all my panties except the ones I was wearing, and I'd no more money till the end of the month. And do you remember the time I was having a bath, and the geyser set fire to the wall, and the only person at home was that man you'd befriended at Film Society, Jean; and I ran out with only the tiniest towel round me, and he rushed in with a bucket and hurled the bathwater at the wall . . .'

There seemed to be no getting away from Cambridge – perhaps for them that time had been so rich that the most trivial incidents were laden with meanings invisible to an outsider.

'. . . and he left so quickly,' Jean was saying; 'but his shadow was so long under the streetlamp when he crossed the road, and he looked so thin and lonely – '

' – and I can still see you,' said Penny, 'running after him and calling: "You – you – come back and have some coffee . . ."'

Jacob was getting bored; he hadn't come to a party in London to talk about a pub in Cambridge. Where should he move next? It would be nice to talk to a woman who was on her own – Jean and Penny were both married.

What about Liz, then – standing beside him, so close he had almost overlooked her? She was one of the most attractive women in the room – not pretty, but striking, her full mouth turned down at the corners, her brown eyes heavy-lidded. An interesting face.

23

Well – make a move. Say something.

But perhaps he should wait? He edged out of the group at the first chance, away from temptation.

Eventually he came across a small, engaging American woman in her forties, who had grey hair wound up in a French knot, warm, shrewd eyes, and blunted Russian-Jewish features like his mother's and his own. She was a journalist, she told him: that was how she knew Oliver. – No, not the same paper. – What did she do? – A bit of this, a bit of that . . . He persisted politely, and she allowed to: 'Some politics, some show business, human interest, travel, backgrounding. All-round hack.' – What sort of places did she publish? – 'Oh . . . here and there, whoever will have me.'

'Hey, hey, hey, Naomi, selling yourself short again.' A stocky man put his arm round her. 'Don't let Naomi kid you,' he told Jacob confidentially. 'This little lady places her stuff in the *very* best publications. The *New Yorker*, the *Observer*, *Vogue*, the *New York Times*, they fall all over themselves trying to get her. World rights, syndication, the lot. I should know; I'm her agent, and believe me it's a pleasure.'

'Oh, you're *that* Naomi Black,' said Jacob. 'When you said your name, I didn't connect – I've read lots of your articles in the *New Yorker*, and I always like them.'

'Say, Naomi, this guy's from back home,' her agent said; 'he'll appreciate. Tell him about the time Joe McCarthy tried to sweet-talk you.'

'Oh, that's ancient history.' But he insisted, and she shrugged and told a couple of McCarthy stories in her cracked, salty voice, wrinkling up all her features like a monkey at the punch lines.

A short, swart man came up. 'Hi, Naomi, how's it going?'

Naomi introduced him. 'Norman Susskind – another expatriate. We've just done a story together, and Norman's got the most marvellous photographs.'

'Yeah, how'd you get them to let you into a harem?' the agent asked.

Norman grunted. 'It seems that infidels don't count as men – I was an honorary eunuch. But what really hurt was working in that light – so dim you wouldn't believe.'

They drifted into a rather technical conversation. Jacob

listened for a while, then, whispering, 'Hope I see you again,' to Naomi, slipped out of the group.

He found himself in the back part of the drawing room. Except for a few couples intent on private conversation, it was almost empty, as if an invisible barrier were keeping most people within the jam-packed front room. He wanted a breather, so he took down a picture book and began to flip the pages inattentively.

Suddenly a name leapt at him from beneath a photograph. Oh. *That* Norman Susskind. The famous one. Two pages on was a photograph by Jean Fuller. One of the articles was by Oliver; Naomi had written the introduction; and the list of contributors, which included several other people he had met this evening, was like a *Who's Who* of photographers and journalists. How odd that he had not recognised their names upon meeting them. Yet not all that odd, really; they wore success so unassumingly, whereas, at his mother's less enjoyable parties back home, similarly successful people in the same kinds of work were, with a few exceptions, febrile and self-promoting and disinclined to give the time of day to anybody who wasn't somebody.

Round him there was a pool of silence. In the front room the chime and boom of conversation rose and fell like the splash of a fountain, words indistinguishable, a civilised harmony. He was light-hearted with gratitude towards England as he looked at the gleaming faces, eager, happy, serious, amused, excited, ironical: all shining with evidence of subtle apprehensions and sensibilities, of lives comparatively unscarred. He was an alien, freighted with knowledge without use or meaning in England, and correspondingly ignorant about the springs of English life; yet he felt safe here – safe, happy, at ease. Not at home: it must be impossible to be at home in a foreign country. But had he been born here – and into the right class, of course – he could have felt at home, as never in America, where he had spent his life in an exile that he had not quite recognised until now.

The crowd shifted, and he saw Imogen standing between her parents, who were talking over her head, slightly exasperated by her arrival, but not seriously put out. She was one of the lucky ones. England was hers, waiting for her. Oliver bent down and whispered; she nodded, and he led her away.

Liz was moving from group to group with a bottle in each hand, pouring red wine or white into proffered glasses, smiling, speaking into the splash of sound, moving on: slowly working her way closer to the back room. Would she cross the invisible barrier? If she came up to him, he would say something – or would he?

She did come into the back room and moved from couple to couple pouring wine. When she reached Jacob, who was solitary and had no glass, she hesitated, perhaps wondering if she should offer to fetch him one. Her face took a greenish tinge from a spotlight trained on the green wall; the corners of her mouth were turned down; her eyeliner emphasised the tragic-mask aspect of her face. About to go – but she could not go without a greeting – she looked up to smile, and her dark eyes caught the light and glowed.

He forgot all about waiting. But just then Oliver drifted by, announcing food. The couples stirred in their corners, and Liz said, 'I'm famished,' and started to move. They went down-stairs together, but the moment had passed, and no other turned up. Perhaps if he could have seen her home – but he was staying with the Standishes, and he had already heard Steve and Ann offer her a lift.

Naomi was among the last to leave. She stopped him in the hall. 'You'll come to my Christmas party, won't you? Saturday the nineteenth at seven-thirty. It's always the Saturday before Christmas, and early so that kids can come too. I'd love to have you. – Good. Take care.' Her face wrinkled up in its funny monkey-smile, and he stood looking after her affection-ately, reminding himself that Americans, too, could be civilised.

The sky was a sepia wash the next morning, but the kitchen was warm and cheerful, and Jacob and the Standishes sat drinking leisurely coffee and gossiping about the party, while Imogen made toast on the Aga and deposited slices on their plates at regular intervals. Frances invited him to spend Christmas at their cottage in Wiltshire, but he had to decline: 'I've already said yes to the Potters, I'm afraid.'

'The Potters?'

'Oh yes, I haven't told you. They're graduate students, Al and Barbara Potter, and they pay the mortgage on their house in Hertford Street by letting most of the rooms. I'm moving into one next week from Pembroke – it'll be more fun than living in college. And they've asked me to spend Christmas with them. Too bad – I'd far rather have come to you.'

'But we'll see you soon afterwards, I hope. Do come soon – for the weekend. But I've just remembered, we'll see you before – at Naomi's party. How nice.'

Chapter 6

AOMI LIVED IN a big white airy fourth-floor flat in Cornwall Gardens. There was no lift; the stairs were punctuated with adults, including the Standishes, pausing to catch their breath, and children, including Imogen, rushing on ahead and calling back: 'Mummy, Daddy, hurry up.' This party was also full of people in publishing, journalism, films and television, as well as a good handful of Naomi's fellow expatriate Americans and a number of children. Penny had a baby in her arms and a sulky flaxen mite hanging onto her skirt. She looked harassed; but Jacob had not forgotten that moment on the Standishes' darkened staircase, and he envied her for already having two children when she was no older than he.

'Oh God, Jude, you're not going to – ' Penny got a paper napkin between her shoulder and the baby's vomit just in time. 'Kids!' she said in disgust.

He laughed. 'Hmm, yes, they're a nuisance. But I wish I had some myself, mess and all.'

She stared. 'You're crazy. If I'd known what I was letting myself in for – well, all I can say is, don't.'

'Don't what?' It was Liz Perrin.

He got her a drink, and they spent the rest of the evening drifting around the party more or less together, talking to other people, but more and more to each other. All the people with children had gone; it was getting late. He would have to leave soon if he were to catch the last train. If. He had somehow missed the moment – if there had ever been one – when it might have been possible to go home with her without telling her about Sheila first; but he had also missed the moment – if there had ever been one – when it would have been easy to mention Sheila. He didn't know how to; he would have to go to his train and forget about Liz.

A silence had fallen. Abruptly she said, 'I, er, I'm, er, involved with someone, maybe I should say.'

'Really?' he replied with stunned aplomb. His heart sank; he had misread the signals. But at least here was his cue. 'So am I, in fact. Someone in America.'

'Oh,' she said politely. 'Will she be coming over?'

'No, we'll get back together when I go back.'

Liz raised her mournful brown eyes. 'Same with me. Patrick's in Buenos Aires – he's just started three years in the Argentinian branch of his firm. We'll get back together when he comes home.'

'Why didn't you go with him?'

'I wanted to keep my job.'

Jacob looked at her. 'I'd uh, like . . .' he said slowly; and stopped.

The corners of her mouth turned even further downwards in a curious smile. 'So would I.'

'To be serious about somebody who understood – '

' – that there's someone else who comes first – '

' – and won't be hurt by it.' He beamed. 'Well, then.'

'As you say, well, then.'

He looked at his watch. 'I have to leave in about five minutes to get the last train to Cambridge – or I could, uh . . .'

'Stay?' they said at the same time, and with the same quizzical note.

When he told Frances about Liz, she leapt to the conclusion that he had broken up with Sheila.

'Good heavens, no.'

'But you sound sort of . . . serious about Liz' – perplexed.

28

'I am. But Sheila and I still feel the same about each other.'

'You don't mean you've *told* Sheila? – You *have*? She must be furious.'

'Not furious – that'd be against her principles. I think she's sort of upset – I would be too – but we did agree, you know, and she's standing by that and saying it's okay.'

She looked even more perplexed. Then her face cleared. 'This is a sort of trial period for you two, isn't it? I mean, you're making sure you've made the right decision about each other.'

That wasn't the way it was, but he couldn't quite think of how to explain. He shrugged, looking through the french windows at Imogen, who, in woolly coat and wellingtons, had been standing at the bottom of the garden for nearly half an hour, hardly moving, in animated conversation with Pan and a rosebush, inclining her dark brown head now to one, now to the other, with gestures she had picked up from Frances.

'What do you think she's talking about?' he asked.

Frances' face clouded. 'I don't know. She does it a lot. The one in the rosebush is an imaginary friend – a woman, I gather. She hasn't told Imogen her name. She has to talk to them every day – it's a nuisance when it rains. And she should have outgrown that stage by now. It worries me a bit; she's so inturned. Probably it's from being an only child. I mean, I keep wondering if I'm doing something wrong. Lord knows I give her every chance I can – I spend half my time chatting up mothers so that Imogen can play with their kids.'

'Doesn't she make friends at school?'

She frowned. 'Yes, but . . . I mean, I don't want to sound like a snob, but the school's got a very . . . mixed intake, and I wouldn't want her to have just the friends she makes there. She picks up the most amazing bits of accent as it is . . .'

'Why not send her to a private school, then?'

'We couldn't do that!' She was horrified. 'It's simply terrible, middle-class parents skimming the cream off the state school intake that way. No, Oliver and I believe in supporting the state system, and we're not going to opt out just because we can afford to. I mean, we're so dreadfully privileged already – it's the least one can do.' She got up, called out: 'Tea in five minutes,' to Imogen and went to put the kettle on.

29

Imogen said thank you politely for her tea when she came in, then asked, 'And may I have a cookie, please?' darting a glance at Jacob.

'A what?' said Frances with heavy patience.

Imogen weighed her tone. 'A biscuit.'

'Please.'

'I said please.'

'You said please cookie, not please biscuit.'

'Please biscuit.'

Frances gave her a biscuit and a mug of weak tea. 'I should have you up for corrupting the language of a minor,' she told him, only half amused. 'Cookie, indeed!'

'Cookie sounds nicer,' said Imogen from her mug.

'Maybe, but it's not what we call them here, and nobody will understand you if you call them that.'

She thought it over. 'I'm going to be a foreigner when I grow up, like Jacob. Then I can say "cookie" and "I guess" and things, and everybody will just have to understand me.'

Frances choked and got up quickly, shoulders shaking, to carry her cup to the sink. Jacob bit his lip and asked, in an almost sober voice: 'What country are you going to be a foreigner in?'

'Oh, England – same as you.'

Chapter 7

ACOB LIKED AND admired the Standishes immensely – they seemed to be splendidly representative of English upper-middle-class life at its best. There was nothing defensive or defiant or embattled about them; they had an ease of manner, a solidity, a confidence about their relation to the world, that derived from their membership in a large, easy, solid, confident section of a rooted, long-settled society. It was not just that they were 'cultured', in his American sense of being well-bred and interested in the arts. They were at ease with their culture and their manners, free to be gentle and unembattled; they fitted into a large context. In a word, civilised – though he had already acquired an English reluctance to use any word at all to describe the quality he sensed in them.

To his pleasure he saw more rather than less of them as a result of his attachment to Liz. He and she spent every weekend together, usually in London – he would meet her after work on Saturday evening, then return to Cambridge on Monday morning – and the Standishes often asked them to a Sunday meal. He also saw Frances on his own; with her encouragement he got into the habit of calling round for a talk on Saturday before meeting Liz. They both benefited from the visits. Frances was bored and isolated by her self-imposed task of being a full-time mother – there were weeks when the only adults she talked to were Oliver, Imogen's friends' mothers, and members of committees she sat on; and Jacob needed someone to talk to about the two subjects he could not canvass with Liz: Sheila, and Liz herself.

Frances was concerned for Liz. 'I do hope she isn't going to get hurt,' she told him. 'I keep worrying that she'll end up caring for you more than Patrick.'

'It's a risk in theory, but I really don't think so, you know. Liz says not – and going by my own feelings . . .'

'How can you be so sure about yourself?'

'Uh, I don't know. It's that . . . even if Patrick and Sheila both, uh, threw us over' – even saying it felt like bad luck – 'and we were both free, I wouldn't want to stay with Liz permanently. She couldn't take Sheila's place.'

Frances was surprised. 'But you say you're in love with Liz too.'

'I am. But – but . . . it's still Sheila that I talk to in my head. I'd never be more in love with Liz than I am now, and that's not enough. But you'd have to know Sheila to know what I mean – I'd want someone as . . . extreme as her. No, the chief danger for Liz and me isn't wanting to chuck Sheila and Patrick, it's caring for each other so much, in spite of them, that splitting up when I go home next June will hurt like hell.'

'But I don't see how you can help it. I mean, just looking at the two of you, it seems to me you're there already.'

She was right. Neither of them was the casual type; they had known from the start that the end of their attachment would be painful. But there was not much they could do about it, except to avoid spending too much time alone together. Sometimes they called on Naomi and other friends on Sunday afternoons; but Jacob usually wanted to be out seeing London, even in the gloomy winter weather, and they could hardly ask friends who were Londoners and used to the place to join their excursions in order to save them from themselves.

That was where Imogen came in handy. They took her along one afternoon in February for a bus ride and a walk in dingy Stepney, and she loved it and asked if she could please go out with them again sometime. So they took her out the next week, and before long she was accompanying them almost every Sunday. It was an arrangement that suited everybody. It gave Liz and Jacob the company they needed; it freed Frances from what she called, wrinkling her nose, 'afternoons with mothers,' adding guiltily: 'Aren't I awful? But really I don't enjoy most women's company very much, I mean, I'm more

32

of a man's woman, really;' and it unfailingly delighted Imogen. She liked everything they did: looking at buildings, visiting churches and museums, calling on friends, strolling in parks, and simply exploring London. They would take a bus to somewhere new, always riding on top at the front for the view, walk about until her legs gave out – sooner than theirs, since she was always running ahead of them and back – then take another bus, and so on until they were all tired and ready for a late cup of tea at the Standishes'.

Jacob was not surprised to find that he enjoyed her company, for he liked children, but he was slightly startled to recognise, sometime in the spring, that she was becoming dearer to him than his own cousins. He liked looking at her, listening to her. She had a sensibility that was marvellously pliant, responsive and open to wonder – and a will of her own, too, beneath her beautiful manners; she fastened upon life with avid curiosity. She was just what he wanted a daughter of his own to be – the daughter he and Sheila would have – and he observed her with hidden intensity, as if by watching he could learn the secret of raising such a child.

She liked the most extraordinary things, with an extraordinary tenacity of concentration. When they took her to the National Gallery in May, she ignored pretty Uccellos and stopped dead in front of Piero della Francesca's austere *Baptism of Christ*; then stood there looking for so long that they grew impatient.

'Come on, young 'un,' he said at last.

'What?' She looked up blankly. 'Oh. All right.'

'Funny child,' he murmured to Liz as they moved on. 'What makes her pick on an unlikely painting like that?'

Two rooms later they missed her and retraced their steps, peering through crowds that seemed to have got much thicker, and beginning to be rather alarmed. Then Liz said, 'I know – she's gone back for another look at the *Baptism*.'

Sure enough, there she was. Her lips were moving slightly, and she did not notice them.

'Hey, you.' He took her by the arm and turned her round. 'You might have told us you were coming back.'

Imogen was bewildered. 'But I never went away.'

'You've been here all this time?' Liz asked. 'We thought you were with us.'

33

'I was coming – I just stayed for a minute to talk to these men.' She indicated three calm, unforthcoming presences in the *Baptism*.

Over her head they exchanged amused looks: it would be as well not to tell Frances, who was not entirely happy about anything that nourished Imogen's taste for solitary pastimes and imaginary friends, that they had lost her daughter in a museum and found her talking to three angels in a painting.

Chapter 8

ACOB'S TUTOR LOBBED a bombshell at him early in June, at their ritual end–of–term interview. Gautrey usually dispensed sherry and asked intelligent questions without listening to the answers. This time, when he asked about Jacob's plans for the academic year after next, he waited for the reply, then said, 'Ah. Going back to America to "graduate school". Are you indeed?' He inspected the ceiling through round NHS spectacles. 'Have you c-considered staying on?'

'Staying on?'

Gautrey let his artificially curious birdlike gaze fall upon Jacob. 'To do research here. G-graduate work. You're doing well, I have good reports of y-you. You wouldn't be un-unwelcome.'

'It's not something – it never occurred to me that . . .' He put down his sherry glass and stared in bewilderment at the skimpy sprigged curtains and the good Persian carpet. 'Uh . . . I don't think . . . I have to go back sometime, you know, and if I'm out of the American system for too long, it'll be harder to get back in. But, uh, thank you for putting the idea in front of me.'

Gautrey bobbed his head. 'I see, I understand. Well,

c-consider it, anyhow.' An unuttered 'my boy' dangled from the end of his sentence, and he beamed, bright and kindly, a life-size wind-up simulacrum of genuine human interest.

Out in First Court, the Wren chapel was fading in the June evening. He shook his head. Stay? Impossible. Like a life all ice-cream. Can't be done.

In King's Parade he thought: Stay, and don't lose all this: England – Cambridge – a flash of a day at the zoo with Imogen – a flash of Liz –

Not Liz. He had to lose Liz, because of –

Sheila. He had to go back, because he wanted to be with Sheila.

So? Sheila could come here.

Sheila would want him to go back.

In the kitchen at Hertford Street Barbara Potter said, 'Why not?' in her throaty whisper, and Al said, 'Why not?' in a tone of offhand contempt for people who let anything come between them and what they wanted. Jacob held his tongue: he did not want to expose himself to Al's merciless rationality. He would talk about it tomorrow with Liz, who was coming up to Cambridge for a party that the Potters were giving.

Then he decided not to say anything to her either. Staying was out of the question, but the person to tell about the crazy idea was not Liz but Frances, sensible, uninvolved Frances. It would have to keep.

There were about twenty people at the party, all – except Al – sitting or leaning on big corduroy cushions on the carpeted floor. There was one leather-covered swivelling armchair. It was Al's; he growled if anyone else sat in it. Slouching back, higher than anyone else, he peered lazily down at his guests like a lion blinking in a tree. By the chair was a dimmer switch for the spotlights. After eleven o'clock Al turned it down a little every quarter of an hour, and by one the room was as dark as a bistro. People were sleepy, or drunk, or a bit of both. Now and then he would bait someone with a sarcastic question, interrupting the increasingly private murmurs and caresses; everybody would sit up and wait for the blood to flow; and for a time the party would resume the chilling liveliness that was the hallmark of intercourse with Al.

Towards two, one of these exchanges led to a discussion

of the taboo upon nakedness. Into a sleepy general agreement that it was silly and outdated, somebody said, 'Silly, maybe, but not outdated. It's one of the most powerful taboos left. We've all got clothes on, and we all keep them on. We're all "advanced"; but there isn't a single person here who'd take their clothes off in public – even among friends, with no danger of arrest.'

Al swivelled back and forth. 'I would – why not?'

'I would,' said Barbara from the shadows beside him.

'Come off it, Al. You wouldn't. Besides, you'd look ridiculous, naked with everybody else dressed.'

'Would I?'

Al took off his shoes and socks, unbuttoned his shirt, and stood up and took it off. He looked down at Barbara. She took off her shoes, and he helped her to her feet.

'Unzip me, will you?'

He unzipped her dress, and she stepped out of it. He took off his trousers, she her bra and tights; they stooped in unison to take off their pants and stood up, together, naked. Barbara swayed back slightly, inviting inspection. Al inspected her, and let his half-erect prick swell into full erection – impossible not to believe that he was in control and did it deliberately. Barbara watched, and smiled, and with that smile sought the eyes of each person in the room, forcing each one in turn first to meet her gaze, then to inspect her body as openly as she offered it. She looked at the men harder than at the women; Al looked at women and men alike, with lazy, malicious, lively eyes, wringing from both sexes a not dissimilar acknowledgement of his power.

They should have been ridiculous; they were not. They were frightening. They had in their power a roomful of people who were embarrassed and ashamed to admit embarrassment, aroused and ashamed to admit arousal. Naked and unashamed they held their guests paralysed by conflicting shames. No one knew what they would do; they could do anything. They might screw each other, or they might invite someone else. No one would dare refuse; and everyone would end up screwing right there in the drawing room.

Al ended it. He had shown his claws; that was enough. He put on his shirt, his socks, finally his pants and trousers, letting his prick jeer out until the last moment. Barbara got dressed too. They had undressed quick and businesslike; they got dressed slowly, seductively, a striptease in reverse, drawing out their power to the last zip and button.

'I hear you've been having orgies in Cambridge,' Frances said cheerfully the following Saturday.

'Hmph. You've been talking to Liz.' He was slightly peeved; he had not really wanted to tell her about the party until he had thought about it some more.

'Yes, and she said something about lurid goings-on, everybody stripping at the Potters' party, wasn't it?'

'Not everybody, just Al and Barbara;' and he described what had happened.

'My, how fascinating. What a – a dashing thing to do. I wish I . . .'

'Yeah, me too.' He met her eye, and they smiled ruefully. He wanted to tell her how much the incident had disturbed him; it was a grain of sand lodged in innocent soft tissue. He felt a confused, turbulent envy of the Potters' fearlessness, a queer abashment when he met Barbara in the kitchen or on the stairs, and scorn for himself and everyone else at the party, except Liz, whose gentleness was incompatible with large defiant gestures. But he could not find words for what he felt; so instead he shrugged and told her about his interview with Gautrey.

'But really, why don't you stay? I mean, you'd clearly love to – and it would be so nice for *us*.'

He mustered all the reasons against it: Sheila might not be able to use her training; she might not like England; they would have to postpone having children; a Cambridge degree wouldn't count for as much as an American one when they went back home.

'I see what you mean,' she conceded at last; 'but think how nice it would be. You're so happy here.'

'Yes – I've never been happier in my life.'

What?

Yes. He had not known that it was true until he said it. Happy away from Sheila, from his country? Yes. He was in England; and, much as he missed Sheila, he had Liz and Imogen.

And *Imogen*? Well, yes. Good Lord, yes. He realised that he was more than just fond of the determined little creature: he had come to love her, both for herself and because she reminded him so much of Sheila – or of the imaginary daughter that he and Sheila were going to make real; he wasn't sure which. With Imogen's company he missed Sheila less than if he had had only Liz.

But he still missed Sheila. Only if she were here would his happiness really overflow.

Chapter 9

'ARE YOU GOING abroad on holiday?' Frances had asked him one day in June.

'No, I want to see more of England – get a feel for the countryside. So we'll hitch around for a fortnight.'

'Wouldn't you learn more about England from seeing a small area thoroughly than rushing about like that?'

'You know, that hadn't occurred to me . . . You may be right. Perhaps . . . But no, it'd be a bad idea. Liz and I need bustle and movement – we'll get too immersed in each other if we're on our own in one spot like that.'

'Oh, of course. But – I know! – come to us in West Horton. That way you won't be alone together. – Yes, for the whole time. – No, you won't be a bother, quite the reverse. Oliver will only be down at weekends – *if* then – and I'll not have a soul to talk to for the whole month. You'll save me from insanity.'

So on the tenth of August they motored down to Wiltshire with Oliver, in time for Imogen's birthday tea-party. West

Horton lay in steep country, deep in a network of narrow lanes, and miles from a main road. It had no new buildings, only lovely plain stone houses dotted over the downs and jostled round a stream and a small green where four roads met at the bottom of the narrow combe.

'It is nice,' said Oliver. 'It's still a real village, thank God. We're spared commuters, and we've almost no weekenders – most people who drive from London don't want to add half an hour in the lanes to their trip. We're the only holiday house, and I pretend we're, er, local, because Broughton – where I grew up – is so close.'

Monk's House was the highest house on one of the downs, up a narrow lane that soon dwindled into a farm track. Frances called it their 'cottage in the country', but it was a good-sized, sprawling house with a seventeenth-century core – long drawing room, big kitchen, dining room two steps down, all low and stone-paved – to which an expansive owner in the Regency had added an airy back wing, as well as fitting the front elevation with the latest thing in narrow, slightly effete Gothick windows.

'Cottage indeed,' Jacob grumbled good-naturedly; 'you could get lost in it. I suppose it's one of these transatlantic differences?'

They all tried without much success to work out the difference between a cottage and a house; then Liz asked Oliver how long they had had the place.

'Ever since we were married – it was part of the family property, and we rented it from my mother for a while, then bought it.'

'It was the only way of keeping Kathleen out,' said Frances with a dry chuckle. 'She was always acting the good landlady, checking that the roof didn't leak and telling me how to do things till I wanted to scream. But since we bought it, she's needed an invitation to cross the threshold, thank God. Gracious, I sound like a traditional daughter-in-law. But we're having dinner with her this evening – more birthday celebrations for Imogen – so you'll see her for yourself.'

Broughton House was set in a modest park; and it was no cottage, but a big Victorian house with vermiculated dressings and an abundance of staring bay windows. The inside was quite different, furnished in severe elegance with the best modern furniture of the past five decades – perquisites of Standish and Sons.

'Surprises you, doesn't it?' said Mrs Standish, watching him look round with pleasure at her drawing room. 'You expected chintz and mahogany, and me in a twinset and tweeds, hey?' – and, when he grinned guiltily: 'Then imagine my surprise when I came here as a bride – wearing a good tweed suit, too – expecting chintz and mahogany, and found most of *this*!'

She was not wearing a tweed suit now, but a beautifully cut fawn linen frock and a long modern silver-link necklace. In most respects, however, she remained as she had been bred, a member of the rural gentry. She was affable, almost jolly, talked a lot in a high, loud, confident drawl, asked a lot of impertinent questions and listened to some of the answers. Her condescension comprehended everyone. Only Imogen was exempt, and only Imogen really seemed to like her.

Over dinner she went to work on Jacob. She blamed him for Jamie's decision to live in Canada – 'I'll never see him. – What, me, visit the *colonies*? Too frightful. And he'll pick up the most dreadful accent, just like yours.'

But he had a lifetime's experience at warding off aunts who habitually made up for his mother's failings as a Yiddische momma by lunging for his jugular with zeal and surgical precision; compared to them, Mrs Standish was an amateur. He dodged and weaved and came up bland and smiling; and after a few passes she treated him with the beginnings of a surprised respect and started quizzing him about America with genuine curiosity. Though her tone was that of a civilised person enquiring into the customs of barbarian tribes, he didn't much mind – he quite liked her. She was a bossy old terror, but he could not see much real harm in her, and there might even be a fund of stifled good will. She was no innocent – she liked sticking pins – but some of her outrageousness seemed accidental: she was too clumsy to tease without drawing blood, and too insensitive to notice when she had done so.

That fortnight was like sliding down days of sunshine. Every day had a simple routine: in the morning, a walk; a picnic; driving to look at villages: in the afternoon, going down the

40

hill for papers and groceries, with Imogen bouncing ahead, downhill and up, down and up; carrying the tea-tray through the dark flagged hall and the sunny drawing room to the garden; drinking tea in a daze of contentment – three pairs of adult legs outstretched, three pairs of adult eyes narrowed against the westering sun, and a child perching briefly to stoke up with tea and biscuits, then off again, up slope and down slope, round the apple tree and behind the garden shed: in the evenings, sitting outside again after dinner, while white flowers, still visible in the deepening garden, fluttered like butterflies in odd little gusts of wind – more than breezes – that were conjured out of nowhere on the stillest days.

The days had an intensity that was out of time. Jacob was frighteningly happy; the happiness of winter and spring was nothing to this. The beauty of the countryside was stirring something in him that only Sheila had reached before now: a recognition. It was not an exotic, foreign beauty; it was in his bones; he recognised it. He had never guessed that anything could be as beautiful as these combes, villages, houses, hanging woods – yet he had always known. It was all strange and new; it was all deeply familiar, deeply known. It was completely satisfying.

And dangerous. His defences were down, his emotions wrought upon; he missed Sheila more than ever, yet loved Liz as never before; and his happiness was beginning to affect her. If he went on treating her with as much caressing tenderness as he felt, she might soon be in the same over-susceptible state as he.

They did not discuss the danger, but they both acted to minimise it. By the second week they were taking Imogen with them on all their morning drives in the old Morris Minor that was kept at Monk's House – and spending more time at home with Frances, in whose company they were constrained by courtesy to act more as friends than as lovers.

In the afternoons, in the garden, they did not talk much; the sun and the scent of the humming borders drugged them into small-talk or dozy silence. But the quiet of the garden in the early evening was conducive to conversation; faraway sounds were clear – children's voices floating up from the combe, cars climbing the downs – while closer sounds were muted, like the colours of the flowers. In that fragrant stillness, watching sky and downs fade, they would talk at length, swapping childhood memories brought back by Imogen's presence, asking and answering personal questions with friendly ease in the indistinct light.

One evening, as they watched Imogen practise somersaults down the hillside, full of purposeful concentration – tuck, roll, up in one spring, climb the hill, tuck, roll, up – Frances said, 'Oliver was never athletic – she must get that from me. I was captain of the hockey team at school, incredible as that seems now.'

'Well, I was swimming champ of Malden High School, incredible as *that* may seem. And I still swim every week, so I won't go completely to seed – '

'Which is even more incredible,' said Liz, laughing.

'Gracious,' said Frances. 'I mean, I never thought of you as the sporting type.'

'Hah. Quite right, I'm not. It was self-preservation – to keep from being beaten up.'

'Why would anyone do that?'

'Because I was short and smart – I stood out like a sore thumb. But I was a good swimmer, so I worked at it and became school champ. That made it bad politics to pick on me – and swimming made me pretty strong for my height; most guys would have thought twice before taking me on. And I played dumb too; that helped.'

'You mean failing exams?' Frances was scandalised.

'No, no, just day to day – pretending I was one of the guys, talking like a slob . . .'

'But how could your parents let it happen?' she cried indignantly.

'What could they have done?'

'What could they have *done*? They weren't poor; why didn't they send you to a good school?'

'But by American standards Malden High *was* pretty good.'

'No, I mean a private school – a progressive one, like Bedales or Bryanston. Only they're boarding schools, and that wouldn't do – but the day-school equivalent.'

He could see how Frances might oppose private education here yet not in America; but why jib at boarding schools? 'Why not a boarding school?' he asked idly.

'Because children shouldn't spend their adolescence herded

42

together away from home,' she said vigorously. 'It shrivels their souls up, that hard, cold, loveless atmosphere. Oliver and I know from experience. I'd never *ever* send Imogen away to school.' She stopped, as if surprised by her own vehemence. 'But I'm off on one of my hobby horses. I was asking why your parents didn't send you to a good private day school.'

He thought about it, watching Imogen, who was still somersaulting, dirty from head to foot, clarity shining from her streaked skin. 'I don't suppose it occurred to them,' he said finally. 'If it had been a bad school, they would have, of course; but Malden High had a very good reputation. And it's so different over there, you know – hardly anybody goes to private schools, except in the most upper-upper classes. You just put up with school.'

She shook her head. 'I wouldn't let it happen to Imogen.'

'But she's going to a state school.'

'Yes, but at her age it's not so important . . . and . . . one's looking ahead already . . . If Islington goes comprehensive . . . It's such a mixed area, and the parents who send their children to the grammar schools now will mostly send them to public school rather than let them . . . And even if it doesn't change . . . the girls' grammar school, I'm not sure if it's what one wants . . .'

But – but – but the Standishes believed in supporting the state system. So what was this about: 'If Islington goes comprehensive', and not being sure whether the girls' grammar school was 'what one wants'?

So? He didn't have anything against private education – unlike the Standishes.

It came to him later. How did a person know when they meant what they said?

Chapter 10

N THEIR LAST day in Wiltshire Jacob and Liz went for a final drive with Imogen. After dutifully admiring Castle Combe, at Frances' insistence – 'It's a show village, but it *is* lovely' – they were heading for Bradford-upon-Avon when they came upon a village so beautiful that Liz immediately stopped the Morris.

'Ducks!' Imogen ran to the pond.

Ducks; dozens of ducks of different sorts and sizes on and beside a big pond in a big irregular green; ducks squawking like a bad telephone connection. Round the green and along the roads that ran from it in three directions there was a harmony of grey houses: a long stone seventeenth-century farmhouse across the pond with leaded windows rippling light from the duck-wavy water; several chaste Georgian houses of grey brick elegantly diapered with red, one with a delicious shell hood over the doorway; plain cottages of rubble-coursed silver-grey stone. Nothing ugly in sight, only English village beauty, unmarred; and Imogen in the foreground, squatting to talk to the ducks.

'What's this place called?' Jacob asked. The ducks were so noisy that he had to raise his voice. 'Is it famous too?'

'Biddestone, the sign said – I've never heard of it. But it's nicer than Castle Combe.'

'Yes – it's more private. It's like somebody who's just a person, and Castle Combe is like Noel Coward or Auden or somebody, acting the part of being old and distinguished, and proud of the lines on their faces because they're an advertisement of character.'

Liz laughed uneasily. 'You're hard on people.'

He was surprised. 'Me? But I'm always being acc-' He stopped; she would know that the person who accused him of being namby-pamby about people was Sheila. Instead he said, 'I always think I'm too easy on people.'

As if guessing what he had started to say, she said nothing. They started to stroll; insensibly their paths diverged.

At the end of the pond he looked back. Liz was standing a short distance off, turned half away from him, hands in her skirt pockets, looking down at the water. On the other side Imogen was migrating slowly towards him, following ducks. They would not talk to her or let her talk to them; they sailed off at her approach, unfussed but unclubbable, nosed in to shore further on, then moved off again as the spindly human animal crept up on them quacking in accents that would move a duckling to scorn.

Liz sat down. He thought of going and sitting beside her, to make up; but they had not quarrelled, or, if they had, it was without words, and he decided to leave well enough alone.

Imogen came across a duck that was either kindly or gullible, for it floated sedately at its moorings while she quacked at it. Bliss. She squatted happily and kept on quacking with her usual persistence until he thought it would be driven out of its wits and sail off. Instead, it circled slowly, came in close and squawked at her.

She squawked back and hugged her ankles with delight.

The duck answered.

Imogen quacked; the duck quacked; they quacked at each other without stopping. Jacob looked to see if the other ducks were scandalised, but they were minding their own business. Perhaps this one was the village idiot.

A flimsy cloud slipped across the sun, and pond and village, woman and child were suddenly leached of brilliancy, like a hand-tinted photograph. He observed them as if from a distance. The cloud slid away, but his distance stayed; they were an image of something . . . not themselves . . . no, not of the past, nor of the future, exactly, but . . . Of a possibility. On one side of the pond, sitting on the grass, Sheila; on the other side, Sheila's daughter, seducing ducks; at the end, himself, Sheila's daughter's father, watching his family; and nearby, perhaps not in view, home. And a thought as clear as if he had spoken aloud: I could be happy living here.

Nonsense. It's impossible, you're American. You don't belong here. Home is somewhere else. Over there, with Sheila. Sheila wouldn't like it over here, not for the long term.

I could be happy living here? He stifled the crazy notion and substituted a careful appraisal of his present state. I'm happy here, he thought deliberately, looking from Liz to Imogen.

Liz turned her head. Catching his eye, she stood up, brushed the back of her skirt and started towards him. He put his arm round her, and they strolled together to where Imogen and the idiot duck were still talking.

'Time to be moving on, pet.'

With a resigned, 'Oh,' she got up; and started hopping about. 'Oh – oh – pins and needles – oh – my legs are falling off – oh – oh . . . Oh. It's getting better.' She stopped hopping and unscrewed her face. 'If I could stand on my head for that long, would I get pins and needles in my head?'

'Maybe, I don't know,' said Liz.

She looked at Jacob.

'My dear child, I don't know either.' He met her hazel eyes and shrugged; and at precisely that moment he decided to do his graduate work in England. After all, why not? Three more years after next year, then back home by, let's see, the summer of sixty-nine. Not such a big deal – probably shorter, in fact, than an American Ph.D. course. Sheila wouldn't mind coming over for just three years; and it would give him time to get England out of his system.

PART II

Chapter 11

N THE LAST Saturday before Christmas Jacob began the long climb to Naomi's flat. Things had not turned out as he had envisaged them by the duckpond in Biddestone five and a half years before. It was 1970; he had not got a Ph.D; he was still in England; and Sheila had left him and returned to America for good. He was stunned and miserable, and unable to imagine ever again loving anyone as he had loved her. In theory he supposed he would, for he was resilient by nature and knew it; but after five months without her he was still flat, sour, cheerless. Why he was going to a Christmas party he didn't know.

He passed a couple pausing for breath, then their children fidgeting on the next landing. '*Do* hurry,' one of them called past him; and he was taken back to the first time he had climbed these stairs. Then, too, he had passed winded parents and impatient children. Right about here he had said hello to the Standishes; and here, to Imogen.

Another memory: standing in the back room at the Standishes', at his first London party, watching people with gentle, open, shining faces; and with that memory, his reason for coming tonight. He wanted to find his way back to the enchanted ground where high civilisation flourished and faces were alight with subtle sensibility. Briefly his heart lifted. He was looking forward to London again, to the world again.

At the door he stopped in panic. The place was packed; and the days were past when he had relished the challenge of conquering a party full of strangers. He was hovering on the threshold in a funk when Naomi bobbed up in front of him.

'Jacob my dear, I'm *so* glad,' she exclaimed in her deep, cracked voice, beaming all over her lovely monkey face, then led him to the drawing room and into a group where someone was just finishing an anecdote.

'. . . then the producer scarpered, and the project was kaput. That was the last time I saw Orson.'

Naomi chuckled. 'Say, Alec, did I ever tell you – or you, Jacob – about the time I interviewed him on the set of . . .' And she was off on one of her stories, gathering everyone in with her smile and beaming at Jacob now and then with special warmth. Then she said, 'I'd better get back to the hall,' and hurried off: he guessed that she had seen his state and stuck with him, guests or no guests, until he got over it. A lady.

The glow she had kindled stayed lit. Half-listening to television gossip, he glanced about and saw several familiar people and, close at hand, a half-remembered face, brown and button-bright – Penny, that was it, with her towheaded children: a girl of about eleven and a much younger son.

She caught his eye. 'Jacob! It's been *ages,* two or three years, isn't it? – Four? Incredible. Oh, I remember, you were with your girl – not Liz, your American girl, she'd just come over. Is she . . . ?' Her round eyes flicked to either side of him.

Drat. 'Sheila and I have split up' – in his best casual voice. 'She went back to the States in July.'

'Oh, I'm sorry I – er, yes, too bad. Still,' brightening, 'she *was* rather, um, fierce, wasn't she?'

Yes. Fierce, formidable, intransigent, extreme, the best of him, the light of his soul: gone. He had given her up for the chance of listening to prattling china dolls at English parties.

Penny was recounting her romances since leaving her children's father: '. . . and his wife ran off with an Arab prince and left him this nice big house; and he's much nicer than Ken or Jack. The children like him too – don't you, Mandy?'

Mandy made a face, provocatively indifferent. 'Bob's okay.' Then she noticed something; stared intently; finally sighed with satisfaction. 'Look, Mum, Jude's just drunk a whole – '

'Martini. My God!' Penny snatched the empty glass from her son and snapped at Mandy: 'Why didn't you – ?'

Mandy looked her straight in the eye. 'I only just saw him, and I said . . .'

Penny shrugged at Jacob. 'I should have been watching. He'll be high as a kite in a minute.'

Below her line of sight Mandy and Jude exchanged glances of satisfaction at a bad deed well done. Then the martini began to dissolve his self-control. A chuckle of triumph rippled down his body and washed back up tremulously in giggles, then spasmodic squeaks; he began to look alarmed.

Penny picked him up. 'There, there, you silly boy.' He nestled into her shoulder, quivering, and she went on talking to Jacob. Except for seeming more humorously resigned to the demands of children, she was unchanged – pleasant and lively, but not someone he had much in common with. Yet, as she talked over Jude's head, with Mandy beside her half bored, half perky, she presented him with a picture of matter-of-fact domesticity that stirred his old futile desire into hurtful life. Would be never get rid of that intense image – first glimpsed on the Standishes' staircase, then by a duckpond with Liz and Imogen; then sustained, hopefully for a while, then with hopeless longing, through years of argument with Sheila – a vision of him, and Sheila, and a child – their child: a holy family, secure against the world?

Jude heaved.

'You're going to be sick, aren't you?' said Penny.

'N-n-no . . .'

She held up his pallid face with her free hand. 'Oh yes you are. Come on, let's get you to the bathroom.' She hurried away; Mandy followed, looking interested.

'Hullo, Jacob.' It was the bird-thin solicitor and her husband, the cartoonist. How nice to see him, they said; how was he? And where was he living? – Still in Cambridge? He must be a don by now. – No? Still working on that thesis, then. – Given it up? A self-employed computer programmer! Ah (blankly). How interesting – with glazed politeness, as if he had confessed to being an accountant or a file clerk.

And that was that. Their eyes slid about, they saw someone they simply must say hullo to – sorry to slope off – they'd be seeing him . . .

Jacob shrugged and went over to Colin Palmer. 'I saw your documentary about the homelands,' he said; 'it was terrific.'

Norman Susskind joined them. 'Yeah. And that townships footage – how'd you get it out? When I was there, just doing *fashion*, for chrissake, they told me I couldn't take undeveloped film out of the country – and they meant it; the fuckers checked every negative and slide on my way out.'

'I didn't take it out myself. What I brought back was camouflage – pretty colour stuff, happy Bantus doing tribal dances sort of thing. Customs practically hugged me.'

'An underground route?' Norman said alertly. 'Hey, man, I'm going to follow you up on that. I want to go back, do a real exposé. South Africa's wide open for hard-hitting photo-journalism, same kind of thing as your movie. It's what I need to change gear with the Sunday supplements. But I need a route for film – contacts – and for all that you're a goldmine.'

Colin did not look happy. 'Isn't that the kind of thing the supplements get Dave Llewellyn to do?'

'SA won't let Dave in; they know what he'd manage to bring out under their noses. It's my chance to get in on his act – and I've had it up to the eyeballs with child models and shoes and famous fat-ass creeps in their fucking studies. So what about it, Colin?'

Colin's eyes wandered uneasily. 'I, er, I'm afraid it's sort of confi-' Seeing a diversion he called over Jacob's shoulder: 'Liz, how nice to see you!'

'Hullo Colin, hullo Jacob, hullo Norman': a soft, familiar voice, too familiar from the intimacy of a past to which there was no returning. Jacob turned round, hoping that his cheeks were not so flushed as they felt.

The last time he had seen her was four years before at the Baker Street Classic. An awkward meeting; he had been with Sheila, she alone. Now it was he who was alone; now, as she introduced him to Patrick and their baby, he knew how exposed she must have felt while he and Sheila were being so friendly. He was acutely alive to her presence beside him, alive as he had not been since Sheila left. Could such a sharp awareness be one-sided? He watched her covertly, but all he could discern was her delicate awareness that this encounter could not be completely easy for him. She was being careful not to single Patrick out by word or gesture, though once in the middle of a story she nearly touched his arm, then, remembering, retracted her hand. With just that quick reminiscent gesture she had often brushed Jacob's arm, and for a moment he wished piercingly that she were not with Patrick; that they could get back together.

Back together? Even in his loneliness he knew better; he could not help demanding a nakedness of spirit that she could not help withholding.

He should move on. Being alive to a woman, to a particular woman, was too painful. He slid inconspicuously out of the group, picked up a martini and drifted here and there saying hello to former acquaintances. They all asked what he was doing and, when he told them, either lost interest in him, as if he had suddenly ceased to exist, or told would-be-humorous anecdotes about the stupidity of computers in slightly aggressive tones. Most of them had met Sheila – once. They said they were sorry she had left him; but he was sure they were thinking: Good riddance.

The bloom of the party was fading fast. At that first party, the Standishes', he had stood back looking at people with gleaming faces and listening to the harmonious splash of their conversation. Six years later, what had changed? Nothing, to the eye; to the ear nothing. Naomi's white ceiling reflected soft light from upturned lamps onto smiling, sparkling faces; the room chimed with laughter and chatter. The same. Yet not, quite. The plash of voices was not entirely harmonious: there were off-notes, harsh overtones; and the faces did not shine from within: the shower of flattering light was like silver dust over jaded, anxious, insincere expressions. Why the hell was he here?

Because this was where he belonged. And what did he think he looked like, sodden with self-pity?

Where he belonged? What a funny thought.

But true. They were not foreign to him, these people; he understood them, shared the movements of their minds, was part of their world: more at home here than in America, and accepted, at least in company like this, as part of the social fabric.

At home here. Yes. Not completely, not like the English; but he was no longer an outsider. He was half in, half out – probably for good: planted on his feet, the water frothing round his waist, while round him the English ducked and bobbed and slid through their native element. 'You belong here,' Sheila had said. He had denied it; but she was right. His point

53

of reference, his primary allegiance, his sense of community had mysteriously shifted. For such expatriate Americans as Naomi and Norman home was still, unambiguously, America; but for him home was now, however tentatively, England, his beloved England. He had a place of sorts in this mixed and muddied world; he belonged, he fitted in. He would be staying for good.

'Well, you're looking better.' It was Naomi.

'Yeah, I've just this minute decided something I've been dithering about: I'm going to stay here for good.'

'Ah, I thought you would. Good. And you're okay for work permit stuff?'

'Yeah, there aren't many people in exactly my line, so that's no problem. It's a pretty crazy idea, though. I don't have anything lined up for after the thesaurus project ends, and I don't know what I'll find. Back home I could get interesting jobs without trying – the field's booming. But here I might have to take any work I can get; and if there isn't much of a market for my, uh, talents, I might be stuck for ages doing tedious routine programming just to eat. I've been letting people know I'm available – but no nibbles yet. It's a terrific gamble.'

'But worth it.'

'Yes, I want to stay.' Saying so sent a jolt of joy through him. 'You know, Naomi, I wanted to thank you for going on inviting me every year when I kept not coming. It wasn't that I didn't want to, but – ' He stopped; he couldn't say that Sheila had wanted him not to come.

Naomi chuckled. 'Oh, I don't give up that easy,' she said. 'And I did have a feeling something like this might happen.'

'You *did*? But you only met her once . . .' Oh. Not so prescient. Like everybody else, she had met her once and disliked her and hoped they would split up.

She surprised him. 'Yes, but I could tell what she was like, and I guessed that she'd want to go back and you wouldn't. I wished I could warn you, because I could see why you were crazy about her – '

'You *could*? Most people couldn't – and she *was* pretty icy at that party.'

54

'Oh, but she was . . . quite something. A force of nature. And you were so obviously right for each other, and everything was so obviously going to go wrong – and I'm *so* sorry you've lost her.' She *was* sorry, beaming friendliness at him out of crinkled eyes; of all the people here, only she had seen what Sheila was. Not only that: had predicted the future from one meeting. Uncanny.

'No wonder you're a great journalist,' he said. 'And as a fortune teller – well, what say I get you a crystal ball for Chanukah?'

'I don't need a crystal ball to tell about you. You're going to be okay.'

'I am?' – startled. 'That's more than I know.'

'Oh yes, you're out of the woods now, just about.' She laughed at herself. 'Madame Naomi has spoke. And now I'd better go on announcing food. You go to the kitchen and have a little chicken soup.'

Chapter 12

CRUSH OF people was blocking the passage to the kitchen. From beyond them there came a large indefinite murmur, with two voices, a man's and a woman's, somehow familiar, now and then rising clear above the rest.

Nearly there. Beyond the thicket of heads and shoulders the murmur swelled as he got closer, and still above it those two voices hovered and sank like balls in a fountain.

Ahead of him one person moved to the left and another to the right; and at the end of a tunnel of people he saw, in the middle of the kitchen, a child with a serious, troubled face, looking ahead, then down, then slightly up, her straight eyebrows puckered by her effort to understand something difficult and important.

Imogen.

Imogen taller, older – she must be eleven or twelve – but unmistakably Imogen.

The crowd shifted, cutting off his view. He pushed, the tunnel opened again, and he was in the big, tiled, echoing kitchen with about twenty other people, some of them helping themselves to food, others standing, plates in hand, in a loose circle, their attention surreptitiously fixed on Frances and Oliver Standish, who were bickering over Imogen's head on the far side of the circle. Theirs were the familiar voices. Frances was flushed with drink and smilingly furious; Oliver was also rather tight, his elegance drawn thin, like veneer, his smile a strained rictus.

Jacob was too far away to get more than stray snatches: 'But *darling* . . .', '. . . and what about the time . . .', '. . . don't you think . . .' But the thing was as clear as a spectacle in dumb-show: under pretence of light public sarcasm the Standishes were quarrelling with polite savagery about a life-and-death issue; and between them was Imogen, listening intently. Nobody but Jacob seemed to see that the discrepancy between their smooth voices and curdled undertones was disturbing her; everyone else was concentrating upon them.

Moving closer, he began to get the drift. They were taking speciously friendly swipes at each other's driving.

'. . . at least I wasn't going as fast as you,' Frances snapped, 'or we'd have been sardines. And it only happened because I was double-declutching – you get so cross if I don't.'

'My dear, that's on the open road,' calmly and coldly, 'or in normal city traffic, not emergencies.'

'But the time that car shot out of a drive, and I changed down fast to slow up – you didn't praise my fast reaction, you just said, "You didn't double-declutch."'

'There was time – *I* could have.'

'*You* have been driving constantly for seventeen years.'

'You've been driving as long as me.'

'But not as much. I hardly ever drive by myself, and you usually drive when we're together. I *like* you to drive, I mean,

I'm awfully traditional, I'm not one of your Women's Lib types. But it does make it hard for women to get as much practice – admit.'

'Many women drive very competently,' said Oliver airily – the accents of experience.

'And just who did you have in mind?' – caustically. 'Our friend in Clapham?'

Imogen's head shot up.

'Among others.' His voice was icy; his lips moved as if preparing a particularly lethal taunt. Then he glanced round at the roomful of witnesses and forced a smile. 'But the point is, dear, how will your driving improve, unless I remind you about things like double-declutching?'

No question about it, something was badly wrong between them – so wrong that discussions of the most trivial subjects turned into deadly arguments about that one thing. Jacob knew that state too well from his own life to mistake its characteristic tones. He listened to the fragmented ice-chips of their talk and watched Imogen, reckoning her age on his fingers. She was twelve: still a child, a carefully nurtured English upper-middle-class child, young for her years, but almost able to grasp that their row was about something more important than driving. Now and then she tried to look up, to take their meaning from their expressions, then did not quite dare face what she might see; her clear gaze, suddenly timid, fluttered as far as Frances' pink chin, swung to Oliver's pale pointed nose, veered away and finally fixed itself on the near distance in a steady, troubled intensity of effort to understand. But the innocence of childhood baulked her comprehension, and slowly she gave up the effort – it was too hard, the result might be too unbearable. A cloud of sulky withdrawal settled on her brow, and she stood staring into space in dogged silence, waiting for the storm to pass – as if she knew that it *would* pass. Were such scenes a staple of life at home; did they row in front of her all the time?

Surely not; not Frances and Oliver; the thought was indecent.

Yet she was shrinking, a dwarf between giants.

Yet nothing was happening: only, a little girl was standing, rather bored, between her parents.

Jacob was seeing with double vision. He blinked: Imogen was standing up straight and still like a good child, not fidgeting. He blinked again: she was shrinking by millimetres and casting another bewildered appealing glance in the general direction of their chins. A voice in his head said: 'That child is in trouble. Rescue her.' Another voice blurred that imperative to the statement: 'Someone should rescue her;' and he stood still, blinking with double vision. Frances was a coarse-faced, tipsy Juno, Oliver a spruce Adonis, slightly squiffy: dapper, not elegant.

Double vision. They were his old friends; they had been emblems of civilised life to him; they were not shouting before the child.

Yet they were ungainly wanton gods laying waste to innocence.

The moment passed. Looking again at Imogen, a little girl unhappy and out of place, he heard again the inner command: Rescue her. Not heroically, from the clutches of inordinate gods: ordinarily, from ordinary drink-fuddled parents. Distract her, or them. Go say hello.

Someone stumbled against him as he started to move forward, shoving him clear across the circle; he would have pitched into the Standishes had not each reached out a steadying hand.

'We meet again.' Oliver cocked an eyebrow as if to suggest that Jacob's headlong arrival was both typical and excessive.

Frances kissed him and plunged in as if the suspension of friendship that Sheila had caused did not signify. 'Jacob, darling, Naomi said you'd be coming. I want to hear all about you, it's been such ages. And you won't recognise Imogen after, what is it, four years; she's *enormous*, aren't you . . .' But Imogen had vanished.

'I suppose she's at a private school – a public school – by now?' he asked politely.

'Not yet – school fees are simply horrendous, so we're keeping her in her local school – well, nearly her local school – till the last moment. But she'll start at the Friends School next year.'

'The Friends School? What an odd name.'

'Quaker,' said Oliver explanatorily.

'A *religious* school?'

He had tried, without complete success, not to sound horrified; Frances smiled as she replied, 'Not the way you

58

mean – not like convent schools. It's very high-minded, if that's the word, and the children have to go to Meeting, but that's as far as it goes.'

'It's very civilised,' Oliver amplified; 'mildly progressive and all that, but children still learn their lessons and good manners. And it's mixed; that's important – we don't believe in single-sex schools.'

'But that's enough about schools,' said Frances. 'Right now I want to hear about you. Naomi told me you've turned into a computer whiz-kid; and about you and Sheila breaking up. Such a pity!' She sounded less palpably insincere than most people. 'But at least you're still over here, which is nice for your friends.' Oliver echoed her sentiments in his drier fashion; they were meeting him as a couple, united, their earlier tension invisible. 'And where are you living?' she went on. 'Still renting rooms?'

'No, Sheila and I bought a house in 1967.'

'Really? What's it like? Where? Do tell.'

'Let's see . . . It's in a terrace, Coronation Place, that's poked away off the road; two up, two down, with a good big kitchen on the back, and – Oh, hello, Imogen.'

'Jacob!'

And there she was, the old Imogen, her unremarkable features little different, except that their infant roundness had been fined away; her dark hair still short with a straight fringe; her hazel eyes, flecked with yellow and green, still poignantly beautiful. She was taller, more substantial, but in aspect and expression she was the child he had taken riding on the tops of buses, and her delight at seeing him left him momentarily speechless with a gust of joy. He beamed at her wordlessly, and she beamed back with the clear gaze that was her salient feature.

Then somebody tapped him on the shoulder; a new circle was formed; and before long he and the Standishes were on opposite sides of the room.

People with children were beginning to leave, and Jacob, who was pleasantly tired, as if a lot had happened in a short time, decided to go too. He paused a moment on the landing outside the flat; and Frances, Oliver and Imogen came out. Frances, Oliver and Imogen: parents and child, old friends all. Frances and Oliver were smiling over Imogen's head. She was not in on the joke, but she did not look excluded, only sleepy.

Old friends all. They stopped and asked him to come and see them next time he was in London.

Old friends. He had half forgotten their covert quarrel, yet it had left its trace, so that unconsciously he regarded the prospect of renewed friendship as if through a smeared glass: not quite sure what lay beyond, and inclined to look away. He actually did look away: and saw Imogen, sleepy Imogen, smothering a yawn and looking aside in the hope that it would go unnoticed if she did not meet anyone's eyes.

Imogen in trammels, turning her eyes this way, that way, in search of understanding or escape: her averted eyes recalled that much of the scene in the kitchen to him, together with a flash of premonition that the child in trammels and his revelation about belonging in England were connected: not by cause and effect, but as part and parcel of the same thing, whatever it was. So when Frances said, 'Do come *soon*; let's not get out of touch again,' and Oliver added his, 'Er, yes,' of agreement, Jacob followed the flash of premonition, against his first inclination, and arranged to come to them after the NFT in a fortnight.

He waited until they had gone, trying to make that premonition of connectedness solidify into something he could express to himself. Part and parcel, part and parcel – of what? But it was gone. Part and parcel . . . All he could catch was a whisper, something to do with responsibility: that if you belong in a place you have responsibilities.

Chapter 13

SUNDAY BREAKFAST WAS late, and afterwards Oliver started going through the newspapers, while Frances and Jacob sat on in the kitchen, exchanging gossip about people they both knew. The old Sunday-morning ritual of talking over late coffee, the old ease; past and present met seamlessly over the hiatus of the years with Sheila – though those years had not vanished quite without trace. Oliver's face was sharper and thinner and had a fretful cast and a few lines. Frances' slow, confident movements had still their old animal assurance, but her creamy skin was beginning to curdle slightly, and her face was no longer almost as composed and self-contained as the portrait bust of a Roman matron, but nervous, expressive, wholly human.

At midday she heated up soup and got out bread and cheese, and Jacob set the table, pleased that he remembered where to find things. The soup was delicious, as always, and he ate two bowlsful as they talked about movies and Oliver's feud with a copy-chopping editor.

Meaty hot soup and crunchy bread; a warm room; leafless trees holding back the sky outside; friendly talk round the scrubbed pine table: seamlessness.

After lunch Oliver and Imogen disappeared upstairs, and Frances and Jacob settled themselves at the table with a second cup of coffee. 'Now,' she said expectantly.

He groaned. 'Okay, okay. What do you want to know?'

'Everything, of course.'

Of course. He remembered how attentively she had always

listened and questioned. 'There's so much . . . I don't know where to begin.'

'At the beginning, of course. I mean, when did things start going wrong?'

He considered. 'Before Sheila ever came, I guess. She didn't really want to – she wanted to use her training. But several people in education said she'd certainly be able to get work teaching deaf children. So she came – but they were wrong: her qualifications weren't recognised after all. She'd have had to do another year's training, and it wasn't worth it, since we'd only be here three years, four at the most. What she could do – '

'I remember – she got a job at one of those language schools that teach English to foreigners; hadn't they found that deaf-teachers were good at language teaching?'

'That's right – the Horn School of English. But she was cross about wasting her training; it was a bad start. And so was living in Hertford Street. She detested the Potters and their friends: if they were the English left, she almost preferred the American right. Actually, she didn't have much time for almost any of my friends, even – ' He felt himself go red.

'Even us,' Frances finished for him.

'Oh no, she liked Im– ' He was getting hotter and hotter. 'Damn. Foot in mouth. Uh . . .'

'Don't worry, I could tell she didn't like us. She was polite, but it showed.'

'I know, it was like that with a lot of people. I hope you weren't – '

'No, no, I mean, if you don't mind my saying so, I didn't really warm to her either, so – '

'You mustn't judge Sheila just from that' – anxiously. 'She was usually very perceptive; but teachers at the Horn were being horrid about her accent, and she got a bit paranoid about the English for a while – and by the time she eased up, she'd already cut us off from most of the people I'd known before.'

'Yes, we hardly saw you after the first few months – wasn't Naomi's party that year the last time?'

'Dear me, yes. She was quite unfair about Naomi, she judged her from that crowd that turns up; and afterwards she said she didn't want to waste, uh . . .'

'Waste time on people like us and Naomi.' Frances was not offended; she was almost laughing. 'Poor Jacob.'

'Hmm, yes, that year *was* pretty dreadful. I was fratchy about my thesis, Sheila hated her job – we quarrelled quite a lot. But things got better the next year. We bought the house in Coronation Place, and it was fun living on our own – '

'And a relief after Hertford Street?'

'Exactly. And then we got involved in the VSC – Vietnam Solidarity Campaign,' when she looked mystified: 'meetings, teach-ins, demonstrations – Grosvenor Square and all that. We made friends in the movement; we were working for something important, and not alone together so much; and we hardly quarrelled at all. We were . . . secure in each other, you know? And I had complicated word counts that I realised I should be doing by computer, so I talked big about the computing courses I'd done at Harvard and got access to the university's Titan, up on the second floor of the maths lab. That got me out of my thesis rut; and I thought I'd be through in jig time, and we'd be able to go home in the spring of 1969. But it didn't work out that way. Computing was so seductive – I kept making refinements to my programme instead of writing up my results. And one day I got talking to a guy who told me about a small institute called the Cambridge Computer Translation Centre that had several projects going, including a thesaurus of Latin – "because it has a fixed vocabulary", he said.'

'A *what*?'

'Yeah, that's what I said. I can explain if you'd – '

'No, no, another time' – hastily.

'Well, he asked me to give the CCTC a talk about my work; and before long I had a part-time job, programming for the Latin thesaurus project. And it was so interesting – fascinating. Then they asked me to work on the thesaurus project full time. I already knew I wanted to get out of classics – if I stayed in it, I'd end up as a don, and I'm not cut out for that: I don't like teaching, I don't enjoy research, and I can't stand academic social life. But in computing I could freelance as a sort of high-level programmer; and the thesaurus project would be a good start. So I dropped my thesis and took the job.'

'And Sheila was cross, I suppose.'

'Heavens, no – she was happy that I'd found work I really liked, same as her.'

'Wonders will never cease.'

She didn't begin to understand Sheila – impossible to explain. 'No, the problem was that she was less and less happy about staying in England, because she wasn't using her training – and because the anti-war movement here seemed to have so little effect: she wanted to get back home to work in the movement there. And it bothered her that I wasn't as keen to go home as she was –'

'Do you mean to say she made trouble about *politics*?'

Frances belonged to another world. 'It was her country,' he said mildly.

'And yours.'

'Yes, but I loved England too. Besides, it wasn't Sheila that started the trouble, it was me; and it wasn't about politics, it was about children . . . and England, all mixed up; and it wasn't anybody's fault. We just wanted – needed – different things.'

'Children?'

Staring past his reflection in the french window at the darkening garden, Jacob tried to describe that painful time. It came haltingly. He had been in a fever of impatience to have children; they had waited long enough already. He told Sheila about that night on the Standishes' staircase, and wanting a daughter like Imogen; and Imogen's nondescript face and extraordinary eyes had risen vivid in his mind, though he had not seen her in two years –

'Did she really have that effect on you? How . . .' Frances gave a little sniff. 'How amazing, and . . . touching.'

At her tone he looked round; her eyes were wet. He looked quickly back at the window, unable to go on. She remained tactfully silent, and before long he recovered enough to resume. 'Let's see . . . where was I? . . . Oh yes, Sheila and children. Well, she wanted them too, but not so soon. She wanted to go home first and get in a couple of years' teaching experience, because having a child would mean at least six months off work –'

Frances choked. 'Little does she know. Nearer six years.'

Remembering Frances the full-time mother, he said with careful vagueness, 'Depends what you're used to, I suppose.

Both our mothers went back to work soon after having us, so we just assumed . . . Anyhow, I wanted Sheila to have a child over here, right away, since the work she was doing didn't matter to her. She said no – because she wasn't sure that I still wanted to go home. I was hopping mad. Didn't she know that I'd make damned sure I was ready to go home – especially if we had a child? She said she knew that – but she didn't want me on those terms. She wanted me to want to go home myself, not because of a promise and a baby.'

The discussion had become a row; others followed. They slipped back into quarrelling constantly; and it was worse than before: they knew better how to hurt each other, and more was at stake. Eventually, exhausted and unable to conceive of life without each other, they fell into a trance of belief that they would somehow affirm their faith in each other and avert mutual destruction by marrying.

But their marriage enjoyed the usual success of futile gestures; far from bringing respite, it encouraged them to think that they could tear at each other without risk. Their rows were soon worse than ever: it was a horrible time.

He wound up his share of the thesaurus project in March of 1970, and for a while they almost stopped quarrelling. Sheila would start teaching in the autumn at a Boston school for deaf children, and he had some lines of contact set up for freelance work in the Boston area; after she finished the school year at the Horn, they would sell the house and go home.

Home?

He called it 'back home', but it no longer felt like that. He went on a great many long walks in the soft, wet English spring, rather guiltily, while Sheila was at work – looking, listening, talking to people he had known before she arrived, remembering the feel of English life. It was very pleasant; he would regret leaving.

Then, at the beginning of June, Camcomp had approached him. They were starting work on a new computer to compete with the PDP-7. Would he be interested in designing some of their systems software? What they had in mind for him would take about a year.

Tempting. Almost irresistible. He couldn't accept, of course –

But what if –

He told Sheila about his idea: 'Why don't I stay, and you go home alone, and I'll join you next summer? Then we'll both be doing what we want, except for not being together – and we've weathered that before.'

'If I go home alone,' she said quietly, 'that's the end of us. What *I* want is to be back home working – *with you there*. I'm not going to go back, and wait, and then, when you come back, keep wondering if you've come because you want to or because you've promised.'

'Of course I'll want to.'

'But just because you want to be with me, not because you want to live back home.'

'Not so.'

'I think you belong here, the way I belong there.'

'No!' he shouted, so violently that they stopped talking about it out of sheer shock. She was cutting his whole life out from under his feet.

The next day she said, 'We can't go on like this. I'm going home, with you or without – you've got till the end of June to decide. – Don't, Jacob. It's for both our sakes. We're killing each other.'

June lasted forever, heavy days dragging out interminably. He tried to make himself say he would go, but the words choked him. He could not understand what made him hold out. It had something to do with those long walks in the spring, and a lot to do with memories of his first two years – a sense of having unfinished business with England. She had to go back to survive; he had to stay for the same reason. They hardly spoke about anything serious all month, and they were very kind to each other.

On the night of the thirtieth they went to a movie, then for a walk, and finally back to the house. It was ten to twelve. He stood on the pavement and looked at his beautiful, beak-nosed, beloved Sheila and said, 'I can't.'

She nodded. 'I know. Me neither.' There were tears in her glossy eyes; she could hardly see to get the key into the lock.

She stayed a week longer. The time for quarrelling was past; they moved in an exhausted, defeated peace of sorts. Then he took her to Heathrow, and at the last moment could not bear to leave her so abruptly, and bought a first-class ticket – all there was available – and flew back to Boston with her.

But not for good. He stayed for a month, then had to go back to the trivial, worthless job he had given up Sheila for. Aline and Isaac took him to Logan Airport; Sheila stayed away, to spare him the misery of waiting in vain for her to buy a last-minute ticket to England.

'So I came back and started work . . .'

Frances was slicing leftover lamb for dinner. She looked up, saw his stricken face and said softly, 'And that was when the world ended. I expect it only really hit you then, what being alone would be like. Being alone and unhappy is so much worse than just being unhappy.'

Jacob started scraping carrots and after an interval of friendly silence said gratefully, 'Yes, it was awful. But now I can talk to you.'

'What's awful?' asked Imogen, coming into the kitchen.

'Not having anybody to talk to,' Frances answered smoothly. 'Here, dear, could you peel these and then set the table?'

Imogen sat down with the potatoes, looking alertly from her mother to Jacob. But her arrival had ended the conversation.

After dinner he lingered in the kitchen, putting plates in the dishwasher, while Frances made coffee. 'It's awful collaring friends for professional advice,' he said diffidently, 'but could I ask a quick question? . . . It's that Sheila and I should get a divorce, and are there any snags I should know about before going to a solicitor?'

'Let's see, why don't we . . .' She poured boiling water into the filter. 'I'd like to talk it over properly. Why not come up next Saturday for lunch? Oliver will be at work, and Imogen's spending the weekend with her grandmother – thank God; she's been moping and sulking and driving me nearly crazy – so we'll have the house to ourselves.'

'But I didn't mean to involve you in –'

'Now let's not hear any of that. Be sure to bring documents.'

'Lord, and I already feel guilty about telling you my life history all day –'

'But I asked – I *wanted* to hear all about it.'

'Well, it *was* a great relief – except for Aline, last summer, you're the first person I've talked to about it.'

Frances stopped stirring the hot milk in surprise. 'But – your friends in Cambridge? All those political people?'

'Friends of both of us – it makes it sort of delicate.'

'Gracious. That's exactly the position *I'm* in.'

His turn for surprise. 'But you must have lots of . . .' He trailed off, realising that it was her first hint at what he had guessed before Christmas about trouble between her and Oliver.

'Yes – friends of both of us; and I've seen so much less of them recently . . .' She picked up the tray, then paused. 'But what about . . . I mean, don't you have, er, a . . . a girlfriend?'

'Not yet.' He shrugged. 'I'll just have to wait till I'm over Sheila more than I am now. I keep looking, but what I'm looking for is someone just like her – and there can't be another Sheila.'

'No indeed.' Frances' tone suggested that that was something of a mercy.

Chapter 14

HE FOLLOWING WEEK they settled down to business directly, and Frances had his divorce wrapped up within an hour. She was practising again and said she would handle it herself – no trouble at all, perfectly straightforward; and she absolutely refused to take a fee. 'You're just getting started; and how you eat I don't know, with that mortgage and paying back what Sheila put into the house – so don't be silly.'

'But I wouldn't ever have mentioned it if –'

'Gracious, I'm glad you did. I've saved you money and bother, and it'll be a pleasure; that's what friends are for.'

In the end all he could do was thank her profusely. She got up and put the kettle on the Aga, and he gazed out at the dismal February garden, the words, 'what friends are for', lingering in his mind, and remembered what she had said about having no one to talk to. 'You know,' he began hesitantly, 'I've filled you in on the past four years of my life – isn't it your turn now? I've, uh, got the impression you aren't . . . as happy as you used to be . . .?'

She ground the beans. 'Dear me, the thing is . . . where to begin.'

He laughed. 'That's what I said, remember?'

'So you did. Still, it's easier to say than . . . I mean . . .' As she made the coffee and heated the milk, she started to talk, faster and less legato than usual. Of course Oliver had had affairs before – but never important, and in a way who could blame him – always meeting glamorous women. Besides, she only learned long after – preferably not at all – so the boat wasn't rocked. But then came Sara. Sara Pettit. They'd both known her slightly, ages before. About her he had kept quiet for months, then, just last October, announced that he was in love and asked for a divorce.

The coffee was ready. 'Let's take it upstairs,' she suggested.

Thin winter sunshine was trickling into the drawing room. Frances stretched out on the sofa, smoothing her long wool skirt, and faced him squarely for the first time since beginning to talk. 'It was a bombshell. I hadn't guessed anything. And – Sara Pettit! I mean, she's so . . . so insignificant, sort of little and pretty and silly . . .'

There was nothing insignificant about Frances. Jacob looked at her admiringly. She was attractive, humorous, confident, sexually alive – like a lioness with her slow forcefulness of bearing and gesture. 'Surely he can't be serious?'

'Not any more, I don't think; but he certainly sounded serious back in the autumn. He even wanted to take Imogen.'

'You're kidding.'

She smiled grimly. 'He said he'd get custody – he could offer her a ready-made family and a home, instead of a working mother and an empty house.'

'But what about his, uh . . . adultery?'

'The trouble is, in my case, well' – she hesitated – 'I'm not in a position to use it against him . . . I've been seeing something of . . . someone . . . and Oliver found out; so . . .' She looked at him closely. 'I hope you aren't, I mean . . . too shocked . . .?'

'*Me*? Good Lord, why should I be?'

'Well, I mean, it isn't exactly pretty . . .'

'But I don't think in those terms. Heavens, half the people I know are involved in things like that.'

'But that's younger people, still experimenting, not couples with children.'

'I wasn't just thinking of young people.' He grinned. 'There's Aline and Isaac, for instance.'

'Your *parents*? How did you find *that* out?'

'I didn't – it was never secret.'

'You knew when you were a *child*?'

'Sure, as far back as I can remember.'

'But that's *terrible*; I mean, it must have been dreadfully disturbing for you.'

'Not that I remember – it was just part of life, you know?' He considered. 'There was a year or so when I was mortified by everything that made them different from other people's parents – Aline's working, their left-wing politics, their lovers – but not by that in particular.' Suddenly he noticed that she was red with embarrassed outrage. 'Funny, you were worried about shocking me – now I'm afraid I've shocked *you*.'

'No, no . . . I mean, I certainly wouldn't want Imogen to know about me or Oliver; but what other people do is their own business, of course – and, I mean, it doesn't seem to have scarred you for life' – with a laugh: recovery complete.

'So what's the state of play now – with you and Oliver?'

'Improving. The thing is, until Christmas I was driving him further and further away by trying to make him stop seeing Sara. So I took hold of myself and stopped, and let him know that he could see her without any more comeback from me . . . and it seems to be working – so far.'

'What I don't understand' – delicately – 'is, you don't sound happy, but you're bending over backwards to make things work. Why? Mixed feelings about Oliver?'

'Mixed feelings . . . yes . . .' she murmured, closing her eyes, then, frowning, opened them. 'Yes indeed. Half the time I

70

hate his guts; the other half I . . . I'm lonely for the old Oliver. He must be there still, people don't just change. And I won't just hand him over to Sara Pettit. Not without . . . And then there's Imogen. Broken homes have the most terrible effect – children need both their parents, don't you think?'

'But surely it's far more upsetting for a child to be living with parents who don't get on?'

'Only if the child gets caught in the middle. Imogen's all right; she doesn't have the faintest idea of what's been going on.' She caught his quizzical look. 'You don't think we quarrel in front of her?'

'No' – hastily. 'But it's hard to keep things from children. She might overhear – '

'Never.'

'Or sense trouble in the atmosphere.'

'She couldn't – we've been very careful.'

So careful that they had quarrelled over her head at Naomi's party? She might not have called that a quarrel; but Imogen had certainly known that something was wrong.

He said nothing and neither did Frances. She looked comfortable, leaning on one elbow and resting her head on the back of the sofa. He was comfortable too, deep in his favourite armchair. The sun had succumbed to cloud; the light in the room was glaucous and hazy. Restful. He yawned, so did she; they apologised simultaneously, then laughed.

'It must be talking about such emotional things,' she said. 'But it's been *such* a relief.'

'Same as I felt, telling you about Sheila;' and they smiled out of the ease of an old friendship.

Jacob soon got into his old habit of visiting Frances when he was in London on a Saturday: every week or two, that winter and spring. He was on his own, and lonely, and talking to her was a way of reconnecting himself to English life. But, although their friendship appeared to flourish, he gradually found that he was no longer completely at ease with her. They seemed to have less in common than they had once had: he had grown more radical in the past six years, she more conservative; and the worlds they lived in, the assumptions they lived by, were different enough to make explanation difficult. It was easier to stick to gossip, and even that had its dangers. By

March he was beginning, reluctantly, to wonder whether they still had enough in common to sustain the kind of friendship he needed.

He certainly hesitated about telling her of his encounter with Barbara Potter. The Potters and four other couples had recently become notorious among the Cambridge left by setting up a commune that pooled money and goods, had rotas for housework and looking after children (and, so it was rumoured, for sleeping partners), and made all decisions collectively at weekly meetings enlivened by denunciation and self-criticism on the Chinese model. Jacob could imagine what Sheila would have had to say about the commune; he wished she were there to say it. Though he often saw Barbara at political meetings – she and Al had been in the anti-war movement from the beginning – he had made no attempt to renew the slight friendship of the old Hertford Street days: she was not someone he regretted losing touch with.

But the possibility of sleeping with her was there from the moment he heard her husky, 'Hi, Jake,' at a meeting about Greece; and it got stronger back at Hertford Street when they took their coffee to her study for a quiet talk.

Barbara wasn't interested in discussing the commune; she wanted to hear about him. 'You've been through a hard time, Jake,' she said invitingly.

He almost confided in her. She was very attractive, leaning forward with arms clasped round her knees – relaxed, receptive, alert, dark eyes glowing, dark hair falling forward onto her arms; her smoky vitality was like a magnet. He would tell her something of his troubles. Not everything – the secrets of commune members were probably communal, and he did not want his history to be all over radical Cambridge within a week – but enough to relieve his chronic loneliness; and then it would be very late, and she would ask him to stay, and they would sleep together, and to hell with Sheila and Sheila's opinion of Barbara. He must get out of Sheila's shadow . . . and he had always found Barbara attractive . . . and never more so than tonight.

But if her smouldering attentiveness indeed meant that she wanted to sleep with him, she took the wrong line about Sheila. He had hardly begun to talk when she said, 'The trouble with you two, Jake, was that you were locked into this incredibly oppressive bourgeois monogamous couple thing.'

'It wasn't that way on principle, you know' – defensively. 'But we were too, uh, busy trying to stop being unhappy with each other to get attached to other people as well.'

'But that's just it – you both put all your energy into an exclusive relationship –'

'But it was only exclusive by accident.'

'That's not what I mean by exclusive. What I mean is, with you, if you were involved with two people, you'd be having exclusive relationships with both of them. Intense, I mean. And Sheila was the same.'

'So what's wrong with intense?' he asked, perplexed and nettled.

'What's wrong is the way you are now, all screwed up. Doesn't that make you wonder about the structures that made you that way – the cult of romantic love? It doesn't work. You need something with a broader basis – friendly, low-key, open-ended relationships that don't privatise you.'

She had spoken with the same throaty voice, still leaning forward and glowing at him. Perhaps that was her idea of low-key friendliness. Golly. He looked at her sourly, annoyed at her for waking him so rudely from his erotic dream of her. It was still possible . . . But she was right; he did have a cult of intensity – needed at least the illusion of intensity – could not make love to her while feeling contemptuous of her theory of sexual–emotional relations.

Barbara went to the door with him, her composure un-ruffled; she seemed secretly amused. Perhaps she was looking forward to telling Al – and God knew who else – that he had not been up to the challenge of sleeping with her.

It was a close escape: he would not have liked himself if she had been the first person he slept with after Sheila.

But he took so much embarrassment and injured pride away with him that, when he saw Frances a week later, he overcame his hesitations enough to tell her about his conversation with Barbara – though not about how near he had come to sleeping with her.

Frances made really-I-have-no-patience noises about the commune, then said, 'Still I've always been sort of fascinated by the Potters – you once told me about a party where they got undressed.'

'Did I? I don't remember telling you – it must have been right afterwards, because it was something I did my best to forget.'

'But why?'

So he told her about the shame and scorn for himself and all the guests except Liz that had lodged in his mind after that strange party. The episode had eventually sunk out of his consciousness; but the irritant speck had remained, forcing him for years, against his instincts, to retain an uneasy respect for the Potters. Then, at a VSC meeting in 1969, something about the way Al imposed silence by his height and massiveness and baleful stare had recalled Jacob to the memory of that long-ago party, and afterwards he had told Sheila about it.

'You pathetic sap,' she had said. 'You thought they were free spirits? Holy catfish. They were getting a cheap thrill by breaking taboos they believed in. – Oh yes, believed in. They thought they were being naughty. And don't admire them for stopping where they did. That wasn't self-restraint – they were going as far as they dared, three years ago. These days they'd have to start an orgy to establish their power.'

'Power?' he said protestingly.

'That's what that striptease was about, silly – making you people despise yourselves – putting you in bondage to them. – Libertarian ideas? Don't make me laugh. That was moral coercion.'

Sheila had been right. 'There *was* a whiff of brimstone about that night,' he concluded. 'What she said suddenly made me smell it; and I was free of Al and Barbara, just like that.'

Frances frowned. 'But you just took over her ideas instead. Isn't it time you started getting free of her?'

'But . . .' How could he explain? 'The thing about Sheila was that she showed me the way into my *own* ideas.' He met Frances' slightly antagonistic hazel eyes. 'Listen, she cut me off from a lot of things; and she was wrong some of the time. But more often than not her intransigence was *good* for me. She made my mind work – she didn't get muddled by always trying to think the best of people, as I do.'

'That's *much* better than trying to think the worst. And you may think it's dreadful, but I sort of envy the Potters. I wish I could be as free as that.'

'But they weren't free. They believed in the taboo as much as the rest of us. Nobody laughed. That was what gave them such power.'

'Well, at least they were the ones that had it. I'd like that.' She spoke airily, but her eyes stayed alight with a dream of power.

Chapter 15

ACOB NO LONGER had much interest in Imogen; she had changed from the delightful mite whom he and Liz had taken on outings into a solemn, almost sullen girl at an awkward age between childhood and adolescence – old enough to want to participate in adult talk, too young to know how. But he felt rather sorry for her. Oliver hardly noticed her, unless she addressed him directly; and, though Frances manifestly loved her with deep-rooted, uncomplicated maternal love, and tried to make up for Oliver's neglect – 'I do my best to compensate by paying a lot of attention to her,' she confided – Jacob thought that Imogen might well be perplexed at getting so much affection, yet so little interest; for what Frances called paying attention seemed to consist of little more than caressing her absentmindedly in passing, like a pet, or putting an easy arm round her while continuing to talk past her – sometimes about the subject already in hand, sometimes about her, usually in the third person: 'Imogen thinks . . .', 'Imogen says . . .', 'Imogen has done . . .', with an occasional, 'Don't you, love?' and a squeeze. She even seemed slightly disappointed in the way Imogen was turning out: too polite, quiet, serious and solitary. 'It's not natural,' she told him fretfully. 'Most kids her age are driving their parents crazy – playing rock at top volume, swearing, smoking – trying pot, even. But Imogen? Not a bit of it. She gets moody, but she doesn't even act provocative, let alone anti-social.'

'Parents are never satisfied. Those ones you say are going crazy, I bet they say, "What did we do wrong? Why aren't our children as nice as Imogen Standish?"'

'But she's *too* nice. It isn't healthy, the way she bottles things up. Children should express their hostilities.'

He let this dubious doctrine pass. 'Maybe she's only good at home,' he offered lightly, 'and does all those terrible things, like playing rock and smoking and swearing, with her friends.'

'If only she did!' – a comical wail, but in earnest. 'But she's turning into a hermit. She's always spent too much time alone, and now it's become a mania.'

'That's not the way I remember her,' he admitted. 'Didn't she have quite a lot of school friends around here?'

'I, well . . . terribly middle-class of us, we pulled strings and got her into a rather better school, so naturally she doesn't see so much of the girls you're remembering . . . and I have to confess that we weren't entirely sorry, I mean . . . And her new school is further away. But if she made an effort . . . She did have a nice friend in the autumn, but she didn't keep it up – she must *like* being isolated. I only hope going away to school next year cures her.'

'Going *away* to school?'

'The Friends School, remember?'

'But I thought it was in London. A day school – '

'Gracious, no. Saffron Walden. She'll be nearer to you than us.'

'But I thought you didn't approve of boarding schools,' he blurted.

'Me?' Frances looked blank. 'Whatever gave you that idea?'

'You did. You said boarding schools dried children's souls up.'

'Did I really? How peculiar.'

'It was to do with your and Oliver's schools.'

'But the Friends School isn't like our schools at all. That's why we chose it.'

She might not remember, but he did; his mind's ear rang

76

with her vehement cry: 'I'd never *ever* send Imogen away to school.' But why be surprised? That was the occasion, he reflected wryly, when he had wondered for the first time how a person could tell when the Standishes meant what they said. Frances' capacity to put her past behind her was still sublimely complete.

When Imogen came down for tea, he said, 'I've just realised that the Friends School is in my part of the world. Saffron Walden isn't that far from Cambridge, you know.'

She looked up from her slice of malt loaf. 'Oh, that's nice – you'll be able to visit me.'

'Imogen!' Frances said severely. 'You mustn't ask people to visit, you should wait till they offer. Besides, Jacob hasn't got a car.'

'Oh.' Imogen buried her face in her mug.

'Well, you never know,' he said. 'I've been thinking of getting a car – if I do, maybe I'll come and see you some time.'

She flashed a glance of triumph at Frances, then beamed at him. 'Oh yes, please.'

Chapter 16

F IT'S STILL nice tomorrow, we'll be in the garden,' Frances had said on the telephone. 'I'll leave the front door open for you.'

The weather still held – unseasonably hot for the middle of April – so he went straight in when no one answered his ring, put his overnight bag under the hall table, then glanced at himself in the looking glass. Less gaudy than usual; the dim light turned his hair auburn and darkened his pink skin flatteringly. He grimaced and was turning to go downstairs and out to the garden when he heard voices in the drawing room. Raised voices: Oliver and Imogen. They seemed to be moving towards the door; as they approached, their angry tones separated into distinguishable words.

'. . . you were behaving . . .' That was Oliver.

And Imogen: ' . . . she was . . .'

Jacob hesitated. They must have heard his ring but assumed that he would go straight to the garden; if they emerged now, they would wonder how much he had heard. But did he have time to get downstairs?

'Imogen, I will not have you speaking to me like that. Lower your voice.'

'I won't,' she said shrilly.

'I am not going to have you disobeying me.'

He moved quietly along the hall towards the stairs; he was passing the drawing-room door when Imogen, just behind it, shouted: 'I hate you!'

Oliver's footsteps moved quickly towards her. Jacob held his breath and froze. Would he hit her? But he only said, very close, quietly but savagely: 'Young lady, *never* say that to me again. You will go to your room now and stay there until you are ready to apologise.'

'I will not.' But Oliver's tone brooked no opposition; already her hand was rattling the doorknob.

'Imogen – this minute.'

The knob turned. Obeying an irrational impulse not to be caught fleeing down the stairs, Jacob retreated back along the hall the way he had come, stooped to his bag and, when the door opened, stood up, pantomiming apologetic embarrassment.

They were startled to see him. Imogen ducked her hot face and rushed along the hall and up the stairs without looking at him. Oliver rubbed one hand along the door-frame. Insofar as the face of so thin a man could bloat at all, Oliver's was bloated with anger – a barely perceptible thickening of planes normally lean and supple. He was flushed, but the end of his long, narrow nose was greenish-white. 'Were you – ' He stopped. 'That is, did you hear that dreadful . . . ?'

Jacob nodded.

'Er, yes. Sorry about that. Imogen's at a . . . she's going through a . . .'

'A stage.'

'Just so. I expect you're looking for Frances,' he added in what almost passed for a conversational tone. 'She's in the garden.' The graceful hand gestured, and he managed a sketchy half-smile before retreating into the drawing room.

Jacob stood still. 'Were you – ' Oliver had begun. He had been going to ask: 'Were you listening?' Damn the man.

He bestirred himself. What if Oliver came out and found him still standing there? But, instead of going downstairs, he started to go up, drawn by the memory of Imogen's suffused face and her: 'I hate you,' which had had the sound of a deeper misery than any mere childish petulance.

Halfway up he stopped. Crazy. He should fetch Frances from the garden. But he kept on going. Frances had not heard Oliver's savage voice or seen Imogen's face; she might think he was making a mountain out of a molehill.

Thus he rationalised his strange course as he climbed the second flight. Only afterwards did he see the primitive need to give comfort that had compelled him upwards.

Imogen was sitting on her bed with a book in her lap. She glanced up at Jacob and back at the book. Her face was puffy; he guessed that she was trying to read in the hope of averting tears.

'Imogen,' he said.

She looked up, tensed as if to take a slap, and waited for him to speak.

'Imogen, what's wrong?'

'Nothing.' She dropped her eyes to her book.

Without premeditation he knelt in front of her. 'Imogen.' He was reiterating her name instinctively, as if gentling an animal. 'Imogen, that's not true; you're upset. What's wrong?'

'None of your business,' she muttered.

'It is my business, Imogen, because I care about you.'

She gave him a surly look. 'You do not, you just care about *them*.'

Led by grace where he would not ordinarily have ventured, he leaned forward and gave her a quick hug, then drew back. 'Imogen, you're an idiot. I don't "just care about them".' What would convince her? Words rose to his lips, and without weighing them he said, 'My dear child, I love you. Ever since

79

you were six years old, remember? You're the only child I've ever loved so much – I could hardly love you more if you were my own daughter.' The words became true as he spoke: his recent indifference vanished, and his old love flowed back undiminished.

She closed her book and folded her hands, still looking down – probably waiting, embarrassed but polite, for him to withdraw his over-emotional presence to a greater physical and mental distance. The thought made him melancholy, almost desolated. Then she raised her gaze to his, and for a moment they looked at each other across a distance too small to be measured, offering over their deepest timidity as earnest of complete trust. Her lips quivered. She blinked; gulped; tears suddenly engulfed her; and she leaned forward and buried her face in his neck and wept so copiously that tickly rivulets ran along his collarbone and down his chest. He put his arms round her, patting her back and murmuring, as his mother had done to him once upon a time, 'There, there; there, there, my poor puchkie; there, there . . .'

At last she ran out of tears, sat up straight and prim, sniffed, found a handkerchief, blew her nose and apologised ' – for being such a nuisance.'

'Not at all,' he said handsomely, squirming back again to a conversable distance. He wondered what to say next, and tried the obvious. 'Imogen, you're unhappy. What is it?'

Silence.

'Why was Oliver angry with you?'

Still silence.

'You don't want to tell on him?'

She nodded and, since he had guessed so much, confessed the rest. 'Daddy said I was impolite to somebody at lunch, but I wasn't, it was her fault; and he wants me to apologise, and I won't.'

'Impolite?'

'*She* started it. She called me "dearie", and I said, "My name is Imogen" – and she called me Imogen for a while, but then she forgot and called me "my sweet little girl". So I said . . . it was part of what Daddy said was rude . . .'

'Yes?' he prompted.

'I said . . . I said: "I am *not* your little girl, I'm Mummy and Daddy's little girl. Besides . . ." Oh dear, I suppose it was awfully childish. I said – I said: "Besides, I'm not little, I'll be thirteen on the tenth of August."'

'Hmm' – non-committally.

'And then she was perfectly revolting. Instead of saying sorry or getting cross, she sort of smiled and said: "Of course you're not little, you're a big girl, but you *are* a sweetheart, and I can't help wishing you were mine." And *I* said –'

'I bet I know what you said. You said: "Well I never will be yours, and I wouldn't want to be. So there."'

'Yes – I was *shouting*,' she confided, half ashamed, half proud. Then a double-take. 'How do *you* know what I said?'

'I suppose because it's exactly what I'd have said at your age. Anyhow, who's this old biddy that called you names?'

'Oh, she's not old – not *really* old. She's sort of the same age as you and Mummy and Daddy.'

Jacob still thought of himself as young; it was startling to hear Imogen place him so firmly among the grown-ups. 'Who's this not-so-old person, then?'

'Mrs Pettit. She wants me to call her Sara, but I won't.'

Ah. Hmm. Go cautiously. 'She seems to have pretty horrid manners towards' – he suppressed 'children' – 'towards young people.'

'Oh, it's not her manners really; I don't like her because she makes Mummy unhappy. But Daddy likes her, that's why he was cross. He wants me to be specially nice to her, you see, and I won't.' She looked at him challengingly.

Was she trying to get him to tell her about Oliver's affair? If so, he was in a quandary, for he had no business telling her things that her parents didn't want her to know. But perhaps she knew already and simply wanted to talk about it. Should he give her an opening? 'Why do you think Mrs Pettit makes your mother unhappy?' he asked experimentally.

'Because Daddy likes her so much.'

Suddenly he remembered Imogen in Naomi's kitchen, trying to understand her parents' veiled dispute, then switching off, as if the effort, or the truth, were too much for her. Probably she still didn't know anything for certain, and didn't want to be told very much – not by him, who was in this context of family secrets an outsider – but simply wanted him to confirm her intuition that there was indeed something (to be left unspecified) in the air: that she wasn't just imagining things. Deep waters. 'Hmm . . . your father likes Mrs Pettit, but your mother doesn't?'

'No, she doesn't. That's why I thought she wouldn't mind if I was rude to her. But she was just as cross as Daddy. Maybe . . . maybe she was afraid Mrs Pettit would think she hasn't brought me up right – because once I heard Daddy telling her she wasn't as good a mother as Mrs Pettit. Mrs Pettit has three children, so I suppose she has more experience.'

'I don't think motherhood works like that. Don't worry about Frances. *I* think' (firmly – this was not the moment for qualifications), 'I think she's a *very* good mother.'

'Oh, so do I, it's just Daddy that doesn't.'

More deep waters. Jacob headed quickly for a harmless question. 'Do you know Mrs Pettit's children?'

She wrinkled her nose disdainfully. 'Hardly at all. Daddy keeps wanting me to visit them, and I went a couple of times, but they're younger than me; Jason is eleven, Zoë is ten, and Adam is only six; and where they live, in Clapham, their house has a park of its own behind, that only the houses round it can use, and they think it makes them special, so they won't play on the Common, though it's much nicer and only just across the road. And – and Daddy isn't like Daddy when he's there.'

He stood up and looked out of the window. Frances, Oliver and a fair-haired woman were sitting on chaise longues in the garden. Really, the Standishes were crazy. If they didn't care whether Imogen knew about Oliver's affair, they should tell her, not leave her to guess; if they didn't want her to know, they should work a lot harder at keeping it secret. She was twelve years old, not an infant: how could they expect her to sit through the tensions of Sunday lunch here with Sara Pettit, or visit her in Clapham with Oliver, or hear coded conversations about her like the one at Naomi's party, without picking up an inchoate half-knowledge more alarming than the truth could possibly be?

'Has she gone?' Imogen asked hopefully.

'Nope.'

'Oh dear. I wish she'd go away and I'd never see her again. Daddy says I have to apologise, but I won't. No matter what. You wouldn't, would you?'

Jacob caught the note of appeal. 'You're wanting some advice, aren't you?' he asked, turning back to her.

She nodded.

'You won't like it.'

She gave a little gasp of desperation. 'That's all right.'

'Okay, here goes. Whatever you want to happen to Mrs Pettit – for her to stop making your mother unhappy, or disappear in a puff of smoke, or whatever – you won't get it by being rude to her. I think she was rude to you first. But she doesn't think so. And rudeness is almost always counter-productive; it makes other people feel right and superior and grown-up. So –'

'You think I should apologise,' Imogen said bleakly.

'I told you you wouldn't like it. You'll have to, in the end, to get out of your room . . .'

'But if I wait long enough, she'll go home, and I'll only have to do it over the telephone.'

'And that'd be easier than seeing her.'

'Yes.'

'And that's what your parents will expect you to do?'

She nodded.

'Then you could surprise them – and take Mrs Pettit down a peg or two, by showing her that you're more grown-up than she thinks.'

'But that won't make her "disappear in a puff of smoke".'

'No, probably nothing would do that, but –'

She got there ahead of him. 'Oh, but it could make Mummy less unhappy. If Mrs Pettit thinks I'm well brought up, then Daddy won't get at Mummy afterwards, and she'll be less unhappy – and it'll be because of me! All right, I'll do it.' She stood up, alight with the resolution of a martyr off to the lions. 'Will you come with me?'

'I will if you can't face it alone, but won't it look as if I put you up to it?'

Imogen bit her lip, then nodded, said, 'Okay,' and descended to the arena alone.

Sara Pettit was short, full-breasted and pretty. She had the higher wholefoods look: long fair hair, no visible makeup, expensive peasant blouse and skirt, sandals, chunky beads, Greek wool shoulder bag. She was tremulously complaisant, smiling a lot, saying little and listening with a round-eyed interest that Jacob found flattering until he saw that she used it on everyone.

Before long she got up to go. 'I told the kids I'd be back by three – it's nearly that already; and you know what the underground is like on Sunday.'

'Don't worry about the tube,' said Oliver; 'I'll run you home.'

There was a moment of silence. Jacob quickly looked at Imogen. She was looking at Frances, who was looking at Sara, who was looking at Oliver, who was looking at – Jacob. Their eyes met; it was Oliver who looked away.

Frances broke the silence. Stretching, she said lazily, 'Yes, dear, what a good idea. It's a terrible day for the tube.'

Sara bestowed solicitous smiles and farewell kisses – she smelt of expensive scent and Johnson's baby soap – then drifted away with Oliver. Imogen, watching her waft through the french windows, commented, 'Silly old cow,' and stumped off towards the house fast, to escape scolding.

'Thank God that's over,' Frances muttered, kicking off her shoes and leaning back wearily.

'It was certainly a surprise meeting *her* here' – enquiringly.

'Yes – our Sara just hates hurting people; and whenever she starts worrying about hurting me, Oliver drags her over here for a meal so that she can see I'm okay. Well, what did you think of her?'

He snorted. 'Not in your class.'

'But very pretty. Admit.'

'Sure, pretty; the effect's impressive. But no personality. Maybe she wears that – that peasant potpourri as a substitute. Me, I prefer . . . oh, either jeans or elegance.'

Frances smiled. 'Sometimes she wears frills,' she murmured drily, smoothing the skirt of her undoubtedly elegant Jean Muir frock. 'Imogen doesn't like her either. There was the most appalling kerfuffle earlier . . .'

'Yes, I saw her in the house' – he did not say that he had sought her out – 'and she said something about it. She seemed a bit upset, and I was wondering . . .' He hesitated, then plunged: 'I was wondering how much she knows about Oliver and Sara.'

'Nothing at all – gracious!'

'Hmm, well . . . you know, I got an impression that she's picking up signals –'

'I don't think so' – dismissively.

'But she's been hearing things she doesn't understand and –'

'Things she doesn't understand. Precisely.' The long shadow of the house had reached Frances' chaise longue; it brushed her toe, and she moved her foot impatiently. 'As long as she doesn't understand, she won't be seriously upset.'

'But –'

'Are you wanting us to tell her the works? – Not necessarily? What, then?' Briefly there was silence in the garden. She twitched her stockinged foot in and out of the creeping shadow.

'The thing is, I think she can tell that you're unhappy. That's quite a burden for her.'

'But I'm not any more; I'm really over it now. So if she's "picking up signals", she'll pick that up too and stop worrying.' She smiled triumphantly.

Jacob held his tongue. It was time to heed the ancient wisdom that one did not tell parents how to bring up their children. Poor Imogen.

Poor Frances too. Of course.

But 'poor Imogen' was the thought he turned over on the way back to Cambridge on the lurching King's Cross train. Their attempt to keep her in complete ignorance was misconceived; she knew too much already. They should relieve her desperate uncertainty by giving her some version of the truth.

Poor Imogen, trying with precocious nobility to deflect Oliver's censure from Frances. It was deeply unnatural; Frances should be protecting her, not the other way round.

Why on earth didn't Frances even notice that she was unhappy?

The thought stirred an echo. He listened for it and found himself in Naomi's white kitchen, thinking: That child is in trouble. Rescue her.

He put the Standishes out of his mind. But between Royston and Cambridge he suddenly thought: She needs a friend – then why not me?

There could be problems, an inner voice cautioned him: Divided loyalties are the damnedest things.

Chapter 17

N HIS NEXT visit he made a point of going up to Imogen's room for a few minutes; and she was so pleased that he got into the habit of dropping in to see her every time he came – sometimes just to say hello or goodbye, sometimes for longer.

It was a hard slog at first; Imogen was so anxious to sound adult that she hardly spoke at all. Then one day he said something about his schooldays; she asked a question – another – another – and the tide turned. The next time he came, she had more questions; and the next: and he mined the long-ago-and-far-away of Malden High for all it was worth, dredging up what he had studied at her age, in the seventh grade; his first dates ('When you were only twelve!' she cried, scandalised); cheerleaders; high-school hops; chug-a-lugging beer ('Not till I was fourteen,' he said quickly); summers as a lifeguard or at his family's camp in northern Maine; what girls had worn; what boys had worn. By the time he had exhausted his recollections, her shyness was gone. They were well and truly back where they had been.

When he found her indoors on a beautiful Sunday early in June, he said jovially, 'You shouldn't be cooped up in here, you should be out with your friends.'

'Oh, I don't have any friends,' she said matter-of-factly. 'Except you, of course.'

'Come now' – still more jovially; he was staggered. 'Haven't you got friends at school?'

'Oh yes, lots – there are super girls there.'

'But you just said you didn't have any.'

'Oh, I meant . . . I meant . . .' She fell silent and frowned, as if realising that what she had meant was not easy to explain. He waited, and she looked up, still frowning. 'It's . . . if I tell you, promise you won't tell Mummy and Daddy?'

'Promise.'

'Really promise?'

'Really promise.'

She sighed with relief. 'You see, this year I made friends with an awfully nice girl, and we'd visit each other. But then, just after Christmas, Katy came to tea; only . . . Mrs Pettit came too, it was the first time she came here. And afterwards Katy asked me if . . . asked me if . . . my parents were going to get divorced, and would I live with Mummy or Daddy. I said of course not, whatever makes you say such a silly thing, and she said that when she went down to the lavatory, she looked over the handrail and saw Daddy – ' Imogen went red and stopped.

She obviously wanted encouragement to say more; but Frances expected him to participate in the fiction that she knew nothing. Drat. He should have listened harder to that voice telling him about the danger of divided loyalties. He hesitated, then said slowly, 'Katy saw your father and Mrs Pettit?'

She looked up sharply. 'How did you – ? Does *everybody* – ?' Then, regaining a precarious composure: 'But you're wrong. Mummy said so. They're just very special friends. Mummy says lots of people don't understand special friendships, so Katy didn't understand when she saw Daddy . . . kissing Mrs Pettit.' She swallowed. 'She didn't understand the *spirit*. But after that I didn't ask Katy home again – or anybody else. I knew what she thought she knew about Daddy, and I didn't want her feeling *sorry* for me. But you understand about special friendships, don't you?' She looked at him intently.

Jacob nodded. She was shying away from what she knew; it was not up to him to force it on her.

Thank God she was going away from this. Frances thought she was shielding Imogen – but did she really expect her to swallow that line about special friends? Why didn't she see that Imogen was unhappy, or realise how much she must already know?

He did not try to answer his own questions. He needed Frances' friendship. She had faults, but she was good-hearted, knew his history, was comfortable to be with. So he worked at thinking the best of her, and went on trying to be Imogen's friend without letting himself know why he considered it necessary.

Not an easy trick.

He pulled it off for a while – until the day before his departure for a holiday in France and Italy. He had come up to London a day early to see a couple of movies and stay with the Standishes, and he was sitting in the sun in Lincoln's Inn Fields, eating a sandwich lunch and watching a little boy and a girl in a flowered smock chase each other round trees and bushes, while their mother sat on the grass in a patch of sun with a clutter of toys and lunch things round her. The boy was still young enough to run for comfort when he fell. His high voice and his mother's soft one would mingle, then he would run back to play with his sister.

Children of privilege; happy; secure; their playground one of the fairest spots in one of the fairest cities of civilisation: they had everything it was possible to give a child. Like . . .

No, not like Imogen. Curious, how he had once thought that, back in his first two years in England, when she had put him in mind of the coloured frontispiece in one of his old *Books of Knowledge*: a girl of about twelve, with flowing red-gold hair, wearing a red-gold embroidered dress and carrying a jewelled casket. 'The Heir of All the Ages', it was called.

Yet she had not changed; she was still like the red-haired girl in the picture, with the same gravity of gaze; still heir of a high civilisation.

But she no longer had everything it was possible to give a child: she was not happy, not secure; her parents were no longer protecting, cherishing, valuing her as they ought.

Unhappiness must have changed them, then; when he first knew them, their care of Imogen had been exemplary. He had watched them with fascination, and her sensibility had flourished in lovingly prepared soil.

But . . .

No, he decided finally. They hadn't changed; it was he who had changed: his sight was no longer dazzled. They had never, in fact, been quite so finely civilised as he had considered them; they had simply been better equipped to care for Imogen at the ages of six and seven than for Imogen now. The warning signs had always been there, and he had ignored every one – in the past because he had made the Standishes into emblems of the civilisation he had fallen in love with; in recent months because he had needed Frances as a confidante, a link with the past, a bridge to life in England without Sheila.

He felt sore, as if Frances had betrayed him by not living up to his ideal of her. Unfair, of course – it was not her fault if she did not correspond to an image of his own creation. Most unfair. They were all right, the Standishes, they were nice folks, sensitive, intelligent, cultivated, even if they weren't in the same league as their daughter. Making a face he crumpled his sandwich bag, threw it at a litter bin, missed, retrieved it, threw it again and succeeded. The young mother smiled at his success with easy wordless friendliness, as people often smile in London parks.

At the edge of the park he stopped dead, shaking his head in amusement. The moment he admitted to himself that he thought less of the Standishes than before, he tried to excuse them by blaming himself, instead, for having had unreasonable expectations. Sheila was right: he would go to almost any lengths to think well of people.

That evening at Canonbury Park South, Oliver, unusually affable, told stories about his early days as a journalist and asked sensible and interested questions about the applications of computers to book and magazine production. Jacob enjoyed himself, but there was something – was it in Oliver's manner? – that left a faint sour taste in his mouth afterwards.

He identified it the next morning while shaving. Oliver had talked to him as an equal – for the first time. Indeed, both Standishes had treated him with more respect of late; the change correlated with their gradual appreciation that his work was much more demanding than routine computer program-ming and would eventually be much better paid: that he was not a white-collar worker, but a professional like them.

The hell with them, if he had to have the right status before they took him seriously.

He nicked his cheek. Their fault. Pah.

He had recovered his temper by the time he was dressed; he had also come to a decision. There was no point in trying to maintain much of a friendship with people who so often made him feel uneasy: in future he would see altogether less of them. He would be away for a couple of months – it made a natural break. It was time he weaned himself of needing a substitute family.

They had breakfast in the garden, talking about holidays.

'I do envy you,' Frances said. 'We've hardly been abroad since Imogen was born. Oliver always said she was cooped up in London all year, and West Horton was better for her than museums and churches, and we'd take her abroad when she was old enough to appreciate things like that. But when I suggested it this year, he said she'd soon be old enough to go on her own. I ask you!'

Oliver smiled and grimaced. 'Not exactly that. The truth is –'

'The truth is,' she cut him short amiably, 'that you go off to the Continent on stories and forget that Imogen and I haven't gone – because you don't ever want to go abroad for holidays: you want to go to Monk's House. Admit.'

'Well . . .' Oliver shrugged and smiled and admitted, self-deprecating, ruefully charming – like the Oliver of long ago, not the remote man of the past few months. Perhaps things were working the way she had hoped; perhaps the worst was over.

'I want to go to Monk's House too,' said Imogen. 'I don't want to go to silly old abroad.'

'Oh, *Imogen!*' Frances cried in mock despair.

Imogen looked mischievous, and she and Oliver exchanged a glance of affectionate alliance in defence of Monk's House. Then the telephone rang. She went to answer it and came back scowling. 'It's for you,' she told Oliver.

'Who is it?'

She affected not to hear.

'Who is it? You're supposed to ask who's ringing. Did you?'

'Mrs Pettit.'

'You mean Sara,' said Frances as Oliver strolled indoors. 'She asked you to call her Sara, remember? It's polite to call people what they want to be called.'

She did not reply. Frances slowly finished her coffee and went in too, carrying the breakfast tray. Imogen watched her out of sight, then stood irresolute, full of anger but with no

90

one to be angry at. Jacob gave a mental shrug. His friendship
was no actual help to her. He was glad she was going away to
school; that would end his useless sense of responsibility, and
the Standishes could become part of his past. He would see
them now and then, but not often.

He looked at his watch. 'Well, I guess I'd better be moving,'
he said, standing up.

Imogen jumped up and stood right in front of him, barring
his way.

'I've got to go, Imogen.'

'But you'll come back?'

'Sure,' he said lightly, not meaning it.

'Really?'

'Sure. I'll visit you at school sometime, when I've got a car.'

'Really and truly? You won't just not come?' It was as if she
had seen into his mind and read his decision to see less of the
Standish family.

He looked at her. She was squinting against the sun, her eyes
more than usual like her mother's – yet not at all alike, except
in shape and colour. Even screwed up, they were beautiful;
Frances' were not, with their perpetual defence of secret
amusement. Perhaps a prelapsarian Frances had had a gaze like
Imogen's – intent and serious, without self-regard; if so, it was
before his time.

'You won't just not come?' she insisted.

With a grunt he relinquished the prospect of freedom from
Standishes and all their works. 'No, I won't just not come.'
Then, when she still stood in front of him: 'Listen, I'll come,
I'll come. Okay?'

'Okay,' she barked back.

They glared at each other, then she backed off to let him
pass, and they walked back to the house together.

Chapter 18

HOUGH JACOB WAS no longer miserable about Sheila, he was not positively happy; he felt dulled, middle-aged, a man of measured and reasonable pleasures. Life was vivid but distant – brightness at the end of a tunnel. He would never get there again; he had been wounded too deep.

But time had been working on him, as he discovered one morning in Versailles, looking at the slant of light across a street of sober, decent, elegant houses. They had an air of doing the sun a favour – for where else could it show its stuff to such advantage? Sedate, above flattery, they needed no gilding; they could manifest their propriety perfectly well without any ephemeral sunshiny flummery. It was absurd, it was very French, it was beautiful. He was amused and delighted, and primitive creating joy surged in his blood, the joy he had feared was gone forever. As suddenly as if a switch had been flicked, he was healed.

For the next two months he wandered footloose through France and Italy, walking and hitching, sleeping in youth hostels and cheap hotels – until Florence. There, after one prodigious look, he abandoned all thought of going anywhere else in the time he had left, squandered the last of his savings on a fairly expensive central *pensione*, then spent ten intense days confirming what he had guessed from that one look: that his mother was right: there was another celestial city besides London, and it was Florence. He had never lived so continuously at full stretch. All he lacked was someone to share it with.

His time was nearly up before he noticed that the someone whose companionship he missed was not Sheila. He really was well again.

And penniless. He had enough work lined up to pay his mortgage, nothing more; he would have to turn computing dogsbody on some university project. Not an appealing prospect: he wanted to work on his own and steer clear of the academic community. However, he had to eat; and it would only be temporary – and Florence had been worth it.

But there were three offers of work in the heap of post on his doormat – two dull but lucrative jobs, one lovely treat. A chain of London estate agents wanted him to debug, probably redesign, their over-elaborate programmes. A business directory was going over to computerised typesetting; would he advise them? And an Italian publishing firm had heard about his work on the Latin thesaurus project and wanted him as a consultant for an Italian thesaurus. He need not worry about not knowing Italian – with his classical training he would easily pick up as much as was necessary. Unfortunately the job would entail a certain amount of travel to Milan.

Unfortunately! Italy! Italian!

He had won his gamble. Three such offers in so short a time meant that word was getting round – that his future was assured. He needn't work on academic projects for other people. If he were lucky, he wouldn't even have to go looking for work: it would come to him. He accepted all three jobs, arranged for intensive coaching in Italian – he was going to wow them in Milan, by gum – and buckled down to work, hoping he hadn't taken on too much.

He hadn't. It was a bit of a juggling act, but he managed it and still found time to buy a secondhand black Mini 1275 GT; to call briefly on the Standishes and Naomi; to go – of course – to movies; to fall intensely but rather unsatisfactorily in love with a doctor who was in any case leaving Cambridge at Christmas for a practice in Liverpool; and, one grey October Sunday, to pick up Imogen at the Friends School in Saffron Walden and take her for a drive in the country.

He went with no intention of repeating the visit; it was a one-off occasion, undertaken solely in order to keep his promise to her. But it was such a success that he suggested another; and that, in turn, was so enjoyable that they lined up another, then yet another. Jacob had an insatiable appetite for the English countryside – even the Fens – and fed it regularly, now that he had a car, by taking drives and walks. But he had had to go alone – no one he knew, not even his lover, wanted to swan about the back roads in one of the dullest parts of England.

Imogen did. East Anglia was new to her, and she had an eye hungry for impressions – a patient, differentiating, demanding eye that seized on structure and teased out significant detail: the cant of a tree, lichen on tiles, the ghostly bloom on ploughed fields in chalk country. They both enjoyed going into churches and round churchyards, and strolling along village streets, and clumping across muddy fields in search of tumuli that were more conspicuous on the one-inch map than on the ground, and stuffing themselves with cream teas, and just driving or walking about; and their response to what they saw was so uncannily identical that he often half forgot how young she was – until her tea-time accounts of life at school reminded him.

By his last visit before Christmas he realised that he would quite like to go on with their trips – 'If you're still game.'

She beamed. 'Oh, I'm game!'

So their outings were resumed and became a fixture on both their calendars – every three weeks on a Saturday or Sunday afternoon.

He did not see much of the Standishes; they still made him uneasy, though they were as friendly as ever, and grateful for his regular visits to Imogen. He did, however, visit Frances for an occasional talk. His long celibate recuperation was over, but his problems were not: neither of the attachments he formed after the doctor left was really so suitable as, in the first flush of infatuation, he had hoped; and it was a help to discuss his predicament with a sympathetic and fairly perceptive friend.

'I wonder,' she commented at last, 'if you've got over Sheila as much as you think. I mean, you only fall for people who can't take her place. Isn't it too much to be coincidence, picking three in a row who don't work out?'

Maybe she was right. But what was he to do about it?

Laura Hackett ended his self-questioning. Laura was the real thing. He met her in May, only a fortnight before going to

America for a month with his parents, and fell in love with her immediately and thoroughly. She was a biochemist and a fellow of King's, but moved as little as possible in the academic social round; she and Jacob belonged to different, overlapping circles of the Cambridge left. She had a deadpan sense of humour, a well-hidden wild streak and an unassuming, almost apologetic absolute honesty. Her head was screwed on the right way; she was an active feminist, involved in a group that gave free pregnancy tests and contraceptive information; and she liked movies – real movies, American movies, not just art films. She had a lovely, compact, composed body, and the most graceful way of moving that he had ever seen, quick and light as a cat, or of standing still – again like a cat, everything effortlessly concentrated on stillness. She had fair colouring, wavy fawn hair, and a face composed of blunt-pointed triangles: sharp-arched eyebrows; tilted cheekbones; a small, full mouth with the points in the middle of the upper lip well defined and very close together; strongly curved eyelids; and bright triangular pale-blue eyes. She looked permanently quizzical, and often formidably inscrutable; her countenance did not reveal the gentleness and tenderness in her nature. Most people would think she looked interesting, but too angular and austere; Jacob thought she was beautiful.

And she was, miraculously, unattached.

But only just. Before her recent move into rooms in King's she had lived for several years with an unhappy man, who had battened on her happiness and vitality. She had been miserable; she was still drained; and she did not want to plunge straight into another attachment: she tried hard to resist getting interested in Jacob. She was glad he was going to America; she needed time alone. Maybe when he got back . . . but maybe not. He mustn't count on it. She just didn't know; she refused to promise anything.

She also refused to make love to him, even after intense late-night conversations and embraces, lest she be precipitated into feeling . . . more than she could bear to.

'It's as bad as dates back in high school,' he grumbled, but not seriously; she was speaking a language he understood. He went away in a state of excitement shot through with panic. Would she be there when he got back? He thought so, but he had learned to distrust his own optimism.

She was there, and she was even better than he remembered. He was home and dry and safe and sound and happy, really happy, for the first time since Sheila.

Not that things were simple; Jacob did not have the knack of picking women who made things simple. Laura's past few years had been so bad that she had virtually lost faith in simple reliability and decency between lovers. They had a few blissful days together; a month of reaction followed.

A bad month. She did not trust him, or pretend to; she never pretended. She was waiting, sceptically, for him to show his true colours: and doing her damnedest to find out what they were, by attacking him with scathing criticisms and coldly searching questions, then refusing to listen to the answers – she actually left the room if he persisted, so much did she fear the very quarrels she was working to provoke. She was trying to make him turn on her; he only hoped she would let up before she succeeded. He held on grimly, but he was beginning to wonder if there were any point: if he had perhaps imagined the woman he had fallen in love with in May, or those few joyful days after his return.

But the worst was over. Slowly Laura was beginning to believe that he would not kick her in the teeth.

Slowly – then not so slowly; she was spiritually robust, and by summer's end he could tell, from the ease of her laughter, from the way she let him read delight in her face, from references to future time that crept into her speech and went uncorrected, that she had rebounded into her natural state. He breathed easy: things were going to be all right.

But still not simple. For a start she refused to live with him. 'I've been living with people since I was nineteen. Now I want a good long stretch – years – in a place that's all mine. – No, don't give me half of your house. – No, I don't want to buy half of it, either. It's not a question of ownership – I don't own my rooms in King's – it's territory.'

In theory Jacob understood; in practice he didn't like it: in practice it was duplicated razors and underwear, and never knowing whether he had left things in King's or at home, and half the time staying with her or she with him, but half the time being left at home or sent back there. It felt like being on indefinite probation.

'But it's not like that,' she said. 'It's just that I can't imagine when I'll ever have enough of living alone.'

When we have children, he thought, but did not say. That was presuming too much on the future; that must wait. No point in risking one of Laura's formidable retreats into silence by raising a subject so freighted with implications of continuity.

It was another sore point that she would neither say she loved him nor let him say he loved her: her last lover had so often made her say the words to reassure him after bitter quarrels that she associated them only with coercion. She couldn't say them yet, perhaps not ever; and she didn't really want to hear them – if he could bear to refrain? Again he understood why; but keeping silent was a torment: to repress the words from his lips was almost like suppressing the feeling from his heart – as if, unspoken, it did not quite exist.

But these were minor problems, born of her still-recent unhappiness. She would come round – he would wait – she was worth waiting for. In the meantime he laid in a large supply of spare socks and razor blades and tried to get used to finding that what he wanted was always where he wasn't: and surprisingly soon – by early autumn – life began to have a blessedly ordinary rhythm.

Chapter 19

N OCTOBER HE took her to meet Imogen – rather nervously: what on earth would he do if they didn't like each other? Visiting Imogen at school was by now an institution that he could hardly stop without hurting her feelings; visiting her without Laura might somehow hurt Laura's. But there was no problem; they took to each other immediately.

They went to see a wool church. In the graveyard afterwards Laura fell behind, reading gravestones, and Imogen said, 'Laura's super. Are you going to marry her?'

'Nope.'

'Why not?'

'We, uh, don't believe in marriage.'

'But you and Sheila were married.'

'Yes, well, that was sort of accidental.' How did one explain these things to children?

She accepted it, however. 'Then you're living together.'

'Uh, sort of.'

Imogen looked enquiring.

'We live half at her place and half at mine and half by ourselves. Laura wants to keep her independence.'

'I think that's a very good idea' – approvingly.

'What is?' Laura asked, coming into earshot.

'Keeping your independence and living in two places like you two.'

'Hah – an ally,' said Laura, amused.

'Traitor,' said Jacob.

Imogen looked from one to the other and decided that nothing serious was the matter. 'You mean that Laura wants to keep her independence and you don't?'

Laura hooted.

He started to answer, then caught them glancing at each other. 'Imogen Standish, are you having me on, you snake?'

'Oh – yes – I suppose so' – demurely. 'But it does seem like a good idea. I get awfully tired of living with people, even Jo, and she's my best friend. I'd like you to meet her, Laura. Jacob hasn't met her yet either, but I've told him all about her.' Her eyes lit up. 'But I haven't told you.' And she sang Jo's praises all the way back to the school.

A few days later the telephone rang. 'Hullo, Jacob? Oliver here, Oliver Standish. I'm, er, terribly sorry, I'd never have rung so late, but, er . . .'

Jacob put his hand over the mouthpiece. 'Oliver,' he told Laura, who was getting ready to go home.

'I know – his voice carries. I can hear every word.' She went upstairs to fetch something; when she came down, he had hung up. 'Something wrong? You look peeved.'

He shrugged. 'Just Standish complications. It's Imogen's half term, and Oliver wants me to fetch her in the morning and bring her here for the day. Don't ask me why, he wouldn't exactly say – something to do with Frances. She isn't ill, and she hasn't had an accident, but she's "in a state", and he has to stay with her. He'll tell me – and Imogen – what's up when he comes for her. In the meantime I'm to tell her that Frances has flu – which she doesn't – and he's held up looking after her.'

'I don't see the complication in that.'

'Just that he was so evasive about what's going on. And Imogen will know I lied to her if I tell her that Frances has flu, and then she finds out it isn't true.'

'I see what you mean – it lines you up on their side, not hers, somehow. Yes indeed – complications.'

Imogen was happy to see him and came away incuriously. Maybe he would get away with not having to explain anything. But, as he drew up in St Eligius Street beside the passage to Coronation Place, she said, speaking quickly: 'There's something wrong, isn't there, or Daddy wouldn't have sent you, he'd have got the school to send me home by train.'

'Oliver said that Frances has flu and he's held up taking care of her.' Not a lie – though she was unlikely to remember, if she thought about it at all, afterwards, that he had spoken the literal truth.

'Why can't I go home, then?'

'He didn't say – he said he'd explain later.'

She gave a resigned sigh, then suddenly gasped. 'But if Mummy just has flu, why can't I go home? She must be dreadfully ill, and Daddy's trying to spare me – maybe she's – she's – *dying* – and what if I never *see* her again? I've got to go home – right away!' She clutched his arm. 'Please will you take me to the station?'

'Listen, pet, you can't go – '

She snatched her hand away, exclaimed, 'If you won't take me, I'll go by myself,' leapt out of the car without her suitcase and set off in the wrong direction.

He caught up with her. 'Listen – it's okay. Frances is all right.'

Imogen kept on walking, head up.

'There's nothing wrong with her, she isn't ill at all.'

'You're just saying that,' she flung at him sideways.

'And the station's back thataway,' he flung back. 'And take your suitcase if you're going – I don't want it.'

She stopped and looked at him uncertainly. 'Mummy isn't ill at all? How do you know? You said she was.'

Jacob grunted. 'Oliver said to tell you she had flu; but I'd already asked him if she was ill or had had an accident, and he'd said no.'

'What *is* the matter, then?'

'I don't know. That's the truth. He said it was too complicated to explain – he'll tell you when he picks you up this evening.'

Her face cleared. 'Okay.' She turned back. 'I'm sorry I rushed off; I didn't understand.'

She didn't understand now, either, and no more did he. But perhaps simply knowing that they were in the same boat was a help.

They had a nice day: a companionable lunch, a walk across Sheep's Green, a look at Queen's and Corpus. Jacob stopped in at the maths lab to check something and show Imogen where he worked; then they got two greedy boxfuls of Fitzbillies' cakes and came back home for tea.

Laura arrived late, muttering about a slow chromatography, and caught them on the point of sharing the last Chelsea bun. 'Pigs!' She grabbed it.

'We left you plenty of other things,' said Imogen disingenuously, picking up an Eccles cake.

'Not the same as Chelsea buns' – Laura licked sticky fingers – 'and you know it.'

The telephone rang. 'Hello – oh, hello, Oliver. – Yes, fine. – Yes, no trouble. A pleasure.'

'Look, Jacob, this is an, er, an enormous favour to ask, but do you suppose you could possibly keep Imogen longer – overnight, in fact? If you can, I'll pick her up in the morning.'

'I can keep her, sure, it'll be a treat' – smiling at Imogen, who was looking perturbed and did not respond; though he was pressing the receiver to his ear, he could tell that she heard every word. 'But listen, how's Frances?'

'Oh, fine, fine. Only it'd be better . . . if you *can* . . .'

'Sure, no problem. But Imogen's right here' – sitting bolt

upright with fear on her face – 'and I think she's a bit worried. Wouldn't you like to talk to her?'

'No, look, there's nothing to say, really. You can tell her, er, that Frances is better, but another quiet night – you can improvise; she trusts you. Look, I'd better hurry. You're sure it's all right? I'll be up by eleven.'

'Okay;' and he hung up before Oliver could do more damage.

Imogen was clutching her Eccles cake; her face was closed tight.

'I guess you heard most of that.'

She nodded.

'Well, is it okay with you?'

She looked up, eyes small with anger. 'It has to be, doesn't it?' she said savagely.

There was nothing to say to that. He and Laura took the tea things into the kitchen and did the washing up slowly and noisily, in order to give Imogen some time by herself. Uncharacteristically, she did not come and offer to help.

'We should *do* something tonight,' Laura whispered, 'not just sit around here.'

When they returned to the sitting room, Imogen was slouching listlessly. 'We were thinking of going to a movie,' he told her. 'Would you like to come?'

She gave a tired sigh. 'Thank you, but I'd rather watch – oh, you don't have television. I – I've got a book, though. You don't need to worry about me, it's a jolly good book.'

Jacob and Laura looked at each other. Laura said, 'Jacob doesn't have a telly because he's a snob; but I'm not – I've got one in King's. Why don't you come back with me after dinner. You can see what my rooms are like, then watch TV all evening if you want.'

'Thank you, that's very nice of you,' she replied with passive politeness; 'but I don't want to be in the –'

'You won't be in the way. The set's in the bedroom, and I work in the sitting room; you won't disturb me a bit.'

'No, but I don't want to make you two miss your film. I'll stay here and read. I'll be all right by myself, really I will. I *like* being alone.'

It was a plea. They exchanged uneasy glances, weighing the risks of leaving her alone (what risks? – she was fourteen) against the impossibility of explaining that they had thought of a movie only to entertain her.

Meanwhile, as if thrusting apprehension away, Imogen turned cheerful. 'It'll be fun staying all night – I can tell them at school that I spent the night with an unmarried man.'

'Alone with him, too,' Laura said.

'Alone? I thought you'd be – '

'No, I mostly sleep in my rooms. *He* snores.'

'I do *not*,' said Jacob automatically.

'*Alone* with an unmarried man – fantastic!'

'Hey, you, stop planning to shock the entire Friends School,' he said, 'or next thing you know, I won't be allowed to take you out for the day or anything.'

'Blast,' said Imogen. 'But *please* do what you were going to do. I'll be okay here, really.'

Easier to go than to explain. After dinner they showed her where the bedclothes were, made her promise not to open the door to anyone, and went.

Chapter 20

 HE WAS SUBDUED at breakfast. At last she said, her tone airy, her look anxious: 'It's fun staying with you' – an indirect apology for yesterday's outburst about having no choice but to stay.

'It's fun having you,' Jacob said with light formality – apology accepted.

She brightened. 'It's like being married, isn't it?' She swept him a languishing look through lowered lashes.

She was joking, but he thought she would be chagrined if he laughed. 'Not the same at all,' he said matter-of-factly. 'If we were married, you'd make your own toast.'

'You didn't make Sheila's?'

'No.'

'Did she make yours?'

'Good God no.'

'Why "good God no"?'

'It was against her principles.'

'Making toast?' – with false innocence.

'No, silly – making mine. She didn't believe in waiting on men.'

She nodded. 'Because she's a feminist. Was that why you two broke up?'

'You mean because she wouldn't make my toast?'

'And things like that.'

'No, I don't want people making my toast, or vice versa. It's nice, of course, but . . .'

'You made mine' – speaking through a mouthful of it.

'That's different. You're a guest.'

'Well, did Sheila *think* you wanted her to . . . "make your toast"?'

This was old ground: she periodically quizzed him about why his marriage had ended, never quite understanding when he explained about the conflict between his need to stay in England and Sheila's to return home to her work, and never quite reconciled to incomprehension. If she were hoping to find clues to her parents' troubles, it was a fruitless quest, for the situations had nothing in common. But he could not violate her indirectness by saying so; instead, he once again told her about him and Sheila.

Imogen listened, frowning slightly. 'Laura's the same, isn't she – about "making toast"?'

'Mm-hmm.'

'And you don't mind with her, either?'

'Nope.'

Her frown deepened. 'What I don't see is – you and Sheila agreed about just about everything, including "toast", but you didn't stay together. So how do you and Laura know you'll stay together?'

'We don't,' he said cautiously. 'We *think* we want to, but we aren't sure yet. We're still finding out.'

'Finding out what? If you, er, love each other?'

'No, we're sure of that.' (He was glad Laura could not overhear him.) 'But we want to be sure we'll . . . go on . . .

and . . . well, we're neither of us kids, you know; we've both had attachments that ended badly – and it makes you . . . careful.'

She set down her mug. 'I can see why you're careful,' she said in a clear, forceful voice; 'but you mustn't be *too* careful, or you'll, you'll, miss it.'

'It?'

Her hazel eyes regarded him seriously. 'Life. What you want.' Then the vatic spell waned; the sybil was fourteen again, and blushing. 'I – I suppose I just mean I like Laura and I hope you stay with her.'

Miss it. Miss it. One of his deepest fears. How did she know? Could she see right into him? 'Very kind of you,' he snapped. 'But you're over your depth; you sound just like an agony aunt.'

Imogen picked up her mug and took a big gulp; another; then got up and took the mug to the sink. He watched her wash it. Her shoulders were narrowed. She started on the plates, and he picked up a tea-towel and went to help her. She kept her eyes down. 'Imogen.' He touched her tight back. 'I'm sorry.' Her hands stopped swilling. 'It was a mean thing to say. And you weren't over your depth at all – you said just what I sometimes feel. I'm sorry.'

She faced him. '*I'm* sorry, *I'm* sorry,' she shouted, bursting into tears and ducking her head, wet-faced and wet-handed, a huddle of woe. He put his arm round her, and she heaved and gulped briefly on his shoulder, then pulled back, looking at him shamefaced.

'It's all right, puchkie, we both got . . .'

'I'm sorry' – for crying, this time. She sniffed and wiped her nose on a paper towel. 'I wanted to apologise for . . . you know . . .'

Jacob didn't.

'For saying I didn't want . . .'

He saw the light. She was still worried about yesterday; her indirect apology had not cleared her conscience. 'That's okay, I knew you didn't mean it.'

'You *did*?' Sniff. She blew her nose.

'Sure. People often say stupid things when they're upset – like me just now. You scared me, saying I might miss . . . whatever it is; and I sort of lashed out at you. Same as you yesterday. I knew you didn't mean that crack about having to stay.'

'Oh. Good.' Looking happier, she fished the J cloth out of the water and began swilling the last plate.

Chapter 21

OFFEE WOULD BE nice, Oliver said with a wan smile, leaning back on the sofa, the very picture of elegant relaxation, except that the end of his nose twitched a little now and then.

Imogen brought him his cup, and he patted the seat beside him. When she sat down, he neither withdrew his arm nor put it round her, but left it extended stiffly behind her back, bunching his hand on the seat to support his slight inclination towards her. The posture was intimate but not affectionate, and he maintained it without noticing that it was uncomfortable for Imogen, who, unable to lean back against that rigid diagonal, but clearly unwilling to reject his gesture by sitting up straight, was having to hold herself in a strained halfway position so that her back brushed his arm.

He drank his coffee slowly, affecting nonchalance (was the show for Jacob or Imogen?) and talking to her about school: the perfect father, acquainting himself with his child's little world. His physical demonstrativeness was at full stretch in that frozen arm and bunched fist; but his voice was caressing, languorous, flirtatious – almost one for wheedling women into bed with insinuations of shared sensibilities and special affinities; and she responded with a gauche, uncertain, but potent flirtatiousness of her own: a smile that appeared only for him, and a soft tone that gave back his caressing notes like an echo.

Jacob had often wished that Oliver would pay more attention

to her; but this performance made him uneasy. She thought she was getting attention and affection; but Oliver was not interested in her as she was: what he wanted, and elicited, was adoration. Whenever she got enthusiastic or earnest, or cracked a joke, his attention turned off abruptly, and a glaze of faintly irritated boredom shuttered his light, narrow eyes, until she noticed she had lost him and, with no more than momentary bewilderment, clicked back into her role.

Oliver accepted a second cup of coffee and looked at his watch. 'We should be going, Imogen. Why don't you take your case out to the car while I finish this – I'll be out in a minute.'

'You might as well just say: "Go away so I can talk to Jacob".' She looked put out, but said thank you and goodbye and left meekly enough.

'Er, I don't know how to thank you enough for –'

Jacob cut him short: it was no bother – a pleasure – a tiny repayment for years of Standish hospitality – but perhaps Oliver could give him a clue about what was going on?

'Yes, yes, you have a right to know – that's why – ' He gestured at the door. 'I don't know how much you know about Frances' life recently . . .'

'Uh, not . . .'

'The truth is that she's been, er, experimenting . . . and, well, frankly, she took some, er, LSD at a party and had a . . . a "bad trip", I believe it's called.' He scrutinised Jacob's carefully impassive face – hoping for signs of shock? 'The first time I rang you, she was still crying and babbling and shrieking – I had to stay with her. I couldn't fetch Imogen, and I didn't want her to come home by train – I didn't want her to, er, see her mother like that. And Frances was the same way most of yesterday, too, sort of . . .'

'Spaced out?'

'Er, yes. She was beginning to . . . come down, is it? . . . but I still didn't want Imogen to see her . . . you can imagine . . .'

'So how is she today?'

'Today?' – momentarily disconcerted. 'Oh. Fine. Fine. She slept it off last night, and she's all right now – a bit weak and dizzy, that's all.'

'Good.' Suddenly Jacob wondered with a sinking feeling

why Imogen had been sent to the car. 'I suppose you'll be telling Imogen about it on the way home?'

'Good gracious, no.' Oliver looked surprised. 'Frances doesn't want her to know, and neither do I. No – she thinks it was flu, and I'll just tell her we didn't want her to catch it.'

Jesus. Imogen already knew that that story wasn't true. 'Uh . . .'

Oliver interrupted him. 'In fact, I told Frances I'd tell you the flu story too, so all this is rather, er, confidential . . . I . . . er . . .' He got up to go.

Jacob followed him, working up his nerve for another, 'Uh.'

But at the door Oliver said, 'Well, goodbye,' and without waiting for a reply quickly let himself out. Jacob was left, mouth open to speak, facing a closed door.

After a blank moment he opened it. But the car had gone. Damn. He'd better let Frances know.

Her 'Hullo' was tired.

'How are you?' he asked anxiously.

'Oliver told you, then. I should have known. Imogen, too?'

'No, that's what I – '

'That's something. He said he wouldn't, but I never know . . .' She trailed off wearily.

'Are you okay?'

'Sort of. I'm just tired out, which is funny. I mean, I've been sleeping practically non-stop for the past two days.'

'*Sleeping*? Oliver said – '

Silence on the line. Then, less wearily: 'Oliver said what?'

Christ, why hadn't he kept quiet? 'Uh, that you were still pretty spaced out last night.'

'Did he, just? And what else?'

Reluctantly, he repeated what Oliver had said about her bad trip.

'He spins a good story,' she said grimly.

'You mean none of it is – '

'No, it's true in parts. I mean, I did have a bad trip, but not screaming or babbling or anything, just, oh, sort of like depressed, only more so. Paralytical with misery. But that was three days ago. I've been okay since the day before yesterday, except for being so sleepy.'

'Then why did Oliver , uh . . .'

She hesitated. 'I don't know if I should tell you . . . But Oliver promised not to tell about *me*, so why not? The truth is, both times that he rang you, he wasn't here taking care of me, the way he said; he was at Sara's. He's got a slack week at work anyhow, and I'd behaved badly by freaking out; so he decided to pay me back by having a little holiday with her.'

Jacob was supposed to be outraged at the way he had been used. He was; Oliver's stock hit the floor. But he also felt a familiar revulsion from both Standishes and their intrigues; he wanted to be done with this conversation. 'Hmm, well, no harm done,' he said non-committally. 'I enjoyed having Imogen to stay. But listen, I should tell you why I rang. It's about telling her.'

'You don't mean about what Oliver – ?'

'No, no – about your bad trip.'

'Oh, that's no problem, she thinks I've had flu.'

'Well, no, she doesn't,' and he told her what he had told Imogen in the middle of St Eligius Street.

Frances clicked with annoyance. 'That's torn it.'

'I couldn't help it,' he said defensively. 'She thought you were dying; I had to tell her something, or she'd have gone straight home. I'm sorry I've complicated matters, but Oliver left before I could tell him, and I thought I'd better let you know, so that you can tell her the truth.'

She hardly hesitated. 'I don't think it's as bad as that. I mean, by now Oliver has said I had flu, so we can't tell her anything else.'

'But –'

'I'm not telling her what really happened' – tartly. 'Out of the question. I do *not* want her to know I've dropped acid.'

'Why not? She knows I have.'

'That's different – I'm her mother. But don't worry, it'll be all right – she'll just think you were trying to reassure her, or that you misunderstood what Oliver told you.'

'You'll tell her that?'

'She'll just assume it, she won't ask. But if she does, I think it's the best line to take, don't you?'

'It's up to you, Frances,' he said in resignation. 'As you say, you're her mother.'

'Fine. Thanks for letting me know.' Still a bit crisp. Then, with tardy compunction: 'Jacob, thank you, really. I mean, I'm sorry you got sort of . . . caught in the works.'

'That's okay . . .' They both apologised again and rang off in a flurry of inauthentic good will.

Caught in the works, indeed. He felt like a puppet whose strings they were both trying to twitch.

Chapter 22

ESUS, I COULD murder those two,' he told Laura that evening after recounting the morning's events. 'Thank God for the school. I met the Head once, last year, and he sees what Imogen's like; he said she's got "a delicate gravity that needs to be respected and fostered". Pretty good, don't you think? But the Standishes only sent her there because it's cheaper than Bedales; it's so modest and un-glamorous that they're always apologising for it. Idiots.'

'What I don't understand,' Laura said rather tartly, 'is why you're so steamed up. Why not just forget about them?'

'Surely it's obvious – I've told you enough about them.'

'Yes, but I haven't met them, and nothing you've told me explains why you keep on being bothered with them. You don't even seem to like them.'

'But they aren't just friends, they're more like . . . like relations – I've known them ever since I came here, you know? I've stopped thinking of them as the, uh, finest flower of civilisation, but there are still ties. Especially to Imogen; I've sort of taken her on. And she's not like them, she is . . .'

'The finest flower of civilisation?' – drily.

He grinned but stuck to his guns. 'Something like that.

Besides, having a . . . a duty to her has been a help to me, too; it's given me a stake – made me feel less rootless. I suppose it relieves this Jewish sense I've got, that a man without family obligations is nothing. And there's something about her . . . It's awfully hard to express, but she's kept me in touch with life, you know?'

'And I don't,' Laura said in a light, cool, detached voice.

Jesus. His big mouth. 'Laura, Laura, of course you do. I meant before you, when I was floundering about. Don't you know what I mean?'

She considered, her face remote. 'Yes,' she said – a judge passing sentence. 'I'll be going now.'

He watched her put on her coat. He said nothing; there was no point: he would only lose his temper and make things worse. She had retreated deep into mistrust; there was no getting her out. She would go away now, and, when he saw her tomorrow, she would be over it; they would not speak of it, it would be through – except that it would not be, not quite. Each of these occasions had its effect.

She turned for a last word. 'You idealise her. Nobody can be that good. She's a fantasy you've made up.'

'Not so.' His voice was as level and deadly as hers.

She shook her head and left. He stayed where he was, tears of self-pity coming to his eyes, so that when a key scratched in the lock, and she came back in and stood at the edge of the sitting room as if she did not belong there, he saw her through a haze.

'I didn't mean it,' she said at last. 'I think I'm . . . jealous of Imogen.'

He shrugged. 'What on earth for? That's one of the feeblest – '

She crossed the room and stood glowering over him. 'Shut up and let me finish.' Her eyes glittered in the unflattering light cast up upon her from the low lamp beside the sofa. 'I – you're . . . she kept you in touch with life, and now you're relying on me to – and – and – I'm *afraid*. So I said you idealise *her*, but what I meant is that you idealise *me* – and you'll – you'll – '

His angry self-pity evaporated. For the first time she was standing her ground, explaining herself, seeing a quarrel through, and it was terribly important for him not to say

110

something stupid. 'You're afraid I'll rumble you,' he ventured.

She nodded.

'What will I find out – that you aren't as – what did you call it – as "good" as Imogen?'

'Yes. After all, it's easier for children to be . . . pure, whatever it is. They've had less . . . less living to cope with. And you – expect so much.'

He could see her clearly now. She was almost trembling with the effort not to turn round again and leave. He wanted to reach out and comfort her with a touch, but he must meet her effort with words, with truth. 'I do expect "so much". That's why I want you. I don't idealise you, I know you've got faults – God knows we both have . . .' He had to do better than that. But he couldn't think of anything. He laughed nervously. 'In fact –'

'What's funny?' she snapped.

'The idea that I idealise *you*. Because I've been worrying that you idealised *me*, and, you know, when you found out . . .'

'Oh.' Laura laughed tremulously. She looked diabolical in the inverted light. 'Really?'

'Mm-hmm.'

'Oh. We're a fine pair.'

'The halt leading the blind,' he agreed.

They regarded each other curiously. Not much of an explanation, on either side; but she had not rushed away, and he had not lost his temper.

'Well, see you tomorrow, then.'

'Yup,' he said, almost easily, though with all his being he wanted her to stay, wanted her to offer, wanted to ask her; and got up to kiss her goodnight. They gave each other a quick brusque kiss and hug. Then Laura moved closer, hugging him with all her might, and they stood still, holding on tight, drawing solace from each other. She would stay if he asked, for their embrace was slowly becoming suffused with –

But she had been intending to go back to King's. What if she got the idea that staying long enough to see an argument through also meant staying all night to make it up? She might feel trapped; next time she might not stay at all. He tried to ignore the idea, but at last, reluctantly, he drew back, smiling quizzically, making the choice hers: and, when she kept the short distance he had put between them and ruefully returned his smile, he guessed that she was wondering much the same thing – damn it.

'Well . . .' he said inanely, in order not to say the 'Stay' that was on the tip of his tongue.

'Well,' she responded, not moving. He leaned forward and kissed her a tender goodnight. She touched his cheek with a regretful, 'Oh dear,' and left.

Progress, he supposed. Maybe next time she would stay. In the meantime – he had read somewhere that you could relieve frustration by punching cushions. He punched a cushion. No joy.

Chapter 23

 TALL GODDESS – five foot eight if she was an inch – waylaid Jacob by the rhododendrons at the edge of the school car park. She had dark skin and hair, protuberant light blue eyes and an emphatic, scornful expression, like a downy young hawk.

'You're Jacob Harris, Imogen said you had red hair. My name is Jo Anscomb, I'm a friend of hers, we take Italian together, and I've decided to speak to you, because Imogen's upset about something, she cries some nights, I can hear because my bed's next to hers, and I thought you could do something about it.'

'Me? What makes you think that *I* – ' He took hold of himself. 'What do you want me to do that you can't do yourself?'

'She hasn't *said* anything – she just *looks* worried – but I think it's about her parents, that's why I thought of you, because you know them, so you can bring them up and see how she reacts.'

112

'I get it. Okay, I'll see . . .' She turned to go. 'Hey. Tell me more. How do you know it's her parents she's worried about?'

'Letters. She's worried before she opens her mother's letters. But I've got to go, or she'll come out looking for you and see me; and I didn't tell her what I was going to do – so don't say you saw me!' She melted into the rhododendrons.

'I'll be jiggered,' he said aloud to himself.

Jacob and Imogen went to a church and poked about until parishioners started arriving for evensong, then decamped to Finchingfield for tea. Imogen seemed happy, but her spirits faded over scones. The dirty-brown day thickened to the afternoon night of December, and she ate and drank in silence and stared through the tea-shop window at less and less.

Her long silence gave him an opening. 'What's eating you?'

She looked from the darkness to him in languid query.

'You're worrying about something.'

'What makes you say that?' she protested – but without denying it.

'You haven't said a word, and usually you're asking a question a minute.'

'You *are* horrid.' But after a little encouragement she admitted to being . . . a bit . . . oh . . . er . . .

'About school?'

No.

'Problems with your friends?'

Oh, no. She and Jo *never* had problems.

'Homesick, then?'

Warm. She denied it, but hesitantly.

'Are you missing Frances and Oliver?'

Warmer. 'I don't exactly *miss* them.'

'Heard from them recently?'

Hot. 'Only ordinary letters' – resentfully.

'Only ordinary – you're expecting something out-of-the-ordinary?'

She half-shook her head.

Jacob leaned back and let his silence force her into speech; in a couple of minutes she was stammering: 'When I was at home at half term . . . I . . . it . . . I've been wondering . . .'

'Wondering?'

'Oh, if something was – wrong.'

113

'What sort of thing?'

Imogen looked down at her plate and pushed her leftover jam into a mound with her knife, then decided to confide in him. 'Something *was* wrong – Mummy and Daddy were . . . strange. Not exactly upset but as if they'd *been* upset. And they both said Mummy had had flu, and you'd told me she hadn't; and they kept whispering; and Mummy stayed in bed; and she looked a mixture of tired and awfully unhappy. Flu wouldn't make her look like that. So I wondered – ' She looked at him suspiciously. 'I don't know why I'm telling *you*; you probably *know*. They tell *you* things.' But she went on anyhow. 'First I thought maybe they – that Daddy was going to leave Mummy, and that was why she was unhappy – and they'd tell me by letter, because it's easier to say bad news in letters. But I've just had ordinary ones, so now I think it's something else, like – ' She looked out of the window. Outside it was so dark that she could not see beyond her own frowning reflection. 'For instance' – addressing the window – 'maybe Mummy had an abortion – she'd think I was too young to know about that; grown ups do.' (How quickly taboos changed; she took abortion more for granted at fourteen than he had at eighteen.) 'Or – or – or maybe she has – cancer or something.'

'Oh, Imogen, no, not that at all, it was only – '

She swung round angrily. 'I knew you knew. What *is* it?'

'I wanted them to tell you, but they thought it would upset you,' he gabbled, then realised that he was an idiot. 'Listen, all that happened' – Imogen steeled herself – 'was that Frances had some LSD at a party and had a pretty bad trip, and – '

'Is *that* all? Really all?' She glowed with indignant relief. 'Why didn't they say so? All that flu stuff, I was so *worried*. But what happened to Mummy, what was it like? Do tell, please.' She leaned forward, all anxiety gone, eager for a good story. Jacob repeated Frances' account of her bad trip, and Imogen listened raptly, making short work of cakes she had neglected earlier, then said contentedly, 'Poor Mummy, it must have been perfectly ghastly.'

'Poor Imogen, worrying about divorce and cancer and things.'

She shrugged away three weeks of distress. 'They thought they were doing the best thing. Older people don't have a sense of proportion about drugs, don't you find?'

Nice of her to include him in her generation. Though that might have been a courteous afterthought: with Imogen one never knew.

Chapter 24

ARLY IN DECEMBER Frances rang and invited Jacob and Laura to West Horton for Christmas.

'We can't, I'm afraid,' he replied; 'we'll be with Laura's parents in Wales.'

'Where in Wales? – Knighton? Then why not make a detour to us on your way back? The thing is, we won't be at Naomi's party this year, and I'm dying to meet Laura – you've been naughty, not bringing her to see us.'

He chuckled guiltily. 'Well, I'll have to ask Laura and ring you; okay?'

When he asked Laura, she said, 'Good – I'd like to meet them. Let's accept.'

'Good heavens. I assumed you wouldn't want to go any more than me.'

'Oh, but I'd like to get a good look at the Standish charm and the Standish mixture of good breeding and vulgarity; I want to flesh out the myth. But not if you'll go crazy . . .'

'No, I'll survive, I'm used to them. Okay, let's go. I suppose you should meet them. And West Horton *is* pretty.'

'Don't worry, they'll probably be a relief after my family.'

Laura was right. Her parents were stiff, humourless county-professional people, visibly suspicious of their daughter's association with an American Jew; Jacob was soon looking forward to Monk's House as to a haven of civilisation.

Which it was, though only in comparison with the Hacketts'. On the day they arrived, Oliver was slightly drunk by mid-afternoon and Frances by tea-time. Jacob and Laura started in on some serious drinking themselves, in self-defence: there was so much hearty good will flying about that they needed lubrication to keep up their part.

Things got better in the evening. Dinner sobered them up, and afterwards they were quietly conversable; for a few hours Monk's House was almost the advertisement for civilisation that Jacob had thought it in the summer of 1965: the modest but good furniture; Boccherini and Haydn on the tape deck; Imogen reading on the Turkey carpet in front of the wood fire and looking up now and then to join in convivial conversation about friends, books, the weather, music, Laura's family, movies, how to keep warm during power cuts, and the best place in Soho for coffee beans.

Almost. There were jarring notes that there had not been – or that he had not noticed – eight years before. Imogen was as usual acting younger with her parents than she did alone with him and Laura; Oliver was treating her with caressing flirta-tiousness; and Frances was looking on almost with an indulgent wife's complaisancy towards a mistress who is not a real threat. And under the surface of their talk there was a flavour of frivolity, of tolerance extended too far. They deprecated enthusiasm and intensity. This compromised life of theirs, in the agreeable firelight, with good music and food and drink and chat, was civilisation as reasonable people understood it; anything more strenuous was excessive, earnest, rather ridi-culous. Jacob looked at Imogen, who was smiling happily from the hearthrug at something Frances had said, and wondered whether her gravity was by now a fixed quality, incorruptible, or whether it could still be undermined. The Standishes and their view of the world were seductive, and she wanted their love and approval so much. Already she was becoming expert at alluring Oliver with false naivety; would their wordless pressure work on her insensibly until she acquiesced in their jaded urbanity? It would be easier all round; and they were, after all, worthy of emulation in many ways; they lacked nothing but the heart of the matter: the highest standards, and an active belief that goodness was desirable and happiness, if not probable, at least possible, and always worth striving for. They had retreated from strife rather than risk failure and now justified themselves by pooh-poohing those who had not. And it was not out of despair that they had retreated: they were not among those so constituted or circumstanced that nothing but despair was possible. Theirs was a case of sheer cowardice, or sheer laziness; he didn't know which. He looked at his old friends – his paragons of civilisation – admiring their subtle, wry, sensitive faces, pleasant and tired in the firelight, and for a moment sympathised with them. They would not find it easy to watch their child career fearlessly towards adulthood, expecting happiness and embracing – already with some dim foreknowledge of possible costs – the discipline of seriousness.

'But at least they gave her the childhood that made her qualities possible,' he said to Laura as they talked it over at bedtime. 'I think she represents the best of them.'

'Huh. Everything they've done for her has been utterly conventional – what's expected from parents in their position: a good education; good manners; certain standards of good taste. Where she got her character is a mystery. All they intended to produce was a nice, well-bred child who was clever and articulate and sensitive and witty – your ordinary upper-middle-class product.'

'That's "all"? It seems like a hell of a lot to me.'

'That's because you're American – you don't expect parents, except special ones like yours, to provide children with anything more sophisticated than straight teeth.'

'Don't knock straight teeth' – conceding defeat. 'They're all that makes those wholesome grins bearable.'

The next day they went to visit Oliver's mother. She was as formidable as Jacob remembered her; to his surprise, she was pleased to see him. 'I've hoped you'd come back another summer. Why didn't you?' she demanded.

Frances rescued him. 'He goes to America every other year, Kathleen, and he was married, and divorced, and he's started up a business and been to France and Italy and places. We hardly see him in the summer any more.'

Mrs Standish said 'Hmph', and gave Frances a cool look, but let him be.

After tea he was alone with her for a time in the handsome,

mortally cold drawing room, while Imogen took Laura on a tour of the house, and Oliver and Frances did the washing up. 'I like your young woman,' she observed. 'Comes of a good family. Suitable partner for you.'

'*I'm* not from what you'd call a "good family",' he said, fresh from four days of Laura's. 'I'm an American Jew. You should be warning Laura against me.'

'Nonsense. You're a gentleman,' ignoring his incredulous snort, 'so you must have good blood. The Jews are an ancient and distinguished race.' She examined him carefully. 'Interesting – you don't look Jewish.'

He flushed with anger, then saw that she meant just what she said – she was interested: unlike most people who made the all-too-familiar remark she did not have the effrontery to think she was flattering him. So he contented himself with saying ironically, 'Yes, typical Jewish cunning, isn't it?' then, when she merely stared, sublimely uncomprehending, shrugged and gave her a potted lecture on differences in physical type among various branches of Jewry. She listened with the same anthropological curiosity she had shown eight years earlier about America. Some of her questions were hair-raising; she was just saying: 'Tell me, what makes you Jews so clever?' when Frances and Oliver returned.

'Kathleen!' Frances exclaimed in horror. Mrs Standish merely glanced at her and returned to Jacob, waiting for an answer.

'Natural superiority, of course – good stock and centuries of inbreeding,' he said lightly. She took him seriously and nodded, perhaps drawing an analogy with her own superior stock. Amazing woman, a dinosaur-like survival; few people nowadays blurted out their racial preconceptions so unself-consciously, thank God. But he found her entertaining; and her habit of saying whatever came into her head, without caring what anyone thought, was at least more refreshing than the Hacketts' unspoken distaste.

Back at Monk's House Oliver started to apologise for her, but Jacob said, 'Don't worry, your mother's okay. She's the kind of dame,' using the word on purpose to make Oliver wince, 'who would have joined the underground if the Nazis had invaded. They'd have offended her sense of justice.'

'In fact, I think of you as just American more than

118

American-Jewish,' said Frances. 'I mean, you don't have the
same turns of speech as Norman Susskind or Naomi.'

'Yeah, they're from New York, it's a whole different world.
Boston is . . .' But he despaired of expressing the difference.
'Besides, we lived in Arlington before moving to Malden.
There weren't many Jews there, and I think I picked up a more
New-England turn of speech, playing with all those Gentile
boys . . .'

'And you aren't religious, so with that background I suppose
you more or less forget you're Jewish, same as I forget I'm Gen-'

Jacob laughed. 'It's not the same, not the same at all. My
parents are atheists, but they made sure I knew what race and
religion I came from. They sent me to Jewish summer camp –
a Progressive Children's Camp, no less – and I went to an
after-school school in somebody's house – they and some
other parents like them clubbed together and hired a teacher to
teach us some Hebrew and Yiddish and Jewish history and
culture, that sort of thing. He also taught us about Papa Lenin
and Uncle Joe Stalin – a free extra. And Aline's family are
Russian Jews – from New York, yet – and I used to go visit my
great-uncle Ira the Talmudic scholar, and hear stories about
the *stetl*, and the lower East Side in the old days –'

'*Stetl*?' queried Imogen; 'lower East Side?'

Jacob explained, and Imogen listened avidly and begged for
more. As an American he was hardly foreign at all, but as a Jew
with a great-uncle from the *stetl* he was a reporter from an
exotic world. So he told her stories from old-world and new-
world ghettoes and jokes about rabbis who went from Minsk
to Pinsk and, at Laura's urging, sang old Wobbly organising
songs that Aline's mother had taught him. Laura demanded
'The Twelve Days of Marxmas' as a seasonal encore, and soon
they were all (except Oliver, who did at least smile) singing
lustily:

> Seven socialist republics,
> Six Jewish doctors,
> Five ye-ar plan;
> Four Das Kapitals,
> Third International,
> Two bayonets,
> And a portrait of Leon Trotsky.

★

After dinner the Standishes started sniping at each other. They had not drunk nearly so much as the night before, but licensed their tongues by pretending they had. Jacob and Laura left them to their barbed small-talk and went to bed early.

'I don't understand how you were *ever* fooled by them,' said Laura up in the low-eaved bedroom. 'I don't mean the way they punch holes in each other, I mean them, themselves. Standish charm, my eye. They must have been like that when you met them – people don't change that much.' She got into bed. 'My God,' she yelped. 'It's freezing!'

'Actually,' he reflected, getting undressed, 'I think they have changed a little – Frances, at least. She was nicer that summer than she is now. It's not just that I was more impressionable; she was, hmm, more good-willed, more open.' He switched off the electric fire, opened the window a scant inch and ran for cover. 'Jesus! Where's the hot water bottle? Boston was never like this.'

Chapter 25

ARLY IN JANUARY they stopped in to see Imogen on their way to London. There was too little time for a proper outing, so they went for a walk in Saffron Walden, looking at dubious antiques in dingy shop windows. As they strolled back towards the school, Imogen's eye was caught. 'Look, that writing desk is just like Mummy's – I mean Mother's. I'm trying to remember to call Mummy Mother and Daddy Father,' she explained self-consciously. 'I asked them if I could and they said yes, because "Mummy" and "Daddy" are so childish. Jo calls *her* parents by their first names, but I don't think that's respectful enough, do you?'

'I think it's your attitude, not what you call them,' said Jacob.

'Oh. Oh, I forgot, you call your parents "Aline" and "Isaac". I didn't mean *you*, just me. I suppose it's different when you're grown up. What do you call your parents, Laura?'

'Speaking about them, mother and father. To their faces it's "Mummy" and "Dad".'

'Oh.' Imogen shook her head at the complexity of life. 'Well, Mother said I could call her Frances, but I said that was a bit *extreme* – and she said it was ironic for her to have a conservative child. She thought I wouldn't understand her, but I did. What *I* think is that Mother underestimates the respectability of conservatism.' She uttered this obviously rehearsed statement very casually, trying to give the impression that such words and ideas were the small change of her mind. 'I'm an embarrassment to her, you see – because of the Women's Liberation Movement.'

'The women's movement?' Laura said faintly.

'Oh – didn't Mu- Mother tell you? She's joined it.'

'*Frances* has?' Jacob asked. 'She didn't mention it at West Horton.'

'Yes, she's in a consciousness-raising group and a group about women and the law. It sounds interesting. But Father doesn't like it at all.' She stopped. Eyes intent on an estate agent's window she said abruptly, 'They were quarrelling a lot in the holidays. I wish I knew why.'

At Christmas she had still been a child, in spite of her adolescent rounding figure and spotty skin and her nonchalance about acid and abortions: the same child Jacob had always known. Now, though her abruptness and averted eyes were childish, there was a new note, tentative, transitional, in her quietly reflective tone. She was leaving childhood behind.

From then on, throughout the winter and spring, she seemed less of a child, more of a girl in her teens, every time they visited. The change was entertaining, and it made her easy to entertain: she was so bursting with speech and discoveries that she hardly cared where they went; all she wanted was a place where they could talk – where *she* could talk, sixteen to the dozen, sometimes about politics and religion and school gossip, sometimes about her parents and their lovers – carefully, one step at a time, testing the ice.

'Mother has a friend named Nick, who used to work in her office,' she told them one day; 'and he came to the house once, and Father didn't like it; I heard him tell Mother afterwards that Nick was –' She broke off. 'Do you know Nick?'

'No,' said Jacob.

'I wonder if he and Mu- Mother are like Daddy and Sara – special friends.' Her gaze just grazed his, knowingly, then swung off.

The next time she chatted in a brittle gossipy way, as if to prove her sophistication. 'I think Nick's all right' – airily. 'I can't really see what anyone would see in him, but he's nicer than Sara.'

But Frances and Oliver had led her to assume that married people loved only each other and that affairs led to divorce; and beneath her flippancy she was puzzled and disturbed. 'If Mother and Father love each other, why do they want to . . . see . . . other people? And, it's funny, I don't think other people make them happy. Why don't they see people who make them happy?'

Her questions had been rhetorical; but, when she next returned to the subject, while walking with Jacob and Laura along a muddy bridleway, she wanted answers. 'What I don't understand is, if Mother and Father are unhappy with each other, why don't they get divorced and marry Nick and Sara?'

'It depends, doesn't it?' said Laura. 'You can be unhappy with someone but not want to leave them, because you love them.'

'I was like that with Sheila,' Jacob added.

But this was beyond Imogen's understanding just yet. She shook her head in irritation, muttering, 'That doesn't make sense.'

'Would you mind if that happened?' asked Laura.

'If Mummy and Daddy – Mother and Father – m-married other people? Yes!'

'They might be happier,' he said rashly.

'But *I* wouldn't be.' She heard the high, childish note; in a more natural tone she added: 'There would be all sorts of things wrong, like having my things in two different places –'

'Hah!' said Jacob in a triumphant aside to Laura.

'That's different,' she and Imogen said almost in the same breath, and looked at each other with startled fellow-feeling.

'And not being at home anywhere,' Imogen went on.

'Wouldn't home be with Frances?' he asked as they turned off towards a stile.

She sat on it, looking down at them with a frown. 'But home is where we live, too – Canonbury Park South. It wouldn't be *so* bad if Mother stayed there and Daddy – and *Father*,' clutching her detachment, 'moved to Clapham with Sara. But what if he stayed at home and Mother moved to Nick's?'

'Could she? Nick's not married?'

'Divorced. Like everybody' – bitterly. She went over the stile.

The footpath was even muddier, and they had to walk single file; but the hedgerow and field were bright with spring green, and there was sun behind the thin cloud. They squeezed through a hedge onto a road, and she said, more cheerfully, 'Marriage is awfully complicated. I'm never going to get married.'

'Good – you can be a spinster like me,' said Laura.

'Not like you – you live with Jacob. – All right, half-live with him. I'm not going to live with people – *or* half-live with them either.'

'You'll be lonely, won't you?' said Jacob.

'No, I won't. That's what Jo says – but she likes being with people. I don't.'

'Thanks' – now it was Laura and Jacob who spoke in chorus.

'Oh – not all the time. I *love* talking and doing things – especially with you – really. But most of the time I like being by myself.'

Chapter 26

SHORTLY BEFORE EASTER Jacob and Imogen drove up to Ely through a fenland afternoon of soft blue sky and towering clouds and planted fields black beside the raised roads. Over tea at the Old Fire Engine House he told her his news: he and Laura were going to Italy in the summer – to Rome, Florence and some places in between.

'Florence . . .' she breathed. He had described the city to her after his first trip, and she had been on fire to see it ever since. 'You are lucky. I wish I could go, and practise my Italian, and see the Duomo and the Baptistry and everything. Lucky old Jo spends part of every summer in a farm outside Florence. Oh, and now that you've met Jo' – she had introduced them formally that afternoon at the school, and they had carefully pretended never to have met – 'what do you think of her?'

'Well, she's got a strong character.'

'And she's so pretty.'

'Hmph. A trifle alarming.'

'Why?'

'She does tower, rather.'

'Oh Jacob – why don't you forget that silly hangup? Nobody cares about things like that.'

'They do where I come from, kiddo.'

'Well, they don't over here – and here,' she said firmly as they got up to leave, 'is where you are.' Out at the car she looked at him across the roof of the Mini – their heads were level. 'But I'm glad I'm not as tall as Jo, because you'd think I was too tall for you.' Ducking quickly inside, she added: 'But that doesn't really matter, because I'm not in love with you any more.'

'Any more? You had a crush on *me*? When?'

'Not a crush' – loftily. 'It was very serious . . . Well, not *very*. Last term, everybody was supposed to be in love with some-body, so I picked you – it had to be a grown-up, you see, not one of the boys, and I didn't fancy any of the masters. I even convinced myself it was true.'

'What unconvinced you?' he asked drily.

'I suppose I just got older. It was an awfully *childish* stage.'

She was brimming with excitement when she bounced down to meet him and Laura after the Easter holidays. 'Guess what? I'm going to Italy too! With Jo! To Florence! And a little while in Rome, too.'

They went for a walk, but Imogen paid hardly any attention to the spring all round them; instead, she chattered about Italy and renaissance art – she had already started reading for the trip.

Back at the school she asked, hesitantly, when they would be in Florence. Jacob had seen this one coming. 'Oh, sometime or other in July,' he said vaguely, before Laura could speak. 'What about you?'

'We'll be in Florence – near, not in, but there's a bus – from the eighth of July to the twenty-second, then it's on to Rome.'

'Ah. Maybe we'll bump into each other.'

'And we could see some of the things you told me about, like Brunelleschi and Donatello, all together.'

'Yes indeed,' he replied, with considerably more enthusiasm than he felt.

His tone was only half successful. She looked at him a little uncertainly and said nothing more about meeting.

Afterwards Laura said, 'I take it you're hoping to avoid Imogen in Florence.'

'Well, damn it, I've got a life of my own. I'm not a nurse-maid. I want to see it with *you*, I don't want her and Jo tagging along.'

She laughed. 'Don't sound so guilty. You don't need to justify yourself; you do quite enough for Imogen.'

He still felt slightly guilty, though, and on his next visit gave her a copy of the *Companion Guide to Florence*. She was bowled over; by the following visit – their last before the summer – she had read it twice from cover to cover and talked so excitedly about what she was going to see that she forgot to ask again when they would be in Florence.

Jacob did not remind her. Dearly though he loved her, he badly wanted to be alone in Florence with Laura, whom he loved far more. The two of them had been together now for nearly a year and had never had, with each other, the giddy romantic exploratory happiness of new love: their beginning had been too fraught; and by the time they were over the hurdles of the first few months, they knew each other – were used to each other. That was a deeper happiness; but they both admitted to a sneaking regret for what they had missed. He did not delude himself that they could find it – but perhaps, in Florence, something like it? He would give her the city he loved, and for the first time they would be completely happy together, carefree, infatuated with Florence and, through it, with each other.

Chapter 27

UT IN ROME Laura caught a cold that developed, as her colds sometimes did, into sinusitis; and by the time they got to their hotel in Florence – the Pensione Strozzi, oddly but conveniently situated on the top floor of a central office building – she knew she was in for a bad bout: up to a week of low fever, nausea and agonising headaches. There was no cure; she simply had to stay in bed while it ran its course. 'Oh *hell*,' she said wanly. 'It's not fair – I'll be like this for *days*; and Florence is what we've looked forward to; and I'm spoiling your –'

'There now, my sweet, it's you that's ill; don't worry about me. After all, this *is* Florence – and you'll be better soon.'

The next day he arranged for Laura to have meals brought in on trays, assured the sceptical *padrona* that sinusitis was not a communicable disease and went out. For a while he was happy; but, as the day wore on, he began to be vaguely dispirited. He could not recapture the bliss of his previous visit; solitary sightseeing was not what he wanted from Florence this time. He was disappointed in himself. To his shame he caught himself feeling disappointed in Laura.

Late the following morning he came across Imogen and Jo in the Uffizi. He was tired and bored and, since he couldn't be with Laura, really quite glad to see them; and they went to the terrace and exchanged travel news over *spremute*. The girls were on their own in the city; Jo's mother, Elspeth, let them come down by bus each day for sightseeing, while she stayed up at the farmhouse near Careggi with her younger two children. 'Elspeth just wants to sunbathe,' said Jo scornfully, 'and all Marcus and Susan care about is playing games.'

When they were through their drinks, they all went and leaned on the parapet for a look round. The sun beat down on their heads and on the wonderful jumble of red-tiled roofs that stretched off as far as they could see, punctuated by church towers and the pretty sugar-stick *campanile*, toylike in front of Brunelleschi's huge, solid, rust-coloured dome.

'You *are* right about Florence,' Imogen told him – 'what you said back in England. It *is* the centre of the whole world.'

Jo groaned. 'Oh no, not that daft idea again.'

'Do explain it to her, please,' Imogen begged. 'I've tried, but I can't remember it just the way you said.'

Jacob protested that his account was too embarrassingly simple-minded for repetition, but Jo said, 'Go on, do – see if you can convince me;' so he gave in and tried to describe his sense that Florence was at the heart of western civilisation. It was a matter of lineage. Of the many strands out of which our high civilisation was woven, the one that bound us closest – that was woven into our deepest roots – was the one first spun by Homer sometime after Troy. The Romans had brought it to Italy, where, during the dark ages and after, it was almost lost from view. But in the fourteenth century – in Florence – Dante and the humanists had rescued it for literature; and in the fifteenth century – in Florence – Brunelleschi, Donatello,

Masaccio and others had reclaimed it for the visual arts. And we were still –

'Where you really want to be is Troy,' said Jo.

'Not really – there's nothing there but some dug-up walls.'

'Rome, then.'

'Well, yes, there's a case for Rome. Wait till you've been in the Forum. Ancient Rome grows up around you in your head, imaginary roofs on real pillars; and your feet tingle because you're standing where the first Brutus stood. But ruins aren't the same: you have to squint to keep those roofs up. Nobody's torn Florence down; it's a real city.'

Imogen said, 'Yes – so real that – that – it's going back from my eyeballs – every stone, and the noise, and the hot smell – and being etched on my brain so that I'll never ever forget this exact place and time.'

'It's the heat,' said Jo. 'It's scrambling your brains, not etching them. Yours too' – to Jacob. 'Imogen's a nut, and now I know where she gets it from. How can you moon on about Rome when it was founded on the labour of *slaves*?'

They ducked out of the brain-addling sun and strolled downstairs and out into the piazza, where Imogen stopped to look up at Donatello's sublime *Judith* – 'My favourite statue so far. But I'm going to see lots more tomorrow morning in the Bargello.'

Then they were off down the Via Por Santa Maria. As he watched, Imogen suddenly ran back. 'Would you like to join us for lunch?' she asked hopefully.

'Thanks, but Laura's expecting me.' He did not suggest meeting them later, though it would be more fun than wandering about alone. Better not encourage them to think that they would be welcome to tag along once Laura was well – as she surely would be by tomorrow.

But Laura was no better, and Jacob went out feeling dumpish, strolled about the streets until the heat grew stifling, then headed for a museum. Any museum, he thought vaguely; but, when it was the Bargello that he fetched up at, he realised with amusement that he was hoping to run into the girls there.

They were in the *salone*, in front of the young *St John* of Donatello's old age. Jacob joined them, and they stood for a while looking at the *Giovannini*'s thin ecstatic face, then went

128

round the *salone* together. When they left, at noon, the girls invited him to have lunch with them, and he thought: What the hell, I've enjoyed the past hour more than the past two days; and accepted. 'I was going to eat out anyhow – I woke Laura up when I went back yesterday, so I told her I wouldn't come in for lunch today.'

They ate *oltr'Arno*, rested for a while in the Boboli Gardens, then went back across the river to the Ospedale degli Innocenti. The little white-walled museum upstairs was empty and light, and there was a big *Adoration of the Magi* by Ghirlandaio – bright, bustling, innocent, wordly, full of loving detail that begged for loving observation: so they sat down on a bench and observed, for a good deal longer than any of them had devoted to greater works in the Uffizi. But in the Uffizi there were always people blocking the view and saying silly things about the pictures; here there was peace and privacy. Jo got up and wandered slowly round the room; Imogen stayed sitting. Jacob met the eyes of one of the fashionable young men attending the Magi; let himself be drawn into the world of the picture; sauntered idly through the peacock crowd – entirely happy, for a while, just looking at the lovely, simple-minded painting.

Humph. He stirred. 'Time to put you two on the bus, pet,' he said. They left the white room reluctantly, looking back at the happy *Adoration*.

Chapter 28

AURA WAS A little better on Sunday, but not well enough to go out; so he joined the girls again, and they went to Ognissanti to look at paintings in the refectory.

The church was locked. They stepped through a doorway beside it, went along a passage into the quiet, empty cloister and walked round it looking for someone to ask directions of. No one came. In spite of the solitude they felt as if unfriendly eyes were watching from obscure windows and through keyholes. They tried a couple of doors – locked – began to get cold feet, retreated to the passage and scanned the walls for some mention of paintings or refectories.

Jo found a bell-pull. 'Shall I?'

'It's like *Alice*,' said Imogen. 'The frog footman will come out.'

Jo pulled. A distant, rusty clanging. Silence. Then shuffle, shuffle, slap-shuffle, and round the side of the cloister there came a short, stout old monk. He was bald, not just tonsured, and wore thick pebble spectacles.

'Not a frog footman,' whispered Jo; 'more like Tweedledum or Tweedledee.'

He growled something unintelligible in a sixty-cigarette-a-day voice.

The girls looked to Jacob, who wondered how to address a monk. Not *signore*; but he didn't quite dare venture on *fratello*. 'Mi scusi,' he essayed, 'cerchiamo i dipinti e gli affreschi del Ghirlandaio e Botti- '

The monk grunted and cupped his hand to his ear.

Jacob said it louder.

The monk cupped his other ear.

Jacob bellowed: 'Ghirlandaio! Botticelli!' so loud that the cloister bounced back the echo.

The monk croaked a hoarse string of rapid-fire sentences, turned and shuffle-slapped back round the corner.

'Did you get any of that?' Jacob asked. 'Do we go away or follow him?'

'I bet he was saying, "You don't need to shout, I'm not deaf".' Imogen suggested.

'I heard something with "chio – " in it,' said Jo. 'Maybe it was "chiostro".'

' "Chiuso", more likely,' said Imogen.

The monk reappeared, holding a key nearly a foot long, repeated the 'chio' sound ('It's "chiave",' the girls whispered together), waddled towards one of the locked doors, let them into the clammy refectory and sat down on a bench to wait.

They stayed for a quarter of an hour, trying to imagine rows of monks eating – had they had fires against the damp? – and admiring Botticelli's febrile *St Augustine* and Ghirlandaio's simple *St Jerome* until they began to feel guilty for keeping the monk from whatever monks did. As they left, Jacob said 'Grazie', and held out three hundred lire. The monk shook his head and muttered incomprehensibly. Oh dear. Maybe you didn't tip monks. 'Per la chiesa,' he shouted, still holding out the money.

The monk pushed his hand back, talking to beat sixty, and Jacob suddenly caught some clue to his dialect – he was saying something about being pleased to show them his treasures – and at the same time saw that the old man's eyes were milky with cataract behind his pebble spectacles. He was nearly blind. Jacob roared his thanks, and the monk locked the door behind them with the enormous key. 'Arrivederci,' they said, but he did not hear them and shuffled away down the cloister. Looking after him, Jacob felt dizzy with the mysteriousness of the old monk's life. What was it like for him – a peasant from the south, surely, with that accent – to spend his whole life in a Florentine monastery, now and then letting strangers from the outer world into a room where they would look, with aesthetic not religious fervour, at works painted to glorify religion. And to be deaf and half-blind and fat – what was it like? What

131

did he mean when he said it was a pleasure – how long since he had been able to see his 'treasures'? Strange, strange, to come face to face, in this century, in the middle of Europe, with someone whose life was as remote as St Jerome's.

Up at Fiesole the breeze was almost cool, and they sat on a shady bench looking out over the city and ate their packed lunches. The dome shimmered in the hot noon air, undiminished by distance.

They were waiting for Elspeth, who was coming by car to fetch the girls for a drive in the country. 'With my awful brother and sister,' said Jo.

'Marcus isn't too bad.'

'That's because he's too young to devil us like Susan. He would if he could.'

'She *is* a bore,' Imogen told him. 'She's only ten, and she keeps wanting us to play with her. Oh – will we be seeing you tomorrow?'

'Uh . . .'

Jo nudged her. 'Laura's getting better – you'll want to be with her, not us.'

'Of course,' said Imogen valiantly.

'Well, yes,' he allowed. 'But she's at her worst in the mornings, and she said she'd rather start after lunch tomorrow. So we've got the morning – and we still haven't seen the Pazzi chapel.'

Imogen glowed at him; Jo groaned. 'More Brunelleschi. I think his churches are heathen – all that grey stone and plain plaster, and no statues or anything to show that it's Christian. And I've been there before. You go, Imogen; I'll stay up at the farm.'

As soon as they entered the Pazzi chapel the next morning, Jacob sat down. He remembered from last time that this was something you couldn't fight. Imogen stood quite still, then let out her breath in capitulation and sat down too.

For the most part they were left to themselves. The purity that made them linger gave no purchase to the scurrying attention of most sightseers. Occasionally an inquisitive tourist walked slipshod down the aisle, turned full circle, audibly or inaudibly registered disappointment and went away, leaving them alone in the lucid serenity of white walls and ceiling, dark grey pilasters and frieze, and wonderful blind arches that enclosed only white plaster: the geometry of white and grey marking out a magical tension between height and breadth. The chapel was austere but not ascetic, plain to encourage contemplation, not mortify the senses; it was the antithesis of dim gothic clutter, being both rational – conceived by a man whose touchstone was the classical world – and informed by mystical beliefs: the idea of approaching God through perfect forms; the idea of God as Light.

After a while Imogen chuckled. 'I'm glad Jo's not here. She'd say it was heathen.'

Jacob smiled absently. 'I suppose she would.' It was hard to imagine. For him, in love with the idea of the Renaissance, the Pazzi chapel was a *sanctum sanctorum* at the secret heart of his holy city. As a shrine it had the advantage of being less frequented than the Bargello or the Uffizi; and here, in as much solitude as it was possible to find in Florence, gazing at bare walls and simple, complex forms, he had the illusion of being, however imperfectly and naively, in direct communion with the spirit of Renaissance humanism.

But there was a limit to how long he could be wrapped up in anything, and he had passed it and was looking forward to the afternoon with Laura when Imogen yawned behind her hand, stretched, checked her watch and said, 'Nearly time to meet Jo.' She too had reached her limit.

Laura felt fine by the time he returned, and after lunch they closed the shutters against the heat and made love, and then discussed what to do. They had intended to make trips outside the city during this second week; but seeing Florence together was what they had most looked forward to for months.

'But now you've seen it already.'

'Not with you.'

'It won't be the way we imagined,' she said mournfully, sitting cross-legged on the bed and brushing tangles out of her curly hair.

'Well, let's just see how things go.'

'Okay. But promise you won't . . . Ouch!' Her hairbrush was stuck in a tangle, and she grinned through the fawn mass.

'Won't·fake it? Sure.' It was the first time she had looked

mischievous for days. Instead of the forbidden, 'I love you,' he said, 'Well, let's get out there and hit the tourist traps;' and they began their tour of Florence, almost a week late.

She was right; it was not the same as the week they had missed. He was not so much seeing the city with her as showing it to her – and to some extent he was faking a shared response, in spite of his promise, and although he knew she could sense it. It seemed impossible not to. But by the second afternoon he began to get excited about what they were seeing. It was not the week they had lost, but it was going to be all right, especially since it was a relief to be with an adult again; with a lover again. He and Imogen were in an uncanny way cats of the same colour, especially in their response to art; but with her there was always the tension of inequality: she looked up to him; and she was naive, earnest, unironical, vulnerable – young. With Laura he could joke without condescension or special care; talk without danger of being taken more literally than he meant; listen without having to make allowances: could also make love to her, hold her hand, touch her cheek, curl up beside her in bed, snap at her, ignore her – all the things lovers but not friends can do.

'It's nice being back together again,' he said as they left the hotel on Tuesday afternoon.

'Yes, and being back in the world. It's such a bore, being ill.'

'My lamb' – tenderly.

She bleated.

'Watch it, Bo–Peep. There are laws about keeping sheep in town. They'll arrest me and deport you to the hills.'

Chapter 29

WO NIGHTS LATER Elspeth rang. Had he seen or heard from Imogen? Nothing to worry about, she was sure, though now that it was getting dark . . . but Imogen hadn't been seen since morning. She'd probably be back soon; she must have gone down to Florence and missed a bus back. Sorry to bother him, she'd ring again in the morning, just to let him know she was safe.

In the morning Jacob was called from breakfast to the telephone; when Laura returned to the bedroom, he was still talking: 'Yes . . . of course . . . and why not send Jo down . . . okay – yes – right away. Goodbye.'

'She's still lost?' said Laura in alarm.

'Not lost – she's run away.'

'She's *what*? Imogen isn't the kind of girl who'd –'

'Oh yes she is. They've been going through her things, and she's taken her passport and travellers' cheques, and her flight bag with night things and a change of clothes and enough Tampax for the rest of her period and so forth.'

'But *why*?'

'Because Jo's little sister Susan got cross yesterday and said something like: "You think that my mummy asked you to come on holiday with us to keep Jo company, but that isn't true. Your mummy and daddy asked my mummy if she'd bring you along, so that they can get divorced while you're away."'

'Good Lord, are they really?'

'Getting divorced? Not as far as I know, or Elspeth. What is true is that they were the ones that got in touch with Elspeth,

135

not vice versa; but they told her they were going to say that it was her idea, and would she please not tell Imogen or Jo. Well, Elspeth thought it was peculiar being asked to take Imogen at all, though she didn't mind – and it *was* company for Jo – and even more peculiar being asked not to tell Imogen about the real arrangement, with no reason given; and she and her husband were speculating about what on earth and why on earth – and Susan overheard them, and remembered, and then spewed it all out at Imogen.'

'Lord, what a mess.'

'You're telling me. Why the hell don't those two tell the child the *truth* once in a while – it's their own goddamn fault that she's run away. Not that they see it that way: Elspeth says Frances was furious at her for letting Susan overhear – as if she did it on purpose. They'll be coming out on this evening's plane. In the meantime, we – uh, well, I speak Italian, and I don't think the Standishes do; and so I . . .'

'You volunteered us to look for her.'

He nodded. 'Specifically, I volunteered me to look and you to stay here, in case she comes to us – '

Laura groaned. 'Another exciting day in my hotel room.'

'Oh, Laura, I *am* sorry. But you still feel awful in the morning, and Elspeth has to stay up at Careggi with the children, and the police have already established that she did come down to Florence, and they've notified the borders, so she's probably still here, and . . . well, Jo's coming down to look; and Oliver's going to wire a photograph of Imogen to the local office of the *Corriere della Sera*, and I'll take copies to the cops – and they'll be able to trace her through hotel registers anyhow: she can't get a room without showing her passport, so the place where she stayed will have a record. Maybe we'll find her quickly.'

'I know – we couldn't do anything else. But when Miss Sensitive comes home to roost, I'm going to wring her tender neck.'

At the first few places Jacob enquired, he explained that the runaway whom he was seeking was the daughter of friends; soon, simplifying, he described her as his cousin. It became his refrain: 'Sto cercando una mia cugina,' at the *questura*, at the Pazzi chapel, the Uffizi, the Ospedale degli Innocenti, the Bargello; 'Ha visto una mia cugina?' at the Pitti, the Giardino dei Semplici, the Medici chapels, the Palazzo Vecchio, the Badia, the Palazzo Davanzati.

Florence was a small place when he was not lingering to look at anything; by early afternoon he had walked along most of the streets in the centre, gone into every major museum and church at least once, had lunch, and sweated up to San Miniato. He was hot, tetchy and bored. By three o'clock the photograph had arrived. He collected it and headed for the *questura*, glancing at it as he went – a good likeness, taken less than a year ago. She was smiling slightly, her eyes clear and serious, and there was a tell-tale pucker of self-consciousness between her eyebrows. Imogen! He forgot that she was a brat who was lousing up his holiday; when the police told him that they had checked all the hotels in the centre without success, he looked so distraught that they made large reassuring noises.

'Non vi preoccupate, la troveremo sicuro, stasera o domani.'

'Domani!' He could not wait till tomorrow.

He must understand, there were many hotels in the periphery, not a small job to check.

'Anche pensioni?'

Only the big *pensioni*, those with signs outside; she would never find the smaller ones. They understood child psychology, leave it to them. His cousin was – looking at the photograph – a 'ragazza distinta'. Every policeman would see the photograph; every policeman would be looking for her. He must not worry.

They wouldn't *arrest* her, would they? he blurted.

'Signore!' They were fathers themselves, the *poverina* would be like a daughter.

He apologised effusively and slunk out to go on looking.

When the museums and churches were shut, he went back to the Strozzi for dinner. Laura had sent Jo home an hour ago.

'Was she out looking all day?'

'Yes, poor girl, right through the heat.'

He finished his *peperonata*, glad that worry did not spoil his appetite for the Strozzi's most delicious dish, and laid down his napkin. 'It's ridiculous, you know. Jo and I didn't even bump into each other today, let alone Imogen. It's useless.'

Nevertheless, he went out again, first to the Piazza della Signoria, where all Florence was taking an evening stroll in the soft artificial dusk reflected from the floodlit buildings, then over the Ponte Vecchio. No, she wouldn't be here, or wouldn't linger; the bridge was too garish and touristy, and the other side suddenly too solitary. She was a girl, she wouldn't – he hoped she had enough sense – he hurried back across the bridge, glancing suspiciously at men selling gewgaws. They looked sinister, jowly, unprincipled; they'd steal a young girl who asked the way or the time as soon as speak to her.

Back in the Signoria he came to his senses and felt ashamed of himself. He had a pricking in his thumbs, as if she must be in the piazza; then, standing under Donatello's *Judith*, he forgot about her in pleasure at the utter relaxation of sleep-sunk Holofernes' dangling arm, the hand curling back luxuriously along the pillow; and the way the soles of his feet arched slightly from the sensual dream that was making him smile in his sleep; while one of Judith's hands held him up by the hair and the other gripped her upraised sword: her resolution was fixed; yet she paused . . .

He turned round sharply. He had forgotten Imogen; so she must be there.

She wasn't. Not anywhere. Not that he could see.

'Oliver rang,' said Laura when he got back. 'He's not coming till tomorrow night, now. He says we're handling the situation very well, and that you're quite right, he doesn't know Florence, and he can't speak Italian, and he'd do nobody any good asking agitated questions in English.' Her voice was dry.

'Humph. This is Friday, Oliver's deadline is tomorrow. He'd miss it if he came tonight – I should have guessed. But what about Frances? Why isn't *she* coming, for God's sake?'

'Frances thinks Imogen's on her way back to England – back to her mother. She says that's why she took her passport – not to register at hotels or cash travellers' cheques – and that she must have left the country before the police alerted the borders. She says she has to be at home when Imogen gets there. Do you think it's possible?'

'I – I don't know. It doesn't seem – but I must admit it hadn't occurred to me. Maybe she *is* going home. By ox-cart, from the time it's taking her.'

Chapter 30

N SATURDAY MORNING the *padrona* set Laura up with one of the Strozzi's four telephone lines and a list of *pensioni*. If those lazy do-nothings of *carabinieri* weren't going to check the smaller *pensioni*, somebody had to. No trouble. A pleasure. Her hard features softened not a whit as she uttered these energetically altruistic sentiments.

Jo reported for duty again; and Jacob returned to the fray, flashing the photograph of his *cugina* at ticket sellers and sacristans. They had not seen her, but some of them remembered him and wasted his time sympathising with him in his loss. As if she were dead, he thought with a resentful shiver. He was more worried today. Yesterday was one day, today was – two days. Twice as bad as one. More ominous. More possibilities. Maybe she had been kidnapped off the streets of Florence. Maybe she had been murdered and –

Maybe she really was dead.

He shot out of his idle imaginings. She couldn't be. The police would have found her.

The inefficient Italian police?

He found a telephone. Had they checked the morgue?

'Senz'altro, signore,' said one of the men he had talked to yesterday. They always did so, it was routine. But – suspiciously – why did he think his cousin would kill herself?

No, no, he stuttered, he wasn't worried about suicide, only about a fatal accident. Or – struck by a new thought – a non-fatal one. Had they checked the hospitals?

'Senz'altro, signore.' No flies on Florentine flics. And none too pleased at being told their business, either.

He went back to the Strozzi for lunch. Jo was there; she had been sick and was drooping on the edge of the bed. 'Sun,' said Laura. 'She wants to go on looking, but I've told her she mustn't.'

'Quite right,' he said. 'Jo, you'll just be a hindrance if you get heatstroke; I'll put you on the bus after lunch.'

It was hot as hell. Doorkeepers and sacristans greeted him with 'Non l'ho vista' – today's refrain as he went into churches and museums for the third or fourth time.

The Duomo, San Lorenzo, the Ospedale. Damn. This is ridiculous, he thought. Frances is probably right, she's on her way home. Why should I spoil my holiday looking for a girl whose own parents can't be bothered? Double damn. Spoiling Laura's holiday, too. Ridiculous.

Another check at the Pazzi chapel. The sour ticket seller had not seen 'la ragazza' and did not offer to let him in free. He paid up, amusing himself with a fantasy of sending the Standishes a bill for museum fees incurred in the course of searching for their daughter.

She wasn't there, of course. The chapel was empty.

No it wasn't. In the back right-hand corner a red-and-blue figure was hunched up on the stone bench: Imogen – dejected, woebegone, cringing into the shade, yet at the same time straining toward him intently, without moving, like a pointing dog.

Jacob closed his eyes; a hot wave of relief made him burst out in sweat. When he opened them, he was furious. He advanced on her, grabbed her arms and yanked her to her feet. 'What the hell are you doing sitting here and not getting in touch?' He shook her. She was limp. 'Do you realise the trouble you've caused? I thought you were dead, you selfish bitch' – shake – 'you two-year-old ninny' – shake – 'you imbecile' – shake – 'you –'

'Hurrumph, er . . .' An English hurrumph.

He turned round, involuntarily giving Imogen the shake that had been going to accompany the next epithet. A grey-haired couple were standing inside the door, embarrassed and concerned. He saw them through a blur of rage. Go away, he wanted to tell them, and let me shake this girl to pieces.

140

The man cleared his throat again, and hesitated. The woman, braver, said, 'Is this man, er, molesting you, my dear?'

Jacob looked at Imogen. The muscles on his swimmer's forearms were standing out; his hands were gripping her hard – big, muscular hands, bright pink with exertion. She was white and frightened and wincing with pain, his prisoner; there were tears in her eyes. One ran down her cheek and into the corner of her mouth; she licked it and blinked.

'No, it's all right,' she whispered.

The woman took a step forward. 'Are you sure?' Jacob tried to loose his grip, but could not.

'Yes, he's . . . he's . . .' Imogen gulped. 'I've been very nau– nau– naughty.' She licked away more tears. Jacob thought he should feel sorry for her, but he didn't.

'Well! I don't know – ' The woman whispered to her husband; he whispered back. In England they would have been wondering whether to fetch a policeman; off home ground they were unsure what steps to take. 'Well . . .' she said, hesitating. The man whispered to her again. 'Well, then,' she said. They both looked witheringly at Jacob and turned aside ostentatiously.

His locked hands loosened of their own accord. 'Let's get out of here,' he said and marched her by one shoulder into the glare of the big cloister. There were people dotted about all over. 'Jesus. Where the hell can I take you?' Somewhere close, so that his anger would stay hot. He steered her towards the second cloister. It was nearly empty. He picked a spot in the shade and sat down; Imogen hovered, waiting for orders.

'Sit down!' She sat. 'Okay, let's hear it,' he said harshly.

She sniffed. Her eyes were red; she had an unattractive hangdog look. 'Er . . .'

'Haven't you got anything to say for yourself?'

She blew her nose and hunched forward, hugging her knees. 'Er . . .'

'You're repeating yourself.'

That goaded her into barely audible speech. 'You know about Susan . . . and Mu– and my parents? Well, I wanted' – she glanced at him and away. 'They were all perfectly beastly, and I wanted to worry them' – in a defiant rush – 'and maybe it'd make Mother and Father stop getting divorced.'

'Do you realise that Susan was just repeating something she heard her parents speculating about?'

'But they've been so tense and quarrelsome all year – it makes sense. They were just waiting to get me out of the way, and they'll get divorced, and when I go back there'll be two houses, and Nick and Sara everywhere, and nowhere for me!' Tears of self-pity oozed down her cheeks.

'Bullshit. There wouldn't be "nowhere for you",' imitating her in a falsetto whine. 'Besides, even if they are getting divorced, so what?' She looked up sharply. 'No, I don't know anything, they haven't said a word to me. But *if* they are, they're considerate to send you away instead of dismantling things around your head, which is what happens to most children. And you have no right, *no* right, to inflict this on Jo and Elspeth. They aren't responsible for your parents' problems. You've frightened a lot of people for no better reason than a child's unsupported gossip.'

'But they were feeling *sorry* for me. Even *Susan*!'

'Listen, you idiot, don't you realise that Jo and Elspeth are worried sick?'

Imogen scowled.

'And Frances and Oliver are frantic.' Pour it on.

'Serves them right,' she said sullenly.

'And me? Does it serve *me* right?' he shouted. '*Me?* I've wasted two days of my holiday with Laura chasing all over this town till I'm sick of it looking for a spoiled brat who wants to spite her parents and hurt her best friend and worry her hosts.' Imogen's lower lip stopped jutting out; she looked stricken and frightened. Jacob ignored her expression, but lowered his voice as a thought struck him. 'Speaking of parents and hosts, I'd better let them know I've found you. Come on.'

He left the cloister without looking back to check that she was behind him and walked briskly back to the hotel. The walk was soothing; being angry at Imogen was soothing; making her trail behind him without looking to see that she was there was very soothing. By the time they got to the Strozzi, he was beginning to think he had been hard on her. Ringing for the lift he met her eyes; she had been crying as they walked, and her face was mottled. 'Imogen,' he said, 'I've been so *worried*.' He touched her patchy cheek. 'Thank God I've found you.'

At the office Laura took off her earphones – she was still

working through the list of *pensioni* – and rushed to hug Imogen. The telephonist jumped up. 'È lei?'

'Sì, eccola, l'ho trovata, sta bene!'

A torrent of congratulations; the *padrona* swept in and kissed Imogen, the telephonist kissed her too; then Jacob and Laura took her to their room, and he telephoned the farm while Laura ran her a bath.

Elspeth said, 'Thank God,' and, 'I'll ring her parents right away,' and rang off.

Laura came out of the bathroom. 'She's crying inconsolably, she seems to think you'll never be friends with her again. What have you been saying to the poor child?' She listened to his summary and said, 'Idiot,' rather tolerantly. 'Can I tell her there's some hope?'

The telephone: Elspeth. She'd quite forgotten to say that she'd be right down for Imogen.

Imogen emerged from the bathroom, dressed, pink and diffident. He covered the mouthpiece. 'Elspeth, saying she'll be down for you.' Seeing her disappointed expression, he and Laura exchanged glances; when Laura nodded, he kept the mouthpiece covered and asked, 'Would you like to stay here tonight? There's a daybed in that cupboard – and we can take you back tomorrow.' She nodded delightedly. 'Okay, I'll ask Elspeth. But then you should say something to her yourself.'

She was dismayed. 'But what?'

'Anything. She's responsible for you, and she's been *worried*.'

When he handed her the receiver, she stammered apologies, then fell silent under Elspeth's torrent of happy chatter, followed by Jo's ejaculations of wrathful relief.

At last Jo rang off. The telephone rang while Imogen's hand was still on the receiver; she picked it up automatically, then remembered that it was not hers and held it out. Jacob gestured to her to answer. 'Pronto,' she said, and turned scarlet. 'Mummy!'

Chapter 31

HE LOOKED QUITE grown-up in the blue voile frock that Laura lent her to wear to dinner. There was a sudden hush when they entered the dining room, then an excited buzz. She was rigid with self-consciousness, and they placed her with her back to the room so that she could look up without meeting curious glances.

'We should have guessed this would happen,' said Laura.

'This isn't like an ordinary hotel restaurant,' he explained to Imogen. 'Everybody who eats here is staying in the *pensione* – they've heard about you, and naturally they're interested.'

'My back has holes in it from people looking. They're thinking: There's the creature that caused so much trouble.'

Jacob was cocking an ear; in English, French and Italian the comments had the same tenor. 'They're saying, "the poor child",' he reported drily, 'and, "so pretty and well-bred", and, "so brave, such an ordeal". I don't know what the Germans are saying, but probably the same.'

Their waiter bustled up and congratulated her in halting English upon her safe return. When she thanked him in Italian, he beamed and, in Italian, made a speech. The hotel had not breathed, neither the staff nor the patrons, since her most unfortunate disappearance; her safety restored them all to life; her presence honoured the dining room; he personally was honoured to serve her; and *la signora* had commanded him to ask whether there was anything special she would like for dinner: if the establishment could provide it, it was hers. He bowed.

To their amazement Imogen bowed back, thanked him for

144

his kindness and said that her gracious hosts had praised the *peperonata* so highly that she longed to try it. Otherwise she had no special requests: the culinary repute of the *pensione* was such that their ordinary fare could be trusted to be superior to the best efforts of lesser establishments.

Her gracious hosts gawped. Was this Imogen, whose speech, even when she was talkative, was full of qualification, hesitation, and English understatement?

'I didn't know you could do that,' Jacob said.

She looked smug. She was relaxing; she was even revelling in the discovery that, though to them she was a naughty girl, to the dining room she was a heroine. 'Only in Italian,' she said. 'It's like being an actress; I pretend I'm not me, I'm someone Italian. It must be easy for you, your Italian is so much better.'

Jacob was good at accents and picking up languages. His Italian was fluent and colloquial, and he harboured a secret ambition to speak it well enough to to be taken for a native: but he had realised, listening to Imogen's speech, that he never would. He lacked the requisite flexibility of temperament, his cast of mind was unalterably Anglo-American. Even though he could think in Italian, he was thinking, and uttering, Anglo-American thoughts: his mental accent would always betray him. It wasn't that he was too old; he had never been young enough. Imogen, stumbling, slow, incorrect, with a wrong gender in every sentence, was streets ahead. 'I don't have your histrionic abilities,' he grunted.

It came out sourer than he intended; Imogen glanced at him keenly and, fine-tuned as usual to his mood, paid a lot of attention to her shallow bowl of soup until he could get over his chagrin. He in turn guessed what she was doing and was momentarily even more annoyed. Laura looked from one to the other, sensing undercurrents, but slow to catch up. Well as she knew him, there were areas in which Imogen intuitively knew him better: such as this matter of pride invested in the mastery of languages.

He came out of his sulk to find Imogen intent on her last mouthful of soup and Laura looking at him with dawning comprehension. He winked; Laura relaxed; and the moment dissolved in bustle as the waiter brought the main course.

The *padrona* herself brought an enormous dish, brimful of

145

peperonata. 'Ecco la peperonata; l'ho preparata io stessa per Lei,' she told Imogen, who thanked her, staring in alarm – were the three of them meant to eat *all that*? The *padrona* signalled to the wine waiter, who handed her a bottle of red wine, already uncorked. A most special wine, she said, presenting it: not – dropping her voice – one of the wines on the list. It was Brunello di Montalcino, the local wine of her village; it was 'tipico, molto caratteristico'. Most was sent away to rich people in Rome; a little the villagers kept. Of this little, she got a very little; and with a little of her very little she wished to demonstrate the affectionate relief and esteem of the Pensione Strozzi. She filled their glasses, waggled a finger viciously at the wine waiter for another, poured some for herself and raised her glass. 'Alla ragazza ritrovata!' she cried. Jacob, Laura and the *padrona* drank to Imogen; so did the other diners.

Her embarrassment returned in full force, but she rallied quickly. 'Sono molto commossa per ciò che ha fatto per me,' she said, raising her glass to the *padrona*. 'Alla Sua salute!' After drinking slowly and attentively, she emerged to say that it was a magnificent vintage, rare as the finest burgundy – who knew, perhaps finer – and that she was ravished to the depths of her heart by the honour. Would not the *padrona* do them the honour of joining them for dinner?

The *padrona* was desolated to refuse, but she must return at once to supervising her cretinous cook or else – disaster. She retreated in full flourish.

'What's this about burgundy, you fast-talking flatterer?' said Jacob. 'You don't know from nothing about burgundy.'

'I do,' she said indignantly. 'Father's training my palate . . . and I've learned enough to know that I was, er, stretching the truth a little just then.'

'Hmph.' He took a heap of *peperonata*. 'Well, at least you've fulfilled a fantasy of mine. I'm going to have as much as I can eat of these peppers.' He ate his share of everything else and, when Imogen and Laura could eat no more, much more than his share of *peperonata*; to their amazement he finished the bowl. 'The past two days were worth it, just for that,' he told Imogen. 'Now the only problem is how to get up. I've got pepper-paralysis.'

'You can recover during pudding,' said Laura.

'Pudding?' – incredulously.

'We'll eat yours,' she and Imogen said in unison; and they did.

'I'm bursting with curiosity,' Laura said after dinner, sitting down cross-legged on the bed. 'There's been so much bustle, we haven't heard what you've been *doing* for the past two days.'

'You don't really want . . .' said Imogen.

Jacob stretched out in the armchair. 'Oh yes we do. Let's have it. The works: how you survived for forty-eight hours in deepest Florence.'

She laughed guiltily and, after some embarrassed ums and ers, and a little more prompting, sat on the daybed and began at the beginning. She had packed her flight bag and run off to Florence almost without thinking why, in a frenzy of angry grief. She had no plan; and by afternoon she had realised that she would have to go back. But then she met four sixth formers from the Friends School. They were staying in somebody's flat *oltr'Arno*, and, when she boldly asked if she could crash with them, said sure, no sweat, bags of room, without asking any inconvenient questions. Good. She wanted everyone to suffer, especially her parents. She'd show *them*.

By the next day she knew how stupid and wrong she had been – this was about ten times worse than anything she'd done in her whole life before. But she couldn't go back ignominiously with her tail between her legs like a naughty infant. People must be looking for her by now – they would have to find her.

'But I never *dreamed* it would take so long – two whole days. I was in *despair*, by this morning I was beginning to think no one was looking for me after all. It was awful; everywhere I went, I'd remember that I'd been happy there a few days ago, but I *didn't* really remember – only the place, not what being happy was like. And then I went to the Pazzi chapel for about the fourth time, and I was sitting there, wondering what to do, but my brain was paralysed, and you came in. You looked round, but I thought you weren't going to see me. I thought if you didn't, I'd die, my heart would stop, it felt like that.'

'If I hadn't seen you, you could have said something.'

'Oh *no*,' Imogen and Laura said together.

★

Before long Imogen was stifling yawns. 'Bedtime, don't you think?' said Laura. 'You've had a long day.'

Accepting the suggestion gratefully, Imogen retired to the bathroom to undress; she fell sound asleep as soon as she was in bed. Jacob and Laura followed her in the bathroom, then sat up in bed for a while, discussing how to spend their last three days – they were leaving for France on Tuesday, and there was so much they had not seen, thanks to Imogen. 'I said I'd wring her neck,' Laura whispered, 'and right this moment so I would.'

Soon they were sleepy. He turned off his bedside lamp; she was reaching for hers when Imogen stirred and said, 'This'll be another barbarian episode.' Yawn. 'Barbarian to the Rescue.'

'What?' said Jacob.

She opened her eyes. 'Oh – what – ?' She sat up and clapped her hand to her mouth. 'I thought Laura was Jo.'

'Oh,' he said sleepily.

'It's only a joke, don't take it seriously,' she added in a placatory tone.

He yawned. 'Don't take what seriously?'

She could still have backed off, but did not know how. 'The barbarian jokes.'

'The what?'

At last she realised that he did not know what she was talking about. 'Oh, nothing.'

But by now he had guessed; the idea that Jo called him a barbarian was curiously unpleasant. 'Come on, cough up, what's this with the barbarian jokes?'

She hesitated, then said in a queer voice, 'They call you The Barbarian, and they make up titles for things you do. The Barbarian Invades Italy, Barbarian in Love, The Barbarian Goes to the Movies – they think it's "uncivilised" to call films movies. The first was A Barbarian at Cambridge; that was way back, when I was little. I don't like those jokes, they aren't very nice.'

'Wait a minute.' Light had dawned. '"They", you said. It's not Jo that makes these cracks.'

'Of course not' – indignantly. 'Jo wouldn't say things like that. It's Mother and Father.' Then, seeing the necessity of defending *them*: 'They don't mean any harm by it, it's sort of unconscious; they're . . . it's being from an older generation – they don't quite know what to make of Americans.'

148

Jacob said nothing.

'They know you're civilised,' she said anxiously. 'Actually, I think they're jealous of how civilised you are, and that's why they make jokes about it.'

Jacob still said nothing. He was sitting up in bed in the shadows beyond Laura's lamp, inscrutable.

'Actually' – the anxious voice from the daybed sounded resigned to having the truth dragged out – 'I think they make fun of you because they want me not to like you, because you don't like them.'

'But I do,' he said in automatic self-defence.

Imogen's turn to be silent.

'Okay, I don't always approve of them. But I *do* like them. They're so . . . charming, it's impossible not to.'

'Yes, but you just said you don't approve of them. They can tell. You condescend to them, so they condescend back.'

'Did they say that?' – astonished.

'No, they didn't have to. I've noticed.' She sounded proud of her spanking-new capacity to understand the things adults did not say.

'You "notice" too much, young Imogen. Be careful you don't notice things that aren't there.'

'It is there. It's in the jokes.' The voice from the daybed was offended.

'Hmph. Well, sticks and stones . . . And "barbarian" is far enough off base not to get to me the way "shorty" would, say.' He yawned loudly. 'Time to go to sleep.'

'Okay.'

Laura switched out the light.

Out of the blackness: 'You're *sure* I haven't hurt your feelings?'

'Sure. Go to sleep.'

But it left a nasty taste in his mouth. The Barbarian. All that time: in years when his affection and respect had been un-qualified; when he had felt like one of the family – when they had *made* him feel like one of the family, damn it.

All very well, telling her that a gibe so far off the mark couldn't hurt. Some taunts always did. 'Liar' would hurt an honest person, 'coward' a brave one. 'Barbarian.' It hurt. He rolled the sour taste on his tongue.

So friendly and affectionate – all sham.

Okay, okay, not *all* sham. He should know – who better? – the mixture of good and bad in most things about the Standishes. Especially Frances. She could easily listen to him with warm interest, or tell him her troubles, or share gossip about their common friends; and afterwards elicit Oliver's narrow smile of pleasure with casual jokes – The Barbarian Loses his Mate, perhaps, or, The Barbarian Hears Confession, or, The Barbarian Mystified by the Customs of the Natives – in that lazy, amused, confidential tone that placed her and her hearer inside a charmed circle.

And they were still doing it. Hmm. They couldn't be thinking of divorce, then: you don't go on sharing family jokes with someone you're about to leave. Not rational, but he bet it was true.

Chapter 32

 AURA FELT QUEASY the next morning. 'Why don't you two do something while I stay still for a while?' she suggested. 'I'll feel better in an hour or so, then we can go up to Careggi.'

'Right – what about a lightning tour of some favourite spots, Imogen?'

'Oh yes, what a lovely idea. And' – smiling and grimacing – 'maybe I'll get the bad feel of the past two days out of my memory of Florence.'

It was a new Imogen who was walking with him. She was calm and self-possessed, but it was not just that; there was something different about her, something that baffled him until he became conscious that he felt almost a tingling on the side nearest to her – a faint, abstract, barely perceptible awareness of a woman.

150

A woman? Imogen, who was fourteen-going-on-fifteen? A glance reassured him that she was still a young girl; another told him that his instinct was not wrong. The depth of her self-possession was new, and something about the tilt of her head suggested greater independence.

In the Pazzi chapel she looked at the ghost of herself in the corner and startled him by saying to herself, 'Poor Imogen' – reflectively, without self-pity, as if talking about someone else. In the second cloister she looked at the spot where he had shouted at her the previous afternoon, said – not to herself – 'Poor Jacob,' and sat down on the wall a little way off. He leaned against a pillar, regarding her quizzically. She looked back, serious, composed, and took a deep breath. 'Jacob, I've been thinking . . . How can I say it? . . . One way and another we Standishes have given you a lot of trouble, ever since' – her tone forbade interruption – 'since that time when I was twelve and I'd just been rude to Sara, and you got me to come downstairs – remember?'

He nodded.

'And I've begun to realise how much you've done – how you've tried to stand between me and my parents' unhappiness with each other –'

'They're not unhappy,' he burst out. 'They're discontented.'

Imogen winced; like anyone at any age she preferred the tragic vein to the shabby-domestic. But she turned the idea over, looking out at Michelozzo's delicate arches. 'You may be right. But whatever it is, you've helped me . . . I was going to say, helped me face it, but that's sort of *dramatic*. You've helped me not mind things so much. You see?' She gave him just time to nod. 'And I've always taken it for granted, but I shouldn't, because you aren't *really* family, you just act like it, but you aren't *obliged* to. So I should be grateful –'

'But –'

Her frown stopped him. 'I know you haven't minded most of the time. But I'm thinking about what *I* should think. In the past few days I've been so much trouble to you, and messed up your time with Laura, and made you worry; and it was rotten of me' – matter-of-factly; her look forbade him to utter a word. 'I've already said I'm sorry, and saying it a hundred times will just make me feel better, not make it up to you.

What I want to say is thank you. That's all, only I couldn't just say it without explaining what I meant.'

Jacob did not know how to answer. He wanted to meet her seriousness, not slide off with something glib like, 'Think nothing of it.' But how? He shifted his weight from one foot to the other. 'Uh, in England, when somebody says thank you, you answer, "Not at all", if you say anything. In the States we say, "You're welcome". So that's what I'm saying,' he smiled at her: 'You're welcome.'

It was all right: Imogen smiled back and stood up – then looked suddenly sober; her eyes filled with tears.

'What's up?'

Snuffle. She found her handkerchief and blew her nose. 'It's okay . . . It's just feeling that . . . that I'm on my own now.' She blew her nose again. 'And now I've got to face Elspeth and Jo, and they'll forgive me – but Elspeth will keep wondering if I'll run away again . . . And then I'll have to face Mother and Father, and – oh, dear, wickedness doesn't seem to be worth it, does it?' She was smiling again; and they headed back to the hotel in companionable silence.

When the three of them got out of the bus at Careggi, Imogen said, 'There's a bus back down in five minutes, then it's an hour till the next. Why not stay here and catch this one?'

'We told Elspeth we'd bring you *home*,' Jacob began doubtfully; 'and we can give you – you know – moral support and all.'

'But you have so little time left for Florence. And I think I should face it on my own, don't you?'

'Not really.'

'You know what I mean. *Please*.'

He gave in. She was right about how little time he and Laura had; right to want to face Jo and Elspeth on her own. 'Okay then. Good luck.'

'Do you think that was wise?' Laura asked as they got on the down bus.

'She won't not go home, if that's what you mean.'

'I know that; but what will Elspeth think?'

'Let's not worry about Elspeth. After all, Florence awaits.'

Florence awaited. The bus swept round a corner, and there down in the valley, rising out of a mass of red roofs, was the

Duomo, overbearing, magnificent, queen of everything. Laura said, 'Look!' and then, with excitement, 'We're nearly there,' and turned from the window to Jacob, happy in the discovery that she had come to love the city as he did. He had given it to her after all.

Chapter 33

Y THE TIME Jacob and Laura returned from Italy they had been together for a year, slowly and steadily growing happier with each other; the anniversary made them realise how far they had come from that uncertain time. Having stayed together this long (in their fashion, for she still would not live with him), they were very likely to go on doing so. Even Laura acknowledged it.

'When we're in the States next summer –' he began one day in August.

'We're going to America, are we?' she enquired, amused. 'Thanks for letting me know.'

'Well, you know, I go to see Aline and Isaac every other year, and I, uh . . . um . . . I did assume that you'd – I do want you to meet them.'

'I suppose it is your turn, after what you've suffered from *my* parents.' She did not add a crushing, 'if we're still together' – she had not done so for some time. And soon afterwards she herself suggested a plan for much further ahead: she was due for a sabbatical in 1976 and wanted to spend it at Stanford. If he'd like to, it would be nice for him to come too – was there any chance that he would be able to buy time on their computer and work from there?

'California – crumbs. Hmm . . . I don't know what I'll

be working on in two years, but if it's like the current lot, I should be able to shift things about and come for part of the time – maybe all.'

In September, emboldened by the summer's contentment, he burst out: 'It's ridiculous, not being able to say I love you – especially since you know anyhow.'

'But I don't feel that way any more. *I've* been wanting to say it to *you* for ages. Like this: I love you.' She said it so crossly that they both laughed.

'So why didn't you?'

'I didn't dare, in case *you* didn't any more.'

'Idiot. Of course I do.'

'Do what?'

'Love you.'

Laura smiled a cat-cream smile.

We're there, he thought. What a relief. The last barrier was down.

Almost the last barrier. There was still Laura's deep, inscrutable reserve. Not that she deliberately hid anything; but she was not very forthcoming. There was too little give and take: he talked about his thoughts and feelings; but, unless he probed – when she would answer freely – she did not often meet him with an account of hers. He resented having to solicit what he wanted her to volunteer; it felt like forcing her privacy.

Yet he also admired her reserve. 'It's rather awesome,' he told her one day; 'I'm such a gabbler compared to you.'

Laura looked up with a peculiarly naked face. 'That hurts.'

'Good God' – aghast. 'I meant it as a compliment.'

'I know, but people have always said I'm reserved, though I don't mean to be – and I didn't think I was, with you. If you don't know me, who ever will?'

'Lordy, love, I didn't mean it that way. And of course I "know you".'

But did he? Until she told him, he had not guessed that her opacity was involuntary. He certainly didn't know her as he had known Sheila. He tried to leave Sheila out of it: people were different – Sheila had had her inside on the outside and no defence except pride against the world's onslaughts; it had been impossible not to know her all too well, impossible not to move with the tides of her moods. He must not find Laura wanting by the measure of someone who had been agonising to live with. Besides, it was Laura he loved, now. She was not fiery, not extreme; but she had a beauty of mind, an active lovingkindness – a *caritas* – that moved and almost dazzled him: in spite of abstract impatience, he wanted passionately to make things work with her.

And she had reservations of her own about him: about work, in particular. She was a good biochemist – 'Not quite first-class,' she said carefully, 'but good' – and she worked hard: he often went to movies alone because she was too busy to come. He was a butterfly in comparison; he worked in his spare time only when he had to meet a deadline. He enjoyed his work and earned a reasonable living, but he was not absorbed in it; the effervescence of ideas that brought him more customers each year was only the natural overflow of his mind, not the result of sustained application. Work was not central to his life – and Laura found his lack of zeal incomprehensible and infuriating. From the beginning she had occasionally grumbled that he was a dilettante, and her sniping was becoming more frequent. 'You only play at your work,' she would complain; 'it doesn't have a grip on you.'

He minded more than he knew how to say. He liked computing – why wasn't he engrossed in it? Sometimes he thought that his lack of dedication was a price he paid for staying in England on the terms he wanted: that his creative effort went into learning English life well enough to put down some sort of roots – but perhaps he would have been just as rudderless in America.

Chapter 34

ATE IN SEPTEMBER they stopped in to see Imogen on their way to London. As they strolled along the Avenue in the school grounds, slowing up to watch a girl and boy toss a Frisbee, Laura said, 'Imogen, I'm dying to know – how did Elspeth and Jo act when you got back? Were they cross? Did they worry that you'd run away again?'

She laughed. 'Oh, I told them not to worry; and saying it straight out was a good idea – they didn't.'

'And what about your parents?'

'They weren't cross either, they were super. And they explained why they'd needed to send me away – they'd been going through a bad patch, and they needed time alone together.'

'So I take it you were generally reassured,' said Jacob a little drily.

Hearing his tone she said, 'Yes, of course,' in defence of her parents. 'And the reason they didn't want me to know that they were the ones who arranged for me to go to Italy was that they were afraid I'd think I was being got rid of. Mother said they should have known I was old enough to understand – but why hadn't I guessed that their motives were good, and trusted them?'

Typical of them to throw most of the blame onto her, instead of saying they were sorry. But he didn't say so. It was time to go; as they turned back, he asked about the rest of her time in Italy.

'Oh, it was wonderful – and Rome was best of all.'

'Better than Florence?' – jealously.

156

'Oh, no. Well – I don't know. Florence is a – a temple; Rome is so full of people, and shabby and homely and comfortable. The buildings and statues and paintings aren't a patch on Florence, but it's such a lovable city. I felt at home there. Oh, and I haven't told you: I've decided to do modern languages for A-levels, especially Italian.'

At the car he said, 'So. Three weeks today, same time, same place?'

'Oh yes,' said Imogen happily, waving goodbye.

A few days later Frances rang. Why didn't he – he and Laura – call in, next time they came up to London?

Laura shook her head vigorously as he relayed the invitation with his hand over the mouthpiece. 'I'd rather not; I don't like them at all. Why not see them next Sunday, while I'm visiting my parents? – you're going to the NFT that afternoon.'

So he arranged to have Sunday lunch with the Standishes. 'I'm glad you can make it so soon,' Frances said cordially. Presumably they wanted to thank him for finding Imogen.

Laura might be impervious to the Standish charm, but Jacob, even now, was not; drawing up in front of their familiar, dignified, comfortable house he was looking forward almost with the old pleasure to a session of chat and gossip. He had not forgotten that he was a barbarian; he did not trust them an inch – but, unscrupulous and untrustworthy though they were, they could also be lively and entertaining, and he wanted to maintain some sort of infrequent intercourse with them. Besides, although he no longer thought of them as friends, in some measure they were still family and always would be.

Oliver led him straight down to the kitchen, where Frances had lunch nearly ready. She came forward holding a bowl of salad and kissed him. 'Jacob – how nice – it's so long since we've seen you,' she said, smiling as she turned to put the bowl on the table.

'Yes, indeed,' said Oliver, rummaging in a drawer for the corkscrew.

It had been cloudy, but the sun gleamed out as they sat down to lunch. There were pale-gold beech leaves scattered over the lawn outside, and late, half-blown, white and yellow roses on Frances' big old rosebushes. As always on sunny

157

days, the kitchen seemed continuous with the garden: lit by the same light, bright with the same colours – russet floor, orange casserole, honey-gold pine table, and the scarlet bulk of the Aga glowing in its dark recess. Jacob sat in the chair he always sat in and sniffed luxuriously as Frances ladled out thick hot stew and Oliver cut slices of crunchy bread. It was all comfortable, familiar. And the Standishes seemed happier, keeping up a flow of lazy banter that was not edged with malice. It did not quite include him; it had an almost loverlike note of private understanding; but the change from their former tensions was so pleasant that he was content to listen on the outskirts. Perhaps they had indeed worked something out during the summer.

Eventually conversation flagged. Jacob watched a patch of sun slide across the salad bowl, irradiating the top layers of lettuce and thin slices of tomato and cucumber. 'We shouldn't eat that,' he said, to fill up a silence that had gone on too long. 'It's a still life, not a salad.'

'Gracious, I hadn't noticed. It'll be baked.' Frances twitched the bowl into the shade.

'More wine, Jacob?' Oliver opened another bottle. Looking through the french windows he said, 'I must rake up those leaves later this afternoon.'

'And I should dig up the bulbs.'

'This year?'

'They want dividing.'

Languid shrug. 'If you say so.'

They're making conversation, Jacob thought; that's not real talk. He listened to it and contributed his bit, as if they were people he had just met; and the sun slid off the table and along the floor towards the french windows. Frances brought out a trifle; Oliver poured more wine. Jacob, with a drive ahead of him, stopped after two glasses, but the Standishes were putting away a fair amount; by the time lunch was over, the second bottle was empty.

Upstairs they drank coffee in almost unbroken silence. The sun was moving round to the front, and the room gradually brightened; Jacob was comfortable, sitting in his favourite chair with his legs stretched out. He knew this room so well: the eighteenth-century gentleman on the wall; the crimson lady's chair; the long, bottle-green, sedately modern Standish

158

and Sons sofa, on which Frances and Oliver were sitting – Oliver leaning back, his long legs crossed and one arm extended so that his fingers just brushed her shoulder.

One by one they put down their cups; and still no one had said anything more interesting than, 'More coffee?' and, 'No, thanks.' Where was the gossip he had been looking forward to?

Then Frances cleared her throat and glanced meaningly at Oliver, who nodded and said, 'Look, Jacob, we thought we'd take the opportunity – while you're here, don't you know – to, er, to have a talk about Imogen.'

'Sure.'

'We were, er, it was a . . . very upsetting business, this summer. We talked to her, and I think she understands . . . But . . . er . . . Frankly, we're rather worried about – please don't misunderstand me – about your influence on her.'

'My influence!' He stopped relaxing.

'She says you don't think we're serious – '

'What on earth? I've never told her anything of the sort – she had no right – '

'She didn't say you *said* it,' Frances interposed; 'I think she deduced it.'

'Even so – '

'Even so' – Oliver smoothly took the words from his mouth – 'it's a question of what Imogen thinks, don't you see. She thinks so highly of you, and she thinks you have a certain opinion of us – and thinks less of us because of what you – '

'But I just said – '

' – because of what she *thinks* you think about us.'

'It's such a nuisance,' said Frances. 'I mean, she disapproves of everything. Not just our . . . private lives.' (So it was 'our' now, was it? No more jealousy?) 'She disapproves of what we think and how we talk – she's got this absolute obsession with "seriousness"; she's turned into a stuffy old maid.'

'Of course we value seriousness too,' said Oliver. 'We're serious people ourselves . . .' An unspoken, 'even if you don't think so,' hovered in the air.

Jacob spread his hands in silent protest. How did one answer? What was he doing in this strange conversation?

'. . . but she's got no sense of humour, no tolerance, and it's partly because of you.' He raised his hand: 'Though not

159

deliberately, as I said. We want to try to undo some of the damage – we want to get our daughter back.'

'Our daughter, not a judge,' Frances said with sudden vehemence.

'Don't you realise that she'd stand on her head for a month to get your approval?' Jacob asked in exasperation.

'If it wasn't against her principles of the moment – which she gets from you.'

He shrugged – he had no words. Nothing in his life had equipped him to get out of the sticky flytrap of their logic.

Frances interpreted his shrug as indifference and flushed with anger. 'She's turning against us; and you're responsible –'

'But that's ridiculous!'

She looked at him out of narrowed hazel eyes. 'No, it isn't. I know it's true, because she went to you in Florence instead of coming home to me.' Her voice curdled on the last words.

'Listen, Imogen didn't "come to me",' he said angrily; 'I found her. And anyhow, I don't know where you get the idea that I have to justify myself to you.'

'Of course you don't,' said Oliver calmly. 'We didn't mean to give that impression. We're just trying to explain our position.'

'Which is?' – belligerently.

'Er, we rather wish . . . we wonder if . . . it seemed to us that you might agree that there was a case for . . . for your seeing rather less of Imogen for a while.'

He went red with amazed anger and made a strangled noise.

'Please don't misunderstand,' Oliver hurried on. 'You've been very good, visiting her; it's been a great help when we couldn't get up there; but right now we think we and the school should be the main influences on Imogen for a time.'

I don't believe this, Jacob thought: People don't behave like this. 'Let's get this clear,' he said pugnaciously. 'You mean, after all these years; and my finding Imogen in Florence; and saving you the trouble of visiting her at school; and the time you asked me to keep her after Frances' bad trip – you're actually forbidding me to see her?'

'Not forbidding: just *asking* you to see her rather less often. We want her to learn to be lighter, more . . . jolly. She's missing out on her youth; she's like a nun –'

'A judge,' Frances interjected.

160

' – and she'll have more chance of developing an attachment to the values of her peer-group if she sees rather less of you.'

Jacob said slowly, 'I was under the impression that you'd be grateful to me. I took a lot of time and trouble finding her this summer. It was no fun for me; and I assure you I wish she *had* gone to you. It would have given me my holiday with Laura, which got messed up looking for *your* daughter.'

Frances' face thickened with anger, 'You expect us to be grateful? Don't hold your breath. If it hadn't been for you, she'd have come to me. You want a child, and you don't have one, so you're trying to steal ours.'

His eyes stared out of his head. He got up and took one blurred look at the Standishes: at Oliver, rising quickly with a, 'Look here – ' dying on his lips; at Frances, huddled forward, arms on her knees, looking up flushed and frightened at the effect of her words. With all his being he wanted to hit her; the inconceivability of actually doing so almost choked him. His tongue was thick in his mouth; a voice in his head was muttering over and over: The end, the end, the end, it's the end, the end . . . He must say something – must crush her –

Oliver moved forward. Jacob stepped back sharply to evade the false-friendly hand already stretching out to detain him, dropped the search for a crushing retort, walked quickly out of the drawing room and out of the house, started the Mini, set off with a jerk – Frances was at the doorway, Oliver hurrying down the steps – drove round the corner into Canonbury Park North, beyond pursuit, and parked – he was not fit to drive – in the first space he found. His hands were shaking. He got out of the car and stood with his elbows on the roof, breathing hard. 'You don't have a child, and so you're trying to steal ours.' God, God, God. He remembered the child his imagination had conceived, in their house, at the party in 1964 – the child with Imogen's delicacy and Sheila's features – the child who had been so real to his mind's eye that for four years he had kept pleading with Sheila to participate in making her real in the flesh – in Sheila's flesh; and the pain of loss rose up in him until he gasped for breath: a lost, real Sheila; a lost imaginary child . . . When he began to get his breath back, he recognised with faint surprise that his grief was only for the child.

Family, he had thought, coming to see the Standishes. Not at all. Family survived scenes like that, because it had to.

Friendship, under no such necessity, did not survive – had not survived. 'You're trying to steal ours.' Those words had swept away the last vestiges of his regard for Frances. Unforgivable, to turn his most secret grief against him.

He was stupefied. He looked at his hands. They were no longer trembling, though they felt too weak to make a fist. He remembered shaking Imogen, in the Pazzi chapel, and being unable to loose his grip. Family. 'You're trying to steal ours.' He thought about some of the rejoinders he might have made. Lucky he hadn't begun; he wouldn't have been able to stop. Amazing, how strong were the taboos against losing one's temper: so strong that three very angry people had not raised their voices – though Frances had come close – or said explicitly things that could not be retracted.

No, he was wrong. 'You're trying to steal ours.' That was beyond glossing over: unretractable, unforgivable. The veneer of civilisation had snapped.

It was time for the NFT. Down on the South Bank he parked in Festival Hall Approach, got out and remembered leaning on the car roof a short while ago, overcome by an old grief. 'You want a child and you don't have one, so you're – '

You don't have a child –

But he did have Laura, and he hoped . . .

He had never suggested it, not yet; only recently had he dared even let himself think about it. What would a child of his and Laura's be like? Not like the lost child; there would always be a pang for her. But think; imagine; hope. A child with Laura's triangular planes and curly fawn hair, with Imogen's delicacy. They might call her Imogen.

Or might not. Don't count your chickens, he told himself as the house lights went down and the big yellow metal curtain slid open.

When he got home, the telephone was ringing. It was Frances. 'Jacob, I'm so glad I've got you. I want – we both want – to apologise for this afternoon.' Her voice was warm and urgent – the old Frances, his friend and counsellor. He raised his eyebrows and stood listening in the darkness of his sitting room. 'I just don't know what came over us – I'd had rather too much to drink at lunch . . . and I do feel threatened about

Imogen, after last summer . . . but still . . . we shouldn't have . . . and of course I was much worse than Oliver – '

'I wouldn't say that. Don't be too hard on yourself, Frances,' he said through bared fangs.

She paused, probably wondering whether he meant to be snide or polite, then, with a vague, 'Oh . . .?' to cover both cases, hurried on. 'I *do* hope you can understand; we've been bottling up our fears about her, and what came out today was our insecurity.'

Insecurity phooey. He was used to the dark by now; he smiled wolfishly at his shadowy image in the looking glass, while she wound up with a plea, in her warmest tones, for him to forget this afternoon and come up and see them soon, 'same as always.' He did not reply, and she went on nervously: 'We're such old friends, after all . . . and between friends this isn't the end of the world . . .' She ran out of words to throw into his silence. 'Are you still there?'

'Mm-hmm – but listen, Laura's just back from Wales' – Laura was no such thing – 'so I'd better cut it short, okay?'

'Certainly,' she said graciously, and waited for him to end on a friendly note.

'Well, keep in touch' – a calculated phrase. 'Goodbye.'

'But – '

The receiver was halfway down to the handset when he heard her protest, and it went right on going: revenge for his loused-up exit line in the afternoon. He went to bed with a light heart, in spite of just having cast off his substitute family for ever, thinking of the future, and Laura, and children.

Chapter 35

HEN LAURA RETURNED, jaded from a week with her parents, Jacob was unexpectedly nervous about bringing up his wonderful idea. He put it off until after the frenetic first week of term – and until he was spending a night in her rooms: such a delicate subject might be better raised on her territory rather than on his.

On his third night in a row in King's he mustered his courage. Putting down on the sofa the book he had been pretending to read and rubbing the top of her head – she was on the floor beside him – he began tentatively, 'Uh, I've been thinking . . .'

'Oh-oh, that usually means something horrid.' The toffee-coloured curls slid out from under his hand as Laura twisted round and looked up alertly.

'No . . . it's just that . . . I told you about the Standishes, and what Frances said, that made me walk out – '

'Insufferable woman.' Her eyes flashed.

'Well, the thing is, it set me thinking . . . I've always wanted . . . thought it would be nice . . . it occurred to me that wouldn't it be nice if we – if we had children,' he finished in a rush.

Her reaction was crisp and definite. She didn't want children yet. – Ever? – She thought so. – When, then? – She didn't know.

He lost a little of his caution: 'But you're thirty-one, you can't wait too long.'

'I've got a few years' grace. Having a child in your mid-thirties is much safer than it used to be – and of course I'd have an amniocentesis done and have an abortion if it were going to be a mongol or whatever.'

'But why wait? The earlier the better, surely?'

'Oh, Jacob. It's my work. I'm full of ideas, and getting more graduate students; my research is going so well: I'm beginning – just beginning – to find my feet. What I need, for at least two or three years, is to get all my beginnings properly established. It just isn't the right time to have children. Do you see what I mean?'

He nodded mournfully.

'Oh dear.' She rubbed her cheek against his knee. 'I've sort of known this was coming, because I know you like children – not just Imogen: all those cousins you send birthday presents to . . . but I didn't know how to say anything . . .'

'That's okay, love – it'll keep.'

'But what if I never want children?' she said a few days later.

'You said you did!'

'But I've been thinking. What if I still feel the same way, three, four, five years from now – that I need two or three more years without interruption? And the same the year after that, and so on?'

'Do you think that's likely?' he asked glumly.

'I don't know. It's funny – I've always thought I'd have children, but I'd never thought of *when*; it's always been vague. Since you brought it up, I've been trying to imagine the effect on my life – and I realised that maybe I'd get more and more involved in work and never want to ease off – and then where would *you* be? The point is – ' Laura stopped; when she resumed, her voice had the declarative flatness that marked things she found hard to say. 'The point is, I've realised I can't *guarantee* that I'll *ever* be ready to have children; and I thought I should tell you, so that . . . would you – do you want them so much that you'd' – she swallowed – 'want to . . . move on to somebody else?'

He thought about it. 'You know, this is the first moment in my whole life that I've even tried to imagine not having children – I've always wanted them so much that I just assumed I would. But, no, I wouldn't want to "move on". It'd be a bit much, going around looking for a breeder of children.'

'You could advertise. One ad in *Time Out* and one in *The*

Lady. I wonder which would get the best answers? . . .
Seriously, though: don't answer now. Think about it – I'll ask
you again in a week or so.'

Jacob tried to think about it, without getting very far.
Not having children was almost as unimaginable as losing
Laura.

A week went by, and another, and she did not ask him; so
finally, one Saturday morning as she was leaving to man a
pregnancy-testing session, he said, 'I'm still sure – I wouldn't
want to move on.'

Laura looked at him with her head on one side and her light
triangular eyes crinkled into slits. 'I'm not so sure.'

'I am. I want to stay with you. Besides, I don't want just any
old children. What I pictured that day in London was a child
that looked like *you*.'

Her face softened. 'Poor Jacob – I'm not a very good bargain,
am I? I won't live with you, and I won't promise to have your
children – '

'Ah, but you're *you*.'

That evening, while heating up a chili con carne he had made
the day before, Jacob had an inspiration. The chili had mellowed
nicely . . . perhaps a little more pepper – perfect. Water for
rice – and here was Laura, lifting the lid of the chili pot and
sniffing lustily: 'If you'll *have* the children,' he began abruptly,
'I'll stay home and look after them.'

She straightened up and looked at him strangely. 'Good
Lord, you're serious, aren't you?'

'Mm-hmm.'

'Not a chance, mate. When I have children – *if* I do – I'll be
their mother myself, not leave it to somebody else.'

He was astonished. 'I don't get it. Don't you believe that
men and women should share taking care of children?'

'You're proposing role-reversal, not shared child-care,'
Laura said tartly. 'Besides, either I'll be a proper mother, or not
at all.'

'What on earth is a proper mother?' He was testy because the
conversation was not going as he had planned. 'You sound
awfully conservative all of a sudden.'

'Quite the reverse,' she said rather fiercely. 'After all, some
feminists are questioning the whole concept of social paternity.'

166

'So tell me something new. Come off it, Laura, don't tell me you're rushing to embrace separatist feminism and test-tube babies and all that.'

'Not in that primitive form – of course not. But ask yourself what this *is* that you have about fatherhood. Would you be so keen on looking after an adopted child? Or if I had somebody else's?'

'No, I guess not' – slowly – 'I want my own children. But yours and mine, you know, love, coming out of both of us.'

'Out of *me*. That's the point. I'd carry it, bear it, feed it – do you think I'd want to hand it over to somebody else after that?'

'You mean you wouldn't use day nurseries?'

'Of course I would, as soon as possible. Harvey Road takes babies after six months.'

'Then I don't understand . . .' He frowned. 'Do you mean you'd want a child to be only yours, not mine at all?'

'Not exactly. Just more mine than yours.'

The telephone rang. Jacob went to answer it and came back looking puzzled. 'Imogen. She's busy again tomorrow; and could we come next Sunday. I said fine.'

Laura checked her diary as they ate. 'I can't come, I've got a meeting. Too bad . . . Oh. That's the second time she's put us off. You don't suppose her parents have told her not to see you so often?'

'I'd believe anything, after that explosion. But Imogen sounded normal, so let's hope not.'

He reverted to the question of children later. 'I wouldn't be trying to steal a child's affections from you – it's just that I do so much work at home anyhow, now that I've got a terminal here, so it'd make sense that way round.'

'You wouldn't get much work done – mothers of young children don't.' There was a sarcastic emphasis on 'mothers'.

'So what? I'd do enough to live.'

'So *what*? What's your life about?' she cried with sudden fury. 'Do you want children to compensate for not having any –'

'Watch it!'

' – any idea what to do with your life?' she finished defiantly.

167

Jacob stood up, clenching his fists. When he found his voice, he said, very quietly: 'That's the second time in a month that I've been accused of wanting a child as a substitute for something. I – I – Go home, Laura, go home, or I'll start saying things I'll regret.'

'No. Say them.'

He glared down at her. She did not budge. 'You stay, then. I'm going.'

She caught up with him in front of Fitzbillies. 'I'm sorry,' she said, pulling him back by the arm. 'Really. I didn't mean it the way Frances did.'

'Perhaps you could describe the difference?' he replied coldly, walking on.

'It's that she was being malicious and I wasn't. Oh dear, how do I . . . I feel as if you're trying to force having children on me – '

'But I'm not. I've told you I'm not. I don't want – '

'I know you don't want me to unless I do too – but you want me to so much that your wanting is like a force I have to resist. And I *do* have trouble understanding why this abstract idea of paternity is so important to you.'

'It's not abstract,' he snapped. In the near-darkness of Garret Hostel Lane he repeated, more evenly: 'It's not abstract.' They stopped on the bridge and leaned on the parapet. 'It's . . .' He pulled his mind together. 'It all began with Imogen, you know;' and for the first time he told her about the imaginary daughter he had conceived before the Standishes' party in 1964, and how hope had kept the idea alive during the years with Sheila, 'until it became part of me. And then, after Sheila left, Imogen kept showing me what the pleasures of parenthood could be. More than pleasures – what it could mean to be involved in the fate of a child. It's not abstract, not for me.'

'The trouble is,' she said, peering at him seriously, 'I don't think you understand what I meant about a child's being more mine. Let me put it this way. What if we had one, and eventually we split up? It would come with me – how would you feel then?'

The pain of the idea jolted him into an involuntary, 'Oh – '

'That's it. That's what "more mine than yours" means, if worst came to worst.'

168

'And never let me see it?'

'No, just that it would live with me, not you.'

Jacob thought it over. 'I'll take the risk,' he said finally.

Laura laughed despairingly. 'First catch your hare. I'm no nearer to having a child right away, or maybe ever.'

'I know. Further, maybe.' It was beginning to mizzle, and they started back.

'No, just no nearer.' It was her last word on the subject that evening, and the last either of them said about it for a long time.

Chapter 36

'WHERE SHALL WE go?' asked Jacob. Imogen was looking more grown up than ever; it suddenly occurred to him that cream teas and country walks were not entirely satisfactory entertainments for a girl of fifteen.

'Why don't we just walk round here, same as last time – if you don't have anything planned? I've, er, something I want to say to you, and something to tell you about.'

They strolled along by the playing field and sat down in the sun, well away from an impromptu soccer game, and within earshot of the Young Farmers Club's chickens. He lay back on the short turf, looking up at a few long, thin-spun threads of cloud high in the milky blue sky. 'Okay, pet, shoot,' he prompted at last. 'You've got something to say and something to tell – whatever the difference is.'

'Oh. You'll see. What I wanted to say is that . . . oh dear, I don't know how to say it. It's been so nice of you to visit me, these past two years . . .'

Jesus. They really had told her to see less of him. They would push it off onto her. 'I enjoy it, you know.'

'Yes, but really it's for me more than you: what you enjoy is making me happy – and what I wanted to say is . . . is that it's not so necessary any more. It's marvellous having you come – our trips, and being able to talk about things that bother me. But I'm more . . . I'm settled into school life now . . .'

This did not sound like a message from her parents – more as if she still thought she needed to win his forgiveness about Florence. 'Is this some kind of sacrifice?' he asked suspiciously.

'Oh no! Just the opp- ' She stopped, smiling awkwardly. 'It's that there's more to do at weekends than there was, and so I don't need visits so much, you see.'

Just the opposite of a sacrifice? Ah. 'Yes, I see – and who's the boyfriend?'

'How did you guess?' she cried. 'That was the something that I wanted to tell you – I thought you'd be surprised.'

'There's always been plenty to do at weekends round here, and suddenly you say there's more. I may be dense, but I get there eventually.'

'I must be dreadfully obvious.'

He laughed. 'No, I just remembered me at fifteen, in love with Harriet Zuckerman – she was the prettiest girl in grade ten, and I'd managed to steal her from the football captain, of all people. Anyhow, tell me about this person of yours.'

'His name is Ben Stephen, and he's in my form – we're doing a lot of the same things for O-level – and he's very nice – '

'Surprise, surprise.'

'You are horrid' – unruffled. 'And he's one of the best soccer players in the school.'

'Since when have you been interested in soccer?'

'Since Ben.' No beating about the bush. 'He also' – drily – 'plays the cello.'

'That's more like it. Is he good at it?'

'Absolutely terrible' – enjoying his discomfiture. 'You are a prig, Jacob.' She scrutinised him. 'And he's extremely good-looking – he looks quite a lot like you, actually. And you needn't fall about like that. He does.'

'Then he can't be "extremely good-looking". Looking like me and being good-looking are mutually exclusive categories.'

170

'Nonsense. You're just obsessed with those movie stars you spend all your time watching. You're perfectly all right.'

'Okay, okay,' he said weakly, sitting up on his elbows. The soccer game had moved closer. 'Is your Ben out there?'

'No, he's – working somewhere.'

He sat up straighter. 'Waiting for you somewhere, you mean.'

She gave an embarrassed laugh. 'Well, yes. But don't –'

He stood up. 'Of course I will. I remember what it's like. Exit Jacob gracefully, saying, "I was just going anyhow".'

'But don't desert me altogether. I'd miss you awfully.'

'Okay, why don't I come every six weeks or so – that's half as often as before.'

'Perfect.' Imogen smiled at him as at a fellow voyager on the high seas of love.

They met once more before Christmas; but afterwards he hardly saw her at all. On their new six-weekly schedule they should have met twice before Easter and once after, but he had to postpone the late-February visit, and then she was busy one weekend and he the next; and after that she was studying for mock O-levels, and he had several deadlines to meet: so that all they managed was a visit in March and another on a Sunday in May, when she rang to say that she was coming up to visit a friend who was ill in Addenbrookes, and could she call on him and Laura afterwards.

She arrived apologetic for being late. 'I made a detour into King's – I wanted to get a feel for my future.'

'You've got it all planned, have you?' Jacob asked, amused.

'Just as far as university,' said the child of fortune. 'Father was at King's, and he wants me to go there too. So I had a look and sort of thought myself into it. It's beautiful, even if it is unfair.'

'Unfair?'

'What you were thinking just then. That everything falls into my lap, that I practically don't even have to do anything.'

He was startled. 'How did you know I was thinking that?'

'Because I think so too' – as if she took reading his thoughts for granted. 'I'm rather worried about it, you see – it *is* unfair; and I want to do something about it. But I can't think what.'

171

'You mean like not going to King's?'

'No – like . . . giving some of it back. Sharing it.'

'Good works?'

'Don't be sarcastic. No – something more . . . connected. I'll have to keep on the lookout; it'll fall into place eventually.'

Her sublime confidence was frightening. 'Don't just wait,' he said warningly.

'You mean I need to work for it?'

'Well, be thinking about it, at least. For instance, do you know what you want to do after university?'

'Not really,' she said hesitantly. 'When I was little, I was going to be a great painter or an actress – the things children get ideas about. But recently . . . I thought I'd wait and find out – at university, maybe. I want to do something that's useful and interesting, that's all.'

That was all. She was very matter-of-fact, gazing at him with unperturbed hazel eyes, but he knew, through the same kinship that had put her in possession of his thoughts, that what she wanted was a life of heroic possibilities heroically encountered; and his heart ached for her. She assumed that the strength of her desire would lead her to a hard, chosen path, equal to her aspirations – but it was so easy to miss; and there was no use warning her about difficulties, bewilderments, discouragements, chances of failure: for, like him at her age, she would think she knew all that already.

'Listen,' he said. 'You want serious advice? Think hard about what you want to do with your life, and do it. You need a vocation – you've got to be able to define yourself to yourself through some sort of dedication to something.'

'Oh, I know. The trouble is, I don't have any vocation that I know about. There are lots of things I enjoy – '

'It's not just a matter of enjoyment – you need to care about your work more than anything.'

Her brow puckered. 'Oh dear, it is difficult.' Then she looked at him with interest. 'You're speaking from experience, aren't you?'

'Mm-hmm. The thing is, I like computing, but I wouldn't make big sacrifices for it. Not like Laura: if she had to choose between her work and me – or anybody – she'd choose her work. Mine isn't that important to me.'

'And you mind.'

172

'Sometimes, yes.' He noticed that her frown had deepened. 'Heavens, pet, don't worry about *me*. I'm one of the happiest people I know.'

Her brow unknotted slightly. 'That's what I've always thought, but you sounded – You're really happy?'

'Really and truly.'

'Oh. Good.' Her face cleared, and she asked for more tea. 'Laura's awfully late – isn't she coming?'

'Uh, no.'

She nodded wisely. 'She does work a lot, doesn't she. Is she at the lab now?'

'No . . .' Jacob hesitated. He was tempted to say that Laura was visiting a friend; but that was a Standish trick. 'No, she's in Norfolk for the weekend with somebody she's, uh, attached to, a guy called Harold – '

'Attached to – you mean having an affair with?' Imogen asked incredulously. 'Poor Jacob! Why didn't you say? I've been chattering, and you two have broken up, and – '

'No, no, we haven't broken up – not at all. Laura's attached to Harold *too*.'

She turned this over, frowning thoughtfully. 'Oh. Like Father and Sara' – not a comparison he relished. 'Poor Jacob,' she repeated. 'You must be fearfully upset.'

'Well, no, not really . . .'

'You mean you don't mind?'

'Hmm, well, not that, either. I do mind, some – especially at first, when I wasn't sure . . . it's always possible, with something like this, that the new person will be preferred, so there's some suspense . . . and there's always a bit of pain. But . . . we talked about the, uh, question when we first started together, and we decided we'd rather put up with the problems of these things than cut ourselves off from – from . . . the possibility of any other attachments . . .' He floundered to a stop, thinking that he had been foolish to begin.

Imogen sat in silence for a moment, looking at her hands. '"Always", you said: "It's always possible". Do you mean that you and Laura are *always* . . . er . . .'

'Having affairs? Heavens, no.' Obviously she was shocked; why hadn't he kept his mouth shut? 'Neither of us would want . . . we don't just sleep with all and sundry, you know – only people we can be serious about: and those sorts of people aren't thick on the ground. In fact, this is the first time that Laura's had another attachment, and I haven't at all, yet, though – '

'Though you're thinking about it,' she said knowingly. Perhaps she was not really upset; she sounded amused. 'And Laura won't mind either – except the way you said?'

'I hope not.'

'But isn't jealousy a problem? It seemed to make such a lot of trouble for Mother and Father.' She was bright-eyed with interest and not shocked in the least.

'I don't know,' he said carefully. 'Obviously it's a problem for lots of people – it's probably an accident of temperament. And what you're used to, too. Aline and Isaac have both had lovers, and jealousy was never a big issue for them, so I suppose that was what seemed normal. I did feel a little jealous at first, as I said, but not enough to make a fuss about.'

'That's very interesting. That's exactly what I've always thought.'

'You! Since when?'

'Oh, for ages. I couldn't ever understand why Mother and Father were so upset about it – I thought maybe it was one of those things you feel different about when you're grown up.'

She seemed to have forgotten that at twelve and thirteen she had been a good deal upset by Oliver's affair; but he knew better than to tease her about stages so recently outgrown. 'They seem to have got over their bad period, though.'

'Ye-e-s . . . well . . . I think maybe they've just got used to putting up with the way they feel.' She pondered. 'May I ask you a personal question?'

It must be a lulu – she had been doing it all afternoon without asking permission. 'Of course. Fire away.'

'Would you be happier if Laura stopped seeing whatsisname – Harold?'

'Hmm. Happier for me, not happier for Laura, which of course affects what's happier for me. On balance' – he weighed it up, not rushing his answer – 'on balance, no, I wouldn't be happier.'

She nodded. 'That's the way I'd feel.'

'Well, if there comes a time when you have to deal with these things in your own life, you must let me know if you still feel that way or – ' He noticed the clock. 'Didn't you say you had to catch the six-twenty? It's gone six now.'

'Oh dear – I *hate* to go; this is so fascinating. Oh, well,' getting up, 'another time. Say hullo to Laura for me; and have a good summer in America.'

He thought he would see her more regularly after the summer, but he didn't. They met occasionally, and they were still friends, but for the time being their friendship did not meet any very urgent needs. She was older and better able to get through troubles on her own, and no longer needed him as an adult friend to confide in; and she was turned towards people of her own age – towards Ben for a while, then someone called Adam, then Tim, then Thurstan.

Jacob was surprised at how little he regretted their drifting apart. He sometimes missed the child that Imogen had been – now that she was older, he recognised that she had made it easier for him not to mind so much about being childless – but towards the girl she now was he no longer felt the protective, quasi-paternal tenderness of former years. Their friendship would abide, for the ties that bound them were too strong for severance – but in any active sense it would have to wait until she was older.

The last time he visited her at school was in the autumn of her second year in the sixth form, when she was seventeen; the last time he saw her at all during her school years was that Christmas, at Naomi's party – the final one; Naomi was returning to America. Imogen's latest young man was with her – but so were Frances and Oliver, whom he never saw nowadays except at Naomi's parties; and for the third year running they were coldly formal towards him. Jacob did not care – he was immune to them by now – but it was unnerving to talk to Imogen with their hostile eyes watching him but sliding away whenever he glanced towards them; so he and Laura just said hello and goodbye and told her that they were off to California for nine months.

The next autumn he rang her a couple of times at school, but did not get down to see her. It was her third year in the sixth form; A-levels were behind her. She had done well and assumed that she would be coming up to Cambridge in the autumn of 1977; in the meantime, Oliver had wangled her a job in Rome as an assistant hotel receptionist – the one who spoke English to the British and American tourists.

In January she sent him a postcard, a reproduction of Piero della Francesca's *Madonna del Parto* – a grave, human woman, solidly planted on her feet, looking thoughtfully at the ground, one hand on her hip, the other touching her ripe belly, waiting for the moment of birth. 'Isn't she wonderful?' Imogen wrote on the back. 'I made a detour to Monterchi just to see her. I've got a place at King's – see you in October. Rome marvellous in winter. Love to you and Laura – Imogen.'

PART III

Chapter 37

OR A MOMENT Jacob just stood on the doorstep and stared at her.

'Don't you recognise me?'

'Of course, it's just . . .'

'You'd forgotten I was coming up?'

'No, I'd remembered – but come in, come in – it's just . . . you've changed, you know.'

'Have I really? What fun. How?' She settled comfortably on the sofa with her legs tucked up and accepted a glass of sherry – dry, not sweet, her father's well-trained daughter. She had become a composed young woman, still slender, but with more substance, more solidity and grace in her bearing. But the change that had surprised him was in the way she was wearing her hair: no longer short with a straight fringe, but grown out to shoulder length and brushed back, exposing her too-high forehead. Not a flattering style.

She was waiting for an answer. 'Uh, it's your hair, I guess,' he said. 'Last time I saw you, it was short.'

'Goodness.' She touched it in surprise. 'Oh, of course, it's been two years, hasn't it. Do you like it like this? I'm wondering whether to chop it off again. – No, don't be polite. What do you really think?'

'I, hmm, I did slightly prefer it short – it framed your face so nicely . . .'

'Whereas – ?'

'Well . . . maybe this pulled-back style looks better on somebody – on somebody older.'

'On somebody like Laura, you were going to say,' she commented acutely. 'Somebody with bones. Mine are the tragedy of my life – I'll never look distinguished like Laura. Oh well.'

'I shouldn't worry about your bones; you look very nice as you are, you know.' A complete change of subject seemed like a good idea. 'So tell me about Rome. What was it like?'

'Just wonderful.' Imogen sat up and sparkled. 'Even the job was fun. Almost everybody on the staff was Italian, and there were several women about my age, so I made some good friends.' ('Women', not 'girls', Jacob noticed, and was therefore not surprised by what followed.) 'Two of them are in the women's movement in Rome, and I got sort of interested, and they took me to a couple of meetings this summer. It was too late for me to get involved, because I was coming back here so soon; but they've promised to take me again next summer. Did I tell you I'm going back? To the same job. It'll be good for my Italian . . .' She talked on blithely for a while, then left with a jaunty: 'See you soon,' almost as much a stranger, he thought, rather bemused, as when she arrived. A confident Imogen, full of easy small-talk, was a new experience.

He did not see her again during her first term; he was busy, and he thought she should be left alone to find her feet in the undergraduate social world.

She found them pretty fast. Three weeks into term she wrote a theatre review for *Broadsheet*. Laura found it – she kept up with undergraduate opinion by skimming through student publications – and brought it to Jacob to read; and thereafter articles and reviews by Imogen Standish appeared regularly in the student press – standard undergraduate fare, callow and strenuously witty. Laura saw her fairly often in King's and passed on messages of: 'Tell Jacob I'll visit him soon'; but she did not come, and he did not invite her.

'Why don't you?' Laura asked in January. 'You haven't seen her except that once.'

'I don't want her to think she's got to visit me just because I live in the city where she's a student. And she can't be all that keen; she tells you she'll come to see me, but she doesn't.'

'I think you're both being excessively considerate. She probably doesn't want you to think that *you've* got to see *her*. And maybe she's shy about calling on you again without being invited.'

180

'Shy? Writing in that smartass tone? Huh.'

'That's bravado more than self-confidence, don't you think?'

'Hmph, you're just being charitable.' He thought it over. 'But maybe you're right.'

A fortnight later he halfway enjoyed something Imogen had written; and, when he met her outside King's one February afternoon, as he was going to Laura's rooms with a pile of printout from the maths lab, he stopped and said, 'I liked your review of Nola Clendinning's exhibition.'

She laughed. 'Yes – it's the only thing I've written that you *would* like.'

For a moment, as she twinkled at him, he felt only chagrin – was he so obvious? Then it faded, and he was left with the old feeling of kinship. She must, after all, know him quite well. On impulse he said, 'Let's have tea,' and gestured towards the Copper Kettle.

'Yes, let's – but come to my room; the Copper Kettle is too dire.'

Jacob dumped his printout, and they crossed the river to her room in Garden Hostel. But, once there, she talked with such unremitting vivacity, as if she must entertain him, that his sense of kinship faded, and he wished he had not come. Perhaps his unease was contagious, for, after refilling their mugs, she stopped talking, and they sat in silence gazing at the gas fire and blowing steam off their tea.

'How are your parents?' he asked eventually.

Imogen looked at him over her mug. 'Fine.'

Her curt tone stirred his curiosity. 'Fine, but . . . ?'

'There's no "but". It's just that it's the first time you've mentioned them, and I wondered if you'd mind if *I* did.'

'Heavens, no, why should I?'

'Well, Mother and Father do. They never talk about you, and if I do, they get edgy and change the subject.'

'You mean they're still cross about – ' He stopped.

She smiled. 'It's all right. I know they quarrelled with you about Florence. I wormed it out of Mother after Naomi's last party, when you were all looking daggers at one another – she told me they'd thought you had too much influence over me and asked you to see me less often, and you'd got huffy and walked out. I said no wonder, and she admitted they'd been in the wrong. But they're still cross with you for holding a grudge about it.'

'What?'

'Mother said she rang and apologised, and you said you'd get in touch, but you never did.'

'Hmph. I didn't say I'd get in touch, I said: "Keep in touch".'

'On purpose? – So you *do* hold it against them?'

Jacob sighed. 'Listen, Frances didn't tell you the whole thing. Some of what they said went too deep to be mended just by saying sorry. But they're the ones who cold-shouldered me at Naomi's parties – I was ready to be pleasant to *them*.'

'How fascinating. What did they say that was so unforgivable?'

He shook his head. 'I don't want to grumble about them to you.'

'Oh, I wouldn't mind; I know they're not perfect – though they're not as bad as all that. I think you're rather hard on them. Coming up here has made me appreciate them more . . . I've begun to see how enlightened they are . . .'

'Mm-hmm?'

'Oh . . .' She was looking down, rubbing her finger round the rim of her mug. 'At school it wasn't surprising that lots of people's parents were awfully strict – we were younger and all that. But it's amazing that so many people up here have to keep their lives secret from their parents. I've never had to do that with Mother.' She raised her eyes.

An announcement. Humph. She didn't need to hang up a sign: she was nineteen, she had been to a coeducational school, her parents were, as she put it, 'enlightened', and this was 1978. He had assumed that she must have had at least one love affair by now – and she should know him better than to be watching him for signs of disapproval.

Then he remembered that he was almost as old as some of those amazingly strict parents – no wonder she was a little uncertain of his reaction. 'Yes, you are lucky,' he said lightly. 'Same as me. The first person I slept with I told Aline and Isaac about. But parents like them were pretty unusual in those days, and I had to work up my nerve, even though I knew they'd be okay –'

Imogen had relaxed with his first words. 'And what did they say?'

'More or less: How nice, and: Do you know about contraception – which I did, because that was in a book they'd left around – and: Be sure you use it. What about you?'

'Me?' – startled. 'I use it.'

'No, dope. What did Frances and Oliver say?' For the first time he felt at ease with Imogen; it was like the old days.

'Well, I told Mother two summers ago, because Thurstan was coming to West Horton, and I wanted him in my room, not us sneaking off and all that.'

'Thurstan? Not Ben?'

'Ben?' She seemed puzzled. 'Oh yes – Ben. We didn't – that was just kid-stuff. Actually there was Tim before Thurstan. I wasn't going to tell Mother about him, but she wasn't upset about Thurstan at all, just interested, so I told her about Timmy, too; and since then I've told her about everyone.'

' "Everyone"? Must be quite a list,' he said teasingly, more curious, and less happy with the idea, than he let on.

'Eleven.' She glanced at him narrowly. 'That's what you're wondering, isn't it?'

Jacob did not like being so transparent. 'Maybe – or maybe you were waiting for a chance to tell me.'

'A bit of both, maybe' – snappishly. 'Tell you what: in future I'll keep you up to date, then we'll both be happy.'

They looked at each other with a touch of hostility, then laughed, backed off and changed the subject – so successfully that it was quite a while before he noticed the time and remembered he had work to do.

He was glad he had had tea with Imogen, he decided on his way back across the river; it seemed that something of their old bond was still there – though he did not know quite what to make of her precocious social composure, or her brittle-bright Cambridge patter, through which the voice of the Imogen he remembered was so seldom audible, or her formidable list. Eleven, he thought, setting his foot on Laura's staircase. At her age he had slept with two girls. Even now only with one, two (Sheila), three (Liz), four five six, seven (Laura was seven), eight . . . nine . . . ten. Double-check. Ten. He knew the number perfectly well. Ten lovers in thirteen years, as against Imogen's eleven in three. Could she be serious about men whom she went through at such a rate?

'I don't see why not,' said Laura. 'It's an average of, what, three months per affair – that's time enough to be serious about somebody. Besides, I don't think you're worried about Imogen's soul; you're envious. – Don't yelp like that.' There was a malicious gleam in her light eyes. 'She's barely started, and already she's ahead of you. You're score-keeping.'

'Oh!' – outraged. Then: 'Uh . . . maybe. Crumbs, how awful.'

Laura relented. 'Well, at least I'm as bad as you. I did a calculation too – and if she keeps on at that rate, do you know how many men she'll have slept with by the time she's our age? Seventy-three!'

Chapter 38

NE MORNING IN March, over breakfast, Jacob brought up the question of children, and he and Laura had one of their long, miserable discussions about when and if – discussions that had changed little over the years, except to grow more painful for both of them. Especially this one: he felt jagged about an attachment she had recently formed, and he was sourer than usual. Laura clearly guessed why; her tone was gentle when at last she said, 'I've a supervision at ten, I've got to go. I'm sorry, love – I wish for your sake that I weren't always so caught up in work –'

'Work – huh,' he replied savagely. 'You're saying no because you're caught up in Dieter.'

The row that followed was bitter – and cut off abruptly because she had to dash off to her supervision. They made up on the doorstep, but so barely and unsatisfactorily that he could hardly concentrate all day and finally, abandoning his terminal at the maths lab, headed for King's. He would call on her briefly, just to apologise better. She would not be put out, though they were not supposed to turn up on each other in the evening without notice; she knew what this stage was like.

But she was expecting Dieter at any moment. 'I can head him off,' she said when she saw the state Jacob was in.

'No, don't bother.' He stumped down the staircase, feeling sore.

'Hullo, Jacob.' It was Imogen. She inspected him. 'You don't look very cheerful.' He was too dispirited to contradict, and she turned him round, whisked him across the river and up to her room, and made him a strong cup of coffee. 'Now,' she said, sitting down on the bed. 'Why so glum?'

'Oh . . .' he shrugged; but she waited in an unrelenting this-will-be-good-for-you silence that eventually drove him to describe his quarrel with Laura. Not the part about children – that was too private; but his worries about Dieter. 'She says I still come first; but I don't know . . . He's tall and blond and handsome and charming. He's a colleague of hers, too; and she sometimes wishes she could talk to me about her work; but biochemistry is sort of like a language – you can't understand anything advanced without lots of elementary training; and if she can talk to him about work, on her own level . . . it's scary. And he even likes star-watching. So do Laura and I – we usually clip the monthly "Night Sky" chart from *The Times* and go out and have a look at what's going on up there. But she's got keener since meeting him – the two of them even go out and use the university telescopes at Madingley.'

'And you feel left out and overtaken.'

'Mm-hmm. I know it's childish – I'm not really *that* interested. But when I'm feeling really paranoid, I worry that Laura would rather even watch the *eclipse* with him than me.'

'There's going to be an eclipse?'

'Next September. Full eclipse of the moon. We've been looking forward to it for ages, praying it won't be cloudy; and a friend of a friend of Laura's is giving an eclipse party to look at it through Newnham's telescope, and we've been invited. But now . . .'

Imogen leaned forward, half smiling, half serious. 'You don't *really* think she wants to see the eclipse with Dieter. It's her being able to talk about work that's worrying you. I'll tell you what I think, though – I think you should trust her. She

185

says you come first, and she won't change her mind just because she and Dieter can talk tenderly about molecules – and certainly not because he's tall and blond and handsome.'

'Yah, he's a walking Hitler Youth poster.' Jacob stopped in embarrassment. 'Jesus, how awful – my subconscious showing – he was hardly born when the war ended – it's just that he's so goyisch you can't imagine.'

'You're jealous of him!'

She sounded so surprised that he laughed in spite of his gloom. 'I am indeed, pet. I don't suppose you know what that's like, you and your eleven men.'

She tensed, then said mischievously, 'You're out of date. Twelve. But that's the point. How can you be jealous, when it was you who taught me that people needn't be?'

'Me?'

'Don't you remember? Years ago. Laura was in Norfolk with some man, and you told me about how you both had affairs and weren't jealous – '

'I couldn't have said that; it's never been true.'

'Oh – not in those words – more that it wasn't as important as being open to other possibilities as well as each other. I remembered *that*: it's been something of, er, a guiding light to me.'

'Good Lord. Do you mean that it's because of something I said that you have this' – he made his tone easy – 'this train of paramours?'

'Of course not. You just put something into words that I'd been beginning to think already.' A wicked light came into her eye; she had heard the disapproval beneath his careful neutrality. 'But when one thing . . . led to another . . . what you'd said was . . . sort of an inspiration.' She was laughing at him up her sleeve, the sly child.

'So I set you on the primrose path. Corrupting a minor, that was.' Light as a soufflé; he wasn't going to be outfaced in insouciance by a youngster. 'But what about you?' he added curiously. 'Don't you ever get jealous at all?'

Imogen acknowledged that she did sometimes get twinges; he said that 'twinges' was just the right word; and they swapped symptoms in high good humour. He had quite forgotten that Laura was with Dieter. Half an hour later, passing the foot of her staircase on his way home, he remembered, and felt

186

excluded and desolate, but comforted himself into a sense of proportion, at least, by muttering: 'Twinges, it's just twinges.'

For a while after that evening Jacob hoped that Imogen was growing out of her new manner. But there were few signs of the old Imogen in her constant stream of articles; and the person who stopped in to say goodbye to him and Laura before going down for the summer was definitely new Imogen, fizzing as if a moment's quiet would bore them – or her – to death.

'*Broadsheet* is giving me a byline next year,' she announced. 'Isn't that fun?'

'Congratulations,' said Laura.

'Oh, it's not my *beaux yeux*, it's the magic of the Standish name. They say Father's an old-fashioned establishment journalist, but it's still me they give plums to . . .' She rattled on, describing the politics of undergraduate publications in excessive detail: though she made only a short visit, she had them suppressing yawns by the end of it.

'Have a good summer in America,' she said on the doorstep.

'And you in Rome.'

'I will – I'll tell you all about it when I get back. Goodbye.'

'No, keep it to yourself,' he muttered under his breath as she walked away down the terrace; and, to Laura: 'This has been going on for a hell of a time to be just a phase. I think she's stuck like that.'

Imogen waved and disappeared; a second later she bobbed back and ran part of the way towards them. 'I meant to say – have a good eclipse. I hope it's a nice clear night for you. Goodbye again!'

'Well, I'll be . . .' said Jacob, touched. 'She's the funniest mixture, remembering the eclipse – it was way back in March that I told her how much we wanted to see it.'

Laura chuckled. 'You've forgotten that that was the night you were feeling so miserable. I was the ogre who wanted to see the eclipse with Dieter, remember? How could she forget? Still, it was nice of her to wish us luck.'

They needed luck: they almost missed it. After America they had gone to Laura's parents in Wales for their annual duty visit. They left in good time on the sixteenth, after an early

187

lunch; but their fan belt broke outside Ludlow, and it was late afternoon by the time it was mended – too late to get to Cambridge for the eclipse party. But there would probably be no moon-gazing at Newnham anyhow; the sky was heavy with rolling black clouds, and they drove across the west country and the Midlands through a sullen twilight into early darkness.

They were bypassing Birmingham on the motorway when Jacob exclaimed, 'I can see stars!'

'Really? Oh, yes! But no moon.' Laura glanced at her watch. 'Of course not, it's still eclipsed.'

Then there was a white haze in the sky before them; a brightness; a radiance; and finally a sliver that might or might not be – damn the lights of Birmingham – yes, definitely was – the moon, sliding out fast from under the earth's shadow. They were too late for the party and the telescope, but at least they could get off the main roads, into the dark. Laura put her foot down, Jacob read the map with a torch and found dark by-roads, and they hared across Bedfordshire after the moon, hanging out of the windows, loonies, as it grew enormous in the cloudless sky ahead of them, waxing from dark to full in an hour instead of half a month, like a flower unfolding on film in minutes by time-lapse photography.

Then, almost at the full, it dimmed. Clouds? No: Bedford. Turn round to get back into the dark, losing sight of the moon in the meantime, or risk missing the end of the eclipse in Bedford's garish maw? They risked it; Laura careered through the empty centre and the orange outskirts, and they gained the dark high road to Cambridge and stopped the car with eight minutes to spare.

The moon was so full that it was hard to believe it could get any fuller. They walked a short way into a field and watched, in clear brilliant silence, the absolute orb. Occasional heedless cars went by; the moon magically fulfilled itself in the sky overhead: an illumination in the stillness by the flat high road. For a quarter of an hour they watched, making awed small-talk. Then they looked at each other and nodded. Enough was enough.

Chapter 39

MOGEN CALLED ON them when she came up in October, still rapturous about Rome, but indignant about the oppression of Italian women by the church – men – the state. England was paradise in comparison. 'I didn't really see how dreadful it was till this year. I went to women's movement meetings all summer – and the things I learned about! I used to think of women's liberation as one of those sensible things Mother does, not something I needed to worry about. But now I see how important it is – and not just in Italy. In fact, I was wondering, Laura . . . you're in the town group, aren't you; and I'd rather join that than a university group . . .' She sounded bashful, for once. 'Do you suppose I could . . . ?'

'Certainly,' said Laura. 'Mind you, it's all small groups – I can't even remember them all. There's women in education, the National Abortion Campaign, a group reading Marx, Women's Aid, the pregnancy-testing group –'

'The pregnancy-testing group is what you're in, isn't it? Would it be okay if I came along to that?'

'Of course. Come next Wednesday – here, I'll write down the details.'

Imogen tucked the paper into her big soft conker-brown bag, unmistakably Italian and elegant, like her sandals and her long striped T-shirt, and, brightening, started talking with glee about the fearsome responsibility of filling up her *Broadsheet* column every week. 'I'll have to do a lot of socialising, it'll be simply dire.'

And that, Jacob guessed, suppressing a groan, was the last he would hear of anything so unfashionably earnest as the women's movement.

It was a good guess. Imogen was no longer shy about visiting him uninvited; and all autumn she called on him at least once a fortnight without ever mentioning the women's movement or the pregnancy-testing group – without, for that matter, speaking about anything serious, or seriously about anything; until sometimes his irritated boredom stayed within bounds only because her high spirits and sparkling good humour were disarming – and because she never stayed long.

He didn't think he was just being priggish. What irritated him was not that she went to dozens of parties in pursuit of copy, but that she frankly enjoyed being lionised as a journalist and was quite a lioniser herself; not the smartass style of her column, but her apparently unironical pride in what she wrote; not even her three new, concurrently running affairs (fifteen!), but the way she spoke of them, so flippantly that he was driven to wonder whether she had not ended up a young libertine.

Why did she come to see him so regularly, anyhow? He didn't provide her with copy, wasn't entertaining – 'fun', to use the word she sprayed at everything that wasn't 'dire' – and didn't know the people she gossiped about – wasn't interested in them – didn't want to hear about them. 'Academic gossip bores me silly,' he told her one day, 'whether it's about senior members or undergraduates. I just don't have any connections with the university any more, don't you realise? – except two indirect ones: one, I buy time on its computer; and, two, I live with a don.'

'Not two: three. You know me,' she said complacently.

'Imp! That doesn't mean I want to know what some creep in the Footlights eats for breakfast.'

There was no doubt that she was sweet and engaging as she rattled out her frivolities. She did not look the way she talked, but like the old Imogen grown up: her expressions delicate, soft, candid, glowing; her flecked hazel eyes as eager as ever, as alert, as beautiful under her straight black eyebrows – and as heart-touchingly, misleadingly serious. How could she look that serious without being so? It was confusing – infuriating:

had she been anyone but Imogen, he would have chucked her.

But she *was* Imogen – even now, not just in memory: flower of a high civilisation, the person whose qualities he instinctively called to mind whenever he tried to explain why he had stayed in England. In almost every way she was as she had been. That was the pity of it now; for, the more he saw of her, as autumn deepened towards December, the more he feared that she was, as he put it to himself, lost: in all her prosperous purity and brightness; flushed with the promise of youth; bubbling with good nature and sweetness; intelligent, educated, cultivated, articulate; sensitive and tender – that with all this she was lost, lost to something he could hardly define, except as a fear that she had forsworn, had fled from gravity: that in the end her parents had been too much for her; that she had not been able to keep up her resistance to their glittering bait: they had won: she had become what they wanted her to be.

But when he said so to Laura, she rounded on him smartly. 'Chuck her indeed. If she weren't Imogen, you'd be more tolerant. From what I see of her in pregnancy-testing group –'

'I thought she was too frivolous to stick with that. Why didn't you tell me?'

'Why didn't you ask? She's also sitting in on the Women in Society paper, and she's in a group that's reading the *German Ideology*. Frivolous, my eye.'

'Why doesn't she ever talk about those things instead of parties and men?' he asked weakly.

'She probably thinks that sounding flip and hyper-cool makes her seem adult and sophisticated.'

'But all those men – the way she talks about them?' – retreating to what felt like firm ground.

'When *I* was an undergraduate, and a graduate student, too, come to that, I talked about my, er, sex life at every chance, to show the world I wasn't an earnest-virgin type. I suppose you were always above such juvenile behaviour?'

She knew the answer perfectly well; Jacob grinned in defeat. 'But at least' – his last stand – 'it was only about one person at a time.'

'Times have changed. Heavens, man, you've thought well of Imogen from the day you met her. Have you so little trust in

191

consistency of character that you've changed your mind just because she's sleeping with everybody in sight?'

Laura was right, all the way. He was ashamed of himself and began to revise his opinion of Imogen.

Chapter 40

HICH WAS JUST as well – though no amount of revision could have prepared him for the bombshell she tossed at him just before going down at the end of term.

It was a rainy evening, and her secondhand fur coat was slick with wet like a drowned rat. Jacob hung it up, and she pulled off her wool cap with a flourish.

'Oh,' he said with pleasure. 'You've cut it.'

'You like it?'

'Indeed I do.' He looked at her: straight dark-brown fringe, straight short hair, a look of mischief, a look of resoluteness. 'Yes indeed. Did you have it done for Christmas?'

Imogen sat down without answering, so he began to repeat his question.

She stopped him with: 'No, for you.'

'What?'

'Not for Christmas, for you.'

'What?'

'My hair. I didn't get it cut for Christmas, I did it because you said you liked it short better.'

'I did? Actually, I do; but did I really say so? How rude of me.'

'Oh, it wasn't rude: I asked you, when I came up last year. You said long hair and no fringe looked better on Laura than me.'

It came back to him. 'And you remembered all this time?'

She nodded, gleaming at him. 'So. What's new?' he asked, smiling benignly and bracing himself for a budget of parties, lovers, and dog-eats-dog on *Broadsheet*.

She curled her feet up in the wing chair and pushed herself well back, as if digging in for a siege. 'I'm going down the day after tomorrow,' she began, 'and I've something to say, and it's hard to say, so you'll have to forgive me if I'm awkward . . . but, you see, I've got to say it, because if I don't, nothing will happen, because you can't, because if you did, it would be inducement or something.' She looked hopefully to see if he had guessed what she was talking about.

Jacob guessed nothing.

She settled herself deeper against the back of the chair. 'Do you remember, when I was, oh, fourteen, and you asked me something, in Ely? Remember?'

He shook his head.

'I told you I'd had a crush on you, and you asked when. Remember now?'

He nodded. Light was dawning, but very faint.

'I said I didn't any more. But that wasn't true. The truth was,' squirming her spinal column back into the chair, 'the truth *is*, I've loved you for years. All along.' Backed up as far as she could go, she looked down at her hands, then, with visible resolve, straight at him.

'My dear child,' he said helplessly. What did one do? 'My dearest Imogen,' he began again, 'it's . . .'

Imogen looked stern in her effort to prepare for the worst.

'It's not *like* that, you know.'

She frowned slightly and said nothing.

'I'm not somebody you should be in love with, really I'm not.'
'Why not?'

'Well, I don't suppose you mean platonic love?'

She kept her eyes on him and shook her head.

'That's why, then. There isn't anything in it for you. The non-platonic variety – I couldn't . . . uh . . . reciprocate . . .'
'Why not?'

'Hmm . . .' Why not was obvious, how to express it was not. 'Because . . . because I've never exactly thought of myself as your father, but you're . . . no, you aren't my imaginary daughter any more, you're too old now – but you were until a few years ago. Lordy, Imogen, I've loved *you* since practically the day I met you, but only as a sort of daughter, not a – a lover. It'd be sort of like, uh, incest.'

'I can see it's a problem, but if it's the only one, I should think you could get over it.' The corners of her eyebrows were puckered up and inwards; she looked forbidding, a young Daniel.

'It's not the only one. For one thing, I'm a lot older than you. Sixteen years.'

'That doesn't matter to me,' she said quickly – an objection she had expected.

'It does to me. I'm a grown-up man, and I like – '

'Grown-up women, not children of twenty?'

'Mm-hmm.'

Her frown deepened. This she had not expected. 'I thought men your age liked younger women.' She was half joking, half not.

'Jesus,' he snapped, 'be your age.'

'That's the trouble, it seems – I am.'

They looked at each other and laughed, and both of them relaxed fractionally.

'The thing is, pet, it wouldn't be on, even if I were tempted to, uh, to seduce babes in arms' – now it was he who was only half joking – 'because – '

'But I'm trying to seduce *you*!'

'Even so, even so. It's not the age difference in itself – that wouldn't be a problem if you were my age and I were . . . let's see, you're twenty, I'm thirty-six . . . thirty-six plus sixteen . . . if I were fifty-two. But you're only just grown-up; and at this point I'm inevitably more . . . I don't know what the right word is – more powerful or something. It would be dangerous for you to . . . to care a lot about me.'

'But I do anyhow. And you aren't the sort of person who abuses power. I do see what you mean,' she conceded – not seeing it at all, he was sure – 'but it's not enough reason. What else?'

'Laura.'

'What about her?'

'I love her.'

'I know *that*.'

'I'm going to go on loving her.'

'Can't you love two of us? It was you that taught – '

194

'Imogen!' – in exasperation. 'Listen, I love Laura for good. There'll be other people probably, but not anybody to displace her. And you said you were in love with me.'

'Oh, is that all?' Her back eased a little. 'That's okay. I'm not talking about anything permanent.'

'Oh, aren't you?' he spoke rather drily. He had been feeling touched; now he was suspicious. Did she simply want to add an older man to her collection?

'I don't want to come between you and Laura,' she said earnestly, 'not at all. I was thinking of – of you and me . . . as something off to the side of you and Laura, like your other – '

'Our other attachments aren't "off to the side". We take them seriously. And we don't collect scalps.'

Back went Imogen's spine. 'Neither,' she said stiffly, 'do I. And by "off to the side" I only meant not dead central. Don't worry, I take you seriously.'

To his surprise Jacob half believed her; but he was sceptical enough to ask, 'What about the fifteen boyfriends?'

She laughed aloud. 'Oh, I take them seriously too.'

'Hmph.'

'It's true – I do. After all, you're serious about other people than Laura – why don't you think I can be the same?'

'It's the – the scale.'

'So many so fast can't be serious? – Yes, I'm beginning to think that myself. In principle it should be possible to be serious about a number of lovers – same as having several good friends. But in practice I'm afraid you're right. This autumn, especially, I've been stretching my feelings a bit thin. But that's not the same as not being serious. I've been serious about almost everybody I've been involved with – *and* loved them' – reading his mind. 'And loved you, too, all the time – and more than anyone else. I'm like you, you see' – looking impish – 'I like grown-up people, and most men my own age aren't grown-up. So I decided to say something. I guessed most of those reasons you've given against, er, you and me; and I guessed they'd keep you from even thinking about me that way, if I didn't say something. So I got my courage up, and I have. Said something.'

So they were back at that. 'My dear child,' he said, unconsciously repeating his first words. 'It's really *such* a bad idea. All those reasons, as you call them – they're real.'

'But what did you bring me up for, if not – ?'

'What a vulgar notion! I've never had any such thought in my head.'

Imogen flushed indignantly. 'I didn't mean it that way. I said it wrong. I know you didn't think anything like that; it's just that . . . that you *formed* me – I'm who I am because of you, more than anything – and so being in love with you, and – and – and you with me . . . seems like such a natural idea *now* – practically inevitable – even though it wasn't what you intended.'

He snorted, queasy at the idea of being spiritual father to a student-yellow-press scalp-hunter. 'I didn't see you often enough to have a big influence. Besides, your parents formed you, not me.'

'It wasn't how often, it was . . . knowing you. The idea of you. You see?'

'Golly,' he said, suddenly quite believing her and reduced to inanity by this glimpse of responsibilities carried almost unknowingly.

She stirred, hitched forward and put her feet on the floor. 'I think I'll be going now.'

Golly. She was setting a pace he was hard put to keep up with. 'Exit hopelessly love-smitten maiden?' He hoped the tone was right.

'Love-smitten – but not hopeless by any means. And certainly not a maiden.' Brisk. She stood up. 'I knew you'd say no; I just brought it up so that you can think about it. I'll wait for you to decide.'

'And you were such a shy little girl,' he said, looking up at her. She seemed remarkably cheerful for a girl who had not only taken the highly unorthodox step – even in these days – of making an advance to a man, but had also been turned down. 'Listen, don't get your hopes up. Seriously.' He stood up too. 'It's not a question of "deciding"; it's what I *feel*, and what I feel is' – he looked at her, his lovely Imogen, who said he had formed her – 'is that it's a matter of – of categories. You've been in one category in my feelings for such a long time that I can't change categories and feel a whole different way about you. You know?'

She smiled and nodded, curiously undismayed. Out in the hall she put on her damp cap and scarf and shrugged into

196

the wet rat with an, 'Ugh,' then said, 'Let's not let my, er, declaration make any difference to our friendship, all right? Oh, and could you please tell Laura from me that I'm not trying to muscle in? Oh dear, you look so solemn. Don't worry about me. I've felt like this a long time, and I'm not pining away.'

'Okay' – dubiously.

'No, I mean it. If your mind stays made up the way it is now, I won't be upset or feel rejected. It's just that I decided I didn't have anything to lose by speaking, except maybe a little pride; and that if I *didn't* speak, *nothing* would happen. I knew it was just a long chance. Really.' And she did look happy and at ease – more so than he: she had the situation in hand, while he was still breathless with surprise.

'Good heavens,' Laura said meditatively, tucked up cross-legged on the carpet. And again, 'Good heavens. I can see what you mean about incest; it's knowing her since she was a little girl. But – now that she's brought it up, do you find yourself thinking it'd be nice, if only . . . ?'

'No, funnily enough. I simply can't imagine it, there's some sort of barrier. Partly knowing her since she was little, yes; but her age is the nub of it. I really do like my women grown-up.' He smiled fondly at his grown-up Laura.

'One thing, though: you misjudged her, with all that worry about men and frivolity. Admit.'

'I admit. She's serious, all right, though Lord knows what about. Saying she's "loved me for years" – what does she think she means by "love" in a context like that?'

Whatever she meant, it was not anything frivolous. 'You formed me,' she had said – 'the idea of you.' He was touched, and flattered; it was becoming remarkably easy to think well of her, even to be glad that she was finding out how to have fun – something she had not learned from Frances and Oliver, who did not have much real sense of humour and were only wry and witty, not gay. He had indeed been a prig to fret because her education in gaiety included lionising and being lionised, and writing silly articles, and fifteen young men.

Chapter 41

ACOB AND IMOGEN had agreed not to let her declaration make any difference between them – but surely it must, especially since he knew that he would not change his mind about an affair with her. However, they met in January with nothing more than a smilish trace of self-consciousness, which soon disappeared; and no awkwardness grew between them as time went by. Her declaration did make a difference, of course, but not an uncomfortable one; it was simply there, making slight eddies in the surface of their converse.

They did not discuss the subject again at length, but to his surprise they did allude to it – and without embarrassment, largely because Imogen set a tone by mentioning it, on her very first visit, in a relaxed, faintly amused manner. 'I was rather tactless when I talked to you before Christmas,' she said as she was leaving.

'Hmmh?' He could think of numerous epithets to describe Imogen on that occasion, but 'tactless' was not one of them.

'You see, I meant to ask you if you were involved with anybody besides Laura, because obviously if you were already up to your ears in, er, romance, you wouldn't be interested in me anyhow, so I wouldn't have said anything.' She flashed him a teasing glance. 'I'd have bided my time. But when I got here, I was so scared I forgot all about it and plunged straight in.'

'You sure did. However, if you're curious –'

'Oh no,' she said, looking intensely interested.

'The answer is, yes and no. There's somebody – but she's married, and her husband doesn't know, which I find disconcerting, and she's moved to Colchester, so I don't see her much – not often enough to keep it alive, really.'

'And Laura?'

'Still with Dieter. But he's going back to Germany in August – poor Laura.'

She looked at him keenly. 'Oh. You don't mind about Dieter any more.'

'Mind? Oh yes – last spring. No, no, I got over that.'

'Oh good. Well, I just wanted you to know that I hadn't *meant* to be tactless, it just happened.'

'It never occurred to me, pet. I hope you haven't been losing sleep over it.'

'Don't worry, if I lost sleep over you, I'd have died of insomnia years ago.' And she was off with a jaunty wave.

A couple of weeks later she told him that she had chucked her three men.

'All three? How extravagant.' Without thinking, he added: 'Not because of me, I hope.'

Imogen laughed. 'I knew you'd think that. No, I told you I thought I was spreading myself thin; and I met somebody I thought I could be very interested in. And even for me four would be too much to handle, so I've made a clean sweep in favour of Adrian. Adrian Willis. He's a graduate student in history.'

'I'm glad your *grande passion* doesn't keep you from getting on with it,' he said drily.

'You are *too* antediluvian. Besides, you don't realise – I met him a month ago, but I didn't sleep with him till last week. That's the longest I've ever waited after getting to know somebody.'

'Such self-restraint!' he teased. 'I went with Sheila a whole year before I slept with her.'

'Because she wouldn't say yes before, I'll bet.'

'Ouf. A hole in one, young 'un.'

Jacob enjoyed her company more than before Christmas, partly because her declaration did make him more inclined to think well of her, but chiefly because she was, at last, growing out of her new manner. She had abandoned breathless extremes of scorn and enthusiasm and begun to talk naturally, in a way that gave scope for shades other than black and white; she no longer chattered uncritically about the undergraduate whirl; and at Easter she decided to give up her *Broadsheet* column. It was getting to be a bore.

That was all she said, but he thought he might have had something to do with her decision. He also suspected the influence of Adrian, who was politically and intellectually fervent and disdained the romps and squabbles of apolitical undergraduates. Jacob liked him . . . well enough – he was all right – a decent guy . . . but . . . He didn't dare voice, even to Laura, his belief that Adrian was not quite vivid or extreme enough for Imogen.

Her growth out of her social-butterfly stage was rapid and thorough; there was hardly a trace of butterfly in the young woman who sat on the deep window ledge in Laura's rooms one pleasant evening in May, talking about what she should do after graduation next year.

'Father thinks I should go into journalism – but unless I changed my name, it'd be *Broadsheet* all over again: I'd shoot straight up, but not through my own efforts; and that's such a bore. Adrian wants me to change to SPS for Part II, then write a thesis on something to do with feminism. But that's not right for me either. I don't have anything I want to *say*. What I want is – is – to *do* something.'

'But what?' asked Laura. 'Hasn't anything appealed to you especially?'

'Not yet. Sometimes I think I'd like to be in Italy, but I can hardly make a career out of that.'

'Once,' said Jacob, 'when you were about fifteen, you said that all you wanted was something useful and interesting to do. Remember?'

'Did I really? What a greedy child I was. But,' laughing at herself, 'but that's still "all" I want. Oh, I remember – that was the time you lectured me about finding a vocation. I've never forgotten *that* – that's why I'm trying to think about things well in advance. It hasn't worked so far – but I'm not fussed; I always *do* land on my feet,' mock-tragically, 'don't I?'

'Sure, pet. Knee deep in cushions.'

'That's me – a princess in search of a pea. Well, I'd better get back to my books. Goodnight.'

By now their friendship had become utterly easy, and very pleasant. He had long since stopped worrying that she would be hurt at his not changing his mind. She had not changed hers – she sometimes referred jokingly to her *grande passion* – but he never caught her so much as glancing at him wistfully; and she was clearly happy with Adrian. All in all he was glad she had spoken; they might otherwise have been a long time reaching this comfortable state that was already, for all the years between them, a friendship between adults.

Before going off to Rome for the summer, this year as English-language tutor to two rich children, she told him she would write to him often – and did in fact do so. In her final letter she announced that she had decided what to do after graduating. 'I'm going to teach English here in Rome, but at a language school, not as a private tutor. I like teaching English, and I think I'm good at it. The job fell into my lap, of course, like everything – the head of the school is my friend Antonella from the women's movement, and she just offered it when I said I wished I could work in Italy. It isn't a vocation, but the point is that, by working half time at the language school, I'll earn just about enough to work the other half of my time, unpaid, at the abortion counselling centre that I told you about in my last letter. I don't know if that's exactly a vocation either, but it's "useful and interesting". And I've got a place to live, too. Antonella's got a one-and-a-half room flat that's part of hers but separate, that she sublets, and I can have it. So I'm all set.'

Chapter 42

O N THE LAST day of September Laura's friend from Newnham rang Jacob. 'Haven't been able to get hold of Laura,' she said in a confident staccato.

'She's in Holland till the eighth, giving a talk and seeing friends.'

'Naughty Laura, leaving you behind! – You had to stay? – Work? – Deadline? Of course, you computer people always have odd hours. Such a pity she's away – you two missed the eclipse last year – there's a full moon on the fifth – I know how the college telescope works now – eclipse party so successful – I thought, why not have a moon party myself this year – just a very few people – a peek at the moon. But why not come anyhow, on your own – unless,' archly, 'Laura would mind . . .?'

Jacob hesitated – he usually avoided academic parties. But this one would be small, and he was rather lonely without Laura, and seeing the moon would be fun – and he really should show this silly woman that he and Laura were independent beings.

There were at least thirty people in the big college room when he arrived, and more coming every minute. 'Quite a party you have here,' he said with well-hidden dismay. If this were just a very few people, he would hate to see her idea of a crowd.

'So glad you like it – last year's such a success – I'm sure – of course no eclipse this year, but – So sorry Laura couldn't come – so glad you could.'

The couple behind him claimed her attention, and he moved on and found the drinks. Ah. Newnham had a decent cellar;

Volnay '70 and Mâcon Lugny '75 would take the worst edge off the boredom he could tell he was in for by looking round the assemblage – all couples, all respectably dressed, all talking shop, though a few polite souls, upon learning that he was not connected to the university, dutifully switched to small-talk: gardens; the weather; the dreadful numbers of tourists this year; their trips to America, since he was American; the coming season at the Arts – the Theatre, of course, not the Cinema. He went to the cinema, did he? – A lot? How interesting. They would go more often, but there were so few good films these days – and babysitting problems – and old films always turned up on the box . . .

He knew the conversation by heart; he had been having it at parties all his adult life. He extricated himself from one, and another, refilled his glass with Mâcon Lugny, snatched a sausage roll from a passing tray and leaned against a wall near the wine table, bored and lazy, to eat and drink in peace. He would just finish this glass, and maybe try the Volnay, then slope off without seeing the moon – which, after all, a solitary stroller along the Backs might gaze upon with the naked eye.

'Jacob – all on your own!' His hostess bore down on him with flapping wings. 'Let's see, there's somebody else – where is she?' – peering about. 'I see her – be right back.' She lunged into the crowd and returned. 'This is – where's she got to? Ah – behind me. Sorry, dear.' She stood aside, repeating, 'This is – '

'Good heavens,' said Jacob. 'Imogen!'

Imogen gleamed all over with delight. 'I didn't expect to see you here.'

'You two know each other?'

'I've known Jacob since I was six,' said Imogen.

'Ah. Childhood friends.'

They both burst out laughing. 'I was twenty-two when we met,' he explained.

Their hostess said to Imogen, 'You don't *look* that old, my dear – Oh!' turning to Jacob, 'I meant – ' She laughed. 'I've already got one foot in my mouth – better retreat while I've still got the other to hop on.'

He regarded Imogen with deep pleasure. Her black-lashed hazel eyes were very light in her Italy-brown face, and her bright yellow jeans and cobalt-blue top were wonderfully

203

dashing in this room full of outmoded frilly frocks. 'You know, you're a one-woman relief team. I'm bored up to here – I was just about to leave. Here, have some of the Mâcon Lugny, it's lovely. So. Why are you up so early?'

'Oh, I got back from Rome last week; and do you remember there was a group of us wanting a flat? Well, a whole house turned up, and we've all come up early to get it ready. It's in Norwich Street, only about three minutes from your place.' She looked about. 'Where's Laura?'

'Holland – ' he began.

But at this point a sea-murmur swept the party: it was really dark by now – time to go and see the moon. The room heaved, and, reluctantly at first, people began drifting in a straggly crocodile down the stairs and along several corridors to the porter's lodge; then through a gate, along more corridors, through the gardens and out of another gate, which the porter unlocked and locked with a big key – several times, as laggards cried that they were locked in; then raggle-taggle across dark playing fields that got darker as heavy clouds began to scud across the sky out of nowhere and pile up in front of the moon. Loud middle-class women's voices, even louder without their faces, kept exclaiming: 'Isn't this exciting,' and, 'Will it ever come out?' Nobody had brought torches – it had been assumed that the moon would light the way – and women in long Laura Ashley frocks and high-heeled shoes were being jolly and pretending that they did not mind stumbling about in the dark. Jacob and Imogen, walking together, passed a stationary couple; the woman was muttering loudly: '. . . my ankle. I really did twist it. I don't want to go on'; and the man was hissing: 'You might as well . . .'

They came to a hedge. An old man popped up over it. 'Your party is going along that way,' he said, pointing with a formal little bow. 'I'm waiting here to show the rest where to go.'

They bowed and threaded the gap in the hedge. 'That's a country accent,' she said after a bit. 'What's a countryman doing lurking behind hedges in the middle of Cambridge?'

They looked back. The old man's arm was just visible, pointing the next group towards the path. 'Like an out-of-doors butler,' said Jacob.

There were voices ahead and behind, but no one in sight; only shapes that defined themselves as not trees or bushes by moving. Then the great cloud hiding the moon began to roll off. Its edges went grey; the sky turned a deep violet with a dazzle to it; now the edges of the cloud were white; then brilliant white; then the moon burst through and sailed triumphantly into a deep cloudlessness. Jacob and Imogen had stopped to watch, and they were overtaken by people walking faster by its light and talking even louder than before.

At the conservatory there was a mêlée. 'Blast, where is it?' said their hostess, shifting the telescope about.

'Shall I look it up in this?' Her husband reached down a book.

'Of course not. I should be able to find the *moon*.'

He opened the book anyhow, went to the door, and looked up at the moon and down at the page, frowning.

'Did you see that book?' Imogen whispered. 'It's called *The Amateur Astronomer*.'

'Not really; you're having me on.'

'Really.'

They went outside, and Jacob, stooping, fiddled with his shoelace and looked up. *The Amateur Astronomer* it was.

Noises of triumph: their hostess had found the moon. Her husband closed the book, with his finger marking the page, as if it might yet come in handy. People crowded round the telescope, taking turns. 'Isn't it *wonderful*,' they cried and, 'You could almost touch it,' and, 'It's so *clear*.'

'This is stupid,' Jacob grumbled in an undertone. 'With all this racket the moon won't be one bit magical. It'll just be bigger, that's all.'

But, when it came their turn, the moon was unquestionably magical: not a flat watermarked disc floating weightlessly through the ether, but an astonishingly three-dimensional ball, globular as any orange, full-bellied and heavy, its edges shimmering a little, its mountains and craters crisp and bold.

At last they gave way to others and, having fought their way outside again, looked at the moon with a sense of being better acquainted with it. 'It can only be downhill from here,' he said. 'I'm going to vamoose. D'you want to come or stay?'

'I'll "vamoose" too. I was in despair till I saw you; I didn't know *anyone*.'

They strolled back over the playing fields, then down Malting Lane and across Coe Fen, all bright now under the moon. Jacob was reminded of walking beside her in Florence, on their last morning there, when prematurely he had felt a faint awareness that she was a woman. He had the same sensation now. Insensibly he walked closer to her. Their arms brushed; he moved away. He glanced at her sidelong. She was looking, now down at the humpy field, now up at the white majestic moon. He looked up at it himself, walking along, feeling happy.

Imogen stumbled. Automatically his hand shot out and grasped her upper arm to keep her from falling.

She righted herself, wincing. 'I've turned my ankle,' she said with a reminiscent chuckle. 'Like that woman, remember?'

He had not let go of her. Seeing his fingers tight upon her short sleeve, he remembered with a shiver his hand locked on her bare arm in the Pazzi chapel, and raised his eyes to her face. It was still half wincing, still half alight with fading mirth: a white face, under the blanching moon; straight black eyebrows under short straight black hair; eyes uncoloured by darkness, with glittering moon-highlights; a face he knew better, he thought, than any other: Imogen.

'Imogen,' he said. She said nothing, only watched him with eyes now quite serious. He looked down again, saw that he was gripping her harder than he knew, and released her. His hand felt bereft. Without thinking, he stepped closer. Thinking only: Just this once, he touched her cheek with the back of his hand and kissed her.

Not just this once. Just this twice, tenderly, kiss meeting kiss. That'll be all.

Just this twice was two too many. He looked at her; she opened her eyes and looked back. If you're going to get out, now's the time, he told himself. Find a light, mature phrase, refer to the influence of the moon.

Now you've done it, said another inner voice, drowning out the first. That's torn it, You're in the soup now. Now was the time – but now he'd done it. By the light of Imogen's grave, blanched face he could read the truth of what he had been feeling all evening, from the moment he saw her, brown and light-eyed and shiny, and as much out of place at the dull party as he, where Laura – he thought treacherously – would have managed to fit in.

'Imogen,' he said again.

She blinked and waited.

'This is ridiculous.'

She smiled.

'It's banal, you know? – moonlight unhinges ageing number-cruncher. Lunacy, as in.'

She chuckled.

'You realise this wouldn't have happened if it weren't for *that*?' – he waved an accusatory hand at the moon.

She nodded.

'Damn it, who wants to act like some idiot out of *A Midsummer Night's Dream*?'

'You do.'

He laughed with a sense of release. 'I guess you're right.' He touched her hair. 'You're a vile seducer, you know that?'

Her head bobbed under his hand.

'Listen – d'you remember what I said last year?'

'You said a lot of things that I remember,' she replied astringently.

'That there's no future in this.'

'Oh yes, I remember that. I know.'

'Seriously. It's a dead end. I'm with Laura, nothing else can be permanent.'

She looked straight at him. 'I don't want anything permanent myself.'

Full marks for spirit. He could still back off, and should; this could only end one way – with Imogen badly hurt. But it was not a time for backing off, not with her hair sleek and cool-warm under his hand. 'Okay then, junior, let's go home.'

'Okay, Grandad.' Smiling with such happiness that he was dumbfounded, she fell into step beside him. 'But I have to go to Norwich Street first, because I didn't come out prepared.'

'Prepared?'

'I don't have my diaphragm.'

'Diaphragm?' – aghast. 'Is that what you use?'

'Yes.' Her voice had a hint of frost. 'Don't tell me you're one of those men who thinks diaphragms are unaesthetic.'

'No, no, not that at all. It's – it's . . . isn't it, uh, *risky*?'

'I suppose, but I've been using it for years without any trouble. I tried the coil, but it hurt; and I'd rather run the risk than muck myself up with the pill. Besides, it's a risk

I choose' – there was still a slight edge to her tone – 'so I wouldn't land you with problems if I got pregnant.'

'Heavens, Imogen, I'd see you through abortions and things – you must know that; it's just . . .'

'If you're really fussed, you can use a nasty old sheath thing.'

'I . . . don't actually have any,' he said uncertainly.

'There you are, then, you see?' – as if that settled the matter. As indeed it did.

Chapter 43

HEN JACOB TOLD Laura, upon her return three days later, her face grew so taut that every triangular plane seemed sharp-edged. 'Jesus,' she said coldly at last. Silence, then: 'Jesus,' again. 'What became of your dozen good reasons for not sleeping with her – abuse of power, not hurting her, incest taboos, wanting grown-up women and all that?'

'You mind. More than other times.' He was surprised.

'Of course I mind. Am I supposed to respect a man whose principles get thrown over by a bit of moonlight?'

'It's not like that.'

'What *is* it like, then? What *did* become of those reasons?'

He shrugged ruefully. 'I haven't got an answer myself yet. I don't know. I was right last year, in the abstract; and in practice – in this particular situation – I think I'm right now.'

'Come on, the reasons. Be specific. What about the way Imogen will be hurt when it ends?'

'She says she won't be.'

Laura snorted. 'Says!'

'And she's still serious about Adrian.'

That gave her pause. 'Ah, maybe she'll be okay, then. Poor Adrian, though – how is he taking it?'

'Imogen hasn't said much – she doesn't discuss him with me any more than I discuss you with her – but I get the impression he's rather mournful, but, uh, resigned: he's known all along that she was, hmm, interested in me.'

'Hmph. But what became of all that stuff about liking grown-up women? You're not going to tell me Imogen has grown up ten years' worth since last Christmas.'

'Not ten years' worth, but quite a lot.'

'Sex will work wonders' – bitingly.

'You know that's not it,' Jacob said huffily. 'Of course she's young; and I'm conscious of it; but, even so, her opinion is more worth paying attention to than most people's of twenty-one – or any age.'

She looked at him hard. Finally she said, 'You're in love with her.'

He screwed up his face. 'You know me, Laura; I don't fool around. I only get attached to women I can be serious about.'

'Do you' – she hesitated – 'do you love her?' In their private language, loving someone was more serious, more soul-engrossing than being in love, and fraught with more danger to their equilibrium with each other.

He wished that this hadn't come up so soon, before he himself knew what he felt. He shook his head. 'I don't – '

'More than me?'

'Oh, my love.' He tried to put his arms round her, but her body was as stiff as her face. 'Not more than you. Listen, I don't understand. Why are you especially upset this time? Surely you see that Imogen is less of a threat to us than anyone has been before?'

'A threat!' She stood up impatiently, disdaining a discourse couched in such terms, then sat down again, accepting it. 'All right, not more than me. As much as me, then?'

'How could I love her as much as you?' he parried lightly. 'She's hardly seen any movies.'

Laura was having no jokes; Laura saw the evasion. 'I'm right, then, she *is* a threat.'

He spread his hands. 'What can I say? No, she isn't. But

209

if you've made up your mind not to believe me, it's not something I can do anything to prove.'

She looked from his hands to his face, and the icy edges of her features dissolved. 'It's not fair,' she wailed. 'It was *our* moon, yours and mine, from last year; you didn't have any right to give it to her.' Tears blurred her bright blue eyes and trickled down the side of her nose.

His arms went round her, his wronged Laura. Yes: he had not done wrong, but she had been wronged, about the moon. 'I'm sorry, I didn't think. I'm sorry. But it's still our moon, it was only coincidence . . .'

For a short time she let him comfort her, then shrugged out of his embrace. 'It isn't still ours, but that's neither here nor there, it's not what's in question.' She was composed, her tears gone: cold, but no longer a snow queen; and in a moment she closed the subject and forced a return to normal by saying briskly: 'Well, enough of that. We're going to the NFT tomorrow, aren't we? – Fine. I'll be off now. Meet you here at six tomorrow?'

Jacob was startled; he had expected her to spend the first night after her return with him, not alone in King's. He did not want to let her go, but he did; it was inadvisable to trespass when Laura drew a line.

The next night she did stay with him, and neither of them mentioned Imogen. (He guiltily wished it were also true that neither of them even thought about her.) But at breakfast she said, 'What about the difference in your ages – is it part of the attraction – older man infatuated with younger woman? After all, I'm thirty-seven; I don't exactly have Imogen's fresh bloom of youth.' She crunched a piece of toast *à l'Anglaise* – cold and hard – and watched him challengingly: not hostile, but not exactly friendly.

'Bloom of youth, phooey. I'll tell you what Imogen's bloom of youth is, it's a damned nuisance: she doesn't know enough, she doesn't have enough experience of life. And don't tell me you're getting sensitive about your age, I thought it was against your principles.'

'You must see why I wondered,' she said defensively. 'One's always hearing about, er, older men who have flings with girls, trying to prove something or other, heaven knows what . . .'

210

'I believe it's often a matter,' he offered helpfully, 'of trying to revive what's called, uh, flagging potency.'

Laura choked on her toast. 'Horrid man,' she gasped, gulping coffee. 'No, don't slap my back. Dear me. Seriously, though, I do find the whole thing hard to understand. If her age is such a disadvantage, then why Imogen?'

Because we're twins, she and I, Jacob thought fleetingly, but knew better than to say so – not while Laura was still nervous about how this attachment might affect the two of them. He shrugged. 'Don't know. Age wasn't on my mind when it started, and – '

'I bet it wasn't.' Her sarcasm was friendly now. 'Let's see. Maybe it's something simple, like sex. Maybe she's "better" than me . . .' She smiled and crunched another bite of toast, amused, confident: but waiting.

'My love, no one could be "better" than you,' he said fervently. 'Not that I think in such revolting terms – rating people for "sexual performance" – any more than you do. But if you positively want me to isolate that element artificially, then I assure you that Imogen doesn't begin to compete.'

'Why not?' She was reassured now, and simply interested.

'Probably because she's only slept with boys before now.' Laura hooted.

'Okay, okay, me superstud. But seriously . . . she's not . . . ripe? – not subtle yet . . . how can I put it? . . . she does very well, you might say, but – '

'I might not; you might' – good-naturedly.

'Yah, yah – what was I saying? Oh yes – that she's still sort of preoccupied with deploying, uh, technique.'

'Technique?' She looked smug. 'I don't ever remember even thinking about it.'

'You wouldn't,' Jacob said fondly. 'Of course I didn't know you in your green days' – she shied her crust at him – 'but I bet you took to it like a duck to water. You're a natural. You know – natural athletes, natural linguists, natural dancers: you're a natural lover.'

After that, knowing the worst, she slowly relaxed. Sometimes she was snappish about Imogen and called her 'your Lolita'; but, as far as he could tell – and he knew her well – she was soon as comfortable as it was possible to be in such situations.

211

The two women got on all right when they met at his house. At first Laura was overly casual, as if only a chance visitor, and Imogen rather tentative and deferential: they offered each other the best chair, apologised for the implicit possessiveness of a book left on a table, avoided or hastily retracted the word 'we' as descriptive of either one of them and Jacob, and scrupulously gave each other precedence at every door. But this formality did not last a week. They were both up to their ears – Imogen enthusiastically indignant, Laura wearily muttering, 'Oh God, not again!' – in the campaign to defend the Abortion Act against the latest anti-abortion private member's bill; and, through working together so much and sharing an important, impersonal common purpose, they quickly became matter-of-fact comrades, if not exactly close friends: by the last Saturday in October the three of them felt hardly a flicker of embarrassment as they squatted on Jacob's sitting-room floor lettering their placards with simple-minded slogans for the NAC-TUC march in London: 'A Woman's Right to Choose', 'Abortion – Keep It Legal, Keep It Safe', 'Hands Off the '67 Act'.

The next day, quite confounding his expectation that one or the other would carefully go off and join other friends so as not to seem to be walking with him as of right, they both marched with him in the contingent behind the banner of Cambridge NAC: Imogen excited by her first demo; Jacob and Laura, jaded veterans, cynical about the heady illusion of a unified Left marching festive through the heart of London a hundred thousand strong, but exhilarated all the same; all three drawn close in unforced fellowship – the way they should always be, he thought on a gust of happiness. They were dissolved into couples when Adrian deserted the Cambridge Labour Party banner in Piccadilly and joined them, and Jacob felt a twinge of slightly jealous annoyance; but it was not enough to diminish his delight in the harmony that, against all conventional wisdom, they were arriving at.

Across the human sea in Trafalgar Square they caught sight of Frances under a banner that read, 'Lawyers for a Woman's Right to Choose'. She waved at Imogen, then, noticing Jacob, dropped her arm and turned away ostentatiously. Even at that distance it was a direct cut, and he knew the reason: Imogen had told her about their affair on a visit home the previous

212

weekend. 'They're both furious,' she had reported upon her return. 'Mother says it's because you're too old for me.'

'Just what I said myself, junior,' he had replied. Privately he thought that his age had nothing to do with their reaction: that they detested him simply because they had behaved badly towards him in that quarrel after Florence. But he did not say so to Imogen. She was pretty clear-eyed about her parents, but made large allowances because she loved them; and it was not his business to disturb her possibly hard-won accommodation between affection and critical insight by finding fault with them unasked. Besides, he didn't give a damn what they thought of him – except now, when for a moment he felt raw with the sting of rejection.

Then, noticing that Imogen was watching him anxiously, Laura quizzically – Adrian had not seen that anything was amiss – he was restored to the happiness of their extraordinary triunity. Too bad that Adrian was slightly imperceptive, slightly peripheral. If only he were older and generally more considerable, Laura might be interested in him; and, for all their harmony, the present situation was hardly ideal for her. In fact, he did rather wish – the idea flashed into his mind fully formed – that Imogen did not have someone so nice as Adrian patiently, dumbly, hopefully waiting for her to turn back to him alone; someone who could offer her an undivided love; someone to whom she could therefore give her whole love in return, without fear.

What was he thinking? Put it out of your mind, he told himself sternly, glancing guiltily at Laura – and felt even worse when she gave him an intimate, trusting, long-time-lovers' smile, which he did not at that moment deserve.

He put it out of his mind: his guilty conscience drove it out. It had been only a momentary aberration.

Chapter 44

UT FROM SOME time in November his sense of an achieved balance among the three of them, and within himself, began to fade. He hardly knew how or when it began; he only, very slowly, became aware that he was moving – drifting – and had been for some time – towards a place he had never been before – or rather, had been once, long ago, when everything, except the most important thing, had been different. A month ago he had admitted to Laura that he was more than in love with Imogen – that he loved her. Now, as he felt himself drifting, swimming, out, out, into something new, new-old, different, he told Laura nothing, because he didn't know what to tell. 'As much,' he had said; 'not more.' Was it still true? If not, he should tell her. But could one measure such things? Of course not: love wasn't quantifiable. Yet also: of course. On the pulse.

He loved Laura too – still – always – but his love for Imogen was a sensation he had not felt since Sheila, of being attached to her by invisible cords when they were apart, and penetrated when they were together by a sense of completeness quite distinct from the familiar tumultuous intoxication of being in love with someone new. The more he found out what she was like, the more he was bound up in her, in spite of the gulf in their experience of life. She was young, she was green; when Cambodia was bombed she had been ten years old; she had not yet been a reasoning being during those crucial years of the late sixties and early seventies that had given him and Laura a background of common ideas and experience long before they met; she had not even seen the movies that provided them with the delectable small-talk of daily life. But he and Imogen did not need to construct a common language. They were like twins, with twins' uncanny ease of communication, moving on the same current, laughing simultaneously at things no one else – not even Laura – would find funny, thinking the same thoughts at the same time, looking at the world with the same eyes, reading each other's minds and sensing each other's feelings without words, but talking about them anyhow, from astonished delight that such deep correspondency should exist; and out of that strange unity of temperament – not at all the same thing as community of opinion, though perhaps difficult or impossible without it – came an out-to-the-edge passion that he had never quite had with Laura. He was living in a state of joy.

So was Imogen; she shone with it, throve upon it.

Ease, joy, peace. But not for Laura. Twins she and Jacob might not be, but from living in close intimacy for seven years they had grown a great deal alike, and in their own way moved in each other's moods and knew each other's thoughts and feelings without asking. She knew him well – very well – too well not to sense his drift into a delight that she was part of, for him, but in which she could not share; and, in response, she herself was drifting away from happiness: withdrawing behind the portals of her eyes to watch and wait. Had she given him that trusting private smile since the day of the demonstration? He could not remember seeing it for weeks now. Would he see it again until – until – hard even to think it – until the end of his affair with Imogen?

But that would be a long time off. He had better control his wilder flights and set about winning back Laura's trust, otherwise he could lose her, since he did not imagine that he and Imogen would end in the foreseeable future. Not unless that damned Adrian succeeded with his dejected persistence in persuading her to –

How did she feel about Adrian, anyhow? Did she turn that shining face upon him as gladly as upon Jacob? He wished he knew, and wished he knew why the question bothered him.

One evening early in December Imogen raised herself on her elbows beside him and said, 'I'm feeling horribly claustro-phobic. – No, not this minute, silly; in general. I haven't been alone one second all term – there's been supervisions, NAC, pregnancy-testing sessions, Adrian, you; and when I get back to Norwich Street, there's always somebody wanting to talk, or a house meeting; and collective decision-making about absolutely everything takes *ages*. I should have known it wouldn't suit a solitary type like me.'

He grinned. 'Solitary? With that social round you used to be up to your neck in? Go on with you.'

'That was different. I had my room to be alone in. But at Norwich Street I actually have to turn off my light to keep people from knocking on my door. I thought they'd go down at the end of term, and I'd be able to *breathe* – but everybody's staying up till just before Christmas. Thank goodness I'll be living alone next year.' She subsided onto the pillow.

'Next year?'

'I told you – the little flat I'm renting from Antonella.'

'Antonella?'

'Dimwit,' she said affectionately. 'She runs the language school I'm teaching at next year. In Rome, remember?'

Rome. Oh. It had somehow not occurred to him that she still intended to go there. He was glad she wasn't looking at him.

'Anyhow, I've just got to have some time by myself. So I think I'll go down tomorrow.'

'Tomorrow!' Double whammo. 'I thought you'd be here another week yet.'

'Yes, so did I; but it's crept up on me. I've got to get away –'

'You might have told me before,' he said stiffly.

'Oh, oh, I'm sorry – I've sort of sprung it on you. But I couldn't tell you before; I only decided today. I've told you as soon as I knew it myself.'

He swallowed. 'If you're getting stir-crazy in Norwich Street, you could – ' No, he realised just in time, she couldn't move into Coronation Place with him; it was Laura's territory too. For a moment he felt irritated with Laura. 'You could spend more time here,' he substituted.

'I don't think Laura would like that.' Her breath was warm on his shoulder. 'Besides, that's not being alone, that's being with you.'

Through gritted teeth he said, 'Being at your parents' isn't being alone either.'

'No, but I've got my room, and they leave me alone – '

'Unlike me.'

216

This time she heard the hurt in his voice. 'Oh Jacob,' she cried, sitting up on one elbow abruptly. 'I don't mean it that way, I'm not getting away from *you*. I'd rather be with you than anybody else. But it's something we're different in – I'd forgotten there *was* anything, so I just blundered ahead, I thought you'd understand. You don't much like being alone, but for me it's an addiction; and I'm practically having withdrawal symptoms. But I'll stay a while longer if you want . . .'

Of course. She had always been like that. He remembered her at six, talking to Pan at the end of the garden; at twelve, retreating to her room to read. And she clearly had no idea that her offhand reference to next year in Rome had made him feel hollow and slightly sick. 'Don't look so worried, puchkie.' He touched the pucker between her eyebrows. 'Go off to your hermitage, I don't mind. It's just the surprise – I thought we still had lots of time before Christmas.'

Her brow unknotted, then knotted again. 'Actually, in a way I do need to get away from you for a while. Seeing you every day, I can't think properly.'

'What about?'

'Oh . . .'

He had a jealous flash. 'About Adrian?'

'No, that's another thing I was going to tell you. I've broken off with Adrian.'

His heart leapt; then he felt nervous. 'How come?' he asked guardedly.

'That's what I want to think about – part of it.' Her frown deepened. 'Whether . . . what the . . . all sorts of things.'

'You're being unusually enigmatic, young Imogen.'

'Yes, well, that's why I need to go off and think. The trouble is, when I'm with you, I think about you, and it makes it hard to think about my life as a whole. And I really must – right away.'

'Sure, pet. But why the rush?'

Her eyes slid away. 'Thinking about the future halfway through my final year isn't a rush; it's practically dilatory.'

He noticed the evasion but did not comment on it. She would tell him when she was ready. 'So it is, so it is,' he said jovially – he had recovered his composure. 'Well, hop to it, junior, off with you to London, set your life in order. No point dilly-dallying. If you're going to do it, the sooner the better.'

Imogen looked startled, then suddenly smiled very happily. 'You may be right.'

What was up? Was breaking with Adrian connected with going home to think? As she had reminded him, her future had been settled – in Rome – since last summer. Why did she need to think about it now?

Perhaps Rome was her defence against loving him too much. Did she keep her head above water by reminding herself that she had somewhere to go to, a new life, a clean break? And had she changed her mind? Did she need time away from him to think about what she would be doing to herself if she gave up Rome and stayed in England, near him – stayed in England, in fact, precisely in order to be near him, expecting nothing beyond what they had already? The thought made him uneasy and elated.

Chapter 45

NCE HE GOT used to the idea of three weeks without Imogen, Jacob was glad she had gone down early. It was his chance to reassure Laura that she still came first. Alone with her he was more concretely conscious of how much he loved her; and they spent a peculiar, tender, mutually solicitous week rediscovering how much they simply enjoyed being together without anyone else about. He hardly missed Imogen.

Not for the first few days. Then he began to miss her quite a lot. It was odd. He was happy with Laura, yet wanted Imogen; missed Imogen, yet was happy with Laura. Happy with Laura. Yes, in that first week – yes, even after he started missing Imogen: on Christmas day, for instance, when they walked all over the blissfully empty town and came home ravenous for their unseasonal feast of steak béarnaise and potatoes Anna.

Happy – yet missing Imogen the whole time: daily, hourly, in the middle of talking to Laura, making love to Laura. Pangs of disloyalty; pangs of bereftness.

And under the surface, working, an idea. The ease, the joy: maybe he had been wrong. Maybe what he wanted above all things was –

No!

– was Imogen –

No! Go away. Away. Away.

– was Imogen for good – Imogen first.

No.

No.

He fought it down, but it was irrepressible; it would well up while he was walking or shaving or sitting at his terminal punching in a programme, and he would be drenched with joy before he could control himself, then shaken with fear. He couldn't face a future that did not contain both Laura and Imogen, but he couldn't imagine one that did, for in the long run he could not be centred upon more than one person.

A few days after Christmas he found himself facing the fact that what he had thought would never happen had happened – that the hypothetical danger of the path he and Laura had chosen – the danger they had scorned to be ruled by the fear of – was no longer hypothetical: that Imogen had replaced Laura at the centre of his life. The realisation put an end to joy. He was terrified. What should he do? What could he? Not give up Laura, whom he loved, nor Imogen, whom he loved . . . more. Not keep Laura under false pretences, nor keep her if he told her the truth: they had been first with each other for seven years; she would not stand for being less than central now.

Nor keep Imogen, either. For there was the question of age. Not age now, when he was thirty-seven, she twenty-one; not age for a long while: fifty and thirty-four would be fine. But eighty and sixty-four? Impossible. He couldn't inflict it upon her. And what madness led to the beguiling idea that Imogen, unlike Laura, might actually live with him? Impossible, insane. What about Laura? What about Imogen? . . . But . . . No . . . Yet . . . Yes . . . Maybe . . .

'Maybe you've got into this tizz just because she isn't around,' his mother told him. She was ringing ostensibly to say Happy

New Year, but in fact because she had just got a letter he had written to her on Boxing Day, describing his confusion. 'It's easy to exaggerate how much you care for somebody you miss.' Her deep voice had a disconcerting hollow resonance from being bounced off the telecommunications satellite. 'You forget the nuisancey things. Imogen's age, in this case. But don't count on it. She must be quite something to make you so *farchadat* when you've got a woman like Laura. Listen, puchkie, don't do anything rash. Take it slowly, whatever you feel. To be sure. And now here's Isaac wanting to talk.'

Yes, Jacob thought, after saying goodbye to his gentle father: a woman like Laura. Being with Laura was real – the meat and drink of life. Maybe Aline was right; he would come to his senses once Imogen was back.

But, when she returned two days later, she was so much more vivid than his memories of her that he said to himself at once: This is real, nothing can be more real than this. He didn't know exactly what he meant, but he knew it was true. He would find out the consequences in due course. In the meantime, to his heartfullness, here was Imogen, alight with pleasure at being back with him. 'Especially after that *ghastly* Christmas. They still don't like it that I'm involved with you, especially Mother. She was quite nasty, really. Poor Mother, she can't help being spiteful sometimes – she hasn't had all she wants out of life.'

'"Poor Mother" will never get all she wants out of life,' he said vigorously. 'She's insatiable.'

'Oh no – just the opposite. I'm the insatiable one. That's why Mother's sometimes jealous of me: she settled for less, and she knows I won't.'

'Less than?'

'Everything' – aware of extravagance, but in earnest.

Jacob grunted. 'You're impossible. What d'you mean, everything?'

She looked him straight in the eye. 'Life on my conditions.'

'Jesus, girl. Life isn't a piece of cake. The world will make mincemeat out of you if you expect things to be easy.'

'I didn't say easy, I said on my conditions. I know I won't have everything I want; but if I don't at least *want* everything, and try for it, then – then what?'

220

Later, when they were in bed, he remembered the tone of her, 'Everything,' amused by her own absurdity but defiantly meaning exactly what she said. 'Everything.' His heart ached with love and fear for her, and he muttered, 'Oh, my darling,' into the pillow.

'What?'

'Just a fatuous endearment.'

'I heard you, actually,' she said, and he felt her quiver with a fit of giggles.

Later still he thought: She lives on the edge. That's why. Why I love her, he meant; why I want . . .

But that was a sentence he could not finish. What he wanted was Imogen and Laura both, for ever. The impossible. Who was he to worry about Imogen because she wanted everything? What else did he want himself?

From the time she got back, Imogen was extraordinarily happy, bearing happiness like a lit torch, full of splendid bobs and bounces and jokes and a most wonderful tenderness towards him. She seemed to have got her need for solitude out of her system; she stayed with him as often as possible – oftener than before Christmas – and on evenings when he was going to be with Laura she usually stopped in briefly to say hullo on her way home to Norwich Street from the library, books and papers slung in a bag, wearing jeans and her disreputable fur thing – the drowned rat, its fur slicked down with secondhand grease and worn bald round collar and cuffs. He sometimes saw the child Imogen in her face for a split second before remembering that she was his lover, a grown woman; and then his heart would flow with gratitude that she had grown up in time, and with joy at the gravity of her eyes even when she was laughing. From day to day he lived in a state of ever-increasing bliss. What were youth, and an unmistakable wetness behind the ears, measured against her austere seriousness? Besides, she was drying off fast – learning from him, she told him, not entirely to his surprise. But nothing he could teach her could match what she had to give; he could not learn from her beauty of soul, only love it.

So, with joy, his hope, irrepressible, would flow. What would her life be after him? Good. Not easy, she did not want easy paths; but good. And his after her? Desolate. It didn't bear thinking about.

Hope, then?

But there were counterweights to irrepressible, irresponsible hope. The most important one by far was Laura. Loving Imogen more did not make him love Laura less.

And age, age: the impossibility of eighty and sixty-four.

On the other hand, the more he thought about it, the more he was convinced that, if he did choose Imogen, she would not stay with him forever. She would drift away eventually, because of something in her – a need to be on her own – of which her self-sufficiency and love of solitude were only superficial indications. He did not understand it – it did not correspond to anything in him – but he knew it was there. They would have a few years together, then that would be it. Say five – no, say ten – say twelve years, twelve at the most. He would be fifty and she thirty-four, still youngish, still shiningly Imogen, able to choose whom she would.

Unlike him. He would be left with nothing, no Laura, facing the rest of his life.

But he could not stay with Laura simply because he was afraid of being alone in his old age. That was his way of living on the edge – he would not let such prudencies govern his choices. He could be influenced by consideration for Imogen – could give her up to spare her from being chained to an old man while she was still in her prime – but could not show the same tender regard towards his own future.

So: hope, fear, certainty, uncertainty, love for Imogen, love for Laura; and all the time happiness.

He could tell that Laura sensed a change in him, for she was strung-up and remote; but she did not guess the real extent of the danger, or she would have upped and offed – or, at the least, pulled all the way back, into the sarcastic, self-defeating distance of their first months together. As it was, she was simply waiting: wary, hurt, displeased, but containing herself for the sake of a future at the other end of all this; and perhaps – as he guessed from something she had said at Christmas – telling herself that what she felt now was no worse than what he had felt in the first weeks of her attachment to Dieter. He realised with a guilty shock that she trusted him – something he had

222

never quite expected after experiencing the depths of her mistrust seven years before.

After a fortnight, however, the pain of self-containment was too much for her; and one night she burst out with a one-word question: 'Why?'

He knew what she was asking. 'I – I . . .' he said helplessly. Then he remembered what he had told himself the night Imogen said she wouldn't settle for less than everything. 'Because she lives on the edge,' he said.

'The edge of what?' Laura asked with daunting scepticism.

'I don't know. Something – something about the way Imogen would rather go down in total defeat than settle for second best.'

'The way I've done, you mean?'

'You haven't. Not with your job, or with your life, or with me – unless I'm your idea of second best.'

'No, you aren't.' She smiled briefly. 'Though you're strikingly immodest about it.'

He smiled back, keeping to himself the idea that the difference between the two women was in Laura's cast of mind, rather than in anything she had done. She had not needed to settle for second best; but, had things so turned out that it had been a question of that or nothing, he thought she might have been willing to do so.

'And actually I do know what you mean,' she went on. 'It's something you and Imogen have in common. The reason you love it in her is that you have a large streak of it yourself. Not as much as her, but a lot, so that you feel as if . . . it, in her . . . as if it ennobles you.'

Jacob looked at her astonished. 'How do you know *that*? I couldn't have said it myself.'

She smiled, almost sweetly. 'Because I'm in the same position with you. I've got a streak of it too, but not as much as you; and I recognise it in you – I'm pulled towards it, it connects me.'

He regarded her tenderly. For once Imogen was not on his mind at all. 'I love you,' he said to the woman he had loved for such a long time.

Laura recoiled. 'Don't say that.'

Still half-forgetting the complexities of the present, he said, 'But I do.'

'I don't know what you call love,' she said sharply. 'Don't say it to me unless you know what you mean, and *I* know what you mean.'

An ultimatum; withdrawal of permission given six years ago.

'You loved Dieter,' he said defensively. 'Not to mention Harold and –'

'Not the way you love Imogen. And' – with finality – 'I don't want to talk about it.'

The next morning she searched him out in the maths lab. 'I've just rung up Dieter, and I'm going over to Hanover for a few days.'

'What? It's term – what about supervisions? And aren't you lecturing?'

'I've got everything arranged,' she said airily. 'I'm just off to the train now. – No, don't come,' as he tried to get up to accompany her. She ran her hand over his crinkly hair and smiled down at him. 'Don't look dumpish. I'm not trying to get at you, and I'm not in a state – I'd just like a break. Okay?'

'Okay,' he got out, and managed a smile 'See you then.' He watched her weave gracefully through the terminals and enter the lift. He raised his hand to wave goodbye, but the doors closed before she was quite, turned round. Damn it, it wasn't okay. It was dangerous to leave him and Imogen alone right now, and she knew it.

But Laura had her own way of living on the edge, and this was it.

Chapter 46

AURA WAS AWAY a week. When she came back, Jacob was happy – very happy. He had missed her. He wanted to talk to her, make love to her, resume daily life with her. But he had had a week of daily life with Imogen, who had stayed with him in Coronation Place the whole time. Laura had hardly been back for twenty-four hours before he realised that during her absence he had decided: for Imogen.

'Take it slowly,' his mother had said. 'To be sure.' So he said nothing to either Imogen or Laura. He gave himself a week – and only grew more and more certain: happiness increasing, increasing, checked only by the dread of what he would do to Laura by telling her – and also, still, by the dread of losing her.

The week was up on the fourth of February, but he could not speak that night, because Imogen was at a NAC meeting, or the next, because both women were going to a national NAC protest rally in London.

But on the sixth Imogen had dinner with him. After they ate, she nestled up beside him on the sofa, and he thought fleetingly: Much nicer to make love than talk love. But only fleetingly. Loyalty – to Laura, to Adrian – had constrained them all these months from talking about love. She had not said she loved him since the night, over a year ago now, when she had begun everything with her still-amazing declaration; and he had never once said so to her, though he had been longing to speak the words, turning them continually in his mind, on his tongue.

So. 'Imogen . . .'

'Mmm?'

'I love you.'

Silence. Imogen sat up straight and smiled hesitantly. 'Why did you say that?'

'Because I do.'

She looked glad, her light brown eyes very alive and alert. 'I love you too. You know that.'

'Yes. I haven't said it before, because – '

'Of Laura.'

'Yes, and because I didn't quite know my own mind. But ever since January I've been sure.'

'Sure you loved me?' – puzzled, as if wondering what he had felt before that.

'No – sure I wanted to stay with you. And you to stay with me.'

Her brow puckered. After a pause she said, 'What do you mean?'

'Just that.'

'I don't understand. What about Laura?'

What about Laura indeed? – Laura, whom he indeed still loved, to whom this would be a deathly wound. 'I love Laura, but,' slowly, so that Imogen would be in no doubt of his seriousness, 'insofar as one can quantify these things, I love you more.'

'More?' The pucker on her forehead deepened.

'More . . . whatever that means. I can't exactly say what, but I want . . . to live with you, have you live with me, all that.'

'But we said it wasn't going to be permanent.' Imogen's voice went up.

'I know. But I've changed; and that's what I want now, if you do.'

'But I don't.' She stood up in alarm, then sat down. 'I don't understand. We *agreed*.'

Jacob had expected resistance, but not quite in this form: he had thought she would protest on Laura's behalf, yet be glad none the less. 'I guess I was pretty abrupt – do you need some time to take it in?' He half smiled, perplexed at the intensity of her frown.

'No. No. I don't need any time. I don't know where you got this idea, I never said anything to make you think – did I – ?'

'No, but – '

'I don't need any time, it's impossible. Please can't we just – oh dear, this sounds silly – just forget you mentioned it?'

'Because of Laura?'

'No' – vehemently. 'It's me. I don't want – I never – we agreed. I wouldn't have . . .'

'Wouldn't have slept with me?' Jacob's confidence suddenly sank, and he spoke in a subdued voice.

'That's not what . . . I wouldn't have . . . Well, I won't, now.' Seeing his hurt bewilderment, she said, 'Sorry, I'm rambling,' then, scrutinising him closely: 'You aren't serious about this, are you? It isn't some . . . some kind of test?'

He shook his head. There must be some misunderstanding. Last year she had said, 'I've loved you for years.' He would try again. 'Are you sure it's not Laura?' he asked.

'You *are* serious?'

'Never more so. In dead earnest.'

Imogen got up again and turned about restlessly in the middle of the room. Finally she faced him. 'It's not Laura. Not at all. If I did want . . . what you're talking about, I'd feel bad about Laura, but I'd say yes. But there isn't any question of it. It's not . . .'

'Why not?' He was beginning to believe it; he didn't believe it; he must say something to clear this up. 'Tell –'

'It's not how I picture my life' – forcefully. 'For one thing, I've got a job in Rome next year.'

'You could do that, and then maybe . . .' desperately: 'a job at a language school here? A Ph.D? A job in London?'

'Oh dear, oh dear, you don't understand. I never dreamed you'd think of this. It's just not on.'

'But you love me.'

'But not *for good*. Not that way.' Seeing him flinch, Imogen came and knelt beside him. 'Jacob, do you remember that night when you said, "My darling", and I said, "What?" to make you say it again, and you said, "Just an endearment"? I wished so much you could say you loved me, and my heart melted just at the word "darling"; and tonight when you said . . . what you said . . . I was so *happy* –'

'Then why –'

'Because I'm . . . maybe I'm peculiar. I don't want to live with anyone.'

'Laura and I don't live together.'

'I don't mean "not live in the same house", I mean that I don't want to be . . . tied isn't the word . . .'

Out of his own vocabulary he offered: 'Centred on?'

'Maybe, yes, sort of . . .' – though she shook her head; it still wasn't right.

Jacob could not believe that. 'It's me,' he said. 'Something about me. My age?'

'No, not your age. Just that I can't conceive of being with anyone for my whole life.'

'Is that all?' He laughed with relief and told her he hadn't thought she would want to stay with him forever, but maybe five years, ten or twelve if he were lucky.

Her hand was on his arm. Her grip tightened. 'You've thought about it that much . . .' she said slowly, and fell silent, wincing and biting her lip, her eyes lowered. At last she looked up, at him, at his naked, fearful, hopeful face; and what she saw made her withdraw her hand, stand up slowly and return to the spot where she had stood a short while before – a safe spot, far enough to put some distance between them, not far enough to constitute retreat or abandonment. 'Look, I don't know how to explain, but I have to make you see. I love you; but I know myself. *I shall move on*, and sooner rather than later. Not ten years from now, not five. Two years; one year; six months – who knows? I don't; I just know that I shall. It's nothing to do with you; it's me. I do love you. Maybe I love you more than I'll ever love anyone else, but that isn't the point. It's not even that I'll stop loving you all of a sudden, or maybe even ever, but that I'll – I'll get restless, I'll want to move on.' Jacob raised a sarcastically inquisitive eyebrow, and she added hastily: 'No, I'm not feeling that way now, not at all. And it's not that I'll get tired of you – it's that . . . I don't know.'

'Isn't it a rather glib life you're mapping out?' He was very dry, very calm. When she did not understand, he said, 'This serially monogamous solitude you propose to live in – aren't you ducking responsibilities?' She was still perplexed. 'Responsibilities, inescapable obligations to other people, mutual dependency. You're trying to leap right out of the net of human community.'

She stared into him, through him. 'Oh, I want responsibilities,' she whispered, 'but – but I'm me, not your idea of me.

228

And you can't, you mustn't, break up your life with Laura for *me* – for me as I am: for someone who could be off at any moment.'

He sighed, tried to think better of it, and went for broke. 'What if I accept your terms?'

'I've made no terms.'

'Two years, one year, six months: you as you are.'

'That's not terms,' Imogen said in dismay. 'That's description. No. I couldn't. I can't. I'd feel captive, knowing the price you'd paid; I'd feel bound to stay, to keep you happy, and so maybe I wouldn't go when I wanted to – and what depths of – of – rancour would that sink us to?'

No hope. But he went on. 'But if I say I'll be content with that?'

'But you won't be. I know you.'

He shrugged. She knew him; he had thought he knew her. He looked at the girl whom he had worried about hurting badly if they had an affair. She was standing on her neutral ground regarding him anxiously, so distressed at hurting him that she might have been the one who was being hurt. Oh yes, he knew her, pretty well. Only in this one, this fatal instance had he not known Imogen.

'It's not that I'm not tempted,' she added. 'I am. Right now the thought of leaving you for Rome is exile. But it *won't last*.'

'You've got addicted to variety,' he said bitterly.

She frowned dangerously, then took a deep breath, visibly restraining herself. 'I don't think so. I wish I could say that it's . . . "promiscuity": then you could blame me for it or something; but it's not, it's something I don't know how to describe, something about knowing more about the world than I can through one person.'

'Even if the next person isn't as much worth knowing as the last?'

'Yes' – definitely, with no hope of being understood.

'It sounds suspiciously like lots of men's excuse for screwing around, if you ask me.'

'Yes.' Flat. She had stopped trying to excuse or explain; if that were his shelter from the pain of her explanation, then she would allow it him.

He could not take the proffered refuge. Whatever Imogen was, she was not a female pelt-hunter. He felt tired, defeated, numb. He leaned back, rubbing his eyes with weariness, still incredulous, remembering how happy he had been such a short time ago. How had it come to this? Surely – but he could feel defeat in his bones. He wanted to throw something at her, smother her, shake her to bits, but it wouldn't make him any happier. Instead, he opened his eyes and offered her a tired, complaisant, defeated smile.

Imogen had gauged the depths of seriousness in his – to her – incomprehensible wish no better than he had at first gauged the depths of hers in refusing; and from the midst of her own dismay she seized on his smile as a sign that he was returning to normal. Moving quickly across the room she knelt by him again, clasping her arms over his thighs, and looked up affectionately.

'I'm awfully sorry we got our wires crossed,' she said. 'I hope you see that it's not you – not you at all – it's me, I'm peculiar, and I'm sorry, but I *am* glad that you love me, and grateful . . .'

'Shut up,' he said ferociously.

She sat back on her heels, stricken and angry.

'Sorry . . .' he gestured apologetically. 'I thought you sounded insincere.'

'Maybe I was, I don't know; I'm so confused.'

She was confused? Jacob rubbed his forehead. 'Tell me something – you went away at Christmas to think about the future. I was foolish enough to think it meant, uh, me . . .'

She drew in her breath sharply and shook her head.

'What was it, then?'

She shook her head again. 'Something I've changed my mind about. I won't bore you with it.' They eyed each other, and she continued tentatively, 'What do we . . . do now? I – I wish we could go back to where we were, but that's me being selfish, I don't know if it's possible for you . . .'

He began to laugh; he was punch-drunk. What did one say? Anything. 'Oh yes, it's possible, anything's possible.' He didn't think it was, but he was too tired to get tangled in more of Imogen's mysterious thought processes.

They were quiet for a while; she leaned against his knees, subdued. At last he said, 'I'm dead tired, let's go up.'

She looked up, her eyes kindling. 'I was afraid you'd want me to go home.'

230

'No, love. C'mon, let's go to bed.'

She scrambled to her feet and stood waiting for him. He began to get up too, then stopped. Her eyes, gazing gravely down, not quite meeting his, waiting; the way she was standing, solidly planted on her feet, one hand resting on her midriff, the other on her hip – 'You know what you look like? That postcard you sent me two years ago – the *Madonna del Parto*.'

'*What?*'

'Piero's Madonna, you know – over there on the chimney-piece.'

Imogen crossed the room and picked up the postcard, frowning. 'I'm not a bit like that. She's blonde under that coif thing, surely.'

'True, but you were standing like that, and looking down that way – from far off, and so sober, not quite at me, but right to the inside of me, too. Don't look so unhappy, pet. I expect my heart will mend.'

He didn't believe it would; he had spoken simply to hide his sore ego and sorer spirit. He would lose his shredded self-respect unless he could convince her that he was reconciled to her refusal – that the matter was not quite so vital as he had made out in the heat of the moment – that he was back on course after a sort of temporary insanity.

For several days after his declaration – his proposal, as he described it to himself, without much humour – Imogen and Laura were so busy with the last push of the campaign against the anti-abortion bill that he hardly saw them. On the eighth of February they both went to a rally in London. Laura came back late, fairly confident that the bill would ultimately be defeated or amended into insignificance; and Imogen stayed down over the weekend. He had gained a breathing-space; by the time she got back, he was visored, in masquerade as himself. Imogen observed him anxiously, antennae quivering, but clearly she never dreamed that he would systematically gull her; and he succeeded in hoodwinking her completely. Though he woke up a week after his proposal thinking: A week ago I was happy, he smiled at Imogen when she awoke; and worry faded from her eyes. He had persuaded her that he was recovering: still a little bruised, but healing fast.

Jacob was more than bruised; he was scathed, and he had no one to turn to. He could not talk to Laura. He would have to tell her eventually, but not yet, not while his voice would be raw with hurt. And there would be no consolation in telling her. For one thing, he would be hurting her as badly as if Imogen had said yes – for what would weigh with her was how he had felt and acted, not Imogen's reply. And then – what would she do? Leave him? Possible. More than possible. But he dared not think about that now; time to reckon consequences when he had begun to feel less like somebody without a skin. So he maintained a cheerful front and brooded by himself over Imogen's refusal. He was not mistaken about the radiant tenderness she had poured out upon him all this time – but what did their attachment mean to her; how could they be like twins, yet so different that she could not conceive of staying with him for long? He was turned towards her with his whole being; what way was she facing? How could she say she might not love him in six months? Such things happened, of course; but how could she so calmly contemplate the prospect of ending an attachment that she was happily in the middle of – one she herself had sought out? Why was she so transparent to him in all else, yet in this one thing completely opaque?

He had fooled her, but inevitably things were not quite the same between them. He less often rang her up just to talk, and she less often stopped in just to say hullo; they met by arrangement, almost conscientiously, and they were not quite comfortable together. He was tense with the effort of appearing happy – and she was noticeably on edge, though she tried to hide it. He guessed that she was afraid of receiving another proposal. The idea that she feared it was the only thing that kept him from trying again, for he had entwined his happiness around the idea of Imogen.

Bitter, bitter.

Yet he was on the mend without knowing. On the nineteenth he thought mournfully: Tomorrow it will be two weeks since I was happy; but the next day he forgot the anniversary and on the twenty-first remembered it with an embarrassed start. Okay, okay. He was getting better. Not well; not happy: but better.

Oh God. Then he must tell Laura – soon: telling things right away was their first rule, and he had been breaking it for a fortnight. Today? No, no, not so fast. He needed a day to prepare himself. Tomorrow? He was seeing a client in London. Saturday, then. Gloomily he put a ring round the twenty-third of February.

Chapter 47

N SATURDAY AFTERNOON he was nerving himself to ring Laura when Imogen telephoned. Was he busy? Could she see him? He almost said no, but her tone was urgent – and he in truth, was grateful for an excuse to put off facing Laura. 'Such formality!' he said. 'I'm an ogre, that you should make appointments in the daytime? Come on over.'

She came in in a rush, pulling off her cap and scarf and the drowned rat and dropping her conker-brown bag. She was wearing jeans and boots and a long sweater striped in dozens of colours, and her cheeks were bright pink. He expected her to come and kiss him and sit beside him on the sofa. Instead, she plunked herself down in the wing chair opposite, crossed her legs, laced her hands on her knees and took a deep breath.

He wrenched his mind from Laura and tried to pay full attention to Imogen. She really did need to talk: she was bursting – and nervous. His heart turned over: perhaps she had changed her mind?

Another deep breath. 'I've got something to tell you, and I don't know – I don't know if you're going to like it, and I can only tell you properly by telling you all at once. Will you promise not to interrupt till I say you can?'

Had his proposal made things impossible; did she want to break with him now? His spirits plummeted, and he nodded wordlessly.

'And stay where you are?'

'Mm-hmm.'

'Really promise?'

'Really promise. Padlock on my tongue.'

'Well, I was doing a pregnancy-testing session this morning, and I' – she had the strangest expression, happy and apprehensive at once – 'I did a test on myself, and I'm pregnant. Six –'

He forgot all about his promise. 'Imogen, my poor love!' – and he leapt up to comfort her.

'You promised,' she said commandingly. 'I've not finished.'

Her look kept him at a distance. He sat down again on the edge of the sofa and waited.

'Do you remember before Christmas I said I wanted to think? Well, that was what I was thinking about.'

'Hunh?'

'What I mean is, I wanted to be pregnant, so you don't need to say, "Oh poor Imogen".'

He stared at her, he could feel his eyes getting wider and wider.

'Don't look so stricken,' she said, smiling. 'I really mean it. I wanted it and I still do.

Power of thought and speech seeped back, blood coursed through his veins. Wonderful beyond belief – beyond anything he had in wildest dreams imagined. 'Imogen, my – ' He was across the space between them and kneeling at her feet, arms on her knees, as she had sat with him on the night of his proposal.

She looked down at him, and, surprisingly, her eyes filled with tears. 'I haven't finished yet,' she whispered.

He nodded and hugged her knees; he didn't want to interrupt her, he was speechless with happiness.

'I really decided before Christmas that I wanted a child, and I wanted – it sounds rather corny and vulgar, but I wanted it to be yours. That's why I broke off with Adrian. But I needed the time away from you to be sure of myself; and I was; so when I came up after Christmas, I stopped using my diaphragm. I only had until summer to get pregnant, and I didn't know how long it would take, so I thought I'd better get going. I didn't really expect it to happen right away' – her voice squeaked with surprise – 'but it did. I'll be about eighteen weeks by Tripos.'

Tripos, good heavens yes, Jacob thought. May. Eighteen weeks, four and a half months.

'But then, after that talk – after you asked me . . .'

Her face was sad and tentative – why, if she was glad she was pregnant? And wasn't there an incongruity between her announcement today and her emphatic refusal of him a fortnight ago?

'. . . after that, I started using my diaphragm again, but it was a case of shutting the barn door after the – ' She gave a small snort. 'No, that doesn't work, does it? The horse hadn't bolted, sort of the opposite, actually – '

Jacob was utterly bewildered. 'I don't understand.'

'That's because I *still* haven't finished' – with a trace of impatience.

'Okay, finish.'

'I started using my diaphragm because . . . because you wanted me to stay with you, and I thought, if you wanted that, you'd be hurt if I got pregnant and then . . . and then went away.' She was whispering again.

He understood it all, at once. Life drained out of him, he clasped her knees like a drowning man. It wasn't possible. She couldn't be doing this to him.

It was possible. She was. She was looking down at him with tears running down her cheeks and saying, 'Oh Jacob, my love, you *are* hurt.'

Hurt? How did one say that there was something so much worse than hurt that it shouldn't be called by the same name, something so close to death that he was almost surprised that he was still alive?

Her eyes were searching his face. 'Oh God,' she said. 'I'm sorry, I'm sorry. If I'd known it would be as bad as this for you . . . I *did* know, after you asked me to stay; but it was too late.'

She didn't know, she didn't know. He buried his head in her lap and heaved with racking sobs. She crouched over him, stroking his back and making smothered helpless soothing noises.

As his tears subsided, he was overwhelmed by incredulous anger against fate. He must ask her. Already he knew it was useless, but he had to try. Perhaps at this moment, if only out of pity, she would relent. He raised his head and looked into her grave unhappy eyes. 'Please,' he said. '*Please.*'

She shook her head. 'I told you, I can't.' Her face was almost as knotted as his.

'But that was before you knew this.'

'But I don't see' – her turn for bewilderment – 'why this makes so *much* difference. I thought you might be upset, but not *this* upset.'

His response was to break down again. For a long time after he stopped crying, he sat with his face in her lap, too drained to move. Eventually, however, he stirred and sat up, muttering, 'My legs are going to sleep.' Shaking his hot head stupidly, he began to hoist himself up, and promptly collapsed in an agony of pins and needles.

Imogen smiled very tentatively. 'Mine have gone to sleep too,' she offered, as if community in a ludicrous form of suffering might somehow be the beginning of a way back to ordinary life. She leaned forward and touched his hair and his cheek.

He winced. 'Don't bother about me,' he said bitterly. 'I've served my purpose.'

She snatched her hand back. 'That's not fair.'

'Oh yes it is. Why didn't you tell me that all I was to you was a – a stallion or bull or something?'

She crimsoned. 'Oh.' Silence. 'Oh. I didn't . . . you're right. But I never thought of you like *that*, and it didn't occur to me that you would – '

'But why didn't you tell me what you were doing? Just *tell* me, for God's sake?'

'Oh – I was going to – but I felt sort of shy about it: it was rather a . . . a delicate matter just to bring up out of the blue, you see; and I didn't think anything would happen so soon; and I'd just about worked myself up to telling you about it, when you asked me . . . to stay . . . and then – but it was too late; it had already happened . . . and . . . You're right, I shouldn't have decided unilaterally at all, it was very wrong of me. But when I was making up my mind, I didn't think you'd be hurt; I sort of thought you'd be a little bit *pleased*, that I wanted your child rather than somebody else's.'

Pleased. A little bit pleased. Jacob lay back on the floor with his hands behind his head and said, from a long way off, his inflection ironic and detached: 'My dear Imogen, "pleased" hardly begins to describe what I felt when you told me.'

'Then why – ?'

From the same long distance he said, 'It seems we've neither of us been telling each other enough. I didn't tell you about . . . because . . . because it involved talking about Laura in a way that would sound critical, and – damn it, we were lovers, and I didn't want to remind either of us too often that I used to think of you as my daughter.' He sat up, gripping his knees, for the moment beyond any emotion except a strong desire to deal out to her a thousandth of the pain she was inflicting on him. 'Do you know what I've wanted, ever since – ' He shook with unpleasant laughter. This was beginning to be a tale told far too often: in the past to women who did not want to have his child – Sheila and Laura – and now to one who did want to – but who wouldn't stay with him. And there was an irony so convoluted that it made him dizzy to think about: that the woman he must now tell it to, who was pregnant with his child, was – had been – the child who was the starting point of the tale. But how else to twist the knife? He began again. 'Do you remember, back in sixty-four, the first year I knew you, your parents had a party in December, and I came up and read you a story about a Russian witch?'

'Oh, the Baba-Yaga.' But she shook her head; she didn't remember.

Why should she? She had been only six years old. Yet her forgetting it was a blow: one of nature's senseless cruelties. He smiled despondently and told her about coming down the stairs and being seized with desire for a daughter: 'One just like you, a daughter Sheila and I would have.'

Her eyes widened; she saw the whole thing from just those words; but he went on, recalling, fondly, this and that incident – the duckpond, the Piero in the National Gallery – that had made him even more want a daughter just like her.

'Never a son?' she asked with a glimmer of amusement.

'I knew I'd have to take what I got, and I knew I'd love a son too, but no, what I always *saw* was a daughter, and I'd give her everything Frances and Oliver were giving you, and she'd be the happiest, loveliest, most – ' He stopped, on the edge of tears. 'But Sheila wouldn't . . . and wouldn't . . . And when she left, I started seeing you and your family again, and you kept reminding me of what it could mean to be involved in the fate of a child.' *Déja vu*; surely he had once said just those words to Laura, only the persons changed. Only. 'Then I had the same idea all over again with Laura – a daughter with her, who'd be like you and her both. That was just after the quarrel with your parents that I've never told you about, because it would hurt you.' Jacob laughed shortly. He would tell her now. 'Frances accused me of trying to steal you from them because I didn't have a child of my own. I'd told her how much I wanted one, and she knew it was the worst thing she could say to me.'

Imogen sucked in her breath and flushed. 'Oh. Oh. How dreadful for you. And poor Mother, too, not knowing how much I . . . But she was right in a way – not about you, about me. I remember, that year, I often wished you were my father instead – ' She looked away and then back; their eyes met in intense embarrassment, almost horror, at the sudden slide and shift of the categories 'father' and 'child'. 'Then why haven't you and Laura had children?' she asked hurriedly.

He shrugged. 'She hasn't wanted to – no, *has* wanted to, but work was more important. It's come nearer than anything to splitting us up. For a long time she'd say: Maybe in two or three years. Recently – well, she's thirty-seven now. There only *are* two or three more years, and that's pushing it, for a first child. I don't even dare ask any more. So that's the way things are – or were. I couldn't just leave Laura and find some-one to have children with, because I wanted her more than I wanted some child in the abstract – I wanted one *with* her – but it wasn't – it isn't – as if Laura – as if *anything* – makes up for not having a daughter: only that losing Laura would have been even worse. And now . . .' He looked at Imogen. What he had wanted so intensely, for so long – how could it be this close, yet as far away as ever? It was not in nature to accept such injustice. There must be something to say – something to do – shake consent out of her – plead until she understood . . . But she saw his expression and shook her head, remorsefully unyielding. His resolution guttered out, and he only said, 'And now I'll *never* have a daughter.'

'You never do think "son", do you?' She was laughing – not at him, but slightly hysterical with the appallingly tangled absurdity of it all.

238

'It just slipped out,' he said defensively. 'I thought "son" too. Anyway, son or daughter makes no odds now.'

'There's no chance that Laura –'

'There's precious little chance she'll have me back at all, let alone –'

'Have you back?' she asked with fear and surprise. 'You haven't – because of *me* – broken off with Laura . . . ?'

'No – I think she'll break off with *me*, though. I haven't told her about my proposal to you yet, and there was a pretty good chance she'd chuck me for that: so wait till she hears about this!'

'Why this more than –' Imogen saw. 'Oh. Oh no. Do you have to tell her?'

'Hmph. In time she'd see for herself,' he said drily.

'No, I meant telling her how you feel about it. I know you have to, actually, it wasn't a serious question – it's just all so awful for you.' She suddenly looked even more horrorstruck. 'Oh Lord, and it's sure to be a girl.'

'Yup.' He lay back on the carpet once more; he didn't want to cry again, and he was getting dangerously close. He closed his eyes. 'Funny,' he said after a while, 'I didn't even know you especially liked children.'

'Oh, I don't know that I do, especially. But liking other people's children and having your own are different.' Her voice was clear and confident.

After another interval he said, 'You won't get much chance to be alone.'

'That's different too – I think. But maybe I just have to give up being alone.'

He ran out of things to say; he was tired and empty. He lay still, throat tight and eyes sore with tears shed and unshed, washed in turn by grief, weariness, anger, boredom – and always, returning, grief, such as he had never felt before, not even for Sheila.

It had gone dark. Imogen stirred and leaned forward. One side of her face glimmered in the fading light from the window. 'Do you want me to go?' she whispered.

Jacob sat up in alarm and said, 'No, don't leave me, please,' then, 'Sorry – sure, go if you want to,' then, 'I don't mean that; please stay; I can't bear to be alone right now.' He leaned across her to switch on a light and sat back on his heels looking at the woman he loved so painfully.

'I'm a crass, stupid, *young* fool,' she said vehemently. 'I come barging into your life that has all these complications that I don't know about, and I don't even consider, I just make unilateral decisions and think they're only about myself, and, oh Jacob, it's so horrible, because I do love you, and what I've done to you is so dreadful, and there isn't anything to do about it. A few minutes ago I thought of offering to have an abortion –'

'No!' he said violently.

'No, I couldn't either, because I wanted to be pregnant and have a child, and I am, and I couldn't go back on that now.' But his outburst had raised her feminist hackles. 'You sound awfully possessive, the way you said "No!" What if it were the way you thought at first, and I hadn't wanted to be pregnant – would you have tried to make me keep it, wanting children the way you do?'

'Heavens, no. Then it would have been just a rather miserable misfortune. I'd have felt the sadness that's attached to killing any living thing, if you know what I mean . . . ' He paused, trying to imagine how he would have felt if she had wanted an abortion. 'Hmph. And probably I'd have secretly felt very sorry for myself – I'd have thought: The only child I'll ever conceive is an accident that's disappearing before it becomes real. But that's all.'

'But it would be so much easier on you. Oh dear, it would have been better if we'd never begun in the first place.' She started to cry.

'Hey, don't *you* start. You'll set me off, and if I bawl any more, I'll . . . I can't think what. Tell you what, let's go to the Peking.'

She stared at him with a smudged incredulous face. 'Now?'

'Now.'

They went, ate – ate hugely, in fact – and even enjoyed what they ate. 'I love this stuff,' said Imogen, scoffing a second plate of fried seaweed.

'You've never eaten *two* helpings before. Are you eating for two, or is this one of those pregnant women's cravings?'

She looked up alertly. She was not mistaken; he had been joking: self-consciously – whistling in the dark – but distinctly joking. He immediately regretted the joke; he wanted her to be miserable. But then again, he was beginning not to want her to be miserable.

'God, I'm exhausted,' he said when they got home. 'Could you bear going to bed this early?'

'I'm exhausted too,' she said, starting up the stairs.

'Sleeping for two?'

She turned back to him, her attention pricking up at another sign of recuperation.

He stopped on the landing and looked up at her. 'Young Imogen, before we went out, you said it would have been better if we'd never become lovers, and I didn't say anything, because I thought you were right.'

'Oh dear.'

'But I've been thinking it over, and I think I've changed my mind.'

'Oh. I'm not sure what that means.'

'Me neither. Just that, in spite of all this, I wouldn't want not to have loved you – to love you. I think. It's too early to tell, I suppose. Maybe someday it'll even be "including all this", not "in spite of it", though God knows I can't imagine it now.'

Chapter 48

ACOB FLOATED DROWSILY to the surface thirteen hours later, puzzled. It was like waking up in a strange room. He opened his eyes. His own ceiling, and Imogen's shiny black head burrowed into the pillow beside him. His scalp was tingling agreeably. Was there a treat in store, or had it already happened?

Memory pounced. Had happened – was going to happen. Both. And no treat. Sorrow and grief. Calamities.

But in his drugged early morning languour he was almost tranquil, contemplating the cleavage down the middle of his life. Before, after. Look back: the past, with patterns converging on the present, somehow predictable. Look ahead: for the first time ever, a future without probabilities, precedents, signposts. The watershed.

Imogen turned over, still asleep, jamming her fist against her mouth. She twitched. Her eyes opened and met his with unreflecting delight; then her pupils contracted as she too remembered.

'There, there, puchkie,' he said softly. 'There, there. Stop biting your knuckles.' She took her hand away from her mouth, and they lay looking at each other, lapped in a temporary stillness.

He made a breakfast tray and took it up. 'You know,' he said, spreading jam on his toast, 'yesterday I never asked you why. Not why you can't stay with me,' responding to her look of alarm, 'but why you decided to have a child now, on your own.'

She frowned in bafflement. 'It's so hard to explain; I almost don't know why, myself. It flicked across my mind in the autumn, not even related to you at first: just something I wished I could do. There are a couple of single mothers in the pregnancy-testing group, and I admired them for undertaking so much, and the way they manage on social security and odd jobs – and I found I was beginning to envy them, too. I wanted a child . . . just . . . wanted one. I couldn't say why, but it wasn't just an impulse, it was . . . a craving. And a conviction. And then I started thinking: Why not do it as soon as possible? It was exciting, the idea of having a child without the whole rigmarole of house and family and being supported and all that – I'd be tied to the child, but not to one place and one set of pre-mapped social relations, you see. The moral and physical responsibility would be my own – I wouldn't be cushioned. It was something worth doing – a terrific adventure, having to pit oneself against anything that came up, because of responsibilities one couldn't get away from.'

He remembered her staring into him and saying, 'Oh, I want responsibilities,' when he had accused her of ducking them. Ducking!

242

'And the more I thought about it, the more I wanted it, especially because . . . because of you.' She looked to see if he were hurt, but he was still anaesthetised and only nodded. 'It gave me a shiver of pleasure like nothing else I've ever felt. But maybe it would be awfully self-indulgent and cowardly – would I be dodging the question of what to do with my life: equipping myself with responsibilities by a simple biological act instead of working it out rationally. On the other hand, if I decided against it, would I just be dodging the struggles of bringing up a child on my own? It seemed I'd be dodging *something*, either way. I thought of waiting a couple of years, till I came back to England, supposing I did – but by then you . . . might be involved with someone else; and I *did* want you to be . . . the father . . . Anyhow, it wouldn't be the same, being in England with a child; Mother and Father wouldn't let it be; they'd cushion everything, give me money, all that – and it's so seductive, comfort and money, that maybe I wouldn't be able to resist, especially if Mother said I should do such-and-such for the child's sake, you see? And I don't *want* to have everything cushy *all* my life – and besides, I didn't want to put it off at all. I want a child now. More than one, eventually – but one now, while I'm young and giddy.'

'Giddy you are not, pet. What d'you mean?'

'Oh . . . not having money and a base and family nearby. The challenge of that – being ready to meet it. And giving the child the happiness and energy I've got right now. Who knows, in a few years my energy might get more . . . spread out, bound to places and people and circumstances. But that's not an explanation. In the end it's something I can't explain – something I came to want. I weighed the pros and cons, and there didn't seem to be anything against it, because I didn't know about your feelings; and I wanted it so powerfully that it's like that sense of vocation we've talked about. Maybe I won't even be any good at it, but . . . And . . . and . . . and I wanted . . . oh dear . . . I so much wanted a child that was half yours – and, oh, now that it's happened, I can't go back, and I'm still glad, for me. But I'm *so* sorry for what I've done to you – if I'd known, I'd never never never have . . .'

Jacob's heart swelled with love for his heroine, who so little knew she was one – who wished for his sake that she could renounce her prize. 'I know, love,' he said. 'And, listen, this'll sound crazy, but' – tentatively, feeling his way with every word – 'but what I think I feel is that I do wish it hadn't happened, but I also don't want it not to have happened. I can't unwish something so – so real.'

She smiled, grateful, understanding him exactly, and drank the rest of her coffee, looking at him over the rim of the cup. Her eyes smote him, as usual, with the surprise of their beauty: the most beautiful eyes he had ever seen or ever would see – unless she passed them on to her daughter – to her *child*, damn it. (Not his – siring it was not enough to make it his.) Would it have her eyes – the finely striated golden-brown irises, dark round the edges, the poignant shape, black-lashed under straight black eyebrows? He hoped it didn't get his ordinary muddy brown ones instead – or his red hair, either.

Self-pity was welling up. To keep it at bay he asked, 'So what will you do? Practically, I mean. Of course I'll want to contrib-'

'No, I wouldn't want . . . it's not . . . I know you want . . . but it's part of the idea, you see, being on my own. *Do* you see?'

He did see that this was not the time to press the point, so he just nodded.

'I *could* voluntarily subsist on social security, but there's no point in going to extremes of self-deprivation if you don't have to – and it seems I can't help having things somewhat cushy. I rang Antonella at Christmas and asked: What if I turn up with an illegitimate baby, and not in September, but sometime in the new year; and she said: Fine, wonderful, congratulations; and I said: Don't congratulate me yet, I'm not pregnant, just hoping to be; and she wished me luck and told me to let her know when it was due, and said she knew a very good creche for while I'm working, and it's very close, so I can feed the ba- the child between classes – and Italians like children so much; I'm sure it'll get lots of affection from the creche people as well as me . . .'

Carried away with her plans for the future, she did not see Jacob wincing at the death of another hope. Until now it had not occurred to him that she could still be intending to go to Rome; the strength of his desire had deafened him to the allusions to Italy that had been strewn through her conversation all morning. He had assumed that she would be in England, in

London probably, living on her own with the child (daughter, son); that he would at least be able to visit them; that over the years he would come to play in the child's life something of the role he had once played in hers, only more so, kindly, avuncular, diminished, taking it to the zoo and riding on buses, having it to stay now and then. But it would be in Rome. She would come home with it for holidays, and he would go to Italy, perhaps more than before: but that would not be enough to establish even as much connection as he had had to the young Imogen, let alone anything closer, 'I take it you're aiming to shield this child from the contamination of knowing its father,' he said acidly when she stopped singing the praises of the Italian attitude to children.

'Don't be silly,' she replied with some asperity; then, repenting: 'No, I don't want to exclude you from – from whatever I can give you. I love you, and that won't stop even when – if – I fall in love with someone else. I'll always want to be able to see you – if you want to see me – and I especially want my child to know you – and know you're its father. Children need roots, a knowledge of where they come from, a sense of being tied to a line. That's one reason I wanted it to be *you*: so that my child will be able to be proud of its father.'

There was an unconsciously pathetic note in these last words, coming from Imogen, who could not be particularly proud of Oliver; and they melted him. He tried to speak, but could not.

She looked at him anxiously. 'You've got sad again.'

He shook his head, not in denial, but trying to shake away the return of pain. Tears sprang to his eyes, and he looked at her with the word, 'Please,' rising irresistible to his lips.

'No, I can't,' she said, gently but forcefully, before he could speak.

'Goddammmit, why not? I won't ever see it, it won't know me –'

'I've told you why – I need to be on my own –'

'Can't you at least stay in England?'

'But my job is in Rome –'

'Damn Oliver and his hotsy-totsy ideas,' he muttered wildly. 'It's that hotel job he got you that started all this –'

' – and it's as important to me as yours is to you. Would

245

you throw up your work to come and live unemployed in Rome with me? Not,' she added hastily, 'that that's an invitation.'

'Yes,' he asserted. Then: 'But . . . oh hell, I've got contracts I can't leave . . . and it would take me years to get established there the way I am here, it'd be back to taking boring jobs just to eat . . .'

'You see? That's the position I'd be in if I stayed in England. I could find something, but I don't want just any old job. In Rome I have work I want to do, and a bit of a life, from my summers – more than here, where except for you I'm not tied to anything, I'm just a student.'

'You wouldn't need a job – I could support you. In London, if you don't want to be here. You in London, me in Cambridge – you'd be on your own then.'

'Oh dear, oh dear.' Imogen sighed. 'This may sound strange, after saying how much I want a child, but I wouldn't want one if I had to be a full-time nothing-else-doing mother, with that amount of isolation. Besides, it's part of the challenge, to make it all work, to do – '

'The impossible. You'll be devastated. Don't you realise how exhausting – '

' – the first year of a child's life is for mothers who are doing nothing else, let alone for one working outside the home as well? Of course. But women all over the world are having children and going on doing whatever puts bread into their mouths. How could I hold up my head if I gave up a useful job to sit somewhere in London doing nothing but nursing a child? And it'd be like being in prison.'

Jacob had got back his self-control. 'Frances will be proud of you,' he said wryly, 'such a feminist you've become.'

She shook her head. 'I'm not so sure. She'll worry. I'd better go home next weekend and tell them – and you'll think I'm awfully childish, but I'm nervous.'

'My dear, the way you've grown up in these three years – childish is the last thing I'd call you.' His Imogen, no longer his Imogen, starting on the adventure of life. She was like Ulysses setting out for the Western Isles. He noticed the time and added absentmindedly, out of a past life: 'Goodness, nearly noon, time to get up. Laura and I are due at the NFT at three. They've got a thirty-five millimetre print of *Gone with the*

246

Wind.' He was on his feet before it hit him. 'Jesus. NFT indeed. I've got to tell her.'

Imogen looked miserably up at him. 'Couldn't you wait just a little, till you feel better?'

'Well, no. Quite aside from the question of when and if I'll ever feel better' – he could not help rubbing it in, though he knew that one did, eventually, recover even from blows as deadly as this – 'I have to tell her now. Today. It's part of our bargain. I've already been wrong, not telling her for such a long time about, uh, proposing to you. But this I mustn't postpone at all, it's a different order of magnitude. And there's no way to make it less horrible.' He sat down again in dismay.

'You don't think she'll stay, do you?'

'God knows. One in four chance maybe. At best. But I'd better have my shower and put on my bib and tucker and go find out.' He hugged her. 'Imogen, I'm frightened. I was so happy, and now . . .'

'And now I've taken *everything* away from you, if Laura goes.' She gulped. 'Oh, I'm awful. I keep trying to act right, and I've acted as wrong as I could do.'

'No, pet. Yes, you were wrong not to tell me what you were up to – even if you thought I wouldn't care, you should have. But everything else is just the way things worked out. You didn't know how much I wanted children, because I never told you, so you couldn't know how much I'd mind. People are responsible for their lives, after all. I don't mean that everything that happens to them is their fault; but if they choose to do certain things, and their choices lead to unexpected results, they're responsible for . . . oh, you know, for living with the results, whatever they are.' He stood up again and stretched. 'There must be life in me yet. I just found myself thinking what a pity it will be to miss *Gone with the Wind.*'

Chapter 49

ELLING LAURA WAS dreadful. He started right away, still standing up in the middle of her room – but the coward's way round: instead of telling her first about his proposal, he simply said that Imogen was pregnant and wanted to be.

Her face closed. 'And that's tipped the balance – you're leaving me for Imogen.'

'No,' he said baldly. 'She's having the baby on her own and taking it to Rome with her.' He was putting off the evil moment, but he repented when he saw her face soften with pity: she had leapt to the conclusion that she still came first with him, in spite of the child. It was unbearable. Speaking slowly, feeling like a murderer, he quashed the look. 'A fortnight ago, more, in fact, on the sixth of February, to be precise, I asked Imogen if she would live with me. Before I knew she was pregnant. I didn't know she was trying to be.'

Laura drew in her breath and turned her head away; when he reached out, she retreated quickly to the far end of the long room and from there flung back: 'What did she say?'

'She said no.'

'*Why didn't you tell me*?' It was the first time she had ever raised her voice to him.

The truth. 'I was too hurt to talk about it. And scared to tell you.'

She turned and went into the bedroom. Jacob stayed where he was; he guessed that she was getting out of sight. In a short time she came back as far as the door. 'And when she told you she was pregnant?'

'Three guesses,' he said bitterly, then, contrite: 'Sorry, this is no time to be facetious –'

'You asked her again.'

'Yes. Not with any hope. Though, the way she told me, it wasn't clear for a while that I was excluded, and I assumed she wanted us to be together . . . But yes, when I got the drift, I did ask.'

'Excluded?' – startled. 'You mean she won't let you see it?'

'No, nothing so drastic.' He told her what Imogen had said, and then, falteringly, the whole story, watching her with admiration while he spoke. She was standing in the doorway, listening: taking horrible blows – the words of pleading love that he had spoken to another woman – and taking them bolt upright without a quaver. Quite a woman. His heart quailed at the thought of losing her. Losing *her*, not losing second best after Imogen. But nothing he could say would make her understand that. He wouldn't, in her shoes. At last he fell silent. It was not that he had nothing more to say – everything was still to say. But he had no right. He waited for her to speak.

She stood there at the end of the long narrow room, in the protection of the bedroom doorway, upright, unmoving, unspeaking, an avenging angel of scorned womanhood. If she lifted her arm, he would see the sword in her hand. Then she said the most astonishing thing. 'My poor Jacob.' Not sarcastic, not gloating: on a note of pure pain and pure pity. She still did not move.

His throat ached from holding back tears. He croaked, 'I should have thought it was, "My poor Laura".'

'Oh, yes, that too . . . But . . . my curiosity is aroused.' She made an odd little gesture with her right hand, the rest of her body so immobile that it was as if a statue had moved. 'I'm surprised you're still in the land of the living – if you still are.' Her voice was neutral, controlled – a statue talking, for all the expression she put into it; but she was asking a question, and one that expected an answer. An important question.

An important answer. What was it necessary to say, not to lose this woman, whom, oh God, he loved? Nothing could possibly meet the occasion. The truth. Not that it would answer; but he had never lied to her and wouldn't know how to begin now: couldn't conceive of beginning now, for the basis of their life together was truth no matter what the cost. So – the truth.

Whatever that was. 'A good question,' he temporised. 'If I knew for sure, I'd tell you. Yesterday I thought not. It was' – tears filled his eyes – 'the worst thing' – he sniffed – 'that's ever happened to me.'

'Worse than Sheila?'

'Yes. Not Imogen's refusing to live with me. That was – is – bad; but the whole idea was . . . I was serious about it, but it was crazy too, because it meant losing you, and that was horrible . . .' She grunted contemptuously, and he hurried on. 'So I was alive after that, no question. But a daughter – oh damn, Imogen kept twitting me about that – a child: it'll exist, somewhere else, but I won't hold it and hear it learn to talk and those things; I won't have any responsibility for it. Maybe it'll want to visit me when it's older, but things won't be the same as if it had been bound up in my life when it was little. Losing all that is so awful that I don't quite know if I'm still – what you asked – still alive. I'm so sorry for myself that I feel like a zombie. But – maybe. Right now I think I must be alive because I –'

'Because you – ?'

He shook his head – he had no right to say it.

Laura did not press him. She came a little way into the room and looked at him. Now that she was out of the shadowed doorway, he could see her better. Her curious triangular face was at its least beautiful: plain, grim, eyes cold, jaw set to hold back wrath – though she had uttered not a word of reproach except that one furious accusation of broken faith: 'Why didn't you tell me?' By their rules he had not been at fault in asking Imogen to stay, only in failing to tell Laura immediately afterwards; even in extremity her strict sense of justice distinguished between what was culpable and what was merely unbearable. With eyes open they had both chosen to live at risk, and what she was suffering now could have happened to either of them: she would bear it without a murmur. Jacob could not have done so; her heroism staggered him.

She made another stiff little gesture with her right hand. 'What now?'

'What now, indeed. What do *you* want?'

'To go and curl up in a hole and die. Aside from that – what do *you* want?'

Impasse. They looked at each other, both stubborn. At last Jacob said, 'All right, all right, I'll say what I stopped saying a few minutes ago because I don't have any right even to say it, let alone ask . . . I was going to say that I think I must be alive because what I feel most is – well, there are two things. One is pain and grief, and the other is that I love you and don't want to lose you, and part of the pain and grief is because I think I'm going to.'

Silence.

It hadn't worked; well, he hadn't thought it would. The truth has no virtues beyond itself, no magical power to put things right. The world is oiled with lies. He should have lied. 'That's it, then, is it?' he said in a small voice.

She came a few steps closer. 'Would you always be thinking: This is all right, but it could have been Imogen and children?'

Oh God, was it possible? Another important question, and the right answer, the only answer, again the truth. 'Can I try to answer by saying that the thing that most of all nearly kept me from asking Imogen to stay in the first place was that the thought of losing you was unbearable? I don't know how to explain it; it doesn't make sense. The thought of losing either of you is unbearable.'

'But you spoke.'

'Yes. What that means I don't know.'

'You decided that losing Imogen would be more unbearable than losing me – '

'No. It's not like – '

' – and now more so, because of the child.'

'Well . . .' He nodded. 'But they're separate issues, losing just Imogen and losing the – the child too.'

'You haven't answered my question. Would you always be thinking: If only?'

This time he tried to answer it head on. 'I don't know; only time would tell. But I don't think so, or I wouldn't be wanting you to stay with me. Every once in a while, maybe – thinking about children, you know. The thing is, people do survive, and feelings do get less, or change, or go away. I thought I'd never get over Sheila; but I did – and now I'm actually glad she left, because life with her was such hell.'

'Aside from the hell, did you love Sheila more than me?'
Laura had never asked that before.

'No,' he said definitely. The question: Is that true? rose in his
mind, but he stifled it.

'But you do love Imogen more than me' – coldly.

He said in exasperation, 'I can't quantify my emotions like
that. It's not arithmetic – so many points for Imogen's on-the-
edgeness, so many for your *caritas*. You're the scientist around
here, go get one of your .00001 of a gram weighing machines.'

They were on the verge of a row. Laura bit her lip.

'Don't let's fight,' Jacob said.

'I was just going to say that,' she replied. Ordinarily they
would have smiled in pleasure at the concurrence of their
thoughts. Now they avoided each other's eyes. She looked off
behind him. 'I don't know. I don't know what to do.'

'What do you *want* to do?'

She glanced at him and away. 'On balance, to stay. But it
seems so *abject*.'

'And in the end would that weigh more?'

'No,' she said doubtfully. 'What would weigh would be
wondering where your mind was, here or there. I just don't
know – what I want to do, what I should do.'

He nodded, thinking with a painful semblance of happiness:
My God, the nearly impossible has happened – if she says now
that she can't make up her mind, surely she'll stay in the end?

Her eyes suddenly glittered. 'I'll tell you one thing you'd
better put on the weighing machine,' she hissed with pent-up
ire. 'If there was anything that would make it certain that I
wouldn't have children, this is it. I won't compete for you
with Imogen by – by pupping.'

This he hadn't thought of. He nodded again – condition
accepted – keeping his expression steady, though he was reeling
from yet another blow. How could one guess that one could take
so much and not start running about gibbering in the streets?

'And if I do want a child, I won't have it with you, I'll leave
you and find someone else.' Pure, undiluted, vicious rage: the
sword in her hand flashing out for one savage stab of retaliation.
Jacob sat down abruptly on her sofa, transfixed, his face crum-
pling with pain – for him, for her.

After a moment she came down the room towards him,
hesitated, then sat down at the other end of the sofa. Not

252

touching him, not close to him: but on the same territory. Letting out her breath in a long sigh she said, 'Well. A pretty fix we're in. Presumably this is the kind of thing people mean when they say that sleeping with more than one person always leads to trouble.'

'Do you think so? I've always assumed they've got much less complicated . . . uh . . . complications in mind. Though I do seem to be in one of the stock situations – older man with seven-year itch making a fool of himself over a young girl. Just the thing you asked about when Imogen and I began.' He turned to her with what passed for a rueful smile.

'Nonsense. If I thought you were like that!' She too mustered something of a smile.

'It *has* been seven years, you know.'

'Well, you're not Tom Ewell, and Imogen's certainly not Marilyn,' Laura returned tartly.

Their ghostly smiles deepened momentarily; they looked at each other in surprise – so life did go on, did it? Then they sank back on their separate ends of the sofa in exhaustion. Jacob wished he could move closer, but he felt as if he had forfeited his right to go within a yard of Laura unless she gave a sign. Then he realised that in the circumstances she would do no such thing. Uncertain as he felt, outraged though she might be, it was he who would have to do the moving, now or later, if they were not to remain permanently six feet apart. Now? He was very nervous, but also very lonely. Now. He hitched cautiously towards her and extended his arm across her shoulders, tentative as a boy on his first date. Laura did not shrug him off. She passively let him gather her to his side, rather awkwardly; and after a while she curled her feet up on the sofa and laid her head in his lap. He put one hand on her back, one on her toffee-brown hair, and they sat there quietly, thinking their own thoughts.

Jacob's were of questions he couldn't answer. After the pain of the last months and days, would he and Laura be able to reconstruct their lives, or would it be too much for them? Would he always be thinking: If only? Did he now, would he ever, think of her as second best? Why had he spoken to Imogen?

That at least was easy: because with Imogen he had had the same sense of being complete that had made him cling to Sheila in spite of their unhappiness: a sense that came to him only with someone as extreme – or as much like him – as Sheila or Imogen. It was neither the same thing as happiness nor necessary to happiness, and during seven happy years with Laura – happier because he remembered the misery of living with Sheila – he had virtually forgotten its existence or his hunger for it.

Had he, then, loved Sheila more than Laura?

Was that even a valid question? One could be pierced through and through with regret for the loss of something without wishing it back in place of what one had now. He didn't want Sheila back – life with her had been too dreadful, the conditions she imposed on it too limiting. But till the day he died he would be wrung with pain at having lost her. Even Imogen, whose extremity of daring was as great, had not made him stop regretting her.

Yet. Though. However. Perhaps. If. His mind swept back and forth over vast obscure questions, without perspective. In order to act right, he needed answers now. But he was drastically off balance: not off his head, but not quite sane either. All he could do was ask himself how he would behave if he were in his usual state, act on whatever answers his unbalanced mind returned, and hope for the best.

Chapter 50

HE NEXT DAY Laura with characteristic magnanimity called on Imogen to tell her she wasn't angry – not at Imogen, that is – and that she would help her any way she could. She went without telling Jacob; he learned of it from Imogen, who had been dreading that Laura would detest her and was surprised, touched, reassured and finally overwhelmed by her transparently genuine tender of help and friendship. 'We were a bit awkward at first, because we don't know each other all that well, and here we were in this somehow frightfully intimate situation; and I couldn't actually think of any help I needed . . . Besides, it seemed indecent to accept help from her when what I've done – and to her, too . . . But she insisted, and got me talking about things that were worrying me, and it *was* a help. Funny, up to now we've really only been friends through you, and in the pregnancy-testing group and NAC; we've known a lot about each other, but we've hardly ever talked on our own. It's so strange that this, of all things, should make us friends in our own right, but that's what it felt like.'

'What did you talk about?' Jacob was a little jealous – of what or whom he wasn't quite sure.

'Not you,' Imogen said quickly. 'About things like why everybody at Norwich Street is so surprised that I'm not having an abortion; and how Mother and Father will react.'

'You're quite worried about that, aren't you?'

'Not really. Mother will be okay, and so will Father, once he gets used to the idea – he's more old-fashioned than he thinks, and it'll be quite dire for a few hours. But he'll come round. After all, they aren't traditional heavy parents, they don't mind about my lovers – that is, I suspect Father does, secretly, but he'd never admit it; and I think Mother's rather proud of my, er, record. She'll be worried about me, but she had me when she was twenty-three, so she'll understand why I want to start young, and she'll get Father to semi-see it.'

But the weekend shook her. Her parents rallied round splendidly when she told them she was pregnant; but, when she said thank you, but she didn't want an abortion, she was keeping the child, all hell broke loose. Oliver had gone white and stormed about the room; Frances had cried and cajoled. They couldn't believe she meant it, or that she had got pregnant by her own choice – that was a story she had invented to whitewash Jacob. Oliver had said he didn't want a bastard in the family; Frances had hushed him – then told her it would be selfish to inflict the stigma of illegitimacy on a helpless child.

'What's so awful,' Imogen said sadly, 'is that Mother's always defending the right of unmarried mothers in court, and she's terribly proud of it – but she didn't make the connection at all.'

On the Sunday they had been less furious, but every bit as determined to make her change her mind. What about her own future, Oliver had asked severely at breakfast. After he'd put so much money into her education, didn't she owe it to him to do decently in Tripos? – and how could she, when she might be knocked out by morning sickness? Imogen was actually feeling rather queasy for the first time; she thanked goodness that she hadn't mentioned it and replied that morning sickness didn't last beyond three months – she would be well past that by Tripos. But Frances said that it had absolutely flattened *her* every day till the sixth month; and Oliver, who had been counting on his fingers, exclaimed, 'You'll be five months pregnant in June? It'll show by then, won't it? You'll miss May Week!'

'Mother saw the funny side of that, but she said rather nastily that I was inconsistent, campaigning for abortion but refusing to have one, and I got cross and said: "The slogan is, a woman's right to *choose*, Mother – don't you support my right to choose?" Oh dear, it was awful: rows, rows, rows all weekend; and they still don't understand that I'm acting on a decision I've made and really won't have an abortion, no matter what. By last night Mother was telling Father – but talking at me – to remember that I was only seven weeks pregnant, and I'd only known for a week, and quite naturally, being so young, I was all overcome with motherly feelings and therefore a trifle irrational. When I'd had more time to think, I'd realise I was being totally impractical. There was still plenty of time for an abortion – five weeks more for the early type; and even after that, if I was very late making up my mind, the techniques for late abortion had improved a lot.

'I said: "Nonsense, late abortions are very unpleasant; all that's improved is the complications rate," and she said: "Then it's important for you to make up your mind soon," and I said: "But my mind *is* made up, I'm keeping it," and she said: "Oh, darling, that's what you think now, but when you've thought about it – " and I said: "Anyhow, Mother, the timing would be wrong. There's that gap between twelve and sixteen weeks when it's too late for early-abortion techniques and too early for late-abortion ones. By the time I'm sixteen weeks, Tripos

256

will be almost starting – you wouldn't want me to sit Tripos just after a late abortion, would you? And by the time Tripos is over, I'll be twenty weeks; and doctors only operate that late if the woman's circumstances are desperate." Mother said: "Woman! You're hardly more than a child. You'll miss out on your youth if you go on with this!" and I said: "I'm nearly twenty-two – you had me when you were only a year older." Poor Mother – she wanted to say that that was different, because she was married to Father and settled; but she couldn't do that without contradicting her feminism. So instead she said: "Obviously you can't have a late abortion, with Tripos in the way; so you'll just have to make up your mind in the next five weeks." I think there's going to be a bit of a siege.'

For the next week the Standishes rang Imogen two or three times a day, urging her to change her mind; they were so insistent and upsetting that by the weekend she was spending all her waking hours away from Norwich Street to escape the telephone.

But they were not so easily evaded. Early on Monday evening Imogen rang Jacob and asked if she could come over. She sounded wrought up. 'I know Laura's there, and I'm sorry to be a nuisance, but I do so need to talk to you – both. It's my parents – they're here, on the warpath.'

Jacob raised his eyebrows enquiringly to Laura.

'Laura says fine,' he answered. 'Come right over.'

In the fortnight since Imogen's revelation there had been a subtle change in relations among the three of them: a new atmosphere of wordless agreement that, though Jacob and Imogen were still lovers, the two who were aligned as a pair were Jacob and Laura, with Imogen slightly peripheral. They were all contributing to the change. Jacob, however much he yearned towards Imogen, was doing his damndest to put Laura first, in fulfilment of the tacit promise he had made by asking her to stay. Imogen, conscience-struck about the devastation she had wreaked, was moving herself away from the centre of his life to make room for Laura; and Laura, having decided – provisionally – to stay, was making it clear where she stood: at the centre or nowhere. So Imogen sat in the wing chair when she came in, leaving the place beside Jacob on the sofa to Laura, who took it without demur, looked with concern at her strained expression and asked her what was up.

What was up was a state of siege. The Standishes had come to Cambridge on Sunday night, settled into the Garden House and rung Norwich Street to tell Imogen to meet them for Monday lunch. In the morning they had called first on her tutor, who had utterly refused to intervene, ignoring Frances' flattery and Oliver's dark hints of exposés that could be written about undergraduate promiscuity at King's; then on her GP, who was quite properly deaf to suggestions that he should coerce his patient; then on a feminist psychotherapist whom one of Frances' friends had recommended. They had thought she was wonderful and arranged for Imogen to see her after lunch – she had had to skip a supervision to go.

'And it was simply disgusting. All she cared about was what was "in" – the fashion for single motherhood was over, and shouldn't I catch up with the times. Then she asked why I didn't believe in abortion, and when I said I did, and told about my job in Rome, she said – oh, I was *furious* – she said I'd be setting an example of fecklessness to the women I'd be counselling; and it would be frightfully arrogant – almost a form of genocide – to have a child myself, then go and counsel women from another culture about how not to.'

'What an utter idiot,' said Laura.

'You think so too? Good, because I've been sort of wondering . . .'

'Not about that genocide bit, surely?'

'No . . . but she told me that what I wanted wasn't a child, but a sibling, and that I'd got pregnant to pay my parents back for having deprived me of one. She said it was obvious because of,' she hesitated, looking apologetic, 'of "this Oedipal thing I was acting out, sleeping with a father-figure".'

'That,' Laura said roundly, 'is the most unmitigated tripe I've ever heard in my life.'

'Really? You aren't just saying that to . . . No, you wouldn't; you don't say things you don't mean.' Her frown slowly unknotted, and she leaned back with a tired sigh.

Laura inspected her. 'You're looking dreadful. Morning sickness still? – I thought so. Plus parents. How long are they staying?'

'Till they realise I won't change my mind, I suppose.'

'Hmph. You couldn't work much last week, with their telephone calls, and you won't get anything done while they're here. Why not tell them so and send them away?'

Imogen shook her head. 'I've got to give them their chance – they think it's for my good.'

Laura made a noise that Jacob recognised as meaning: 'God grant me patience,' and said, 'In that case, you must come and tell us about it every day while they're here, to let off steam.'

Imogen shook her head again. 'I don't want to be a nuisance after tonight – '

'You won't be. Really. You mustn't take *everything* by yourself. Okay?'

She saw that Laura meant it, nodded in awe and went home looking much better and promising to do some work before bedtime instead of fretting about her parents.

On Tuesday Frances visited Laura in King's. 'She was insufferable,' Laura told Jacob afterwards. 'She commiserated with me for being an older woman, a third wheel, and childless; and she even tried digging to see if you'd thought of throwing me over – "I know how much Jacob wanted children" – just *dripping* sympathy. Thank goodness Imogen hadn't told her about your proposal, it was bad enough without. She says Imogen doesn't know what she's letting herself in for – that her own youth was spoiled by having a child so young instead of having a good time and getting her career established. She thought I'd understand – and then she actually asked me to persuade Imogen to have an abortion for *my* sake!'

'You're kidding.'

'Not a bit. She says that Imogen would do it for me, if I told her that the child would break you and me up. Revolting woman. What I don't understand is, why make all this fuss if she never wanted her in the first place?'

'Well, she does love her, you know. She doesn't know how much she's hurting her; she wouldn't do it on purpose for the world.'

'Humph,' said Laura in disbelief.

That was not the Standishes' only manoeuvre on Tuesday. While Imogen was working in the library, they were in Norwich Street suborning her house-mates, a good-natured group who had been unthinkingly on her side, but did not begin to understand her decision. 'When I got back tonight,' she told Jacob over the telephone that evening, 'they called me to a house meeting and asked me if I was doing the right thing; and they all sounded so much alike that I suddenly guessed my parents had got at them. I asked why they paid more attention to them than me, but it didn't do any good – my parents' position is so much more *reasonable*. I tried to forget about it – but Trojan horses within the gates are a bit much, and I just sat here brooding, till I remembered what Laura said . . . And it *is* a help, talking about it – but after what I've done to you and her, it seems so wrong to turn to either of you . . . Wouldn't it be easier on you if I didn't?'

'Listen, Laura always means what she says; and as for me . . .' He paused. It was over a fortnight since her announcement, and he still felt as if a suspension of ground glass were coursing through his veins instead of blood; the only thing that would be easier on him would be if she were to change her mind. But he could hardly say that with Laura sitting stony-faced in the wing chair – and, in any case, what would be the point? 'As for me . . . well, now that we're in this situation, I'd rather be a help than not. Really.'

'But –'

'You'd feel the same if our positions were reversed, admit.'

'Oh . . . I suppose . . . You're *sure*? – All right.'

Laura had been watching his face; when he hung up, she said, 'I try – I try – and God knows I like and respect and care for her, this mess wouldn't be tolerable for a moment if I didn't – but it's so hard to forgive what she's done . . .'

'To you?' he said gently.

'No, no – to you. The selfishness – the stupidity – of not *telling* you –'

'I don't know, selfish isn't the right word. Thoughtless . . . but even that –'

'Don't make excuses for her' – sharply.

'I'm not. She was wrong not to tell me – appallingly wrong, as it turns out – but it was sort of accidental, too. After all, most men would simply be flattered to be, uh, chosen like that, and she thought I would be too; she didn't know . . . And now that it's happened, what else *can* she do? No matter what I may have . . . asked in the heat of the moment, she can't be expected to change her whole life just because . . .'

'I suppose you're right,' she said grudgingly; then, her sense of justice reasserting itself: 'Yes – I suppose it's understandable, what she did: ninety-nine men out of a hundred would be tickled pink to become fathers without coming in for any of the responsibilities as well. It's just hard luck on Imogen – on all of us – that you're the hundredth.'

The next morning Imogen found out where her parents had gone after Norwich Street. 'They went and saw *Adrian*,' she wailed, bursting in on Jacob at noon. 'And he didn't even know – I haven't seen him since before I knew, because he gets mournful whenever we meet; I was going to tell him *gently* – and they just *told* him, and he came to see me this morning and offered to *marry* me, and he was so *sad*, and . . . ' It was the last straw; she dissolved in noisy tears.

He switched off his terminal and said, 'There, there,' to her, not too sorry for Adrian, but very much annoyed with the Standishes. 'When the hell are they going to let up?'

Imogen wiped her nose. 'Tonight, I think. They'll spend the rest of the day brainwashing me, then go home. Father says they've neglected their jobs on my account for as long as they can possibly afford – thank goodness.'

Chapter 51

ATE THAT AFTERNOON, their armoury exhausted, the Standishes rang Jacob and proposed a meeting. His first instinct was to refuse; he could hardly manage to be reasonably businesslike and cheerful with clients, let alone to hide his wretchedness from such wily tacticians as Frances and Oliver. But it was probably inevitable: if they were determined to see him, they would manage it one way or another. So he gritted his teeth and invited them to come to Coronation Place after dinner.

He had not seen them in so long that he had turned them into monsters in his mind; he was almost surprised to find them a mild-mannered, mild-faced couple in early middle age, familiar-looking, Frances with coarser skin and some grey in her dark hair, Oliver with deeper lines down his thin cheeks, and his fairish hair faded but not grey. He made them coffee, and they gave him news of Jamie and Mrs Standish and admired his sitting room, clearly ill at ease.

'You wanted to discuss Imogen,' he said at last, bringing them to the point. 'I gather you think she shouldn't have her child.'

'It's up to her, of course,' Frances said quickly. 'But . . . but it's not what we wanted for her.' For a moment he was touched. Parents naturally wanted to stop their children from doing difficult, irreversible things – things they might come to regret. Were he not Imogen's lover, and so painfully the father of her child, he himself might now be wanting to shield the girl who had once been his imaginary daughter from danger, difficulty, hardship, responsibility. But Frances' patently synthetic friendliness soon checked his sympathy. She hoped he understood that they weren't urging Imogen to have an abortion because they minded his being the father. After all, their friendship with him was of many years' duration; and that misunderstanding – well, it should be forgotten, didn't he think? And they didn't mind the child's illegitimacy, either. Gracious, so many of one's friends nowadays . . . one couldn't keep track of whose children were legitimate and whose weren't. But the timing was so bad. They had hoped that she would give up that Roman job after a year or so. A break after university was all very well, but there was no future in a language school – or an abortion counselling service, useful though it admittedly was. 'And if she goes to Rome with a baby, she'll get linked into the social system there – she's already talking about creches and nursery schools. The kid will speak Italian more than English, and she won't want to come back here to live; and there's no real future for her in Italy.'

'What would you suggest, then?'

'She should have an abortion now,' said Oliver, 'have her fling in Italy, then come back and find a job. I can help her if she goes into journalism; she's clever enough, and she did well on *Broadsheet*. She'd be established in a couple of years; and then if she still wanted a bas- a kid on her own, she'd have enough money to live in some sort of comfort.'

'It's my impression that she wants precisely to see what it's like to do without "enough money".'

'Yes, and she's daft. She doesn't know what it'll be like, trying to manage on what that language school will pay her. And she won't take anything from us!' His voice was querulous with injured pride.

'Yes, well, she won't take anything from me either, and I'm the, uh, the father, so I guess she really is determined to see how the other half lives.'

'Slumming isn't something you inflict on a helpless infant,' Frances said sniffily.

At the same moment Oliver snapped: 'She could sue you for support, you know.'

In the interests of peace he answered Frances. 'Listen, she isn't inflicting slumming on the child. She's got a decent place to live, in one of the most beautiful cities in the world, and she's made sure that the child will be well looked after while she's working. And surely you can understand this money business – why she wants to make a go of things without the help of well–off parents? We even discussed it once, remember, Oliver? I said I was refusing money from Aline and Isaac, and you told me you'd made a point of living on your salary and not taking money from the firm.'

'But we're men. It's different for Imogen – she'll get married in the end anyhow, and – ' He caught Frances' expression. 'All right, I can understand wanting to be independent. What I can't forgive is her stupidity. She says it was deliberate, but she's just trying to protect you, God knows why. She was *stupid* to get caught. It's ridiculous, in this day and age, and it makes us ridiculous, bringing up a kid who doesn't know enough to go on the pill and whose idea of a career is having a baby.'

'Gracious, Oliver,' Frances said quickly. 'You're full of unworked–out resentments. We're here to discuss Imogen, not your private feelings. I'm sorry, Jacob – every once in a while Oliver loses his temper and says things he doesn't mean at all.'

263

Jacob indulged himself. 'Or maybe when he's angry he tells the truth for a change, like people who say what they think when they're drunk and then try to take it back when they're sober.'

She looked at him without speaking, unpleasantly.

Oliver took a grip on himself and tried to mend matters. 'In this case it really is true, though. I *am* sorry – it's being so worried about Imogen. The question is, what can we do to help her?'

'Leave her alone till she asks for help.'

'I mean, help her to see that she's being misguidedly stubborn.'

'It's her child,' he said mildly. (And mine, and mine, he thought desolately.)

Oliver lost control again. 'And yours,' he exclaimed, as if Jacob had spoken his thought aloud. 'You got her into this, what are you going to do to get her out of it? Or are you only too pleased with what you've –'

'Shut up!' He stood up – it was the only position from which he could tower over Oliver – and towered. 'Get this straight. I'm shorter than you, but I'm probably stronger, and I'll start throwing you about the room if you bloody well say another word about me and Imogen.'

Oliver did not look scared, only incredulous. 'Did you hear that, Frances? He's actually threatening me.'

Jacob was mortified. Such a crass physical threat. Pure bluster, too – he had not hit anybody since he was a boy and was not going to begin now. He composed himself enough to ask, in a bad imitation of his normal voice, 'How about a drink – brandy, perhaps? Or I've got some passable claret left from dinner – Château Chauvin.' He hoped they would refuse.

But Oliver knew the name. He perked up in spite of his anger and said, 'Claret would be nice.'

'Brandy for me please,' said Frances brightly.

What next? Jacob wondered. But the Standishes had said their say – or else were as much unnerved as he by the violence of the discussion. They finished their drinks and left, Oliver carrying off the farewell with a compliment on the claret that would have been perfect had there not been a just audible note of surprise that Jacob should know claret from Coca-Cola.

Halfway down the little pavement leading to St Eligius

Street Frances stopped, came back and, touching his arm, said, 'I know you care about her and what becomes of her. I mean, don't get the wrong idea about us.' She patted his arm, looking almost as if, given encouragement, she might kiss his cheek.

He smiled weakly. 'Thanks, Frances, I know you care about her too.'

She nodded, as if something had been settled, said, 'Fine, then, goodnight,' and rejoined Oliver. The first stage of the siege was over, after only three days – and nothing in it more surprising than that final note of Standish-Harris truce.

Chapter 52

IMOGEN DID NOT go down when term ended; she planned to stay up for the whole Easter vacation. She was nine weeks pregnant. Not until the beginning of next term would she be safely through her thirteenth week, and therefore well past the time when her parents could urge an early abortion upon her; and she was too far behind in her work to dare risk trying to study under their harassment at home. Pregnancy had already cost her much more time than she had expected: a dithery fortnight of suspense between missing her period and doing her pregnancy test; a harrowed, guilty week after telling Jacob; a frazzled, nervous one after telling her parents; then three wasted days during their invasion of Cambridge. A whole month. She could catch up only by working flat out until Tripos – and she was even now losing time from morning sickness and a deep lethargy that turned studying into a constant battle. She hoped that, like most pregnant women, she would be better after the twelfth week; in the meantime she felt weak, stupid and vulnerable – and she was still under siege, chivvied by a constant dribble of communications from her parents, whose surprising persistence upset her so much, in her lassitudinous, dispirited physical state, that after every telephone call or letter she sat worrying, unable to work and trying without success to pull herself together.

Jacob and Laura did the obvious: thrust aside their separate miseries and the question of their future together and rallied behind Imogen; the three of them became a military alliance for the duration. Laura firmly got her to do most of her studying at Jacob's place rather than at Norwich Street, so that her parents could not harass her by telephone – and just as firmly made it clear, without saying a word, that she was executing a tactical manoeuvre, not bowing out of the centre. She also made her promise to ring or visit one of them after every telephone call or letter that did get through to her.

The strategy worked. Most of the time the Standishes could not reach her; when they did, Laura and Jacob were able to assure her that she was not neurotic, immature, selfish, un-feminist, or whatever else Frances had thought up or picked up from some friend. She would have survived without their help, but with more loss of precious time – 'And we can't have that,' Laura said forcefully. Another woman would have said: Serves her right; she chose this, now let her stew in it. Not Laura.

The alliance helped them to make the transition from the white heat of the first weeks after Imogen's announcement – the heat of revelations and decisions and extremes of hope, fear, despair, joy, grief, disillusionment, reconcilation, all huddled on top of each other as if the whole of life must be crowded into as short a span as possible – to . . . to whatever things were going to be like from now on. Already, before they were aware of it, in the four weeks of the Easter vacation, things were beginning to return to a semblance of normality, as they have a way of doing, little as it seems possible in the heat of high events. Things were not the same, of course. They were different, and all three of them, in their separate minds, were never more aware of the difference than when everything seemed most eerily just the same as before the recent tumults. Imogen was still stunned at the unhappiness she had unwit-tingly wrought in the lives of a man she had always loved and a woman she had come to hold dear. Laura was still wry, dry, cautious, humiliated, and tempted to be quit of her treacherous man and his wantonly self-willed lover. Jacob still woke up, spent his days and lay down again at night in what seemed like unremitting pain, the likes of which he had never known, and about which he dared speak to no one: neither to his tired, peaked, gravid young lover, whose every moment was just now so precious and whose equilibrium so easily disturbed, nor to his other lover, who was waiting, in her own pain, to find out whether his would fade enough to make their lives together possible.

Yet sometimes, when he was sitting at his terminal in the evening, with Imogen sprawled on the floor among her books, and perhaps Laura cross-legged on the sofa reading a journal and making notes, he felt . . . out of pain; detached; comfortable; almost . . . normal. Life would go on: different; the same. Different: Imogen would have gone. The same: Laura would be there. He was beginning to believe that his life had not stopped short on the twenty-third of February.

The Standishes had been getting other people to ring Imogen in order to reason with her. At last, desperate, they tried to enlist the aid of Oliver's mother. But Grandmother Standish had a mind of her own. She rang Jacob one night. 'I hear you've made my granddaughter pregnant, young man.'

Mrs Standish's voice carried, like Oliver's, and Imogen, who was in the room, rushed across and snatched the receiver. 'Grandmother, don't you dare say things to Jacob. He did not make me pregnant –'

'Someone else?'

'I decided to get pregnant all by myself.'

'Like the Virgin Mary?'

'*Grandmother*. I mean that if Father's been telling you that I'm covering up for Jacob, he's wrong. Jacob didn't know I was trying to get pregnant. I *chose* it. You won't be able to understand that, but –'

'Young lady, your knowledge of me is strictly limited. Now. I rang Jacob Harris, not you. Be so good as to give him back to me.'

'All right, but don't you dare –'

'Imogen. At once.'

Imogen surrendered the telephone meekly.

'Now, Jacob. If we can keep Imogen off the line for ten seconds, I'll say what I rang up to say, which was to congratulate you on getting my granddaughter pregnant and to tell you to keep up the good work.'

'You mean get her pregnant again?' he asked solemnly. Imogen was in fits.

'No, dolt. I mean backing her up against those damnfool parents of hers. Jolly good show she's making of it, and I'm surprised Frances and my son don't realise it. No, I'm not surprised. Imogen's always had good ideas that they don't like. But I'm glad she has someone to back her up.'

Imogen grabbed the telephone again. 'Oh Grandmother, you *are* nice.'

'You're back,' said Mrs Standish tartly. 'I told you to keep off the line. However, now that you're here, I was going to ring you too. I don't know what people do about unmarried mothers nowadays; in my day young women hid themselves away in the country, and I thought that if Oliver and Frances are worried about their reputation in London and don't want you there, you might want to come here to have your baby.'

Imogen kept a straight face. 'Actually, I think it'll be all right with Mother and Father if I have it at home – at a London hospital, that is: nobody lets you have first children at home any more. But thank you *so* much for offering. And it's nice of you to ring poor Jacob – Mother and Father have been perfectly beastly to him.'

'Hmph, I thought so. I like that young man, always did. You've got good taste. You're sure about Oliver and Frances?'

'Yes, they'll be okay once it's past the time when I could have an abortion, and that's only a week now.'

'You're probably right. Oliver said you'd be frightfully gross by the time you're sitting your exams, but it didn't seem to worry him, only whether it would affect how well you did. All right. If you need me, ring. Thank that young man of yours for me again – and now I'll stop. This is a trunk call, after all.' She rang off without saying goodbye.

'You have to be very rich or very poor to worry about the cost of a trunk call these days,' Jacob said.

268

'And as much out of the world as Grandmother to call an STD call a trunk call.'

'My dear child' – a phrase he still occasionally used, out of habit, momentarily forgetting its multiple inappropriateness – 'that shows the difference in our ages. Unless I revert to American and call it "long distance", *I* still call an STD call a trunk call – as, indeed, I just did. I also call Radio Three the Third Programme; and I wouldn't be caught dead calling Cumberland and Westmorland Cumbria.'

'*Toujours* more English than the English, eh, Grandad?'

His face sobered in mid-grin. 'I've just realised: you told your grandmother you'd be – be having it in London. Do you really want to? I thought you'd have it here, in Cambridge.'

She examined his anxious, hopeful face. 'Oh dear, I never seem to tell you things the right way. In fact, I hadn't quite decided – but the way you look right now . . .'

'What is it?' – impatiently. 'You don't want to have it here?'

'No, I *do* want to. But' – she turned about restlessly – 'well, it'll make Mother happy if I – '

'Frances doesn't want you to have it at all, let alone in London.'

She faced him squarely. 'Okay, I was fudging. The real reason is that, if I stay here, I'll hurt you more and more with every week of pregnancy, once I start getting big; and if I have it here, which was what I wanted in the beginning, you with me and everything, it'll kill you. I can't just do what *I* want, I've got to give you and Laura a chance.'

'I'm not asking for it – neither is Laura.'

'Jacob, go look at your face in the glass. Right now – over here.' She pushed him. '*That's* what you look like at the very thought of my ba– the child. You can't keep showing that face to Laura for the next six months and expect her to stay with you. I'm not doing you a favour, or Laura. *I* can't stand to see the pain I've caused – and I won't be able to live with *myself* if I stay here, and you and Laura break up as a result. I'm going home after Tripos and staying there.'

'And I can't see you?'

'Of course you can. But visiting. Not living here, right in the middle of your lives.'

'All right,' he said listlessly, then: 'Well . . . that was another of your pots of scalding water . . . but I guess . . .' he paused, then made the effort: 'I guess you're right.'

Imogen dissolved in one of the little fits of tears she had been having in the past few weeks – 'pregnant tears', she called them; and, as he went to comfort her, he realised that he was almost as much relieved as desolated by her decision. Good Lord, he thought: maybe I *am* getting better.

Chapter 53

ASTER WEEKEND MARKED the end of Imogen's twelfth week, and Frances and Oliver motored up without warning for a final big push, caught her at home and inflated their distress at her haggard, lank-cheeked face into a factitious frenzy of reproachful woe. Laura happened to turn up a few minutes later and found her weeping nervously and the Standishes intent on their job and rather pleased with themselves – they probably read her tears, rare before her pregnancy, as a sign that she was weakening. Laura took one look, told her to scram to Coronation Place and laid into the Standishes so effectively that they slunk off back to London directly.

'But how did you do it?' Imogen asked in amazement when Laura arrived with the news.

'I told them you're struggling against morning sickness to study, that you have only a month and a half till Tripos, that every telephone call loses you a whole day's work because you're so upset that they're upset –'

'That's laying it on thick.'

Laura grinned ferociously. 'Pardonable exaggeration. And I said that, if they want you to get a good job when you come back to England, they'd better leave you alone, because you need a good Tripos result to get a good job. Then I told them that if you didn't do well, I, Laura Hackett, would hold them personally responsible.'

It had been an overwhelming tirade; it was magnificent; it ended the siege.

Imogen's morning sickness lifted in her thirteenth week; suddenly she was full of energy, addressed herself to her books with gusto, and all in all felt so thoroughly recouped that at the end of April she went home for a long weekend, to give herself a break and reassure her parents that she was all right.

Her absence gave Jacob and Laura their first uninterrupted time alone together since Christmas. They spent the entire three days together, trying not to talk about Imogen, trying to find their way back into the rhythm of their life before her. It was a bit peculiar; they were unnaturally polite and considerate, and unnaturally reticent, since they were both nursing pain that in the old days it would have been natural for them to tell each other about and comfort each other for. And whatever balance they achieved now was provisional; they could not know whether their bond would survive his reaction to the birth of the child. Would Laura simply not be able to endure what Imogen had called the look on his face? Possibly. Or would his yearning towards his child and its mother be so strong as to leave no room for Laura at the centre of his life? Possibly. Anything was possible. But the long weekend was – provisionally – encouraging. Their old life, in which they had been deeply happy, was still important to them both; and its rhythms were still there, waiting to be picked up.

Imogen came back much happier about her parents, who, now that an abortion might jeopardise her examination prospects, had accepted the inevitable with the grace she had expected of them from the first, but had latterly wondered if they would ever arrive at. Frances was already shopping round for the best maternity hospital and gynaecologist as thoroughly and cheerfully as she would have searched out the best doctor for an abortion if Imogen had let her. She was even beginning, furtively, ruefully, to be pleased about the child. Oliver was still miffed and huffy, not because Imogen was going to gum up her future by traipsing off to Rome with a child, but because Jacob was its father: 'I don't think he'll ever really like you,' she said regretfully. 'But I told him he'll have to put up with you if he wants to see *me*.'

Every time she said something like that, Jacob's heart pounded with momentary hope that she was changing her mind about staying with him, even though all she meant – as he knew, and as she usually made clear – was that, although she would be living in Rome for the next few years at least, she wanted him to be able to see his child whenever there was a chance – on his necessarily infrequent trips to Italy (he could hardly make regular pilgrimages to Rome with Laura, and still less without her), and on her more frequent trips home to see her family – which now included him – and that, therefore, if Oliver wanted her to stay at Canonbury Park South when she visited England, he would have to put up with seeing a lot of Jacob. But still there was the surge of hope against all reason. He was still in pain. He had not stopped loving Imogen, not stopped wanting with all his being to be with her and their child, in spite of also and almost equally wanting to be with Laura. Time after time he almost said, 'Please'; it was only because he had asked Laura to stay that he was not every day abjectly begging Imogen to change her mind. But he had asked Laura, and as often as the plea rose to his lips, he chewed it back; and so they went on from week to week.

Imogen's pregnancy had changed things between him and her as surely as between him and Laura, if less dramatically. They had moved a long way from the blissful simplicity of the autumn; and for them, too, the future was uncertain. They would go on meeting, for Jacob would want to see the child – and her; and they thought that perhaps they would always be lovers when they met. But maybe not; he might find it too painful to be with her only temporarily as the father-yet-not-father of her child. And God knew what he would feel when she had another.

'But not by me,' he told her angrily one day. '*I* won't go on siring your pups.'

'I know,' she said sadly. 'I wish it weren't that way, but . . .'

'Don't worry, you'll find another stud; the world is full of them.'

'The world isn't full of men like you. But it *is* probably true that you aren't the only . . . nice . . . man in existence.'

So there was another delicate balance. They were still lovers, still intensely intertwined, readers of each other's minds and eyes; yet there were secrets between them, open secrets, things they knew but could not say: for him, the word, 'Please', for her, the words, 'If only': if only he hadn't wanted children so much, hadn't loved her too much; if only she had asked before taking her own way; if only he could put his hand on her thickening belly with simple delight rather than with an expression of joy shot through with misery that it wrung her to see.

As far as possible she kept him out of the various concerns of her pregnancy, turning rather to Laura for talk and counsel. He saw that putting him at a distance did not come easily; he also saw her wisdom in trying to save him from getting more bound up than he already was in her and the child. In the long run, the more he was able to see her only as his lover, not as both that and the mother of their child, the less he would suffer. In the short run, it hurt.

Imogen sat Tripos and did all right – rather to her surprise, after the distractions of the past months. Then she sorted out the accumulation of three years in Cambridge, left her room in Norwich Street and spent a final, heartrending weekend with Jacob. From now on she would be living at home, where it would be awkward enough just visiting her, let alone sleeping with her. She would come back to Cambridge before October, 'often, as often as you want me to,' but it would be different: a special occasion, freighted, without the easy informality of daily contact.

Final, final – provisionally final; everything was provisional these days, nothing really ended.

But this was an end. He drove her home, chattering with manic inconsequence, and pulled up two streets short of Canonbury Park South because she had burst into tears. He did, too, and they filled the Mini with gulps and wails so loud and abandoned that at almost the same moment they heard the theatrical note and started to laugh instead.

'Oh dear, they'll be able to tell I've been crying,' she said ruefully, looking at her swollen eyes in the car mirror.

'They won't, you know. In the past few weeks your whole face has been getting, uh, roundish –'

'Pudgy, you mean; it's too dire.'

'Well, plump, then; and they'll think it's just the way your eyes always are now. It's me they'll be able to tell has been crying.'

She inspected him. 'No, with your pink skin –'

'Nasty creature, that's your revenge for "plump", is it?'

' – nobody can ever tell you've been crying.' She winced. 'As I've had some opportunity to learn.'

They smiled at each other, putting their best face on it; and he drove round to the house, helped her unload the car – rather, helped Oliver, who rushed out saying, 'You shouldn't be carrying heavy loads,' and took the first armful from Imogen – braved the resentment behind the Standishes' attempt at welcome (tea in the drawing room, the four of them risibly stiff, like total strangers), bade Imogen a quick brushed-kiss goodbye on the front step and drove off.

Chapter 54

ACOB AND LAURA had been going to skip their regular biennial visit to America so that he and Imogen could see each other over the summer; but a few days after her departure they decided on the spur of the moment to fly over anyhow.

It was his idea, and neither of them was sure whether it was a good one. He had said, 'Let's try to re-establish ourselves right now, not wait till October.'

'Are you sure you aren't just trying to get away from the misery of seeing Imogen get more and more pregnant?' Laura queried doubtfully.

'Maybe, but I don't think so. I *want* to see her. But it's more important to start getting straight with you.'

And so they went, and it was all right. He had the comfort of pouring his heart out to Aline, and so, separately, did Laura; she and Aline liked each other very much. Laura also had the satisfaction of at last meeting Sheila and being able to see exactly what he meant: that she was formidable, wonderful, and quite impossible.

Talking to Aline did more to restore him than anything else could have. In all this time he had discussed the business with no one who was not one of the principals in it; and she was the perfect audience, concerned for him, yet never thrown off balance in her judgment by mother-love.

'Before this, I felt as if my life hadn't quite taken its final form,' he told her as they sat together one blue-bright July day, she in a cane chair on the verandah, he on the top step, 'as if all sorts of vague possibilities were open to me. I think it was something to do with not having children with Laura, and something to do with that sense I've told you about, of some sort of limit to . . . to how much I can know her . . . something about the way there's a point beyond which she isn't . . . wild, extreme, call it what you will. I wasn't conscious of it, but I think I was free-floating a little, all those years.'

Aline nodded. 'Not looking for someone else, but not entirely ruling out the possibility.'

'Then I attached myself to Imogen, and she wouldn't have me –'

'And that forced the issue. Asking Laura to stay, in the same breath as telling her you'd liefer be with Imogen, and not only because of the baby. Some chutzpah. You're a lucky boy, Jacob Harris – I'd have booted you from here to Maine.'

'Laura nearly did – all the way from England, too. But she didn't. She didn't even say a word about conditions. But they're there – it was implicit in asking her. I was giving her an undertaking not to be quite so open to the possibility of falling in love with anybody else as shatteringly as I did with Imogen.'

'That certainly does narrow things down,' Aline said dubiously.

'Sure. Asking Laura to stay with me means that I've damned well got to do my best to stay with her.'

She frowned. 'Are you sure you aren't talking about . . . compromising?'

Compromise was one of her blackest words. Jacob looked up at her, frowning in turn, then picked up a stick that was propped against the steps and weighed it in his hands. 'No,' he said at last, definitely. 'Compromise would be putting up with second best because I couldn't face having nothing. But there's no question of putting up with Laura or of her being second best. I wanted Imogen even more, but I'm staying with Laura – if she'll let me – because I want Laura; and that means I have . . . responsibilities towards her that I didn't quite face up to before.'

'You don't mean cutting yourself right off from – ?' she exclaimed anxiously.

He laughed. 'No, no, I'm my mother's son – and Laura wants that freedom too, as much as she ever did. There will always be the possibility of other attachments – for us it's the way of living that comes naturally; we couldn't change it and still be us, you know? But I can lower the risks; stop free-floating – take more care.'

Aline made a sceptical noise.

'It's possible, you know.'

'Hmph. I'm inclined to be suspicious of good resolutions to stick with people who aren't quite right. Won't you be up and off with the next extreme person you meet? I'm worried that you're using Laura as a stopgap.'

Jacob idly stirred the earth in the flowerbed beside the verandah with the stick. 'You like Laura a lot, don't you?'

'Yes. That's why I asked. And stop messing with my nasturtiums.'

'So you can see why I love her. She's not a stopgap – and what I call a limit is something I was hardly aware of until Imogen. Listen – twice in my life, once with Sheila, once with Imogen, I've been with someone who was . . . my twin . . . something . . . I don't know . . . But that's twice in going on for twenty years. You're right, of course: if another comes along, I'd be tempted, and, knowing me, I'd probably

276

succumb, no matter what. But the law of averages is against it. Twice in twenty years, so far. Twenty years from now I'll be fifty-eight.'

'And therefore past it,' said his mother drily. She was sixty-two and had a lover at that moment.

'Oh come on, ma.'

Aline picked up the stick and poked him. 'I've told you not to call me "ma".'

'No, seriously. Laura isn't second best; she's just not . . . whatever it is . . . my twin. And do you understand when I say that, even when I was most besotted with Imogen, the idea of not having Laura was unbearable? That it nearly stopped me from speaking to Imogen?'

Aline looked at him, her long, sallow, sardonic face sadder than he had ever seen it. 'Oh, yes. I've been there myself. Only my story had a happy ending, because when I found my twin, it was Isaac, and he wasn't hell-bent upon solitude, like Imogen. I'm so – I wish I could do something.'

His mother was rarely at a loss. 'Wring Imogen's neck?' he suggested.

'No, I only wish I could see a neck that wanted wringing. Not Imogen's – she couldn't have done any different. No, no . . . I just have a feeling that you've missed, in the end, and through no fault of your own, just the way things happen. You have Laura, and England, and interesting work, even if it isn't that vocation you wanted to find. Actually I think you did – I think England's your vocation – but that's neither here nor there. You've got a lot. More than most people. But . . . I'm your mother, and I want you to have everything. The "everything" you say Imogen wants.'

He looked up, startled by her mournfulness, and grinned to shake off the gloom that had settled on them both. 'That's the most sentimental speech I've ever heard you make, ma. I didn't know you felt that way.'

'I'll "ma" you.' She gave him a really vicious poke in the ribs with the stick.

'Hey!' He lifted up his shirt. 'You've grazed my rib! Monster!'

'Band-aids in the medicine chest. And put on some mercuro-chrome.'

277

'Mercurochrome doesn't do any good. Doctors don't use it any more.'

'Put it on anyhow,' she called after him. 'What do doctors know?'

Chapter 55

IMOGEN'S BABY WAS born early. Jacob had asked again if he could be there, but she had again refused, because it would add to his hurt in the end; and he had known she was right.

'But how will I know when it's born? Your parents won't tell me,' he had protested to the nine-months-pregnant Imogen, who was enormous, and puffy all over – not a woman made more beautiful by pregnancy.

'Don't worry, Mother will. She's gone quite soft about you; she keeps saying I should have married you. I tell her you didn't ask me.'

'True, I didn't.' They could joke about the past months now, just about.

Frances rang him at eight in the morning on the fifth of October, breathless with excitement, to tell him it had happened. Wasn't it wonderful, it had been so easy, only five hours, Imogen had a talent for it, and –

He cut her short. 'Well, what is it?' he asked; and held his breath.

'What – ? Oh, what sex. A boy.'

He breathed again. Thank God. He had not been able to decide ahead of time whether his desire for a daughter was strong enough to outweigh the pain of having one in existence whom he would have almost no connection to. Now, flooded with relief, he knew the answer. Thank God. One mercy granted.

'How soon can I see Imogen?' he asked. 'And the baby. Both of them.'

'Any time. This afternoon? Tomorrow? Queen Charlotte's are very good about visitors.'

When she rang off, Jacob sat and thought. He could go alone, or –

He rang Laura, and they went together.

Imogen was not wan, weary, languid, ethereal, all the things new mothers are supposed to be. She was bouncing and gleeful and triumphant. She reached out to Jacob and kissed him, then to Laura and kissed her, and, holding on to them both, said, 'Well, I did it,' gloryingly, as if nothing like it had ever been done before, and then, with a laugh at her own absurdity, and squeezing both their hands: 'We've made it!'

Laura obviously thought this effort to enrol her as an equal in Imogen's and Jacob's relation a bit much. Mildly but definitely she said, 'More accurately, you and Jacob made it – him – and I'd like to see him. Where is he?'

Chastened, but today irrepressible, Imogen pointed to the cot. Jacob, coming to Queen Charlotte's with assumptions drawn from American movies, had expected to be shown the baby by a gauze-masked nurse through glass nursery walls, not to find it in the room. He hung back, then steeled himself and went and looked.

It was just a scrawny little tad with a scrunched–up purple-red face and a lot of black hair; he felt momentarily ridiculous for having expended so much emotion on a creature that could be considered as human only by an effort of belief. A remark was called for. 'Nice dark hair, like yours,' he came up with. 'I was afraid it would be red.'

'Oh, that's not proper hair, it'll all come off,' she replied. 'You aren't safe yet.'

'He has your chin,' Laura told him.

'You could have fooled me.'

'You can pick him up,' Imogen said from the bed. 'If you want to.'

'How do you pick a baby up?' he asked Laura.

279

She reached down and picked up the tadlike scrap. 'Like this. Hold his head.'

Jacob took the bundle. Laura was watching him; Imogen was watching him. He didn't feel a thing: he was too much on view; the occasion was too much overfreighted with what he had expected to feel, what he was expected to show, what he would have felt had the baby been going to stay in his life. He smiled at it – at them – and said, 'It's got nice hands.'

'*He*,' Imogen and Laura said together, and Laura asked, 'What's his name?

'I rather thought of James – Jamie, in fact, after my uncle Jamie,' Imogen said, 'and . . . and it depends on you,' she told Jacob. 'I'd *like* to call him James Jacob Standish – but only if you won't mind.'

His heart heaved; he almost dropped James Jacob Standish. 'My dear, I'm so honoured,' he said.

At his tone Laura stiffened, asked rather suddenly which way was the lavatory, and went out.

Alone with Imogen, Jacob didn't know what to say or do. He approached the bed, looked down at her. Her face was still puffed up, a moon-face, only her eyes the same, grave, hazel, beautiful under straight black eyebrows.

'I'm glad it's a boy,' she said with a hesitant smile. 'I wanted a girl for me, but a boy for you, if you know what I mean.'

'Oh, I know. And I'm glad too. This is . . . better.' Then, trying to recover a normal tone of voice: 'If anything quite as ugly as this can be called "better". It must have inherited my looks; that would have been a dreadful thing to pass on to a girl.'

The baby woke and yelled. 'It knew what I was saying,' he said in alarm. 'Here, take it.'

She took it and gave it her breast, and it shut up. Laura came back from the lavatory, and Jacob decided he should go: watching Imogen suckle the baby was making his heart turn over dangerously.

In the lavatory he looked at himself in the glass, poking his chin and thinking: Will he look like me? Well, he would find out in due course. Imogen wasn't cutting him off completely from James Jacob; she was giving him, would continue to give him, all she could. He practised a nonchalant expression and went back.

There would be no more moments overcharged with emotion today: Frances and Oliver had arrived. Frances smiled at him benignly, and Oliver with unprecedented expansiveness actually shook hands and said, 'Well, congratulations are in order, old man.'

The inappositeness of this in the circumstances sent Jacob, Laura and Imogen into stitches. The Standishes looked on mystified, Oliver clearly unable to decide whether to feel insulted. 'We'd better be going,' Jacob told Imogen. 'I'll be back. We both will,' he added, turning to Laura, who, still in the aftermath of laughter, beamed and said yes of course; and they left in a little flurry of gay exclamations.

Leaving the hospital – leaving behind one beloved, and his son; walking beside his other beloved to the car park – he remembered what Aline had said. Yes. In the end he had missed the completeness that a relation with Imogen would have had: whereas Imogen, Imogen with all her peculiarities, her quirks, her inability to stay centred on one person, had sailed through into completeness, rightness, gravity, happiness. She would not have an easy life; she would uncushion it at every opportunity; but she knew what she wanted and what she was doing, and there she was, magnificent, dead on course.

And here he was. He and Laura drove home in near-silence. When they got to Coronation Place, she came in, took off her jacket and said, 'I'm glad it's a boy – for your sake.'

'That's what Imogen said.'

'I guessed.'

'I'm glad too – for my sake.'

'I guessed.' She came up to him. 'Are you all right?'

Jacob smiled, a sort of confidence in himself coming back that had been absent for a year. One more stage in recuperation. Yes, he was all right. Not as all right as Imogen, not mounting the upper air wide-winged, but all right. Perhaps even happy.

Happy? Yes.

'You know,' he said, 'I think I'm happy.'

'Happy?' Laura looked at him closely, stroking his cheek. 'Really?'

'Really.' He put his arms round her. 'Oh, my love, such storms, such seas.'

'Not happy, then?'

'Oh, and in despair, but at least happy too. It's a change from only in despair. What about you?'

'Me too.'

'Really?'

'I think so . . . I don't know. I still can't promise . . .'

'I know.' After a moment he said, 'I'm exhausted.'

'Me too.'

They went upstairs, but it was too early to rest. They made love, and afterwards he said, 'Yes, happy. My love.'